A MATCH MADE IN . . . HEAVEN?

"You've finally convinced me," Alex said. "None of this is your fault. And your father is a bad man. A truly rotten man, as a matter of fact. You're right. I was wrong."

To his surprise, she bowed her head. "I'm sorry." Her voice had sunk to a whisper. "I didn't want this to happen."

"Good Gad." He couldn't stand it any longer. With two long strides, Alex crossed the room and took Kate in his arms. He held her close. "Kate Finney, you're the most infuriating woman I've ever met in my life."

"I am not."

"Don't argue with me. You don't know how many infuriating women I've met."

"I guess not."

Alex's heart swelled when she gave a soft laugh. Kate didn't laugh enough. "You're also the bravest."

"I am?"

She lifted her face to look at him, and Alex saw tears in her eyes and a tremulous smile on her face. "Yes," he said. "You are." And then he kissed her.

Dear Romance Reader,

In July 2000, we launched the Ballad line with four new series, and each month we present both new and continuing stories set everywhere from medieval England to the American West—the kind of passionate, romantic stories you love best, written by the most gifted authors. At the back of each book, we tell you when you can find subsequent books in the series that have captured your heart.

This month, Alice Duncan concludes her charming *Meet Me at the Fair* series with **A Bicycle Built for Two**. When a young woman with no illusions about love tells fortunes for a living, she's bound to meet some interesting characters—but she never thought she'd meet a handsome city swell who would fall in love with her! Next up, the fabulous Annette Blair introduces the second book in her wonderfully sexy *Rogues Club* series, **An Unforgettable Rogue**. The day of a wedding is no time for the bride's first husband to show up—especially when he's supposed to be deceased! Can a couple who missed their first chance at happiness find it a second time around?

Kate Silver takes us back to the glittering adventure of the Three Musketeers' era with the second book in the *. . . And One for All* series, **A Lady Betrayed**. Can a young woman desperate to prove her father's innocence take vengeance on the young soldier who accused him . . . especially if he's the man she loves? Finally, the always talented Susan Grace concludes the *Reluctant Heroes* with the alluring tale of **The Runaway Duke**. Escaping from someone who wishes him harm, a rebellious nobleman finds that his savior is a most seductive woman . . . and one who harbors dangerous secrets of her own.

These are stories we know you'll love! Why not try them all this month?

Kate Duffy
Editorial Director

Meet Me at the Fair

A BICYCLE BUILT FOR TWO

Alice Duncan

ZEBRA BOOKS
Kensington Publishing Corp.
http://www.kensingtonbooks.com

First Printing: October 2002
10 9 8 7 6 5 4 3 2 1

Printed in the United States of America

One

"But that's outrageous!"

Alex English stared, aghast, at his fellow members of the World's Columbian Exposition's Agricultural Forum, the body of men in agricultural pursuits who had put together so many of the magnificent exhibits fair-goers flocked to see daily. Alex himself had donated the oats, wheat, and barley, grown on his own Illinois farm, that had been used in creating a reproduction of the Liberty Bell.

"We can't have that sort of thing going on here. This exhibition is meant to be an arena of education. It's a place where families can see for themselves what a great country America's become. It's supposed to be wholesome and moral. It's not supposed to be a . . . a . . . " But Alex couldn't find words egregious enough to describe the disgraceful event that had just been related to him.

"True, true." Gilbert MacIntosh, railroad magnate and weekend farmer sighed. "To be fair to the girl, she did ask the gate men to keep an eye open for the man, and to refuse him admission if he showed up. It's not really her fault that he managed to get past them."

"But to very nearly strangle his own daughter?" Alex could scarcely take it in. "What kind of family does the girl come from? Are we sure we want her sort working at the Exposition?"

All of Alex's sensibilities rebelled at the notion that somebody could attempt murder—and upon his own daughter, by Gad—at the fair he'd worked so long and hard to create. He had no patience with people like this girl, this so-called "dancer," this benighted "fortune-teller." He'd fought against admitting that dashed fortune-telling booth to begin with, believing such truck inappropriate for so high-minded an enterprise as his cherished World's Columbian Exposition. Only reluctantly had he been coerced into accepting Madame Esmeralda's trashy enterprise, and only so long as she confined it to the Midway Plaisance.

"What exactly is her sort?" Gilbert asked, an ironical twist to his voice.

But Alex entertained no such moral ambiguities as his friend seemed to possess. "The bad sort. Great jumping cats, Gil, you can't honestly believe the girl is of sound character with a father like that, can you?"

"I think it's her father's character that's in question here, Alex. Not hers."

"Humbug. The acorn doesn't fall far from the oak tree. No matter what the so-called psychologists that are popping up all over the place say, such moral laxity runs in families." He pounded the table. "It even says so in the Bible. Unto the seventh generation!" The Bible was an excellent resource, and Alex felt no qualms about using it as a reference. Not even Gil, who occasionally entertained bizarre notions, would dare refute the Bible.

"I don't think it's as easy as that." Gilbert rubbed a hand across his eyes, as if he were exhausted, which he probably was. "In spite of the Bible, her father isn't her fault, Alex."

"Bah. His sort breeds his sort, and she's his daughter." Alex knew it to be true. He was sure Gil did, too, but was being stubborn for some unfathomable reason. Alex had the Bible on his side, for crumb's sake.

"You're not being fair to her, Alex," Gil insisted.

The Agricultural Forum members spent long hours, together and individually, overseeing events in the

Agricultural Building and making sure displays inside were kept up to snuff. Alex had worked like a demon all his life to propitiate the farming enterprise his great-grandfather, grandfather, and father had begun and maintained. He'd added his own genius for business, a far-sighted and creative mode of thinking, an interest in new ideas, farming methods, unique uses for his produce, and boundless energy and ambition to his inherited green thumb. He had, therewith, created the largest, most prosperous farming enterprise in the middle west. He wasn't about to let a low-bred, low-class girl from Chicago's worst slums disrupt his cherished Exposition.

"What do you mean?" he demanded of Gilbert Mac-Intosh. "If the girl is a menace to the rest of the Exposition, I say get rid of her."

"Hear, hear," said Mr. Farley Pike, another wealthy Illinois farmer. "We don't want her type soiling our project."

Alex nodded. "Exactly." He didn't much like Farley, considering him a stuffed shirt, a bore, and assuredly a hypocrite into the bargain, but he appreciated his support at the moment.

Gil eyed them both with a jaundiced air. "You're not being just, gentlemen. It's not the girl's fault that her father is a drunkard." He aimed a gaze at Alex that hit its target like a jab on the jaw. "*She* isn't the problem. Her father is the problem. And she took the precaution of warning the gate-keepers that he might well make trouble. I believe she ought to be lauded for her foresight and trying to better herself, not kicked in the teeth for having been cursed with a bastard for a father."

A general gasp went up around the table. These gentlemen, these salt-of-the-earth farmers—granted, they were a good deal more prosperous than most farmers—weren't accustomed to hearing profanity spoken in their presence. Somebody, Alex didn't see who, muttered, "Well, really."

Alex pressed his lips together briefly. He didn't approve of cursing, either. However, it was Gil's prodding of his conscience that irked him more than Gil's unconventional language. He didn't like to think of himself as the sort of fellow who would condemn a person out of hand. An urge to defend his stand, however, assailed him. "Now, listen here, Gil, old fellow. We all know that there are certain types of people who can't be helped."

Gil eyed him without favor. "And how, pray, can you be sure this girl is one of them? Have you met her? Spoken to her? I haven't, so I prefer to withhold judgment until I have. I know you're a good man, Alex, but I think you're not behaving like one in this instance. At least talk to the girl and determine her soundness of mind and character before you deprive her of the means of making her living."

Scores of epithets, most containing words like "bleeding heart" and "soft touch" flitted through Alex's brain. He knew he was being unkind to Gil. Gil was as hardheaded a businessman as any of them. And he was only being reasonable. Alex knew it, even though he hated acknowledging the truth, because the truth in this instance was not to his credit. He liked to think of himself as the reasonable one in any gathering of gentlemen.

After a longish pause, during which Alex pondered how he could get his own way and rid the Exposition of this girl, this Kate Finney, who was clearly devoid of morals or worth, without seeming, even to himself, irrational and ill-tempered, he said, "Very well, Gil. You're correct." He felt magnanimous admitting it. "I'll visit the girl and talk to her. If I think she ought be kicked out, however, you may be sure I'll recommend doing so to the Fair Directory."

"Fine, fine," Gil said upon a heavy breath of air.

"That's fair."

"Thank you." Alex rose. "Shall we retire to luncheon, gentlemen? I hear a hamburger calling my name." He smiled and his co-agriculturalists laughed, whereupon the men all left their meeting room in the Exposition's Administration Building. He clapped Gil on the shoulder as the two men met at the door. "Would you care to visit Miss Finney with me, Gil?"

But the other man shook his head. "Can't, Alex. I've got to see to my Guernseys. My man said one of them isn't feeling well. Can't have sick cows at the fair."

"Good Gad, no!" The mere thought of a sick cow, a diseased cornstalk, or a patch of mildew on one of his pumpkins made Alex's skin crawl. Once, several years ago, Alex's mother had laughingly told him he was too much of a perfectionist, but Alex didn't think it was possible to be too careful. It was his attention to detail that had increased his family's fortunes so greatly. Besides, he knew his mother had only been joking.

Gil grinned at him. "Don't take it so hard, Alex. If the cow's sick, I'll take care of her."

Alex gazed sharply at his best friend. Was Gil making fun of him? He didn't want to think so, but he frowned slightly. "Of course, you will," he said more stiffly than he'd intended.

Placing a hand on Alex's shoulder, Gil stopped his friend's forward progress. Alex turned and gazed at him quizzically. "Yes, Gil? You want to say something?"

Gil looked troubled. Alex hoped nothing was amiss at home. Gil had recently married a charming woman. Alex had been best man at the ceremony, an event that had started him thinking about setting up housekeeping himself. His mother could use some help on the farm. Not that Alex didn't provide her with a full household staff, but still, managing such a large home and grounds could be tiring to a lady no longer in the first blush of youth, especially now that his father had passed on to his just reward. "Is something the matter, Gil?"

"Yes. No. Aw, hell, Alex, I don't know."

Alex allowed his eyes to open wide for perhaps two seconds. It was unlike Gil to swear this much. In order to make his friend relax, he smiled. "Out with it, Gil. If something's wrong, perhaps I can help with it."

Gil's smile slipped sideways and he chuckled softly. "Actually, you're the only one who *can* help."

"I don't think I understand, Gil."

"No, I'm sure you don't."

Alex was puzzled by Gil's air of distress. Cocking his head to one side, he waited, figuring his friend would get to the point eventually.

"Alex . . ." Gil trailed off.

More confused than ever, Alex said, "Yes?"

"Alex, you're turning into a fussy old man before my very eyes, damn it!"

Alex blinked at him. He didn't know what to say. He didn't know what Gil meant, for that matter. "Um . . ."

Gil's hand tightened on Alex's shoulder. "Listen, Alex, I'm saying this all wrong, but try to understand."

"I'm trying."

"We've been best friends for years. I love you as I would a brother." Frowning slightly, Gil amended his comment. "Actually, I love you a good deal more than I do Henry."

At last Alex found a reason to smile. Henry was a stuffed shirt and a crashing dullard. Everyone who knew him agreed.

"But, dash it, Alex, you're getting to be as bad as he is!"

"I beg your pardon?" Alex was certain he'd misunderstood.

"Take this girl, for instance."

"I'd rather not, thank you." A good deal put out with his friend, Alex felt himself tense until his posture was . . . well

. . . rather like Henry's, actually. The realization forced Alex to calm down and relax his rigid posture.

"But that's just it, you see. You're willing to condemn Miss Finney before you know her story. You've never even met her, yet you're talking about forcing her out of the Exposition." Gil's eyes told an eloquent story that Alex didn't want to read. "It's not like you to condemn a person out of hand, Alex. At least, it's not like the Alex English I grew up with. I hope to God you're not turning into another Henry, Alex, or I might just be forced to take action."

He said the last few words with a smile on his face and a laugh in his voice, but Alex still read the truth in his eyes. A mixture of indignation, fury, and absolute, bone-deep hurt kept him speechless.

Gil took note of his silence. "Damnation, now I've wounded your feelings. I'm sorry, Alex. But, dash it, I'd hate to see you turn into an intolerant old fusspot before you're even thirty. You used to be a generous, good-hearted fellow, old man. I know you've always worked like the very devil to achieve your success, but you used to have a sense of humor and an even deeper sense of honor and integrity."

"Integrity?" Alex gaped at his friend. "Are you insinuating—"

"No!" Gil passed a hand over his eyes, as though he wanted to clear them of fog. "You're still full of integrity and honor. You always have been. But you used to care about other people, as well. You used to possess a gentle nature and a sense of fun. You used to possess a sense of goodwill and tolerance for those less fortunate than you."

"Fortunate!" Alex knew that his anger was justified at last. He bridled. "Good fortune had nothing to do with my success, Gil. You know that as well as I do."

Another sigh leaked out of his friend's mouth. "I do know it. You've worked damned hard, and your success has been well-earned. But, dash it, Alex, you're . . ." He hesitated again, as if he didn't want to create a rift in their friendship. "Damn it, Alex, you're losing your humanity!"

Alex fought a sneer and lost. "My humanity? Are you suggesting I'm wrong in wanting only wholesome and morally sound displays and educational entertainments at this fair, Gil?"

Gil slumped. "No. I'm not suggesting that. I'm only suggesting that your heart might be hardening with your success, old man. I hear that happens to people's arteries. They get hard as the people get old, and their circulation stops. I don't want your heart to get so hard around the edges that you can't see the good in people of all walks of life, Alex. You used to be the most open-handed and openhearted of men." Gil shrugged. "That's all."

"I see. In other words, I'm turning into Ebenezer Scrooge before your very eyes, is that it?"

Gil ran a hand through his hair, then clapped his derby upon it. "Now I've offended you. I'm sorry, Alex."

"Not at all," Alex said, offended to his toenails. He drew his gold watch from his pocket and glanced at it for show. "But I see I must be going now, old man. Give my best to Suzanne."

And he stalked off. Reflected in a window, he saw Gil staring morosely after him.

Kate Finney absently rubbed the black-and-blue marks on her throat as she contemplated the various jars, bottles, and boxes set out on the dressing table in Madame Esmeralda's Fortune-Telling booth. The bruises hurt awfully, and she wasn't sure her windpipe hadn't been permanently damaged. The problem now, however, was how best to hide the bruises her father's fingers had made so that they wouldn't distract the people who entered Madame's booth to get their fortunes told. Kate grinned thinking about a fortune-teller who'd been unable to foresee an attack by her own father. The grin didn't last long.

"You ought to see a doctor, Kate," Madame said around a mouthful of bread and cheese.

"Can't afford it," said Kate. She tried to accompany the words with a careless laugh, but it hurt so much to talk, she quit on the laugh.

Madame huffed and snorted, two things she did when disgusted or upset. Kate was used to it. She absolutely adored the feisty old Romanian Gypsy lady who'd taught her how to read palms and crystal balls and the Tarot cards. As far as Kate could tell, neither one of them believed for a minute that a body could tell the future by gazing at any of those things, but that didn't stop either lady from making as much money as possible purveying the mystical arts.

Whatever it took; that's the way Kate had learned to deal with life. And if it took misleading a gullible public, so be it. Far be it for Kate Finney to balk at the chance to earn a buck or two. Especially not now that her mother's health was in such a catastrophic state.

"Ma needs medical attention more than me," she added when Madame looked as if she were going to pursue the subject. "You know that."

"Fah. You're every bit as important as your mother, Kate Finney. If your health suffers, your mother will suffer, too."

"Stop it," Kate demanded, only partially in jest. "You're making my blood run cold."

"Huh. That girl should have killed that man when she had the chance." After this semi-enigmatic comment, Madame stuffed another bit of bread and cheese into her mouth and followed the bite with one of the hot peppers she loved so well.

Kate understood Madame's intent. She sighed and picked up a pot of light-colored facial paint as she thought about Belle Monroe. Belle had come into the

booth as Kate's father was in the process of strangling
her and had battered him with her parasol. "She tried.
She might have, too, if her umbrella hadn't broken." It
still made her grin to think of that most proper of all
proper southern ladies, Miss Belle Monroe, trying to
stab Kate's drunken father with her broken parasol.
"Too bad, that."

"I should say."

But wishing her father dead didn't pay the rent. Or
the medical bills. Kate knew her mother would get better if only she could keep away from Kate's father. The
doctor said there was no hope, that Hazel Finney had
consumption in an advanced state, but Kate didn't buy
it. Hell's bells, Kate herself had beaten tough odds. Who
was the doc to tell her that her mother couldn't?

Besides all that, the thought of her mother's possible
death made Kate want to curl up and sob. No, sir. Kate
was going to fight her mother's tuberculosis tooth and
nail. And she *was* going to get her mother better one of
these days, even if she had to take her out West, where
lots of lung patients were going these days. Heck, Kate
could work out there as well as she could here. She had
faith in herself. Anyhow, the notion of singing or sling-
ing beer in a wild, western saloon made her chuckle.

The chuckle only aggravated the pain, so she hung it
up and concentrated on covering the bruises without
killing herself in the process. "Ow." She winced when
her fingers smoothed greasepaint over the livid bruises
on her throat.

"I cursed him, you know," said Madame in a matter-of-
fact tone of voice.

"Beg pardon?" Kate paused with her fingers on the
rim of the paint pot.

"I cursed him." Madame took another bite of hot
pepper.

"Pa?"

"Umph." Madame, chewing, nodded.

Kate caught her eyes in the mirror and grinned. "Yeah? Thanks, Madame. I appreciate it." Getting back to her job, she murmured, "Only wish stuff like that really worked."

Madame shrugged. "Sometimes it does."

Kate's gaze snapped back to the reflection of Madame in the mirror. Every now and then, Madame's voice would take on an odd, mysterious timbre. When she spoke thus, Kate was never quite sure whether or not to believe her. According to Madame, she'd taught Kate only the rudiments of the Gypsy's panoply of mystical arts. Such things as Madame believed to be out of Kate's realm of comfort, she'd discreetly kept to herself. "Say, Madame, can you really curse a guy?"

But Madame only smiled at her and broke off another piece of bread. Kate sighed, knowing she'd get no further information from that source. Madame never opened up and spilled her guts unless she darned well wanted to.

The door of the booth opened, and Kate muttered, "Nuts." She'd been hoping to get her bruises covered before she had to face any clients.

"I'll see who it is." Madame stood up, dusted crumbs from her brightly colored skirt, and slipped through the curtains to the front part of the booth.

Kate hurried with her makeup job. She had to get herself presentable now, because she wouldn't have time to do so later. Pretty soon she'd have to leave Madame's and go to her other job, which was dancing as a stand-in for Little Egypt. Although she probably made more money dancing, Kate preferred telling fortunes.

She'd learned when she was a tiny child to present herself to the world with bravado. That was the main reason she, among all the girls who'd auditioned for the position, had been selected to dance: because she looked uninhibited. Inside, where no one could see, she didn't enjoy exposing so much of her body to public view. Doing so made her feel cheap, and she didn't like the feeling; she'd been fighting the image of a cheap slum girl all her life. It also opened her up to comments and rude suggestions from the gaggle of stage-door Johnnies who always flocked around the Egyptian Palace, lurking in wait for poor unsuspecting dancers.

They hadn't reckoned on Kate Finney when they'd commenced lurking. Kate hadn't been gullible since she was a baby, and she suspected pretty much everyone of pretty much anything. Especially men. She didn't trust the average man farther than she could throw him. So far, she'd had no trouble ridding herself of hangers-on.

Long ago she'd decided she'd do anything, except things she found morally repugnant, in order to help her mother. "Ah, gee, Ma, please don't die." The words slipped through her lips in spite of the pain in her throat, and they were as close to a prayer as Kate ever got.

"I'll see if she's available." Madame's words penetrated the curtain to Kate's ears, and Kate's fingers stilled as they reached to put the lid on the pot of makeup. She tilted her head and looked into the mirror, wondering if Madame had meant herself, Kate Finney. *Am I available for what?*

The curtain parted, and Madame, casting a glance back at the booth, slipped in. She jerked a thumb over her shoulder. "Man. Says he needs to talk to you."

Kate lifted an eyebrow and reached for a damp towel to clean her hands. "What's he want?"

Madame shrugged and headed to the small table where the remains of her bread, peppers, and cheese lay.

Understanding that she'd get no further elucidation from Madame, Kate checked quickly in the mirror to make sure her bruises were as invisible as she could make them—not very—grabbed a bright red-and-green-striped scarf and wound it around her throat to cover what the makeup didn't, snatched up her multicolored shawl and flung it over her shoulder, and headed for the curtain. As soon as she saw who awaited her, she stopped in her tracks. "I've seen you," she blurted out before she could stop herself.

The tall, elegantly clad young man turned, frowning. Kate's heart pounded out a threatening beat in her chest.

The man said, "Have you?" He finally removed his hat, and Kate realized he ought to have done so sooner. Her heart thudded faster when she understood that he hadn't done so because he didn't consider Madame or Kate worthy of polite, gentlemanly gestures. Kate didn't, either, for that matter, but she'd die before she admitted it.

"Yes. Around. Here at the Exposition." She gestured vaguely, then straightened her spine. Blast it, *nobody* could treat Kate Finney like dirt and get away with it. "Did you have some business to discuss with me?"

"Yes, if you're Miss Kate Finney."

"I am." He was being deliberately rude, or Kate missed her guess. Because she'd made it a policy not to take guff from anybody, even rich men, she snapped, "And you are?"

The bastard bowed. Kate, recognizing the irony intended by the gesture that should have been gentlemanly but wasn't, didn't open her mouth, but stared, hoping she appeared as rude as he.

"Alex English," he said, straightening. "I am a member of the Agricultural Forum at the Exposition."

Kate's frown didn't abate. "Oh. In other words, you're a farmer." She gave the last word a slight special emphasis and curled her lip.

He didn't like that. Kate was pleased.

"More than a farmer, Miss Finney. I am one of the directors of the fair." He walked farther into the booth.

The blasted man was tall and broad-shouldered, he had pretty blond hair that waved like Kate wished her own hair would do, and he took up too darned much space. Kate, who was short and slight of build, wished she'd spent more time cultivating her mystical-Gypsy presentation. If she couldn't out-bulk him, she might have out-mystified him if she'd practiced more. She said, "Yeah?" in as insolent a tone as she could summon. She wished her throat didn't ache so badly; it was difficult to be insolent when she could hardly talk.

Alex glanced around the booth, as insolent as Kate. Kate wished Belle Monroe would come back and hit him, as she'd hit Kate's father. "So. This is where you perpetrate your trade, is it?"

Perpetrate your trade? Kate continued to stare at Alex, thinking what an ass he was. It was too bad, too, because he was a fairly good-looking man. Unfortunately, he was also a pompous poop. "This is where Madame Esmeralda and I tell fortunes," she corrected.

"Same thing." Alex waved a hand at the mystical hangings on the wall. "Do these symbols mean anything?"

Kate watched as his gaze went from a picture of the Hanged Man to the Three of Cups to the Emperor. Kate had asked Madame to remove the picture of the Devil because she didn't want any clergymen taking umbrage, and Madame had done so. Now Kate was particularly glad that Madame was such an easygoing spiritualist. But she wasn't sure how to answer Alex's question, mainly because she didn't know why he'd asked it. Her sense of self-preservation was a finely honed instrument, and she smelled a rat here.

Instead of answering him, therefore, she said, "Why do you ask?"

"Curious. That's all."

"I doubt it."

His smile held no amusement. "Do you mind if I sit, Miss Finney?"

"That depends. You want your fortune told?"

"No." He said the word gently, as if he were humoring a lunatic.

"Then state your business, please. I have work to do."

"Yes. Well, that's the difficulty, you see."

Oh, Lord. Kate felt it coming. He was going to kick her out because of her damned bastard of a father. As if the lousy son of a bitch was *her* fault. Because her knees felt shaky, she pulled out a chair and sat. "Sit down and get to the point," she commanded sharply.

To her surprise, Alex did so. She'd expected him to refuse to do anything she suggested. Even sitting, he took up too much room. "I've come here today because of the incident that happened yesterday."

"Yes. I'd already figured that one out."

His smile was short and cynical. "Ah, I see. Well?"

"Well, what?"

"It was a very unfortunate incident."

"You said it." She resisted the impulse to finger her bruises. Her heart screamed that none of this was her fault, and that if Alex English had a shred of human compassion in his soul, he'd be nice to her. But that was silly. Kate knew better than to expect compassion from rich businessmen.

In the face of her defiance, Alex seemed to be getting annoyed. Kate hoped so. His cynical smile vanished, his eyebrows lowered, and his frown looked more heartfelt. "Miss Finney, I'm sure you realize that we can't have such things happening at the World's Columbian Exposition."

"Yeah? Well, I can assure you that I'll never try to strangle anybody, if that's what's got you worried."

His lips pinched together briefly. "I never expected that you would."

"And," Kate went on, "I've never once stolen anything from anyone or tried to gyp anybody out of anything. If that's what's bothering you, you can forget it. I earn my money honestly."

Another sneer marred the clean lines of Alex's face. "By telling fortunes and dancing in a lewd costume?"

"Lewd?" Kate, who'd had her own qualms about dancing in her modified version of Little Egypt's costume, did a creditable job of gawping at Alex. "You'd better not tell any of those Egyptians that you think the costume's lewd. That's the way they dress. I don't think they'd like it if you accused them of being lewd—and they all carry really big scimitars." She smirked at him. "That's a kind of sword. And those Egyptian fellows are really protective of their ladies, too." She wished American men were more like them.

"You know very well what I mean," Alex growled.

Kate stood up. "Yeah, I know what you mean. You don't want my kind working at your precious fair." She pointed a finger at Alex. "Well, let me tell you something, mister. I may have been born poor, and I may have a disgusting drunkard for a father, but I'm not my father. I'm a hardworking girl who's only trying to make a living for my mother and myself."

"Now see here, Miss Finney, I—"

"No, darn it! *You* see here! *I* didn't do anything wrong! It's not my fault my father's an ass! If you want to punish somebody, punish him. I didn't ask for him to be my father. Believe me, if I could have chosen, I'd have chosen to be born to a nice family with lots of money and a pretty little farm somewhere in the country. I didn't get the choice."

"Really, Miss Finney, there's no call for—"

"No call for me to say these things? Like heck there isn't! You come sauntering in here like a king, sneering at me and what I do for a living. You treat me like dirt, and—"

"Now, see here! I didn't—"

"You did so! You sneered and smirked and wrinkled your nose and acted like Lord Whosis who just discovered ants on his salad plate! Well, for your information, Mr. Alex English, I'm not a darned ant! I'm a girl who's trying her best to overcome her beginnings and create a life for my mother and myself. And if you dare try to kick me out of this Exposition, I'll—I'll—"

But Kate didn't know what recourse she'd have should this awful man try to expel her from the Exposition. The realization was so bitter, and her need to keep her jobs at the fair so great, that she actually almost came to within an inch of crying. She'd never be so weak. Rather, although tears welled in her eyes and her throat ached as if her father's fingers were still tightly squeezing it, she slammed her fists on her hips and glowered at Alex.

Alex rose from his chair and clapped his hat on his head, thereby covering all of his pretty blond waves. "There's no need for this hysteria, Miss Finney."

"Hysteria! *Hysteria?* You come waltzing in here, threatening my only means of income, and you accuse me of being hysterical? You're a louse, you know that, Mr. English?"

"Really, Miss Finney, I didn't intend to—"

"Like heck you didn't!"

Alex squared his shoulders. Kate might have been impressed by the broadness thereof if she didn't feel so utterly desperate. "I can tell that you're not fit to undertake a polite discussion at the moment, Miss Finney, so I shall leave you now."

"Good." She was glad to see his eyes snap with anger.

"I'll be back." And, upon that dire warning, Alex English left Madame Esmeralda's fortune-telling booth.

As soon as the door closed behind him, Kate collapsed into one of the chairs at the table holding her crystal ball, shaking like a leaf on an aspen tree in autumn. She'd used the ball only the day before to bash her father over the head. The memory of that awful incident, and the possible repercussions thereof as represented by

Mr. Alex English and his ilk, made despair flood her. She buried her head in her hands and prayed for some sort of miracle. "Or even a fair shake, God. Can I have maybe just *one* fair shake for once?"

As usual, she didn't hear a word from God, and her innards told her that, as usual, fair shakes were not handed out to the likes of her.

Two

Alex was more disturbed by his encounter with Kate Finney than he'd expected to be. In truth, he hadn't expected to be disturbed at all. After all, it was he who was the rich, successful fair backer, not she. She was a mere nothing. A girl of questionable moral character who owed her continued presence at the Exposition to his goodwill.

Dash it, she hadn't been at all what he'd anticipated. As he'd approached Madame Esmeralda's Fortune-Telling booth, he'd expected to find a woman who more nearly resembled what he'd pictured a low-class girl like her to be. He'd anticipated encountering a disreputable-looking specimen, a blowzy degenerate, a hussy. In short, he'd expected to find the real Kate Finney's antithesis.

The real Kate Finney hadn't fit his assumptions at all. Not one little bit. Well, except for her sassy attitude and disrespectful manners. But she hadn't used poor grammar. And she hadn't been painted up like a scarlet woman. And she hadn't worn anything particularly scandalous. Granted, those silly looking Gypsy garments had been outrageous, but they had covered her from top to toe. She'd even had a vibrantly colored striped scarf draped around her neck. Alex shook his head, frowning and thinking about that slender, delicate neck.

It was difficult to imagine a drunken man's hands encircling the small white column and attempting to squeeze the life out of it. And the girl's father, at that.

Thinking about it gave Alex a sick feeling in his middle, which was most unusual. What was it Gil MacIntosh and Kate had both said? Her father wasn't her fault? In spite of himself, a reluctant laugh escaped Alex's mouth. Kate Finney had spunk; he could give her that much at least.

Still and all, he didn't think her sort belonged here, at his precious fair. He walked down the Midway Plaisance away from Kate's booth, and glanced with satisfaction at all the wonders presented therein. The Libbey Glass Works exhibit was a particular favorite of his. He'd stood for over an hour one day, watching the workers blow glass into gorgeous pieces of art. He'd bought a couple of them for his mother. And he and Gil had dined more than once in the Polish Village, where a fellow could get a good Polish sausage sandwich, complete with sauerkraut and mustard, and wash the whole mess down with a pint of delicious, light-colored beer.

And hadn't the fair introduced the delectable new treat, Cracker Jacks, to the public? And the hamburger? Why, there were new innovations everywhere here, even when it came to food! This was what education was all about. This was what the Fair Directory aimed to present to the public. And if Sitting Bull's camp surrounded an ostrich farm that drew interested people by the thousands, wasn't Buffalo Bill's Wild West an educational enterprise? In a manner of speaking? Granted, the fair directors hadn't allowed the great Colonel Cody to occupy space within the fairgrounds itself, still, the Wild West had become an integral part of the total fair experience.

Then there was the art and music that proliferated everywhere. J.P. Sousa was performing his rousing marches daily in the White City. Flags waved everywhere, and patriotism was rampant. This was America's fair. This was the culmination of two hundred years of American ingenuity and cultural and industrial prowess.

And then there was the Street in Cairo. Alex permitted his smile to fade. He had no quarrel with Egyptians or their culture, no matter what the pert and saucy Kate Finney claimed. If such scanty costumes were part of the Egyptian heritage, so be it. Alex might consider such costumes an indication of a backward and morally corrupt culture, but he knew that Americans found it both interesting and educational to witness the backwardness of other nations. Indeed, viewing such sights was good for American morale, because doing so could make a man proud of how advanced his own culture was.

The problem was that unlike the venue in which Kate worked, there were no scanty costumes worn by women on the Street in Cairo. One had to go out of one's way to see the scandalous dancing of Little Egypt. And Kate Finney. Alex discovered his hands bunching into fists as he recalled Kate, and forced them to relax.

Imagine! A little person like that getting his goat. Such a thing had never happened before. Nobody talked back to Alex except his sister Mary Jo, because he was the most reasonable and considerate of men. And Mary Jo only did so because she was fourteen years old.

He remembered sneering at Kate and not removing his hat when he entered her booth, and he cringed inwardly. Very well, he'd made a mistake there. He ought to have approached her differently. But how could he have known that she was such a—firebrand? Outrageous bit of goods? He couldn't find the precise phrase to describe her. This was due in part to her very unexpectedness. She hadn't looked cheap and she hadn't sounded like the product of the slums. Rather, she was fairly short, perhaps five feet, two inches or thereabouts, and as slim as a boy. She had dark brown hair that she'd dressed neatly in braids which, he presumed, was a Gypsy style of hairdressing. The hairdo made her look like a small girl, not at all like the conniving harpy Alex had assumed her to be.

And spunky? He got angry just thinking about how impertinent she'd been to him. He hadn't anticipated that quality. He'd expected cringing and crying, not overt belligerence. Gil's accusation came back and socked him in the jaw. Alex stopped walking and grimaced.

Had he been too hard on the girl? He didn't like to think so. He liked thinking of himself as a good man, a tolerant one, a man who didn't judge people without evidence. The fact that he'd judged Kate before he'd met her didn't sit well with him, and he wondered now if he'd hoped to have his preconception of her confirmed by his visit.

"Dash it." Alex scuffed the toe of one of his brand-new, hand-sewn, French-calf walking shoes, for which he'd paid the extravagant price of five dollars, and pondered the intricacies of life. Perhaps Gil was right. Perhaps Alex had become the tiniest bit complacent as his fortune had grown. Maybe he was becoming stodgy. Maybe he was developing into an intolerant man, unwilling to give the Kate Finneys of the world a chance to earn a living. He didn't like to think that, either.

Lifting his chin and straightening his spine, Alex came to the conclusion that he was being much too hard on himself. It was, after all, his responsibility to see to the wholesomeness of the Exposition. If the presence on the premises of Kate Finney threatened good taste or public morals, it was his duty to rid the fair of her besmirched presence.

With that in mind, and feeling generous and forgiving, he decided to visit the troubled and troubling Kate again. Perhaps he'd even watch her dance. Maybe he was being too critical of her. If he were to be absolutely honest, he'd have to agree that she wasn't responsible for her father being a drunkard. If Alex discovered, however, that she was a disruptive influence, and if he found her to be a magnet for the kinds of unruly behavior of which neither he nor his fellow agriculturalists approved, then she'd have to go.

He felt better about himself after that, and his step picked up as he walked toward the Polish Village. He felt the need for a restorative sausage, kraut, and, most particularly, a glass of beer.

Kate tied a wide, black velvet band around her throat and gazed into the mirror, dissatisfied. Darn her father, anyhow. It was bad enough that he refused to shoulder his responsibilities for his family, but to interfere with her efforts on her family's behalf was too much. Not that she expected anything better from him. He'd always been a louse. She wished he'd fall down drunk in front of a milk wagon someday and get himself run over and killed. But Kate knew he'd never do anything so obliging. Why didn't justice prevail in this stupid world was what she wanted to know. It wasn't fair that her mother was sick and her father, who was as worthless a specimen of humankind as ever lived, thrived.

Philosophical questions only confused her so she chucked them out. She had more important things to do. Getting ready for her dance number, for instance.

"That looks sort of funny, Kate, that black band."

Kate turned to grin at Stephanie Margolis, one of the legion of women hired to sweep up and mop out the exhibits on a daily basis. "I know it, but it's better than black-and-blue marks."

Stephanie didn't grin back. "I'm awful sorry about what happened, Kate. If you need any help, you just come to me, all right?"

Touched by the offer of generosity from a woman in Kate's own low station in life, Kate nevertheless gave Stephanie the response to offers of help that had become natural to her. "Thanks, Stephanie, but I'll be all right. And so will Ma."

The older woman smiled at last. "I'm sure you will. You have heart, Kate, and that's the important thing."

"Thanks, Stephanie."

Stephanie moved on, plying her broom, and Kate adjusted the black ribbon, trying to make the velvet strip cover all the bruises. She gave an internal snort. Why was it, she wondered, that poor folks like dear old Stephanie offered to help, and rich folks, like that ass Alex English, offered to kick her in the butt? "It's the way of the world," she muttered.

Giving up on adjusting the ribbon—maybe nobody would notice the bruises peeking out from behind it— she picked up her cymbals and fitted them onto her fingers. She clanged them during her dance whenever she remembered to do so.

No expert in the art of the so-called "genuine native muscle dance," Kate nevertheless knew how to perform when she had to. She'd watched Little Egypt often enough, and practiced long enough, that nobody else knew she was a faker. They might suspect something this evening, however. She frowned at her reflection and again fingered the black band. The lights were dim when she danced. Maybe nobody would notice the bruises.

As a rule, Kate wore a short, strapped top with beads and tassels dangling therefrom, along with a gauzy skirt that was split up the side to reveal her left leg—shocking, that—which was encased in black stockinette ending just above her knee. Thus, people could occasionally catch a glimpse of her naked upper thigh if they stared hard enough. She figured they were even more titillated by the white garters she tied about her thighs to keep her stockings up. They'd be a darned sight more titillated if she danced as she'd heard real Egyptian ladies did: barefoot and bare-legged. That would call the Purity League down on the fair in a heartbeat. Alex English would never hear of it. She sniffed at the thought of the stuffy Alex.

She'd unbraided her hair and now it lay in waves over her shoulders, as formerly braided hair will do when left to its own devices. She wore a metal head ornament that reminded her of chain mail, which covered the top of her head. Dangly ornaments hung from the chain mail and jangled around and banged against her forehead when she was particularly energetic, which she tried not to be because it hurt to be banged by bangles. The headpiece was so outré as to divert people from her blue eyes.

Little Egypt herself, who was actually Syrian and whose real name was Fahreda Mahzar, had once told Kate in an accent so thick Kate could hardly understand her, that nobody paid attention to a girl's face when she was dancing. Kate, who chose her alliances carefully, believed her.

The saving grace of the outrageous costume, to her mind, was the sheer scarf she waved around as she danced. It was probably a provocative item of drape, but Kate used it more to cover her assets than to reveal them. She was sure Alex English wouldn't agree. But, then, he was too proper, too much of a decorous gentleman, too much a blasted snob, to visit her performance. Drat the man. She wished she could stop thinking about him, but he worried her. A lot.

Alex English, however, was neither here nor there. She had to prepare for her act, and that dratted black velvet band around her neck looked stupid. "Oh, who cares?" she said at last. Better an article of clothing that looked out of place than a series of black-and-blue finger marks. Besides, she was pretty sure none of the Americans in the audience would know an Egyptian costume from one from Outer Mongolia—or even Mars.

Turning, she picked up her scarf, a pretty peacock-blue number that shimmered like fish scales in the electrical lights. The whole effect of her clad as she was, when combined with those weird bagpipes and drums of the native musicians, was exotic, to say the least.

The peculiar wailing of the Egyptian music had irked Kate when she'd first heard it, but she was becoming used to it. She'd learned, much to her sorrow, that a person could get used to darned near anything if her livelihood depended on it. Therefore, she walked from the dressing room to the stage and waited behind the curtain, tipping winks and grins to the people working behind the scenes. They all liked her. Kate had made sure of it.

The bagpipes which, Kate had been told, were made of goats' bladders, at last squealed out a familiar tune, the drummers started whacking on their drums, and Kate took a deep breath. She was always nervous before she danced, although the state didn't last long. Her cue came rattling at her on a drumbeat, and she whirled out on stage, making sure her scarf did its duty. Thunderous applause greeted her. Kate didn't take it personally. The fools all probably thought she was Little Egypt herself instead of Little Egypt's American stand-in.

Kate danced her heart out, as she did every evening, and left the stage as she'd arrived upon it, in a whirl of peacock-blue scarf to the sound of cheers and claps and funny, squealy, Egyptian music. "Phew!" She winked at one of the drummers, who grinned back at her.

At first, she knew, she'd shocked these men who took their art so seriously with her free-and-easy ways. Those guys didn't know they were from a backward nation. All they knew was that they were sharing with interested American persons their culture, which they loved every bit as much as any American loved his. Strangely, Kate identified with them. Often she felt as though she were participating in an American culture with which she had little, if anything, in common.

She went to the dressing room and took a glass of water because dancing made her thirsty. She danced twice on a typical evening, in order to give Little Egypt the opportunity to have a little supper. Or a lot of supper. Little Egypt was a meaty dish. She was a lot meatier than Kate, but nobody watching seemed to mind.

By the time she'd told fortunes all day and danced half the night away, Kate was always tired. After her second performance this evening, she was particularly worn out, probably because of her ordeal the day before and her constant, nagging fear for her mother's health. Not to mention the possibility that her only source of income might be cut off at the whim of that idiot Alex English. She washed every smidgen of makeup off and gladly exchanged her costume and dancing shoes for more comfortable garb.

Clad in a dark skirt and jacket, white shirtwaist, and neatly tied ascot, she left the Egyptian Palace. She'd knotted her hair up and plopped a hat on top of it, and looked like neither Gypsy fortune-teller nor Egyptian dancer. Thus clad, she was seldom recognized by the public she served, which was the whole point.

Therefore, Kate was startled when a small boy ran up to her and shouted, "Miss Kate Finney?"

Taken aback, she said, "Who wants to know?"—which was the question people in her neighborhood always asked before admitting identity. After all, the person asking might represent a bill collector or an officer of the law.

The boy said, "Jerry O'Hallahan, but I don't really care who you are unless you're Kate Finney. If you're Kate Finney, your brother told me to give you this." He thrust a grubby wad of paper at Kate.

At once, Kate's heart gave a painful spasm. If one of her brothers was trying to get in touch with her, it probably meant that something was wrong. Jerry O'Hallahan, the urchin, held tight to his prize until Kate fished a penny out of her handbag. "Here, kid. Now get lost."

The boy saluted smartly, accustomed to such pleasantries from the gentry, and sauntered off whistling "Daisy Bell," one of the latest popular songs. With trepidation in her heart, Kate unfolded the paper, which was damp with sweat from Jerry's fists.

Her heart sank like a boulder in a pond as she read the words: *Took Ma to hospital. Come quick. Billy.* "Nuts," she whispered, and wished she wasn't too tough to cry.

She very nearly shrieked when she heard a voice come to her out of the dark.

"Miss Finney? I need to speak with you."

Whirling around, she beheld none other than Alex English. She frowned, sensing more trouble. "What do you want?"

"To speak with you." He looked grim.

His looks were nothing compared to the savagery roiling in Kate's own bosom. "Yeah? You got a carriage, Mr. Rich Guy?"

He blinked, obviously surprised by this reaction. "A—a carriage? Why, yes, but—"

"All right. I'll talk to you. But it's going to be in your carriage, because you're taking me to the hospital on Fourth and Grand Oaks."

Kate wasn't surprised when Alex's mouth opened and closed a few times, making him look like a particularly elegant variety of the trout family. But he led her to his carriage, which is what Kate needed.

Alex wasn't quite sure how it had happened, but not five minutes after he'd spoken to Kate Finney on the Midway, he was directing his driver to make haste to Saint Mildred's Hospital. Although he told himself he didn't really want to know, he said, "Are you ill, Miss Finney?"

"No. I'm fine. What do you want to talk to me about? My morals? My father's morals? My Aunt Fanny's morals?"

Alex frowned. This woman was very difficult to talk to,

perhaps because she seemed to approach all conversations as a soldier might approach a deadly battle. Her attitude offended Alex, who had been feeling put-upon ever since Gil McIntosh told him he was turning into a fussy old man.

"Really, Miss Finney, there's no need for such an attitude."

"No?" She kept glancing nervously out the window.

Alex got the impression of tremendous energy trapped in Kate's small body. He sensed that she'd like to get out and shove traffic out of her way so that his carriage could make better time. She was definitely worried. Deciding it might behoove him to discover the source of her trouble before telling her his impressions of her so-called "dance," he muttered, "If there's something the matter, Miss Finney, I'd like to know what it is. Perhaps I could help."

That got her attention. From staring out the carriage window, her head whipped around, and she commenced staring at him. Her scrutiny made Alex uncomfortable even before she spoke.

"You? Don't make me laugh."

After her words smote him, his discomfort turned into ire. "Now see here, young woman, I don't understand your hostility. I only asked a civil question."

"Yeah? Why do I get the impression you're only asking because you think you have to? Sort of a gesture, you know? Before you kick me in the teeth, you'll lull me into thinking you care."

"Now, really! There's no call for that sort of thing." Why was it that every time he encountered this woman— which, he realized, had only been twice so far—she outraged him? What had he ever done to her that he should earn such enmity? Well, except for questioning the propriety of her working at the Exposition.

"No?" She tilted her head and surveyed him from top to bottom. Alex felt like squirming. He hadn't felt like squirming in his entire adult life, and he found the sensation extremely unpleasant. "Listen, Mr. English, why don't you tell me what you want to talk about? If it's about my father, I can't help you. I don't know where he is. If I'm lucky, they've got him locked up, but I'm not usually lucky."

Good Lord. Alex had never heard anything like this before in his whole life. He couldn't imagine so young a woman being so hard and cynical. "It's not about your father. It's about you."

She seemed to slump for no more than an instant, then straightened her spine again. "Yeah? What about me?"

Drat the woman. A person would think he was the one at fault here, when it was she who was the one performing salacious dances and telling fortunes. Everyone knew fortune-tellers were no better than criminals.

"I saw your performance this evening."

"Yeah? Pretty good, aren't I?"

"For heaven's sake, Miss Finney! That dance is scandalous!"

"It's not scandalous. It's Egyptian. How come you've never talked to Little Egypt about how scandalous *she* is? How come you're telling *me* I'm a hussy?"

"A hussy?" Alex felt himself flush and could only be glad the carriage was dark inside. "I said no such thing."

"You thought it," Kate said baldly. "And I'm not."

"Of course not." He didn't believe it. He thought she was a hussy. The truth smacked him like a blow. Gil's accusation taunted him, and he tried to shake it off.

"Listen, Mr. English. I'm only trying to make a living however I can. It's not my fault I wasn't born with a silver spoon in my mouth, like you were—"

"Now see here—"

"Darn it, listen to me, will you? I work hard. Very, very hard. And it's not easy, what I do. I'm trying to support myself and my mother, and believe me, the world isn't kind to women who are trying to support themselves."

"You ought to get married. That's what you should do." Alex was sure of it. Marriage and motherhood were the roles established for women, no matter how poorly this present example of femininity might fill the roles. Until her face set like granite, he hadn't believed she could look any harder.

"Yeah? My mother got married. See the result?" She yanked at her scarf, and Alex winced when he saw the dark, brutal bruises thus exposed. "Marriage isn't for me, thanks anyway."

"You know very well such a marriage as that is uncommon, Miss Finney."

"Not where I come from, it isn't. I've got better things in store for my life than marriage, believe me."

"You sound like a suffragist," Alex said stiffly. He didn't hold with woman's suffrage. What did women know about the world and politics?

"Suffragist, my foot," Kate scoffed. "I don't give a hang about suffrage. I don't have time to think about suffrage. All I'm trying to do is put food on the table. And I won't let you stop me, if I can help it."

"I'm not trying to stop you from putting food on your table." He was becoming annoyed. This little chit was trying to make him out to be some kind of ogre. "What I'm trying to do is maintain a proper tone at the fair I helped to create."

"Yeah? Well, somebody said it was all right for Madame Esmeralda to set up a booth on the Midway, and somebody else said it was all right for Little Egypt to dance there, so I guess we don't really have anything to talk about, do we? I guess everybody else thinks our tone is proper enough." She turned and resumed looking out at the street.

Alex saw that her fingers were tapping out a nervous

tattoo on her handbag. He got the impression her state of anxiety didn't concern herself, but someone else. The person at the hospital? "Are you worried about someone at the hospital, Miss Finney?" He was surprised when he heard the question since he hadn't intended to ask it.

Again, she turned and gave him a look that told him what she thought of him. Not much, if anything.

"Yeah," she said sarcastically. "You might say so."

"May I ask who it is?" That was polite, wasn't it? He'd sounded as if he cared, even though he didn't, really.

"You can ask. I don't choose to answer."

"Dash it, you're a very rude woman, Miss Finney!"

"Gee, I'm really sorry. I usually try to be nice to people who are trying to ruin my life." The carriage pulled up in front of the hospital. Before it came to a complete stop, Kate had opened the door and leaped out.

Alarmed, Alex lurched to the door after her. "Miss Finney! Miss Finney! Wait!"

She didn't wait. Furious, Alex decided he didn't need to lower himself to Kate's level and charge after her, but waited until his driver had guided the horses to the curb. Then he descended from the carriage in a dignified manner and spoke to Frank, the coachman. "Wait here Frank. I'll be back as soon as possible."

"Sure thing, Mr. English." Frank touched his cap in a short salute and set the brake. "I'll be right here."

Tugging at his expensive, worsted frock coat to eliminate any wrinkles, Alex started up the walkway toward the front doors of the hospital. To his irritation, Kate had already vanished into the building. He, however, wasn't through with her yet, no matter what she thought. He was going to get to the bottom of the puzzle that was Kate Finney, whether she wanted him to or not, dash it. Alex hated being thwarted. And to be thwarted by an unlettered, unsophisticated girl from the slums, at that—well, it was too much, and he wouldn't stand for it.

* * *

It took Kate only a minute to ascertain that her mother had been taken to the Charity Ward. She'd expected it would be so, because that's where her kind always ended up, if they ended up in hospitals at all. Generally speaking, they just died without the diversion of a hospital stay.

She ran up the staircase, holding her skirt in her hand, heedless of the gaping hospital orderlies staring at her flashing ankles. Her mother's ward was number 3B. Kate jerked the door open and stood, panting, staring in distress at the rows upon rows of cots with their pathetic occupants. She had to swallow a cry of mingled rage and pain before she stepped, with more seemly aplomb than she'd heretofore exhibited, into the room.

Her heart raged as she walked down the first row of cots, searching for her mother's haggard face. It wasn't fair. Nothing was fair. That her mother, a blameless, pure soul, should have been deceived into marrying her father, a devil incarnate who could put on a good show when he wanted to, was one of life's more bitter ironies. Her mother hadn't deserved such a brute as Kate's father. Kate knew that Ma would have left the bastard long since, except that he'd threatened to injure the children in retaliation. So she'd stayed with him, and he'd only injured her.

That was before Kate was old enough to take matters into her own hands. The last straw had been one night when her father had come home reeling drunk after having spent all the money he'd made doing odd jobs. He'd been mad and mean, and, needing someone to take out his anger on, he'd headed straight for Kate's mother. It was Kate who'd beaned the beast over the head with a cast-iron skillet. And it was Kate who'd dragged her mother out of the house and to her own small room over the butcher's shop.

Hazel Finney had been terrified, but Kate had lectured her long and hard about the wisdom of finally, after far too many years, getting away from her husband. "He's no good, Ma. You know that better than anyone."

Her mother, already sick with consumption, not to mention in a general agony of spirit and soul, had broken down and sobbed. She'd nearly broken Kate's heart with her moans of apology, as if it had been *her* fault she'd married a wretch and a drunkard.

"I swear to you, Katie, that I didn't know," she'd cried. "I swear on my mother's Bible."

"I know it, Ma. I know it."

Kate had never been much good at being a child, having spent her youth figuring out how to survive in an uncertain and often brutal world, but it had been then that she'd taken over the mothering of her family. Her siblings had left home by then, driven away by the misery her father perpetrated.

Since home had never offered any succor but that which their mother could sneak them behind their father's back, Kate's brothers had taken to visiting Kate when they needed a good meal or a shoulder to cry on. They were all overjoyed when Mrs. Finney joined Kate in the room over the butcher's shop.

Every time any one of the children ran into Mr. Finney on the street, he threatened to kill them if they didn't tell him where his wife was. Fortunately, all the Finney children were spryer than the old man. It was embarrassing, they all agreed, to be cursed at and threatened with death by their own father, but it was better than living with the mean old son of a bitch.

He'd meant the threats, as Kate had recently discovered. If it hadn't been for the unexpected arrival of Belle Monroe into Madame's booth, Kate would be dead right now, and her mother would probably be back under her father's thumb. The idea made Kate shudder. She didn't even consider that the police should have arrested the old man for attempted murder. The police didn't pay much attention to what happened to people in Kate's station in life. They spent all their concern on the Alex Englishes of the world.

"Ma!" Kate's relief at finding her mother still breathing was only lessened by the dismal surroundings and her mother's obvious distress. She fell to her knees beside the cot. "Ma, what happened?"

Her mother's eyelids lifted, revealing watery blue eyes that held a world of pain and disappointment. Yet the woman managed to smile at her daughter. "Katie. I'm fine, really. I told Billy not to bring me, but he insisted."

"Nuts. I ordered Billy to bring you whenever he thought you needed help when I wasn't around, Ma." She wouldn't tell her mother so, but Kate understood why her brother had insisted Mrs. Finney go to the hospital. She looked even worse than usual. In truth, she looked like she was already dead and was only still talking by pure chance.

Her mother's smile made Kate want to scream imprecations against the Fates or God or whoever was in charge of things. That her mother, who was the gentlest, most loving human being in the world, should have to suffer like this wasn't right, and Kate resented it. Nevertheless, she smiled back, as cocky as ever. "Tell me the truth, Ma. What happened?"

Hazel Finney tried to sigh, which precipitated a spasm of coughing. Kate held her breath and gritted her teeth as she watched her mother's affliction. "It's okay, Ma. Take your time." Kate dug a clean handkerchief from her handbag and wiped tears and perspiration from her mother's withered cheeks. Hazel Finney lifted the stained handkerchief she'd been holding and discreetly mopped the blood and spittle from her mouth. She still had her pride, Kate knew, for whatever good that had ever done her.

"I had a little coughing spell," Mrs. Finney told her daughter when she could.

"I see." Kate hated feeling helpless. Unfortunately, no matter how much grit and determination she had—and she had tons—she was helpless when pitted against the white plague. That didn't stop her from fighting it tooth and nail, however.

Hazel smiled through the tears that still pooled in her eyes, left over from her coughing. The coughing spasms took everything out of her. "And how about you, Katie? Did you dance tonight?"

Kate gave her the sauciest grin in her repertoire. "You betcha, Ma. I gave 'em a great performance."

Hazel patted Kate's cheek with a hand that looked too heavy for its arm. "That's my Katie." Her vague smile faded and died. "But what's this, darling?" She reached for the scarf tied around her neck, and Kate cursed herself for loosening it in her pique at Alex English.

Quickly reaching for her mother's hand, Kate drew it away from the scarf. "It's nothing, Ma. Just a piece of my costume. I guess I forgot to take it off."

Her mother's troubled eyes told Kate that Hazel didn't believe her. "Kate, if Herbert did that—"

"Ma, I'm fine." Kate made her voice go hard, as if with irritation at Hazel's prying. "It's nothing."

Mrs. Finney stared at her daughter with eyes that told Kate she knew exactly what had happened. "Oh, Katie. My precious Katie. Don't let him hurt you, Kate. Please."

Kate knew that if her mother wasn't so weak, she'd rise from the cot and try to tackle the world for her children. Fighting the world and Herbert Finney for her children's sake was what had ruined her health.

"Nuts, Ma. It's nothing. Honest. You just stop thinking

like that. Here, take some water." Kate knew the spasms left her mother weak and thirsty. "I'll lift your head."

With a sigh, Hazel Finney gave up. "Thank you, Katie. You're the best daughter anyone ever had."

"Nuts." As ever, Kate swallowed the bitter tears clogging her throat as she poured water from a cracked pitcher into a cracked glass standing on the table beside the cot. Then she very carefully lifted her mother's head and raised the glass to her mouth. Hazel drank a few sips before her eyes closed, and Kate could tell she was too exhausted even to drink more water. Without speaking, she lowered Hazel's head to the pillow.

"Thank you, Katie," Hazel whispered without opening her eyes.

"Sure thing, Ma. I'm going to talk to the nurses now. You tell me if they don't treat you right, you hear?"

Without opening her eyes, Hazel managed a gurgling laugh. "They treat me fine, Katie. You just don't worry about me."

Fat chance. Kate wouldn't say so. Rather, she squeezed her mother's hand, rose from her kneeling position, and squared her shoulders. Feeling rather as she expected knights of old felt when preparing to go off to war, she marched back down the row of cots in search of the nurses. Kate knew they didn't pay much attention to charity cases. Why should they? But she wasn't going to let them get away with ignoring *her* mother.

Three

Alex had never been to this wing of the huge hospital. He'd visited friends at Saint Mildred's occasionally, and once or twice had visited on behalf of an agricultural charity or benevolent association. He'd donated lots of money to the hospital, but he hadn't actually observed the ward at which his charitable donations had been hurled.

The cold walls, which had once been painted white and were now fading to a creamy yellow, made him shiver. The hospital board hadn't wasted any pretty scenic prints on these walls. And there was no flutter of nurses eager to be of service to the patients. There were no flowers, no boxes of chocolates, no baskets of fruit, no pretty dressing gowns. For that matter, there were no rooms.

When he opened the door to ward 3B, in fact, all he saw were several straight rows of small, cheap cots, each one filled with a huddled form. The room wasn't quiet, as he expected a hospital room to be. Rather, moans and coughs and sobs greeted his ears. He saw one white-clad form bending over a cot that seemed like half a mile away, and he took the form for one of the nursing sisters.

With a feeling of impending contamination, Alex steeled himself and ventured forth into the room. It seemed to take him forever to reach the nurse. He tried not to look at the people on the cots, but he couldn't help himself.

Looking was a mistake. Alex had never been this close

to absolute desperation and hopelessness before. He didn't like it. How did people sink this low? Was their destitution their fault?

He'd always believed poverty to be a man-made condition, and one in which only the meanest of souls wallowed. But most of these people were women, and the few men he saw didn't look particularly debauched. Rather, they looked sick.

But surely, they had family members who could help them. Didn't they?

Alex discovered that all of his preconceived notions about good and bad and wealth and poverty were getting muddled up, and he decided to think about them later. Right now, he wanted to discover what business had taken Kate Finney to this awful place. And in his carriage, too. Alex managed to work himself into quite a respectable huff when he considered how kind he'd been to bring her here and how rude she'd been in return. She hadn't even thanked him.

The nurse looked surprised to see such a well-dressed gentleman in the Charity Ward. "May I help you, sir?"

Alex presumed the woman was a nun, since Saint Mildred's was a Catholic institution. He didn't hold with popery, although he was tolerant enough to allow Roman Catholics to exist in his city. "I'm looking for—" He stopped speaking all at once, realizing he had no idea whom he was looking for.

"Yes?" The nun smiled kindly upon him.

"Um, Miss Kate Finney was visiting—someone—here. I, er, wanted to know . . ." Good Gad, he hadn't until this minute realized how flimsy his motivation was.

"Oh, Kate." The nun laughed softly. "Dear Kate. I'm afraid that no matter how hard she tries, or how much she prays, her mother still has consumption. And I'm also afraid that even if Kate had a lot of money, there's only so much that can be done for Mrs. Finney."

"Her mother?" Alex swallowed. "Er, yes. Mrs. Finney. Exactly."

"Are you here to visit Mrs. Finney?" The nun looked skeptical, as if she couldn't credit such a fine gentleman having anything to do with a member of the Finney family.

Alex hesitated for a moment, then discovered his mouth making up his mind for him. "Yes," he said, surprising himself. "I'm here to visit Mrs. Finney."

"Are you a member of the family?" The nun eyed him strangely. She reminded Alex of an all-white penguin, with her arms folded and her hands tucked into the sleeves of her habit.

"Employer," he said promptly. "My name is Alex English, and I'm a member of the Agricultural Board at the Columbian Exposition. Miss Finney works for me." In a manner of speaking. At least she worked at the Exposition at his whim. The notion gave him no comfort. Actually, he was beginning to feel like Little Red Riding Hood's Big Bad Wolf, and the sensation was not to his taste.

The nun's air of confusion vanished and was replaced by one of pleasure and surprise. "How nice of you to take time to visit, Mr. English. Most employers don't care, I'm afraid. It's such a comfort to know there are kind hearts in our city."

Guilt attacked Alex. He fought it off as if it were a mugger in the park. Dash it, he *was* a kindhearted person!

"Follow me," the nun said, still smiling. "I think Mrs. Finney is asleep, but she might be able to see you. She is," she whispered confidentially, "in rather poor shape, I fear. She's had quite a difficult life, I understand."

Alex said, "Mmmm." He didn't want to hear about Mrs. Finney's difficult life.

"This is her cot." The nun stopped beside a bed that looked as if somebody had just climbed out of it and left a jumble of covers in her place.

Slowly, reluctantly, Alex walked up to the bed. He didn't want to look down for fear of what he'd see, but he forced himself.

Damn. His worst fears were realized. What had looked like a jumble of covers was the sheet-clad body of a tiny, emaciated female form. "My God," popped out of his mouth before he could stop it.

The nun gazed down at the woman on the cot, her sadness clear to read on her gentle features. "I fear she's awfully sick, Mr. English. It's kind of you to visit."

That was the second time the nun had accused him of being kind. It was the second time Alex knew he didn't deserve the word, and he hated the knowledge. "Isn't there anything that can be done for her?"

Beside him, the nun sighed. "I'm afraid we have no cure for tuberculosis yet. I understand scientists have isolated the bacillus that causes it, but a treatment is still years away. The best we can recommend is rest and quiet, preferably in warm, dry, peaceful surroundings."

Alex dragged his gaze from Mrs. Finney and cast a glance at the Charity Ward. "These surroundings aren't very peaceful."

"No," the nun agreed. "They aren't. They're all we have to offer people like Mrs. Finney, I fear. Taking care of consumptive patients is a costly business, Mr. English. Unfortunately, most families can't afford to send their members to a sanatorium in the countryside."

"No. Of course not. I didn't mean—"

She laid a hand on his arm. "Of course you didn't. I wasn't criticizing. I think it's wonderful of you to take an interest in the family. They're a hardworking, good lot, except for the father. And we keep praying for him."

"Hmmm." Any man who'd allow his wife to linger in this hellhole needed more than prayer. He needed a bullet in the brain.

An idea was beginning to take root in Alex's head, and

he wondered if a bullet to the brain might do *him* some good.

Mrs. Finney stirred on her cot. A small hand reached out from under the rumpled sheet. "Kate? Katie, love?" The hand moved, as if it were feeling for another person. The hand looked like a claw and the voice was like a soft scrape on the atmosphere.

"Oh, dear." The nun sighed deeply. "Miss Kate was here a few minutes ago, but she's left already."

"She's gone?" Alex asked. It was all he could do to resist reaching for Mrs. Finney's hand.

"Yes." The nun laughed softly. "After giving us strict orders on the care of her mother. As if we could do any more than we're doing."

He couldn't stand it any longer. He took Mrs. Finney's hand. It was small and dry and it made him want to holler. "Calm down, ma'am," he said, striving for a gentleness he didn't feel. In truth, he felt savage. "Miss Finney has gone home."

Hearing a new voice seemed to stir Mrs. Finney. Her eyes opened, and she turned her head to search for the voice. As he knelt beside her, Alex got the strong impression of a man up to his thighs in quicksand. If he didn't wriggle out soon, he feared he'd be in way over his head.

Nevertheless, he spoke in a soft, quiet voice. "It's all right, Mrs. Finney. My name is Alex English. I, ah, work with your daughter."

A smile transformed Mrs. Finney's features. Alex thought he could detect the girl she used to be in that smile, and it made him want to add a few curses to his holler. She'd probably looked like Kate when she was young. Say, a hundred years ago, or so.

But that probably wasn't so. She might be only in her early forties. Perhaps even her late thirties. It had been life that had withered Mrs. Finney. Damn, damn, damn.

"You know my Katie?"

"Yes, ma'am." He decided to leave it at that, since he was certain his opinion of Kate Finney differed considerably from Kate's mother's opinion of her.

"She's a good girl, my Katie. She takes care of me, you know."

Not very damned well, Alex thought, knowing as he did so that he was being unfair to both women.

What had Kate said to him? Something about women having a hard time making a living in this world? Ah, yes. It was something like that. And then he'd told her she ought to get married. He cringed to remember that conversation now, as he held Mrs. Finney's hand. How could he have tossed her such a flippant suggestion? Kate had been right about marriage in her mother's case. It hadn't been her salvation; it had probably been her doom. Small wonder Kate didn't want to get married.

"It's so nice of you to visit me, Mr. English."

Mrs. Finney's voice was soft and harsh, as though it hurt coming out of her mouth. Alex forced himself to smile at the sick woman. "Nonsense. I wanted to meet you."

Her eyes opened wider. "You did? I mean . . . How kind of you."

Alex was beginning to react negatively to that word, *kind,* perhaps because he'd begun to reevaluate his own claim to own it. Was he kind? He'd always thought so. Perhaps, however, his own brand of kindness didn't deserve the name. He'd made it a point to contribute to charitable causes. He'd always donated surplus foodstuffs grown on his farm to the Chicago soup kitchen run by some Catholic order or another. He couldn't even remember the name of it.

Was that true kindness? For only a second, Alex tried to envision his own revered mother in this horrible cot in this horrible ward. He couldn't bear it much longer.

Yet Kate Finney bore it all day, every day. Kate, who was half his size, but who had the determination of a lioness, worked at two very odd jobs in order to keep her mother in food and away from her brutal husband.

Suddenly Alex felt extremely small—about half the size of Kate Finney, in actual fact.

"Have you seen my Katie dance, Mr. English?"

The question took Alex aback, mainly because he had trouble justifying the note of pride he heard in Mrs. Finney's voice. "Er . . . Yes. I watched her performance this evening, in fact."

Mrs. Finney nodded, as if she were pleased that her daughter was exhibiting herself so shockingly to the public. "She taught herself how to dance that way after watching that other dancer. The foreign girl. What do they call her?"

"Little Egypt."

"Yes. That's the one. My Katie only saw her once, and when they posted a notice that they were looking for another dancer to fill in for her—she's become very popular, I guess . . . "

"Yes," Alex confirmed. "She has." He tried to keep the note of condemnation out of his voice.

"Yes." Mrs. Finney sighed. "My Katie practiced for a day and a night, and then she marched right over there and danced for the men who were doing the hiring— and they hired her! Just like that."

"Ah." Alex didn't know what else to say.

Mrs. Finney sighed again. "She bought me a woolen scarf that night with the money she made. I didn't really need one, because I still had one, but Katie said it was old and moth-eaten, and she gave me the new one. It's so pretty."

Alex felt like dirt when tears trickled from the sick woman's eyes. "That was nice of her." Feeble. He assessed his comment as approximately as feeble as Mrs. Finney.

"Oh, Katie's more than nice. She's been my salvation. And she takes care of her brothers, too."

"Good Gad." Alex hadn't meant to swear. He glanced quickly at the nun, but she'd turned away to resume her duties.

"Thank you for visiting me, Mr. English." Mrs. Finney broke into a spasm of coughs.

Alex fumbled for a handkerchief, but he wasn't quick enough. Blood oozed from the woman's mouth, and his nerves nearly gave out. He'd never seen anything as pathetic as Kate Finney's mother. She broke his heart. "Here," he said gently, finally managing to haul his handkerchief from his pocket. "Use this, please."

"Oh," Mrs. Finney gasped between racking coughs. "I'm so sorry. I don't want to spoil anything so fine."

"Nonsense. It's yours. I just gave it to you."

She tried and failed to smile at him. After another hard spasm, she gasped, "Thank you. You're very good." She seemed to collapse, and Alex knew she'd exhausted her puny strength.

He rose, feeling more ghastly than he could remember ever feeling. "I'll visit you again, Mrs. Finney." He wanted to offer her luck. Or hope. Or something.

But he couldn't make himself lie to the woman. "I'll see you soon."

"Thank you."

He barely heard her thanks. As soon as he figured he was out of her sight, Alex increased his speed. He was practically running by the time he got to the hospital's business offices.

"What?" Kate stared at Sister Mary Evodius.

"She's been moved to a private room, Kate." The nun beamed at her, as if she considered such a circumstance normal and nice.

Kate knew better. "But . . ." She wasn't even sure what to ask.

"Your very agreeable friend made the arrangements,"
Sister Mary Evodius said, still beaming.

A benevolent beam was no less than Kate had come to
expect from this source, but she still couldn't account
for the words she'd spoken. "Um . . . My agreeable
friend? What agreeable friend? Which agreeable
friend?" Kate had friends, sure, and they were all more
or less agreeable, but not a single one of them could afford to move her mother into a private room.

"That pleasant gentleman, Mr. English. He came here
last night shortly after you left."

"Mr. . . . ." But Kate couldn't say it. She couldn't think
it. Shoot, she couldn't even *conceive* of Alex English—
that was the only Mr. English she knew, and he wasn't
anywhere even approaching agreeable—doing something so generous for her mother.

Unless he planned to kick her out of the Columbian
Exposition, and was doing this as a salve to his conscience. Kate sucked in a gulp of air.

Sister Mary Evodius peered at her closely. "Is something the matter, Kate? Are you unwell?"

"Unwell?" Kate blinked at the nun, wondering what
she was talking about. "No. I'm fine, thanks." Or she
would be once she figured out what in Hades was going
on here. "Do you know what room Ma's in, Sister?"

"I believe they wheeled her to number 22A, dear, although you might want to check at the front desk."

"22A. Okay." Kate nodded briskly. "Thanks!" She
waved at the nun as she turned and hot-footed it out of
the Charity Ward. Taking Sister Mary Evodius's advice,
Kate stopped at the front desk. Any time she had to face
a person in an official capacity—*any* official capacity—
Kate put on her toughest demeanor. She knew what the
general lot of women in this world was, and she didn't
aim to be the recipient thereof.

Her tone of voice on this occasion was so sharp, she

made the young man at the desk jump and turn the pages in his registry book so fast, some of them crinkled under his flying fingers. Kate was satisfied with this response. If it had been anything less brisk, she'd have had to get sarcastic. Over the years, Kate had developed a blistering tongue to go with her brusque manner. She was proud of both attributes, because they disguised her feelings of inferiority rather well.

Sister Mary Evodius had been right. Kate had wasted a lot of time in the hospital, but she needed to see her mother before she went to work. Maybe Ma knew what had possessed Alex English to pay for a private room. Kate visited every morning and every evening when her mother's tuberculosis got out of control and she had to remain in the hospital for a time. Unfortunately, Mrs. Finney's hospital stays had become more frequent of late.

Kate found herself tiptoeing as she approached room 22A. She'd never been in this part of Saint Mildred's. This was where the rich people stayed. Kate felt out of place and nervous, although she didn't show it. She paused in front of the door to 22A, wondering if she was supposed to knock. Rich people liked their privacy—and they could pay for it. But this was her mother's room. "Aw, heck," she muttered at last. Then, squaring her shoulders, she shoved the door open so hard, the door handle bumped against the wall. "Blast it." She hadn't meant to push it *that* hard.

Her precipitate entry woke her mother with a start that set her to coughing. Kate felt terrible. Rushing to Mrs. Finney's side, she hurried to apologize. "I'm sorry, Ma. I had a hard time finding you this morning."

Mrs. Finney pressed a handkerchief to her lips, but Kate saw she was smiling in spite of everything. She reached for the hand not holding the hankie. "I'm real sorry, Ma. Didn't mean to make so much noise."

Her mother only shook her head, a gesture Kate knew

was meant to reassure her. It didn't, but Kate wouldn't let on. Instead, she glanced around the room. "Say, this is swell." Her heart hurt a little, although she couldn't have said why. She wasn't jealous that Alex English could provide her mother with better medical care than she could. Was she?

Kate, who didn't think it was a good idea to fool oneself because life was hard enough even when you admitted your foibles and follies, wasn't sure. She'd have to think about it. But she really didn't think it was jealousy, *per se,* that made her heart hurt. She thought rather that the pain was a manifestation of her limited ability to cope effectively with the cards life had dealt her.

After her mother's racking coughs stopped and she lay exhausted on the bed, smiling up at her daughter, Kate gave herself a hard mental shake. She didn't want to upset her mother. "So, Ma, when did you move to these grand quarters?"

"Last night. That wonderful Mr. English came to visit me right after you left, and he made the arrangements."

"Ah." Kate hated to add, "That was nice of him."

"It was the kindest thing in the world, Katie. I don't remember hearing you talk about him."

"No. I didn't even know him until yesterday." Should she have admitted that? Ah, nuts.

Her mother looked puzzled. "Really? I'm surprised. I mean, I thought you and he were old friends."

"Now where would I meet a gent like him, Ma?" Kate laughed at the notion. "He's rich, for Pete's sake."

"I know." Her mother's washed-out blue eyes scrutinized Kate's face until Kate would have blushed and squirmed—if she did things like that. She didn't. "But . . . Well, I guess I don't understand, then, Katie. Why would he pay for a private room for me, of all people? He said the two of you worked together, but . . ."

"Beats me, Ma, but I'm glad he did." And she was

going to find out the answer to her mother's question, too, as soon as she could run Alex English to ground. Whether or not she explained the answer to her mother, Kate would decide later.

"It's too much, though." Mrs. Finney's gaze swept the room. "It's too fine. It's too good for me."

Kate bridled. "Nothing's too good for you, Ma, darn it! It's not your fault we're poor."

Mrs. Finney sighed and started coughing again. Kate winced inside, although she kept her cheerful demeanor in place. When she'd quit hacking, Mrs. Finney whispered, "Of course, it's not. dear."

Kate patted her hand, but Mrs. Finney still seemed distressed. "It's my fault I married your father, though, Katie. If that wasn't wrong, it was at least stupid. And even you have to admit it was a horrible mistake."

"Oh, Ma, hush up about that. You didn't know what he was like when you married him."

"I knew soon enough afterward that I should have done something, though."

"Don't be daft. What could you have done?" Kate hated when her mother blamed herself for things. Everyone knew that women were the slaves of men, even in the United States, where life was supposed to be easier than it was anywhere else and where slavery wasn't supposed to exist any longer. Kate knew better. Maybe women didn't have to walk around veiled from head to toe, as Little Egypt had told Kate Egyptian women were forced to do, and maybe they weren't shackled to their husbands, but women in the good old U.S. of A. had precious few rights of their own.

If Kate's mother had left her father, and if her father had wanted to, he could have kept Kate and her brothers. He'd probably have done it, too, the monster. Her father didn't give a rap about any of his kids, but he'd have kept them in order to torment Hazel Finney. He was like that, the son of a gun.

"Oh, Katie, I'm so sorry."

"About what?" Kate asked briskly. Sometimes she deemed it appropriate to nip these guilty apologies from her mother in the bud in order to avert a frenzy of self-recrimination. None of her family's misery was Mrs. Finney's fault. Kate knew it, if her mother didn't. "About trying to do your best? If you keep apologizing, Ma, I'm going to have to take steps."

As usual, when Kate pretended to get on her high horse, her mother's worries seemed to fade. She smiled at her daughter. "You're a jewel, Katie. You're the best daughter any mother ever had."

"I doubt that." Kate wrinkled her nose. This time, Mrs. Finney chuckled softly. Kate held her breath, but her mother didn't start coughing. Thank God, thank God. "Say, Ma, I've got to get to work. Gotta tell those fortunes, you know."

"I wish I could watch you work, Katie. I'm sure you make a beautiful Gypsy."

"I make a very silly looking Gypsy, actually, but Madame lets me use her makeup so I can darken my skin. Nobody seems to mind my blue eyes. Anyhow, the booth is dark, so they probably can't even see them. It's spookier that way."

"Ah, Katie, I love you so."

"I love you, too, Ma." Kate rose, leaned over, and gave her mother a quick peck on the cheek. "I'll be back tonight, Ma. Don't let 'em give you any guff."

"Never." Mrs. Finney chuckled again. "They wouldn't dare. Not with you and Mr. English both looking after me."

"Right." Kate waved merrily and left the room with her usual lightness and grace. As soon as she closed the door behind herself, she expelled a gust of breath and leaned against the wall for a moment.

She hadn't anticipated her own reaction to her mother's new surroundings, but the truth of the matter was that she, Kate Finney, a young woman whose entire focus in this life was to overleap the barriers of her birth and class, was pure-D, absolutely, positively, no-doubt-about-it intimidated by all this fancy stuff. She glanced at the walls in this wing of the hospital and noticed all the pretty pictures hanging there, and the bright white paint. Kate would have bet anything that the Charity Ward of Saint Mildred's hadn't been painted since the Civil War.

This place scared her. She kept expecting some rich matron to walk out of one of the rooms adjoining that of her mother, observe Kate in the hall, and call a nurse or an orderly or somebody to escort her out. She didn't belong here, with respectable people. Kate Finney wasn't respectable. She was trash. People had been telling her so all her life, and no matter how much she denied the label, resented it, and rebelled against it, she believed it.

She straightened and took on another cargo of air. Intimidation was no excuse for slacking. Nor was being trash. If Alex English was paying for that room, then even if Mrs. Hazel Finney didn't deserve the benefits that came with first-class accommodations, Alex English's money did, and Kate was going to be darned sure her mother got them. She marched to the nurse's station, willing to be nice about it, but prepared for a fight if anyone challenged her.

By the time she got to Madame Esmeralda's booth at the fair, Kate felt as though she'd already worked a twelve-hour day. She heaved a sigh as big as herself when she saw Madame Esmeralda, dressed to the hilt in her Gypsy suit and swigging a carbonated beverage from one of the Exposition glasses the concessionaires sold on the Midway. Tossing her handbag onto a chair, Kate sank into another one.

Madame cocked one black eyebrow. Kate wished she could do that: lift only one eyebrow at a time, because the gesture was great for quelling the opposition. She'd practiced, but she hadn't succeeded yet in duplicating the eyebrow-lift properly.

"Rough morning?" Madame asked.

"Yeah." Kate's feet hurt, her head hurt, her heart hurt, and her eyes were gritty from lack of sleep.

"How is your mother this morning?"

Kate recognized Madame's intensified expression as one of concern. Madame wasn't like most of the people Kate knew. Whether she'd been through more rough times than most, or her attitudes were a product of her being a Gypsy, or what, Kate didn't know, but Madame never fussed at her. Kate appreciated her for it. Madame didn't dither, and she didn't weep and wail. Madame was, in short, as practical a person as Kate was. "She's okay. Mr. English moved her to a private room." Since she couldn't lift just one of her eyebrows, she raised both of them to let Madame know what she thought about *that*.

Madame's reaction was exactly as Kate expected it to be. "What does he want from you? He gonna make you quit your jobs here at the fair?"

With a shrug, Kate forced herself to get up and head for the makeup table. "I don't know. I was going to search him out, but I was running late—it took me forever to find Ma's new room at Saint Mildred's—and I decided to let him come to me. I'm afraid he will, too," she added glumly.

"Mmmm," said Madame.

Kate recognized the sound as one of agreement. "I guess it would be a good idea to wear that silly black band I used to dance in last night until these darned bruises go away, even in the booth."

Madame nodded and grunted.

And, with explanations taken care of, Kate got busy with her makeup. She expected Alex English to show up sometime this day, and didn't know whether she wanted him to or not. She knew she probably should thank him for improving her mother's lot in life, but she didn't want to. She also couldn't imagine what his motivation had been.

If he thought Kate Finney was one of *those* women; if he expected her to do something of which Kate disapproved, he'd learn his mistake in no time flat. She might even add a touch of physical emphasis. It would feel good to smack his insolent face.

A notion that she might be the least little bit unreasonable when it came to Alex English crossed Kate's mind, but it didn't stick around to plague her.

Four

Alex was feeling rather proud of himself when he left the Agricultural Building and headed for the Midway. Not even Gil MacIntosh could accuse him of being anything other than an open-handed, generous man now. Not after he'd paid to have Mrs. Finney transferred to a private room.

His insides gave a small shudder when he recalled meeting Mrs. Finney for the first time, and of walking down that row of pathetic cots with their pathetic human contents. He almost wished he could rescue all of those afflicted souls, but he didn't have *that* much money. He felt better about Mrs. Finney, though. Much better.

Of course, Alex couldn't very well go around boasting of his benevolent deed, but he had no doubt whatever that Kate Finney would spread the word. She'd have to. After all, Alex was helping her out, wasn't he? He was feeling so good about himself, in fact, that he even broke into song at one point. No one else was around at the time, or he'd never have done such an unconventional thing.

"Daisy, Daisy, give me your answer, do. I'm half crazy, all for the love of you." He liked the tune. It was bright and perky and fitted his mood today. When he got to Madame Esmeralda's fortune-telling booth, he hesitated for only a moment. He didn't know why he hesitated even that long, unless it was because he was slightly nervous about being the recipient Miss Kate Finney's exuberant thanks. Not that he didn't deserve them.

He pushed the door open slowly, not wanting to interrupt anything if there was a fortune being told inside the booth. The lighting inside was so dim, it took several seconds for his eyes to adjust to the change from bright sunlight.

When he could see again, he discovered, in fact, there were two fortunes being told. Without making any further noise, he stood in the darkened booth and watched the goings-on with interest for a few moments.

Kate, who sat across from a hefty matron at the far table, had lifted her head upon his entry, but hadn't acknowledged his presence by doing anything else. She didn't even give a smile or a nervous start. After he removed his hat and set it on the rack conveniently placed beside the door, Alex frowned and took a seat on one of the hard-backed chairs lined up against the front wall.

"You see this line?" Kate asked her victim—rather, her client—tracing a line on the older woman's palm as she spoke. "The depth of this line indicates that your family connections will remain strong throughout your life. Anytime you see a line this deep and well defined, you can be sure it means permanence—or as close to permanence as one can get in this life." A smile flickered across her pretty mouth.

The older woman's smile came and stayed. "Oh, I'm so glad. I do so love my children and family."

"Yes." Kate lightly tapped the woman's palm. "I can tell. And this," she went on, indicating another part of the woman's fleshy hand, "indicates to me that you don't want for much in the way of material goods."

"My husband is a very generous man," the woman said, her voice complacent.

"I can tell." Kate, on the other hand, sounded as if she'd just drunk vinegar. "How lucky you are."

Alex wasn't sure what to make of it. On the one hand, he found the older woman's smug air of self-satisfaction hard to take. To judge by her tone, she believed wealth and comfort her due, as if her station in life was something she'd created with her own soft hands; hands that were unused to hard work. Alex imagined Kate found people like this woman trying, at best. He recalled the face of Kate's mother, and his own innards squinched a little.

Poor Mrs. Finney. He'd done a good deed yesterday; there was no denying it. He was proud of himself. Now *he* had good reason to feel a degree of self-satisfaction today, because he'd earned it. Unlike the woman simpering there across the table from Kate. Kate's voice interrupted his thoughts.

"You will be happily married for many more years."

"Oh, my." The woman giggled. "I'll be sure to tell Godfrey that."

Godfrey, Alex supposed, was the woman's husband. Poor bastard.

But that was unkind. Alex didn't know but that Mrs. Godfrey Whatever was an admirable specimen of womankind under her layers of fat and complacency. He eyed the woman again and doubted it.

"And I do see a long trip for pleasure in your future, too." Kate's voice was like the purr of a cat, Alex decided, when she was telling fortunes. When she spoke to him, she sounded more like an infuriated tigress.

"Europe," the woman said with conviction. "I'm sure Godfrey is going to surprise me with another trip to Europe. Or perhaps this time we'll go to Egypt."

"Really? I'd love to go to Europe. Or Egypt. I'd love to see the Sphinx and the Pyramids." Kate's voice had taken on a wistful quality that made Alex's heart twist uncharacteristically. "I love reading about all the discoveries people are making there."

"It's terribly dirty in Egypt," the woman declared, as

if dirt were something she cared not for. "Although Shepheard's is a rather nice hotel."

"Ah," said Kate. She sat back in her chair and released the woman's hands. "That's it, Mrs. Gentry. I see nothing but good times ahead for you—barring the natural unpleasantnesses that life has in store for all of us."

Mrs. Godfrey Gentry's chair scraped as she pushed it away from the table. She got to her feet amid a fluff and rustle of bombazine and petticoats. Aiming a glorious smile down at Kate, as if she were bestowing a blessing upon an underling, she said, "Thank you so much, Madame Katherine. You're a wonderful fortune-teller, my dear. I do believe you deserve more than you charged me." She fished in her large handbag and produced a coin, which she held out to Kate.

Although he wasn't sure why, Alex bridled on Kate's behalf. That dashed Gentry woman was speaking to her as if Kate were a servant in her mansion or something.

"Thank you very much. I appreciate your generosity." Kate rose, too, without scraping her chair and without a rustle or a fluff. Alex wasn't surprised. She was amazingly graceful for a girl out of the—Alex stopped himself before he could pass another judgment on Kate Finney because of her unfortunate birth. Her family, as she had been quick to point out to him more than once, wasn't her fault.

And, really, her mother had been quite pleasant. Obviously, the woman had deplorable sense and no discernment, or she'd never have ended up with Kate's father, but she still seemed a congenial woman. Unlike her daughter, who was approximately as genial as stinging nettles. Alex rose from his chair and bowed as Mrs. Gentry swept past him and out the door.

"Come with me."

To his shock, Kate grabbed him by the coat sleeve and

tugged at it. He stared down at her in bemusement. "Where? Why?"

In a harsh whisper, Kate said, "Darn it, we need to talk, and we can't do it while Madame's working."

Alex glanced around the booth. He'd managed to overlook Madame and her client entirely, so engrossed had he been with Kate and hers. He didn't understand his oversight, either, since Madame was much closer to his chair than Kate had been. "Oh." He reached for his hat. "I see."

Kate marched him out of the booth, around to the back, stopped walking, and turned to face him. Alex had been rather hoping she'd guide him to a concession-aire's stand and take a cup of tea with him or something, although he had no idea why. He didn't even like her. It was illogical for him to want to take tea with the girl.

He didn't understand why she'd narrowed her eyes into mean-tempered slits and was now frowning up at him. It was quite a way up at that, since he was a little over six feet tall, and she was only slightly over the five-foot mark. It was the first time he'd taken note of her lively blue eyes. They snapped and sparkled in the sunlight, and made for an odd but intriguing contrast to her Gypsy attire and dark makeup. Although he didn't really know anything about Gypsies, he'd always assumed they had dark skin, dark hair, and dark eyes. Kate's hair was a dark reddish brown and her skin, except when she painted it, was fair. And she had eyes the color of a clear summer sky. At the moment, she also had her fists planted firmly on her hips and was standing braced like a boxer about to punch an opponent out of the ring.

"How come you put my mother in a private room?"

Alex caught his breath. He hadn't anticipated such a sudden and stark attack. Actually, he hadn't anticipated any kind of attack. He'd rather hoped for some thanks. His lips thinned when he realized how silly it had been of him to expect thanks from this quarter. He tried to keep his temper in check. "Your mother is a very sick woman, Miss Finney."

"You think I don't know that?"

"Of course you know it. But you can't pay for the best medical care for her. I can. It's simple, really."

"It's not that simple, Mr. Alex English, and you know it. Until yesterday, you didn't know me from Adam—"

"Eve," Alex corrected.

Kate stamped her foot. "Darn it, don't you dare laugh at me!"

He held out his hands in an I-give-up gesture. "I'm not laughing, believe me. I've seldom felt less like laughing."

"Then answer my question!"

Alex gazed down at her for several uncomfortable moments before he crossed his arms over his chest. He wanted to understand her attitude, but it wasn't easy to do. "Why are you being so belligerent, Miss Finney?"

"I'm not belligerent!" she shouted. Realizing she'd raised her voice, she hissed, "I'm not a fool, either, Mr. Alex English. I want an answer."

"Why do you call me Mr. Alex English, Miss Finney? I don't understand why you need to use my name as a bludgeon. You may call me simply Mr. English, if you like. Or even Alex, if you want—"

"I don't."

Alex smiled wryly. "Yes, I imagined you wouldn't, although I'm not sure why."

"You're not sure why?" Kate did a fairly good job of looking incredulous, although Alex imagined nothing much ever surprised her. She'd grown up in surroundings that killed off most people before they got to be her age. He imagined she went to great pains not to be surprised by anything—which might, he thought suddenly, be one of the problems here.

"Listen, Miss Finney, I know we got off to a rocky start—"

"Ha! You tried to throw me out of the Exposition!"

He nodded with some comprehension. "I didn't, actually, but I understand why you might harbor that opinion."

"Nuts. You were going to make me leave without even meeting me first, and you know it. You were going to deprive me of my livelihood because my father's a no-good son of a bitch—er, gun, I mean. Darn it, don't lie to me! And I want to know why you put Ma in a private room!"

Alex hesitated and glanced at their surroundings, hoping no one he knew would walk by. Dash it, why was the woman getting so overwrought? It was embarrassing, standing out here with her screaming at him like a fishwife. "Keep your voice down, please, Miss Finney," he whispered, hoping to inspire her by example.

"Very well," she whispered back. "Why? Why? What do you want from me? Darn it, if you think I'm one of *those* women, you'd just better think again!"

Alex goggled at her. "What in the name of heaven are you talking about?"

Kate's lips pressed together once more, and Alex could swear he saw the color creeping into her cheeks under all that outlandish Gypsy paint. "Just answer me, will you? Why did you put Ma in a private room?"

Hoping that honesty would keep her from yelling again, Alex decided to tell the truth—as much of it as he himself understood. In a loud whisper, he admitted, "I— Dash it, I felt sorry for her." Because he felt compelled to, he added, "And you."

The play of emotions on Kate's face was fascinating to behold. Alex clearly saw fury, shame, and pain chase each other across her expressive countenance. He wasn't happy to see any of them.

Kate's voice shook when next she spoke. "Don't you *dare* feel sorry for me, Mr. Rich Man English. I don't need your damned pity!"

Alex, who never swore himself unless he was alone,

and who was shocked when he heard profanity fall from the lips of gentlemen, was aghast when the word left Kate's mouth. "Well, really, there's no need for—"

"What?" Her body had taken to shaking in time with her voice. "What is there no need for? Me to say *damn?* Or your pity?"

"Dash it, I don't pity you! I do feel very sorry for your mother, and whether you want to admit it or not, I can afford to pay for better medical care than you can!"

"But *why?*" Kate shouted. "*Why* are you paying for it?"

Damned if he knew. But Alex couldn't say that. Especially not after being shocked at Kate for swearing. "I like your mother, Miss Finney. She's a—a very nice woman."

"Yes," Kate said, her voice still wobbling precariously. "She is. But she's nothing to you."

"That's not true. I met her. She's in my life now. I couldn't . . . I can't . . ." Alex felt helpless. He didn't know what had compelled him to help Mrs. Finney. "Dash it, she deserves better."

His astonishment when Kate wiped a tear from her eye was totally unfeigned. He hadn't believed the wench had a tear in her.

"Yes," she said. "She deserves better. She's always deserved better. But not from you."

"Oh, for heaven's sake, Miss Finney! You're being ridiculous!"

"Am I?" Obviously, Kate Finney wasn't one to wallow in emotion. That single tiny tear was the only one she allowed herself. She was back in full form immediately, and as cranky as ever.

"Yes. If I want to pay for your mother to have more comfortable surroundings, why should you object?"

"Because I don't trust you."

The flat statement, rendered in a toneless voice, deprived Alex of thought for a moment. "You—you—*what?*" Never, in his entire almost thirty years of life, had anyone dared to say such a thing to him, because he'd never given anyone reason to speak those words. He prided himself on his trustworthiness. His honor. His integrity. His word was his oath, dash it.

"I don't trust you," Kate repeated. "I don't believe anybody in the world, and especially not *you,* would do something like that for my family."

"For your mother," Alex growled. The dashed woman refused to understand. The fact that he didn't understand, either, didn't make the situation any more comfortable.

"She's my family."

Alex acknowledged the truth of Kate's statement with a nod, although he didn't want to.

"So," Kate continued in her curiously flat voice, "what I want to know now is, what do you want from me?"

Alex threw up his arms. "Nothing! For heaven's sake, Miss Finney, what do you take me for?"

"What do you take *me* for?" she countered. "I'm not going to play house with you, if that's what you're driving at."

Alex's mouth fell open. Kate's color deepened.

This time Alex's voice shook. "I have never, ever, been so offended, Miss Finney. If you think I'm the kind of man who would—who would—who could—Oh, dash it!"

Kate didn't say anything. She stood before him, glaring up at him like some kind of madwoman, her small body trembling with rage. And she believed him to be a cad. A depraved rake. A bounder. He couldn't stand it. "Come with me."

And he took her by the arm and began marching her off to a concession stand or a restaurant. He didn't care which, as long as it was nearby. She dug in her heels, but she probably weighed a good fifty pounds less than he did, she was at least a foot shorter, and she was no match for him when it came to physical strength. Alex, who had never forced a woman to do anything at all, dragged her along like a pirate of old might have taken a hostage. He was so angry, he didn't even look to see if they were being observed by other fair-goers.

"What are you doing?" she screeched.

"Be quiet." He glanced over his shoulder at her; she was hanging back as if she believed he was taking her to be executed. "And if you value your shoes, you'd better pick up your feet. I'm sure you wouldn't want to have to buy another pair of shoes just because you're being stubborn."

"Stubborn? *Stubborn!* How dare—*Darn!*" She picked up her feet and, trotting, caught up with him. "What the heck do you think you're doing?" She'd stopped yelling, thank God.

"I'm taking you to get a cup of tea. We're going to talk like civilized human beings."

"I have to work!"

"Dash it, I'll pay you for a fortune-telling session! You won't lose any money, I promise you."

"Hmph."

A surge of triumph swept over Alex. He figured it was premature, but he could at least congratulate himself on getting the obstreperous Kate Finney to do something he told her to do for once. He'd bet not many people could say that. That this would undoubtedly prove to be the only time he succeeded didn't matter.

He didn't let go of her when they reached the Polish restaurant. It was pure luck that Alex had headed in this direction, and he was glad of it. He could use a sausage and kraut. And a beer. Good God, but this woman was an infuriating baggage. He held on tight and marched her to a table in the middle of the outdoor beer garden. "Sit," he commanded, pressing her into a chair.

Kate looked around, her fury transforming to bewilderment, if Alex read her face right. "I've never been in here before." Her voice was low, as if she didn't want to be overheard.

Alex sincerely hoped he was right about that. He didn't want her hollering at him, especially not in a public restaurant. "They have delicious sausage sandwiches with sauerkraut."

"Sauerkraut?" She squinted at him for a second before her expression eased. "Oh, yeah. Sure. I know what that is. Mrs. Schlichter used to give my ma that sometimes. It's some kind of sour cabbage, isn't it? German?"

He nodded. "German, Polish, Prussian. I suppose they all make it over there."

"Ah."

Alex waved at the waiter who had served him a couple of times before. The portly man smiled broadly as he waddled over to Alex and Kate. He bowed to Kate, who stared at him as if he were something new to her. Which he might be, Alex perceived suddenly. Where she came from, she probably didn't get bowed at every day in the week. He spoke to the waiter. "Good day to you, Herr Gross. Lovely day, isn't it?"

"Ach, ja!" Herr Gross's voice was as loud as Kate's had been minutes earlier, but much more friendly. "Anotter beer for you, Herr English? And for the lady?"

Alex glanced at Kate. He noted with some surprise that she seemed to have shrunk in her chair. It struck him all at once that she was uncomfortable here, in this very commonplace restaurant, and he felt a stab of pity. Because he couldn't imagine feeling out of place anywhere, much less a restaurant, he smiled at her, trying not to come across to her as patronizing, although that was probably beyond his power. She perceived everything as patronizing, when it came from him. "Miss Finney? Would you care for a glass of beer?"

Her eyes grew huge, until they reminded Alex of the sapphire-blue crystal Christmas ornaments his parents had bought one year when they traveled through France. "Beer? Are you out of your mind?"

Alex recollected Kate's father, and cursed himself. Because he didn't want to make a scene, he asked, keeping his tone pleasant, "Would you prefer lemonade?"

She opened her mouth, and Alex braced himself to receive a splash of vitriol. But Kate only cast one apprehensive glance at the jovial Herr Gross, looked away again just as quickly, and said, "Yes, please."

Alex smiled at the waiter. "One beer and one lemonade, please."

"Ja, ja. And will you be having another of our delicious sausages and kraut, Herr English?"

"Yes, please." Alex glanced at Kate. She was looking around the restaurant as if she expected to be attacked by marauding Huns any second. He opted to decide for her. "And one for the lady, please."

With a last exuberant bow, Herr Gross went away to fetch the provender. Alex watched Kate with mounting curiosity for several seconds. Although he'd rather shocked himself when he'd first started hauling her away from her booth, Alex was glad now that he'd done it. If he'd known how easy it was to get her to shut up, he'd have taken her to a restaurant sooner. Folding his hands, he placed them on the table, leaned over slightly, and spoke to Kate in a soft voice.

"Now, Miss Finney, perhaps we can hold a conversation without shouting at each other."

He saw her lips tighten, but she still looked nervous. "I won't shout." Actually, she'd lowered her voice so much that Alex could scarcely hear her. Another jolt of sorrow for her circumstances went through him. He thanked God he'd been born of a good family in respectable circumstances, and wondered why he'd never thought to do so before.

"Thank you," he said. "And now I'd like to clear something up, because I want there to be no mistake about my intentions regarding you or your mother."

She watched him like a bird being stalked by a hungry tomcat. "Yeah?"

"Yeah." The word felt funny on his tongue. "I want nothing from you in payment for helping your mother, Miss Finney. Nothing. Not a single thing. Is that clear?"

She hesitated. "I guess." Her lips pressed together again for only a moment. "But I still don't understand."

Alex felt his anger stir and strove to keep it in check. Unfolding his hands, he poked the table with his forefinger. "I am not a monster, Miss Finney. Nor am I an unreasonable man."

She opened her mouth, but didn't use it to speak. Rather, she huffed softly and shut it again.

"I am very sorry your mother has had such a hard life. I'm also sorry that your own circumstances have been so difficult."

"Huh," she said, as if she didn't believe him. "I don't need your pity, darn it."

Alex sighed. "Of course you don't. I'm not offering you pity. I'm trying to understand how difficult life must be for you. You have to bear far too much responsibility for so young a woman."

She eyed him slantwise. "A lot you know about it."

Alex gave up on that tack. She wasn't going to give an inch. He could practically see the chip on her shoulder grow as he spoke. "I went to the hospital yesterday not because I wanted to dig into your private life, but because you asked me for a ride there. I wanted to find out why, although I acknowledge your life is none of my business."

"Right," said Kate.

Alex didn't take the bait. "I found out, and I met your mother. The poor woman is very ill, as you know." He added the last phrase because he didn't want her to smite him with her well-developed sense of sarcasm. "I wanted to help her. I suppose that in helping her, I'm also helping you, but that wasn't my intention, in case you wondered."

She eyed him sullenly. "I wondered."

"Well, then." He sat back in his chair, glad to have cleared up the doubts in Kate's mind. "Now you know."

"And you don't want anything from me in return?" She still looked skeptical, although not quite as much as before.

"Nothing. I want nothing from you."

"Huh."

Herr Gross showed up with Kate's lemonade and Alex's beer, and the two stopped talking. Alex sipped his beer, glad to have something to do with his mouth besides talk.

Kate took a delicate sip of lemonade and looked at him again. Her expression was wary, and again Alex got the impression of a small animal being stalked by a large one. He decided a smile wouldn't be out of place under the circumstances, so he gave her one. "Do you like your lemonade?"

She nodded and gestured at his own foamy glass. It was a small gesture. Alex got the feeling she didn't want anyone else to notice her, although that was impossible since she was presently garbed as a Gypsy fortune-teller. Her costume was, to say the least, exceptional among all the fashionably clad folks dining in the Polish Garden. But people were, for the most part, polite, and no one gaped at her after taking a second glance. "Do you drink much of that stuff?"

The question startled him. "Beer?"

"Yeah. Do you drink much?"

"No. I enjoy a glass of beer with these sausages. Otherwise, I guess I don't drink anything at all. Why?"

She looked away from his face. "No reason. Just wondered."

Alex remembered Kate's father, and understanding smote him. "I'm not like your father, Miss Finney," he said stiffly.

She gave him a glacial stare. "No, you're not. You're rich, and you're not a pig."

Alex felt his eyes open wide. "Thank you. I think."

She didn't smile, but sipped more lemonade. Herr Gross brought two steaming platters heaped with food and set a plate in front of Kate, and one in front of Alex. "Enjoy!" he commanded them with a merry laugh before trundling off to wait on others who'd entered the restaurant. Taking out his gold pocket watch and squinting at it, Alex realized the day wasn't far advanced. It was, in fact, rather early for luncheon, but he still considered this move a brilliant one on his part.

He dug into his lunch with relish. He hadn't realized how hungry he was. Kate, he noticed, looked slightly daunted at the huge amount of food Herr Gross had set before her. "Don't worry about finishing it," he said, feeling benevolent. "I won't scold you for not cleaning your plate." He'd thought he was being funny.

Evidently, he'd thought wrong. "This could feed my brothers and me for two days, Mr. English. I guess we haven't learned how to waste food yet. Maybe when I get rich, we will."

Alex expelled a breath of exasperation. "Perhaps when you get rich, you'll learn some manners, as well." He stabbed at another piece of sausage, delivered it to his mouth, and followed it up with a bite of potato. Miss Kate Finney was possibly the most exasperating female he'd ever met in his life. He absolutely hated it that she viewed him with contempt.

His astonishment was real when he saw the wretched female appear to be ashamed of herself. He was even more taken aback when she said, "I'm sorry. I didn't mean to be hateful."

Since he was still chewing, Alex grunted.

"I'm not used to people doing nice things for me. Thank you." It sounded as though the last two-word sentence nearly choked her.

Alex decided not to prolong the argument with a bitter retort. Rather, after he'd swallowed, he said, "You're welcome. Now eat your lunch."

She apparently couldn't make herself thank him again, because she only nodded, cut off a small bite of sausage, roll, and sauerkraut, and lifted it to her mouth. It was a pretty mouth. Alex had noticed that before. He didn't dare watch her closely, for fear of igniting that ghastly temper of hers, but he did study her surreptitiously as he sipped more of his beer. She was still ill at ease; that much was plain, and it made his interest in her and her circumstances grow. He doubted that she'd ever feel at ease in his company, but he decided he'd make a push to get her to relax. As long as his association with her mother was a fixed thing—until the poor woman died, he thought unhappily—he couldn't very well avoid Kate.

In an attempt to achieve détente, he said, "I like to put some of this mustard on my sausage and kraut. It brings out the tang."

Kate lifted her gaze from her plate, where it had been stuck. "Yeah?" She shrugged with a fair imitation of her usual insouciance. "Maybe I'll give it a try. It's pretty tangy already." A fleeting grin decorated her face.

Alex took heart. Maybe she wasn't a hopeless case. He grinned back. "It is that, all right. I like it." Taking a chance that speaking of his own mother might make her feel more comfortable, he said, "My mother doesn't make sauerkraut. I guess that's because my family's from a different part of Europe, and it's not in our heritage."

Her mouth twisted wryly. "You mean your mother cooks? You haven't hired somebody to cook for her?"

He laid his knife and fork on his plate, lifted his napkin, and patted his lips, glaring at her the while. When he set his napkin back in his lap, he said, "Dash it, Miss Finney, do you always have to say something provocative every time anyone says anything at all to you? I was attempting to forge some kind of bond between us."

She looked at him cautiously. "A bond? Why a bond? What sort of bond?"

He flung his arms out, barely missing Herr Gross. "*Any* sort of bond! I have, if you'll recall, begun caring for your mother. I don't expect your thanks or your gratitude, but life might be more pleasant if you'd stop snapping at me every time I extend a comment in friendship."

A lengthy pause preceded her next word. "Friendship?"

If he *ever*, God forbid, met another female as unpleasant and caustic and downright ill-natured as Kate Finney again in this lifetime, he prayed that he'd have enough sense to turn tail and run away from her as fast as he could. Even holding a civil conversation with this woman was next to impossible. "You have, undoubtedly, the world's largest chip on your shoulder, Miss Finney. I hope you know that."

Her gaze fell first. She muttered, "Aw, nuts," and resumed eating her lunch. She did spread a little mustard on her sausage first. Alex wondered if that meant anything, conciliation-wise. He doubted it.

Five

Kate peered around the doorjamb before she dared enter her mother's room that evening. She didn't want to run into Alex English, mainly because she had nothing to say to him. He scared her.

But that was silly. Kate could take care of herself in any situation. She'd grown up fighting for survival, and Alex English was sure no match for some of the thugs she'd bested in her short career as a human being. Besides, he'd never make an untoward advance. It had become painfully clear to Kate earlier in the day that he'd rather die than think of her as a woman. She was just a poor little, not-quite-grown-up street urchin whose mother was sick.

The knowledge ate into her guts like a canker.

"Darn him," she muttered under her breath as she surveyed the room. He wasn't there, thank goodness, so she entered, sauntering and jaunty. She'd die sooner than let her mother perceive even a hint of her inner turmoil.

Tiptoeing to her mother's bed so as not to awaken her if she was sleeping, Kate looked around at the room. Somebody—she knew who—had sent Ma some flowers. Her heart twisted slightly, knowing that Alex English could afford to send her mother flowers, when Kate herself couldn't. She tried to think charitable thoughts about him. After all, her mother loved flowers. Kate was glad she had that pretty bouquet of roses and daisies and baby's breath to cheer her.

But darn it all, Kate wanted to be able to do nice things for her mother. She didn't want some rich stranger doing them.

Even working two jobs, Kate didn't have the spare change for a bouquet like that. The best she could ever come up with was a bouquet plucked from bushes in the park—and that was provided the groundskeepers didn't see her doing it and make her stop. She sighed and sat in the chair beside her mother's bed.

Mrs. Finney looked awful. With a feeling of doom in her soul, Kate gazed at her, thinking once more that she looked dead already. *Please, Ma, don't die.* She'd never say those words aloud.

When Kate contemplated her mother's death, she felt as if she were disintegrating from the inside. She didn't know what she'd do without her mother, who had been her rock and her mainstay for her whole life. Hazel Finney had loved her children with everything she had, ruining her health as she'd done it. Kate knew that her mother had gone without food and warm clothes in order to make sure her children didn't want for necessities. Luxuries had ever been beyond her, but she'd made sure her children had the necessities. While Kate's father drank his family's food money, Hazel had taken in laundry and done anything she could to keep potatoes in the pantry. Potatoes and beans and cabbage. That's what the Finney children had eaten.

Recalling the gigantic lunch Alex English had bought for her earlier in the day, Kate felt like crying. She'd been unable to finish it, and would have liked to have taken the rest home to give to one of her brothers, but she'd been too embarrassed to ask if such things were done in fancy restaurants. Darned fool. She ought to have just come out and asked. Alex already knew she was poor as dirt. Kate knew better than to shy away from the truth because avoiding it didn't put food on the table. She'd thought she was long past pride, but she guessed she was wrong.

"Katie? Is that you?"

Her mother's papery hand reached for Kate's, and Kate's attention snapped back to the here and now. "It's me, Ma." She strove to keep her voice light and cheerful. "How're you feeling?"

"I'm fine, Katie. That nice Mr. English sent me those beautiful flowers. Did you see them?"

It worried Kate that her mother didn't open her eyes, although she was smiling. Kate guessed the smile was some sort of a good sign. "Yeah, Ma. I saw them. They're real pretty."

"He's a nice man, Katie."

"Right." Darn it, he *was* a nice man. At least to her mother. Kate hated to admit it. Because she thought her mother would like to know, she said, "He took me to lunch today."

This snatch of information opened Mrs. Finney's eyes. "Did he?"

She appeared troubled now, and Kate cursed herself. "He only wanted to assure me that he didn't want anything from me, Ma. Don't worry." Kate knew how much her mother fretted about her children. With good reason. Kate wouldn't have been the first child from one of Chicago's worst neighborhoods to go to the bad. Kate knew girls she'd grown up with who worked as prostitutes, and more than one of them took drugs and drank to excess, probably to forget what they had to do for a living. "I swore years ago that I'd never do anything you wouldn't want me to do, Ma. You know that."

Her mother's smile wavered and fell. "I know it, Katie."

"Aw, Ma, please don't cry. I'm having a great time

working at the fair. You don't have to worry about me or the boys. We're fine."

More or less. Kate's younger brother Bill worked in the butcher shop under Kate's little apartment. Her older brother Walter worked in one of Chicago's slaughterhouses. It was smelly work, but it paid pretty well. Bill had also started investing a little bit of money, which was all he had, in the stock market. So far he'd been lucky, and Kate made sure he didn't take chances.

Neither of the boys drank, either, which was probably more of a miracle than anything else, in Kate's opinion. Their abstinence might be due in part to Kate's threatening both their lives if they ever succumbed to the lure of booze. Kate hoped so. If either boy took to drink, Kate would never speak to him again, and she couldn't afford to lose family. There was so little of it left.

"Walter came to see me last night. He said he's started keeping company with Geraldine Kelly."

"Yeah. He and Gerrie are tight as anything these days. She's working at that big department store downtown. Wanamaker's. They're going to be fine, Ma. You'll see."

Her mother hesitated a moment before saying, "I hope so."

Kate knew what she meant. She didn't think she was going to live to see her children truly established in life. In her more depressed moments, Kate feared it, too.

"Good evening, ladies."

Kate had been so busy holding her mother's hand and trying to keep the conversation light, that she hadn't heard the door open behind her. Darn. She'd been hoping she'd get out of the hospital before Alex showed up. Her luck was running uniformly bad these days. With a sigh, she stood up, glad she'd washed off all of her Egyptian makeup and was now clad in a sober-hued skirt, shirtwaist, and jacket, and that she'd brushed her hair into a prudish knot. She *really* didn't want Alex English thinking she was a strumpet.

Alex patted the air with his hand. "Don't get up on my account, Miss Finney. Please. I'll just pull up another chair."

Mrs. Finney smiled wanly, but seemed to brighten a little bit. "Oh, Mr. English, thank you so much for the beautiful flowers."

"Yeah," said Kate, wishing she didn't have to, "thanks. That was nice." It was no use Alex telling her she didn't owe him anything. If he didn't know it, Kate did. She'd owe him for the rest of her life for the generosity he was showing to her mother. Kate hated being in debt.

"You're welcome. I thought you might like them, Mrs. Finney."

"I love roses. And daisies." Mrs. Finney sighed. "I always wanted a garden where I could grow flowers."

Kate's heart twisted. If her mother hadn't made the dreadful mistake of marrying Kate's father, she might well have had her garden. But Kate's father wasn't the type to grow things. Rather, he destroyed them. "Someday, Ma. We'll get you a flower garden someday." Even Kate knew that wasn't true, but she couldn't bear to think about it.

"Do you like the country, Mrs. Finney?"

Kate turned to eye Alex with some doubt. While she might, occasionally, offer her mother false coin, as she'd just done, she didn't appreciate anyone else whetting her mother's appetite for things that couldn't be.

But Mrs. Finney didn't seem to mind. She smiled more strongly. "Oh, yes. I remember, when I was small, we lived in a village in County Cork, in Ireland. It was so green and pretty there. And there's some lovely country outside of Chicago." She cast a sorrowful glance at her daughter. "We never got to travel out there very often. My children didn't have—advantages."

"I see." Alex patted Mrs. Finney's hand. "Maybe we'll see if we can do something about that."

All of Kate's instincts for survival went on the alert. She pinned Alex with a hard glance. "Yeah? Like how?"

"Katie," her mother said gently, her voice taking on an imploring quality. "Mr. English is only being nice."

"Nice?" Kate glanced from her mother to Alex. She didn't believe it for a second. Because she didn't want to upset her mother, however, she said, "Oh, of course." When her mother shut her eyes, Kate sent Alex a don't-you-dare-mess-with-my-family glare.

Alex deflected the glare—and it was one of her best—with a smile that made her want to smack him. "Your daughter can be a little touchy sometimes, can't she, Mrs. Finney?"

To Kate's utter astonishment, her mother chuckled. "More than a little, I'm afraid." The sick woman heaved a sigh that set her to coughing. After the spasm passed, she went on, "Kate hasn't had a very pleasant life, Mr. English. I hope you make some allowances. Although," she added, glancing at Kate, "I hope she's not rude to you."

Darn. "I'm not," Kate said, knowing she was lying.

"Not at all," said Alex, thereby sending Kate's instincts on the alert again. Offhand, she couldn't recall anyone else to whom she'd been as rude as she'd been to Alex English, although she'd had good reason to be. She thought. Maybe.

"I'm so glad."

Kate was distressed to see the relief on her mother's face. Did Ma honestly think Kate was rude to people on a regular basis? Recalling one or two incidents that had occurred recently, Kate feared she might have given her mother that impression. Aw, nuts.

"Hi, Ma!"

The cheery voice at the door made all three inhabitants of the room jump a little. Kate whipped her head around and smiled. "Billy! You rat. You scared us all."

Her younger brother, the apple of Kate's eye, swaggered into the room. Kate was pleased to see that he'd bathed and changed clothes before visiting his mother. Bill's job was a dirty one, and smelly, and since nobody in the Finney family could afford indoor plumbing, Bill had to pay to take a bath. Kate was proud of him that he'd done so before visiting his mother.

Bill winked at her. "I was hoping I would."

Mrs. Finney laughed and held out a hand to her son. Alex, looking uncomfortable, rose from the chair he'd pulled up. With a sigh, Kate did what she knew she ought to do.

Speaking first to Alex—he had the money, after all—she said, "Mr. English, this is my younger brother, Bill Finney." When she looked then to her brother, she grinned broadly. "Billy, this is Mr. English, the man who's paying for all this luxury." She swept out a hand, indicating the private room.

Bill evidently didn't share Kate's doubts about Alex's morals and motives. His smile vanished as he held out his hand. "Mr. English, I can't thank you enough for what you're doing for Ma." Irrepressible and unable to be serious for more than a couple of seconds at a time, Bill winked. "She's worth it, believe me."

"Billy," murmured Mrs. Finney, pleased but embarrassed from the look on her face.

"I've already found that out," said Alex, grinning back at the boy.

Well, maybe he wasn't a boy any longer, exactly. Kate herself had reached her twenty-second year without being killed by her father or any of the undesirable people who populated her sphere in life. Bill was only a year younger than she was. He could vote in the next election, for crying out loud. Sometimes Kate contemplated the miracle that had allowed her mother to rear all three of her children to adulthood. That sort of statistic didn't happen very often in the slums, where babies died every day of anything from starvation to diphtheria to abandonment.

She listened to Bill as he sweet-talked their mother. He'd brought his own little bouquet, picked, Kate had no doubt, from some rich person's garden or in a park somewhere. Bill didn't seem to mind that Alex's bouquet was grander than his. In fact, he thanked Alex for thinking of doing so nice a thing, and without the sarcasm Kate often heard in her own voice. Dratted boy. He could charm the apples from their trees.

After a few minutes, right before Kate interfered because Mrs. Finney looked as if she was wearing out, Bill gave his mother a smacking kiss on the cheek. "Say, Ma, I need to talk to Katie for a minute."

Mrs. Finney actually managed a creditable twinkle. "Investments, Billy?"

Her son winked again. "You got it, Ma."

"Investments?" Alex, who had been watching the interplay between mother and children with what appeared to be genuine interest, glanced at Kate and Bill.

Kate didn't want him butting in almost more than she didn't want her mother to think she was rude. The latter sentiment prevailed, however, and she reluctantly said, "Yes. Billy has invested some money in various enterprises."

"Really?" Alex stood up. "Ah, would you mind if I join you? I dabble in the investments myself."

Yes. Kate would mind a whole lot. The darned man was taking over every aspect of her life.

Mrs. Finney whispered, "How kind of you, Mr. English."

Which pretty much put the kibosh on anything Kate had been contemplating saying to the man. She muttered, "Sure. Why not?"

"I could use some advice," Bill said, overflowing with goodwill and gratitude. His was the sunniest nature in the Finney family, perhaps because Kate and her mother had kept him away from his ogre of a father as much as possible. Kate, who valued his good disposition but believed it was overrated under certain circumstances, wished they were still little kids so she could kick him.

"I doubt that I can offer any advice," Alex said modestly. "I was hoping to get some from you."

Liar. Kate turned around so her mother couldn't see the grimace she adopted for Alex's benefit. He only grinned at her. Figured.

"If you don't mind, everybody, I'm going to rest now," Mrs. Finney said.

Kate's attention instantly snapped back to her. Hazel Finney was the important one here, she reminded herself, and she mattered a whole lot more than Kate's uncomfortable sensation of being overpowered by Alex and his money. Bending over her mother, she kissed her on the forehead. "Sure, Ma. Rest up. I'll put Billy's flowers in water while the gents gab about stocks and bonds."

Mrs. Finney's eyes remained closed, but she smiled. Kate took that as approval of her plan, picked up Bill's pathetic bouquet, and marched for the door, past her brother and Alex.

Bill held out a hand. "Wait, Katie, I want to ask you a couple of things."

Sure, he did. As if Kate knew beans about stocks and bonds. She snapped, "Be right back," and kept walking.

Before she reached the door, Alex was there, opening it for her. As she stomped past him, he said, "Don't worry, Miss Finney, I won't squander the family fortune."

She felt her face blazing with fury and humiliation as she walked down the hall.

* * *

The colors and scents of spring rioted in the country-side. The grasses growing alongside the highway were as green as sun-sprinkled emeralds, and the wildflowers shouted their presence in bright reds, yellows, blues, and purples. Birds sang. Crickets chirped. In green, green pastures, cows lowed and bulls pawed the ground, wanting to get at the cows. Sheep dotted the far hills like flecks of ivory, and the apricot, peach, and pear trees were radiant with blossoms.

Chicago's filth and stinks lay behind Alex like a bad dream. This was where he belonged: in the country. The city was good for a change of pace every once in a while, but *this* was what he loved. He breathed deeply and contentedly of the clean country air as his traveling coach neared the family farm.

"Family farm," he muttered aloud. He wondered what Kate Finney would say if he referred to these acres and acres that had belonged to the English family for generations as his "family farm" in her presence. Nothing nice, he was sure.

The girl was driving him crazy. He'd known her for two weeks now, and he still couldn't fathom her. She didn't appreciate anything he did, she had a chip on her shoulder the size of the Rock of Gibraltar, and she treated him with absolute contempt. What was her problem?

Kate hasn't had a very pleasant life, Mrs. Finney had said. *My children didn't have advantages,* she'd said.

Alex guessed that must account for Kate's cursedly insufferable attitude, but it was still hard to take. It crossed his mind that his own attitude might not be so genteel if he'd been reared in the slums of Chicago rather than the glories of this clean, green countryside. He was still brooding about Kate when the coach barreled through the iron gates and approached the house.

Because he'd been puzzling over the Kate Finney problem since he'd climbed aboard the carriage in

Chicago, Alex observed the English farmhouse with a new and critical appreciation, thinking of it in terms of Kate, Bill, and Hazel Finney.

The house was typical of those built in the early days of the century. Two stories. White paint. Green shutters. Huge front porch with an awning that extended the entire length of the house. Lots of big, shady trees lending their loveliness to the picture. Cows in the pastures that surrounded the landscape. Alex couldn't see the chicken coop, but he knew the chickens were in back of the house, scratching and clucking. The barn, painted red out of adherence to tradition more than anything else, stood a few yards from the house. It looked mighty tidy, considering it was a barn. The pigs resided behind the barn, far enough away from the house so that the family didn't have to smell them, but close enough to slop, even during the snowy winter months.

Alex was proud of the appearance of his family estate. He'd worked hard to keep it up and make it better. Still, it was basically a farmhouse, and he was basically a farmer.

He shook his head. Judging from her reaction to that simple little Polish beer garden, Kate would probably be stunned into silence if she were invited into what she would certainly consider such a grand home.

He couldn't suppress a grin at the delicious thought of Kate being stunned into silence. It might be worthwhile to bring her out here for the mere pleasure of shutting her up. He was sure she'd think Alex and his mother and sister resided in a great and fabulous mansion, complete with grounds and servants.

To Alex, the English farmhouse was a comfortable old family home. Big enough, certainly, for a family of six or more, and with quarters for a household staff, but it didn't come close to mansion-size. In fact, the place was pretty much a typical farmhouse, if one operated a prosperous farm, which Alex did. And, dash it, that hadn't happened by accident. It had been he, Alex English, who had built the family enterprises to their present level of prosperity.

Recalling Kate's brother Bill, Alex acknowledged that he was attempting to do the same with *his* family's assets, such as they were. Bill had to work on a much smaller scale, but still . . . The boy should be commended for attempting to dig his family out of the gutter.

Alex had told Bill so, more diplomatically, of course, when they'd spoken in the hospital two weeks ago. He had also given Bill a couple of tips he'd garnered from his investment-minded friends and associates, and had offered him the opportunity to profit from the World's Columbian Exposition, as well. Since Alex was in a position to do so, he'd offered Bill shares in his own Agricultural Cooperative at a greatly reduced price.

Bill, unlike his sister, had thanked him for the information and the offer. He'd made arrangements on the spot to take advantage of the Agricultural Cooperative offer. Bill's appreciation had been overt and absolutely genuine. Every time Kate thanked Alex for anything, Alex could tell it just about killed her to do it. Dratted woman.

Conky, Alex's no-account bird dog, set up a frenzy of barking that jolted Alex out of his broody mood. The dog was a total failure as a hunter, but his rapture at seeing Alex again cheered him up a little. "Hey there, Conky!" he called out the window. The dog, leaping joyously and making a horrible racket, trotted alongside the carriage, jumping up and scratching the door panel every now and then. Alex sighed. What did it matter if the animal scratched the paint? Conky might be worthless, but Alex counted him as a friend, and a man couldn't have too many friends.

"Alex! Alex!"

His mother's happy shout yanked Alex farther out of his mood. He leaned out the window, cupped his hands around his mouth, and hollered, "Ma!" like he used to do when he was a boy. Conky barked, too, as if he were echoing Alex's shout.

Kate Finney called her mother "Ma." Maybe they weren't so fundamentally different from each other as surface indications would lead one to believe.

"Don't be an ass," he advised himself.

When the coach horses drew up to the huge front porch, Alex saw his little sister tripping merrily down the steps. Mary Jo, the youngest of the five English children, was fourteen years old. The rest of Alex's siblings were married and living in or near Chicago. Mary Jo thought she should be married and living away from home, too, but everyone knew that was only her age determining her attitude.

Alex loved her even if she was going through adolescence. He also gave her some extra latitude because he knew she missed their father, the elder Alexander English, who had passed away only two years earlier. Alex missed their father, as well, so he tried not to be too hard on his little sister.

"Alex!" Mary Jo screamed. "Alex! Minnie had her kittens!"

Minnie, the barn cat who kept the rodent population under control on the English farm, had been doing her duty for years now, supplying kittens on a regular basis to serve in the feline rat patrol.

"Are they as ugly as the last batch?" Alex called as he opened the door and let down the carriage steps.

"They're *beautiful!*"

Before he could properly brace himself, Mary Jo threw herself into his arms, propelling him back through the open coach door. He ended up sitting on the steps with her in his lap, Conky leaping on both of them, and unable to catch his breath for laughing.

"Mary Jo, you little fiend, are you trying to kill me?"

"Mary Jo, really," their mother said, trying to sound stern. She couldn't. She'd never been able to, actually, which was probably one of the reasons her children loved her so dearly.

The haggard face of Hazel Finney intruded into his mind's eye, and a notion that had assaulted him several days before in the hospital tapped him on the shoulder again. He wondered what Kate would have to say about it, provided his mother approved. Nothing good, he imagined.

But to hell with Kate Finney. Alex had become quite fond of Mrs. Finney and Bill Finney. If Kate didn't want to accept Alex's offers of friendship and help, he'd just take his suggestion to the other, more amiable Finneys. Dratted woman.

What with the general hilarity of his homecoming and Mary Jo's insistent questions about the World's Columbian Exposition—"For heaven's sake, Mary Jo, I *told* you I'm going to take you to the fair!" "Yes, but *when*, Alex?" "Soon, soon."—it wasn't until almost midnight, after his pesky sister had been trundled off to bed in spite of her protests, that Alex got the chance to talk to his mother.

"I met a girl, Ma."

Mrs. English clasped her hands to her bosom and beamed at him. "Oh, Alex! I'm so happy for you. When are you going to bring her home to the family?"

Blast. He'd obviously begun this conversation the wrong way. "Not that kind of girl," he hastened to assure his mother. "For heaven's sake, Ma." In spite of his embarrassment, he laughed.

"Oh." His mother's face fell. Then it looked worried. "Alex, you're not taking up with the wrong sort, are you?"

"Wrong sort? What the devil—"

"Don't swear!"

Alex rolled his eyes. It took approximately five seconds of being in his mother's company for him to turn from an almost-thirty-year-old man into a five-year-old boy again. "Sorry, Ma. But, no, I'm not taking up with the wrong sort. And I'm not about to marry the girl I just met." What an uncomfortable life *that* would be.

Only seconds later, it came as a shock to Alex to realize that he'd pop anyone in the jaw if they dared question Kate or Bill Finney's moral worth. How had that happened? And when? Good Lord. He'd better start watching his step around the Finneys, or anything might happen. He shuddered at the thought.

"Good." His mother patted him on the knee. "I hope you won't marry anyone for a while yet, Alex. I think you need a little . . ." She stopped speaking.

Alex frowned. "I need a little what?"

She patted him on the knee. "Alex, you're the best son any mother could have, and I love you dearly. I know you're a generous, kindhearted man, too, but . . ." She stopped talking again.

Dash it, if she was going to tell him he was turning into a fussy old man, as Gil MacIntosh had, Alex might just have to do something. He didn't know what. "What, Ma?" he demanded. "Do you think I'm a selfish pig, too?"

His mother's eyes opened wide until they looked like blue marbles against a white background. "Alex! Whatever are you talking about? You're no more selfish than I am a Greek! It's only . . . Oh, Alex, I don't know. It's only that you sometimes act as though you've forgotten there are other, less fortunate, people in the world."

"Good Gad," he muttered. "Not you, too."

She smiled sadly. "Please don't hate me for saying that. Nobody could be kinder or more generous to his family than you are, Alex."

He gazed at his mother, feeling abused and put-upon for several seconds. He didn't know what to say. Anyhow, if he *had* become, perhaps, the least little bit complacent in his success, any hint of complacency had been battered out of him by the Finney family, blast them. "Believe me, I know there are less fortunate people in the world, Ma." He did now, at any rate.

"I'm sure of it."

Detecting a lack of sincerity in his mother's tone, Alex felt himself getting peeved. "Are you through, Ma?" he asked rather stiffly.

"Oh, there, now, I've hurt your feelings. Alex, please forget I said anything. I didn't mean it. You're the kindest, most wonderful boy in the world, and I should be ashamed of myself for even mentioning . . ."

There she went again. She didn't want to tell him to his face that he was a selfish, uncaring son of a bitch. At least Kate Finney didn't have any trouble expressing herself when it came to enumerating his shortcomings.

"Please, Alex, forget I said anything."

A likely chance of that happening. Nevertheless, Alex inclined his head in acquiescence and decided to let his mother off the hook. After all, she *was* his mother. "But I need to ask you something, Ma."

"Certainly, my dear. What is it?"

He wondered how old Hazel Finney was. From the respective ages of the Finney and English children, Alex imagined she was a good deal younger than his own mother. She looked at least thirty years older. Life certainly didn't play favorites.

So Alex told his mother about the Finneys, putting most of the emphasis on Mrs. Finney. He didn't have to exaggerate when describing her condition or her life, a fact that struck him as unfortunate. "Anyhow, I wondered if you'd be willing to have the Finneys visit you over a weekend, Ma. I don't think Mrs. Finney has much longer to live."

It didn't surprise him that, before he was halfway through with his story, his mother had to dab at the tears leaking from her eyes. His mother was a very compassionate, kindhearted woman. He'd inherited his own compassionate, kindhearted nature from her. He wished he could get Kate Finney to acknowledge that, dash it. And his mother.

"Oh, Alex, I'd be happy to welcome the poor woman here. And her daughter, too. Poor dear thing, having to work so hard to keep body and soul together and support her mother and all." She blew her nose with a good deal of vigor and smiled tremulously at her son. "You're such a good man, Alex. I knew you'd grow into your legacy."

Whatever that meant. Alex said, "Hmmm."

His mother went on. "I just hate to think of people living like that. I hope they'll stay for several days. I'm sure Miss Finney can use a rest from her many duties and chores and jobs."

Uh-oh. "Um, if Miss Finney comes, too, there are a couple of things you probably ought to know."

His mother lifted tear-drowned eyes and gazed at him. "What things, dear?"

She's a hard-nosed, sarcastic, ill-natured, contemptuous witch. Alex knew he couldn't say that. "Um, Miss Finney tends to be a little defensive about her relative lot in life." He was proud of that sentence.

His mother, as he might have expected, read between the lines. "The poor dear thing! Of course she is. Why, if she grew up on those horrid streets, she must have learned how to be as hard as nails in order to survive!"

"You hit it on the head, Ma." Now Alex was proud of his mother.

Mrs. English's glance sharpened considerably. "I wasn't always your father's wife, you know, Alex. I lived through some mighty hard times before we were married."

Good Gad. "But—but—Surely, you didn't—"

"Grow up in the slums of a big city? No." Mrs. English smiled gently. "But there are plenty of poor people outside of cities, Alex." She heaved a big sigh. "I was so happy to get away from my own poverty that I sometimes think I didn't give you children a broad-enough picture of the world and of life. That's what I was trying to tell you before. But you've learned for yourself, through the Finneys, I suppose." She shook her head and looked as if she were recalling unpleasant, faraway times. "It's no fun being poor and hungry, Alex, believe me."

Good Gad again. "Ah, I didn't know you went through that sort of thing, Ma. You were poor?"

"Dirt poor."

The same words that applied to Kate Finney. Would wonders never cease? He tilted his head and peered at his mother with renewed interest. He'd always loved her. She was his mother, for heaven's sake. But he'd never actually thought of her as a—well, as a person. He imagined most people failed to take their parents' humanity into consideration when they thought about them.

"You grew up in Kentucky, didn't you?"

Mrs. English nodded. "Yes. Near Bowling Green. My mother and father had moved there from New England as pioneers in the thirties. It was a hard life, Alex." She heaved a sigh and her face took on a thoughtful cast. "Although, I must say that I think growing up poor in the country must be at least a little nicer than growing up poor in a big city."

"Why?" As far as Alex was concerned, poverty anywhere would probably be uncomfortable, to say the least, and not at all something to be desired.

"I'm not sure. Perhaps because there are all the green growing things in the country. One can grow one's food, and my brothers used to shoot birds and game to keep meat on the table."

"Maybe. But you don't have the museums and art galleries and so forth. Libraries. Culture. You know what I mean."

The expression of humor that lighted his mother's

eyes didn't give him any comfort at all. "Alex, do you really believe that Miss Finney and her mother have time to visit art galleries and museums? You've already told me that Miss Finney has to work at two jobs. I have a feeling most poor people in the city are too busy working to appreciate culture very much."

"Maybe. Not to mention dodging their fathers."

Drat. Alex knew he'd made a mistake as soon as he saw his mother's eyes pop open and the look of shock on her face.

"Their fathers? What do you mean?"

With a sigh, Alex told her.

His mother lifted a hand to her own throat. "Good heavens. You mean he tried to harm his own daughter?"

"Miss Finney says he's a drunkard. I guess she's spent the last several months trying to hide her mother from him."

"Good heavens. That poor child. How horrid."

Yeah, as Kate Finney might say. It was horrid, all right. He gave a little start when his mother grabbed his arm and held on tight.

"Alex, you must be sure he doesn't get into the hospital."

Alex blinked at her. "Ah . . ."

"You *must!* And do bring her here, please. Bring both of them. You must, Alex. You know you must."

"Um, I guess so. That's what I wanted to ask you."

He reflected that getting his mother to agree to his scheme hadn't been difficult at all. In fact, he anticipated having more trouble persuading Kate to go for it.

On Monday morning, when his big, expensive traveling coach headed back toward Chicago, he began plotting strategy.

Six

Kate knew that if she didn't get some sleep soon, she'd fall over in a heap. Then what good would she be to her mother? None, that's what. She yawned anyhow.

Madame eyed her with a mixture of amusement and concern. "Kate, what did you do yesterday? Did you work again? I told you to rest on Sundays. You need your rest."

"I know, I know." Kate yawned again. "But when the White Stockings play in town, they pay a lot of money to the people who throw bags of peanuts to the folks who watch the game. And yesterday they played a double-header." Discerning from Madame's expression of confusion that she didn't know what a doubleheader was, she elaborated. "That's when they play two ball games in one day."

"How nice," Madame muttered. "Your health is worth considerably more than a few measly dollars, Kate. If you don't know that yet, you'll learn soon enough when your health breaks down."

Darn it, of all the people in the world, Kate had expected Madame to understand her need to earn as much money as she could, however she could. Her mother was still in the hospital, after two whole weeks, and Kate was beginning to worry that Alex's money or patience would run out, and her mother might be returned to the Charity Ward. Even the Charity Ward cost a bundle, if you made a living like Kate's. "Right."

"And what about your brothers? Do they work all day and all night and on Sundays, too?"

"Darn it, Madame, leave me alone."

But Madame didn't leave her alone. "No." She answered her own question. "They don't. And why don't they? Because they understand that life isn't all about money."

"Darn it, I know life isn't all about money, but money matters. In fact, money matters more than about anything else in the whole world when you don't have any."

Madame laughed, and Kate eased up on her some. "Shoot, Madame, you don't need to tell me what's important in life. I know, believe me."

"I know you do, sweetie. Here, have a pickle." In her thick Romanian accent, the word came out sounding like "peekle."

Good old Madame. For Madame, anything that went wrong could be fixed if you ate something. "Thanks, but I haven't had breakfast yet. I don't think a pickle would sit well." The mere thought made her purse her lips and feel queasy.

Whoops. Kate realized she'd said the wrong thing when Madame's laughter stopped abruptly and she frowned at her.

"Kate Finney, before you put on any makeup, you get yourself out of this booth and grab something to eat. I won't have a starving child working with me."

"Darn it, Madame, I'm not starving, and I'm not a child."

"I don't care. Go eat something." She pointed with a dramatic flourish at the door.

"Aha, it sounds as if I arrived at precisely the right time."

Kate whirled around. Hell and damnation! "No," she said to Alex, who was looking much too chipper and handsome in another one of his expensive suits. "You didn't arrive at the right time." No time was the right time for him. And where in the name of holy Jesus did he get all those fancy suits of his, anyhow? She'd known him for two weeks now and could have sworn he hadn't worn the same one twice. They made him look too darned good, and Kate didn't approve.

"Nonsense. I distinctly heard Madame Esmeralda tell you to get some breakfast. Please allow me to go with you. I'm hungry, too." He patted his elegantly vested midsection.

"Good idea," said Madame, grinning like a cat. She looked kind of like a cat even at the best of times, Kate thought sourly. "You take Kate to breakfast. I don't want to see her again for an hour."

"An *hour*? How the heck am I supposed to earn a living if you won't let me work?" Kate, who was furious and feeling beleaguered and outnumbered, glared daggers at Madame, who deflected the vicious look with one of her more inscrutable grins. Kate was so angry, she stamped her foot. Which did about as much good as shouting. "Oh, bah!"

As ungraciously as possible—and Kate had learned how to be ungracious when she was quite young—she snatched up her small handbag and shawl. It was only seven o'clock in the morning, and the air was slightly chilly. "All right, all right. I'll go with you, but I want to be back sooner than an hour." She shot a scorching glance at Madame, who smiled sweetly. Next thing, she'd start licking her paws, Kate thought bitterly. Kate had never cared much for cats.

"It's such a pleasure to be in your company, Miss Finney," Alex purred as he held the door for her.

"Huh," said Kate.

She stomped along at his side, resenting him and Madame and her mother's poor health and life and everything else for some minutes, while neither of them spoke. She hadn't changed into her Gypsy suit yet, so she still wore a plain, gray walking skirt and white shirtwaist, both of which she'd made with her own ten fingers. The collar of her shirtwaist was high, which was why she'd selected it this morning: it covered the now-yellowing bruises on her neck. She'd bought the fabric at Chinese Charley's. Charley sold whatever he found in big, cheap lots, and Kate appreciated him for it.

She made all her clothes, mostly from material she got at Charley's. This skirt and shirtwaist were her staples. She'd worn the gray jacket that matched the skirt this morning, and was glad she'd done so since at least she was coordinated and probably didn't look *too* incongruous walking next to her wealthy escort.

Big deal. Kate was tolerably certain that her entire wardrobe, if she piled up every garment she'd ever owned from birth until this day, wouldn't fetch as much money in a store, provided a store would offer such shoddy merchandise for sale, as the suit on Alex English's rich body. It wasn't a thought calculated to instill confidence in a person who wasn't awfully comfortable with herself to begin with.

"It's a lovely day," Alex ventured after several moments of mutinous silence on Kate's part.

He, drat him, looked perfectly at ease with himself, her, the day, and everything else. Naturally. Money did that to a person, Kate supposed. She, of course, had no personal experience with the confidence money brought. Bought. Whatever.

"Here, Miss Finney, let's dine here. I've eaten breakfast here several times. The food they serve is quite tasty."

Feeling rebellious, she asked, "How much does it cost?"

"My treat. I more or less kidnapped you. The least I can do is pay for the privilege."

"Privilege? Right." She stormed into the small eating establishment, which was operated by two black men who served Caribbean fare. "I'll pay for my own food, thank you."

"Not this morning, you won't."

He didn't sound angry or perturbed, only reasonable. Kate absolutely *hated* people to be reasonable at her when she was in a temper. She also didn't know what to say, so she flounced over to a table the waiter indicated and sat in a fluff of gray wool. Alex smiled at the waiter for both of them and took the chair across the table from her. "That's a fetching outfit, Miss Finney. May I ask if you made it?"

She gave him one of her best scowls, which he ignored almost as effectively as Madame had done. "Yes. What of it?"

"Nothing. I'm impressed that you have the skill to do so many things, and do them well."

Kate stared at him, speechless, for a moment before she said without as much spirit as she'd heretofore demonstrated, "Like heck."

Alex grinned and didn't leap to defend himself. Rather, he glanced up at the waiter, who was smiling down upon them like a benevolent black Buddha. "I'd like some of your special Caribbean coffee, please, Pierre."

And that's another thing, Kate decided bitterly. How come he knew the names of all these food people? Stupid question. Because he was rich enough to dine out all the time. Rich people dined. Poor people ate—when they could afford to. Kate sneered inside, but didn't show it because she was feeling small and unimportant and stupid.

Her stomach took that moment to growl, embarrassing her nearly to death. Shooting a you'd-better-not-say-a-word frown at Alex, who pretended he hadn't heard the indelicate noise, she forced herself to smile at the waiter. "Me, too, please." She hated eating in restaurants. She'd had no practice. She didn't know how to go about it. Darn it, they scared her.

And if there was one thing Kate hated more than Alex English, it was admitting that so many things intimidated her. Nuts.

"I recommend our potato cakes, sir and madame," the waiter said in a soft, musical accent that appealed to something deep within Kate's battling innards. "With some of our fresh sausages, eggs and a fruit parfait and coffee, it's the best breakfast you'll ever eat." He kissed his fingers and gestured like Kate had seen a Frenchman do once. In spite of herself, her smile became more genuine.

"Sounds good to me," she said to the waiter, guessing it wouldn't hurt her overall state of being as it related to Alex English if she were nice to this guy. He, after all, was only trying to make a living. Kate could claim some sort of kinship with him, as she couldn't understand or appreciate in Alex. Except for his kindness to her mother, she amended, because she was honest even when she didn't much want to be.

"And me," said Alex, sounding suave and man-of-the-worldly.

Not that Kate knew anything about men of the world except that she'd had to dodge advances from several of them who'd managed to spot her in spite of her sober attire after dancing for Little Egypt. The bounders. The cads. The lousy bastards.

At least, she told herself, she could be glad that Alex didn't want her to do anything unseemly in payment for his generosity to her mother. After the waiter walked away, she gazed surreptitiously at Alex as she flapped her napkin out of its folds and placed it on her lap.

He was a good-looking man, darn him. Kate wouldn't really mind it if he found her attractive, she supposed, although she'd kill him if he offered her any lewd suggestions. Still and all, it was sort of pleasant to know that handsome men found a girl desirable. With renewed rancor, she pondered the unpleasant fact that she couldn't even get *that* much satisfaction out of Alex English. He offered Kate nothing at all. Except as it related to her mother.

Kate called herself at least six bad names as she considered what a selfish, self-centered person she must be to want Alex to desire her. Her only consideration should be for her mother.

Nuts. Alex English drove her crazy, and that was all there was to it. She couldn't even think properly around him.

"Thank you for taking breakfast with me, Miss Finney."

She glanced at him, seeking signs that he was about to spring something on her. She didn't see any. Nevertheless, she knew better than to think a man like Alex English would bother to take a girl like her to breakfast unless he had an ulterior motive. "Right. What did you want me for?"

He tipped his head slightly and gazed at her in calm deliberation. If Kate was able to do anything she wanted to do just then, she supposed she'd first throw a few table implements at him, then jump up and down and scream, and then run away somewhere and cry. Then she'd take a long nap. She was so tired, her eyes felt like somebody had thrown sand in them.

Since she was presently sitting in a public restaurant and was supposed to be a civilized adult human being, she did none of those things. Rather, she sat calmly and without flinching and watched Alex think. Her palms itched. She *really* wanted to fidget.

"I must say, Miss Finney, you don't believe in giving a fellow a break, do you?"

She frowned. "What's that supposed to mean?"

He sighed. "I don't know how often or in how many ways I can say this, but I wish we could be friendly acquaintances. If we can't be friends. I'm trying in every way I can think of to help your mother. I'm not doing it because I have any interest in—in showing you up, I think is the expression."

"Hmmm."

"Rather, the fact is that I met your mother, I like your mother, and I'm sorry she's so ill. I thought when I met her, and I still think, that she deserves better than the Charity Ward." He held up a hand as if to ward off an attack from Kate. "Not that there's anything wrong with the Charity Ward. It's a swell place for people who have no other choice, and I donate a lot of money to the hospital on a yearly basis in order to keep it running. Your mother, as of the day she met me, acquired a choice. I have the money to help her, and I'm doing it. I'm sorry if you don't want your mother to receive the best medical care—"

"Nuts!" That stung, darn it. "I do, too, want Ma to have the best medical care!" How nice it must be to have so much money you could afford to toss heaps of it at a hospital on a yearly basis. She bit her tongue so as not to say so.

He nodded. "But you can't pay for it, and I can. Therefore, I don't understand why you persist in being so rude to me."

She couldn't, either, although she feared it had something to do with wanting to be his equal and knowing she wasn't. Which wasn't her fault. Or Ma's. Or Bill's. Or even his. It was her father's, she guessed, although she wasn't even entirely certain about that. Maybe they'd have been poor even if her mother had married a decent man. She almost laughed when that thought crossed her mind. If Ma had married a decent man, Kate, Bill, and Walter wouldn't exist today.

She heaved a sigh, thinking that would probably be better for the world and her both. She gazed at Alex, wondering what to say to him. She knew she shouldn't be rude to a man who was being of such benefit to the person she loved best in the whole world. Because she felt obliged, and a little guilty for giving him such a hard time, she mumbled, "I don't mean to be rude. I'm not used to people doing stuff for me. I—I don't know how to take things, I guess."

He nodded, folded his hands together, and put his elbows on the table. Kate was surprised to see him do that, since she'd always assumed rich people were taught proper manners from the cradle and would, therefore, never put their elbows on a table. He didn't speak, and she got nervous so she fiddled with the napkin in her lap.

After several seconds of fiddling, her nerves started snapping like the electrical current she'd seen in the Mechanical Hall. Darn it, why didn't he say something? She'd apologized to him. Sort of. Darn it, maybe it hadn't exactly been an apology, but it was as close as Kate generally got to one.

And still he didn't speak.

Finally, Kate decided it was either speak herself or leap up from the table and bolt out of the restaurant, so she decided to speak since it would be less humiliating than her other option. "Er, what's a parfait?" She'd never eaten a parfait before, but she guessed if it was made out of fruit, it couldn't be too bad.

Alex gazed at her for several seconds before he lowered his hands to the table and spoke. Kate would have sighed with relief, only she didn't want him to know how unnerved she was. "I imagine this one is going to be a mixture of different kinds of fruits."

She nodded. "Ah." That sounded all right. Kate liked fruit. She didn't eat it very often because fruit was expensive unless you got it outside the fruit stalls before the markets opened for the day or after they shut down. Since she was currently working two jobs and visiting her mother in the hospital morning and night, she didn't have time to do that, but still, she liked fruit.

The waiter showed up with the coffee, and Kate thanked him with genuine gratitude for delivering her from having to be in company with Alex English and not knowing how to behave.

Alex didn't offer his thanks aloud, but he smiled at the waiter. Kate guessed it was okay to have spoken her thanks aloud. Darn it, she was going to have to visit the new public library and see if she could find a book on etiquette.

"And here are your parfaits," the waiter said after pouring the coffee. He set pretty, stemmed glass bowls in front of Kate and Alex.

"Looks delicious," Alex murmured as he picked up a spoon.

It looked kind of strange to Kate. She dipped her spoon into the glass, scooped up some fruit, leaned over, and peered at it. She discerned bits of orange and apple. Those were easy. There was another fruit in there, too, and Kate thought she recognized it. "Is this a piece of banana?"

Alex, who was chewing, lifted an eyebrow, which made him look astounded. Instantly, Kate bridled. Before he could swallow, she said sharply, "People in my neighborhood don't eat this kind of stuff all the time, you know."

"I beg your pardon? I didn't say a thing, Miss Finney. Why are you snapping at me now?"

"Oh, nuts." Kate felt like crying. Again. Darn it, why was she always assuming the worst of this man? "I'm sorry." There. She'd outright apologized to him. "I didn't mean to be rude."

"I accept your apology, and thank you for offering it," said Alex. "Yes, that's a piece of banana. Try it, Miss Finney. It's really quite good."

He didn't sound sarcastic, although Kate couldn't imagine why. He was probably storing up a trainload of sarcasm and would hit her with it later. "I will." She did. It was very good. "I like it."

"Good." He smiled at last. "Have you eaten bananas before, Miss Finney?"

She nodded. "Ma and I used to go to the produce market early in the morning when the stuff was coming in. You can get some great bargains then because the grocers are selling off their produce from the day before. Every now and then, Ma would find a banana or two. I like them when they're not soft and squishy."

"Mmmm," agreed Alex, chewing.

Kate dipped into her parfait dish again. Thus far, she'd identified the banana, the orange, and the apple. She thought the other orange fruit was a peach, but there was some white stuff in there that baffled her. Holding up her spoon, she said, "What's that white stuff?"

Alex leaned over and perused her spoon's contents. "I think you mean the coconut."

Kate was genuinely surprised. "Coconut? You mean that white stuff is what's inside those round brown things with all the hair on them?" Interesting.

With a chuckle, Alex nodded. "Yes indeed. Astonishing, isn't it?"

"I had no idea. Since neither Ma nor I could figure out what you're supposed to do with one, we never bought one. They're hard as rocks, though." She grinned, feeling the tiniest bit more confident. "I know that because I dropped one once. On my foot. It hurt for a week. My foot, I mean."

"They grow on palm trees in the tropics. Like dates. Have you ever eaten a date?"

She shook her head. "No. Too exotic for the likes of me, I guess. Like coconuts."

"I doubt that."

She glanced at him. "Beg pardon?"

"I don't think either coconuts or dates are too exotic for you. You're an Egyptian dancer, don't forget. If anything's exotic, I'd say that is. Not to mention telling fortunes. That's pretty exotic, too."

"Guess I never thought of it like that." She was glad he had, however, because she liked the notion that she was at least equal to an exotic fruit. Which was pretty silly, she supposed.

The waiter brought the rest of their breakfast. The succulent aroma made Kate's mouth water. She guessed she hadn't eaten a whole lot lately. She didn't have time, what with two jobs—sometimes three—and running to the hospital a couple of times a day. It took a lot of restraint for her not to gobble her food, which was the most delicious breakfast she'd ever eaten, but she managed. She really didn't want Alex to think any worse of her than he already did. Her mother had taught all her children good table manners, and Kate used them.

"This is delicious," Alex muttered after polishing off most of his eggs, potato cakes, and sausages.

"Yes." Kate dabbed at her mouth with her napkin, a linen number that was probably laundered after each use. She hated even to think about the soap and laundry bills this place must have to pay. The coffee was good, too. Kate lifted her cup to her lips and sipped a little more of it.

"I have a proposition for you, Miss Finney."

Kate's cup hit the saucer with a loud clink. Her head jerked up. "You what?"

Darn it all, if he was going to prove himself to be a rat just when Kate had almost decided he wasn't, she didn't know what she'd do. Throw something at him, probably, thereby causing a public scene and disgracing herself.

He held out a placating hand. "Now don't get all upset, please, Miss Finney. My proposition is a purely— pure one." He frowned. "A person really has to watch his step around you, doesn't he?"

She scowled back. "When men offer women propositions, they usually aren't pure. I know you're real high-class and all, but even *you* must know that."

His lips thinned. "There's no need to be ugly, Miss Finney. I am not the type of man to make an impure proposition to any female. Not even you."

She gripped the table. "And exactly what is that supposed to mean?"

"It means that you take every single thing I say in the worst possible light. For God's sake, Miss Finney, will you please just relax and listen to me? And stop twisting everything I say until it means something else, will you? It's an aggravating trait, and one you ought to conquer if you expect to get anywhere in this life."

Kate held on to her mulish mood for a couple of seconds longer, then eased up a bit. Without lowering her guard, she said cautiously, "I'll try."

He cast a beseeching glance at the ceiling before looking at her again. "Thank you."

"So, what's this proposition of yours?"

He sucked in a deep breath, as if he still didn't trust her. Well, that was fine with her. She didn't trust him, either.

"It's about your mother."

She relaxed a little bit more. "Oh."

"She mentioned that she liked the country."

"Yeah?" *So what?* She didn't say that, though, since Alex might think it sounded challenging. He might be right.

"I went to see my own mother yesterday. She lives on our family farm about twenty miles southwest of Chicago."

"A farm?" Kate wrinkled her nose. "Oh, yeah, that's right. You're a farmer, aren't you?" Kate couldn't reconcile the elegant, dapper Alex English with her mental image of a farmer. And that, she figured, only went to show her yet once more how little she knew about anything.

"Yes." He sounded a trifle defensive. "I run a very successful farming operation. The English farm has become a byword in the grain and beef industries."

"Oh." Whatever that meant. The only thing Kate knew about grain and beef was that you could make bread out of the one, and you ate the other on special occasions that were too good for beans and potatoes and cabbage.

"I'd like to take your mother to visit my mother. On the farm."

Kate gaped at him. "You what?"

He spoke again, and again he sounded slightly defensive. "I'd like to take your mother to visit the farm. She said she enjoyed the countryside. I think the fresh air would do her some good."

"Yeah," said Kate. She didn't want her mother deserting her to go to the blasted countryside. "It probably would."

"Good. I was hoping you'd consent."

"Consent?" As if he needed her consent. All he needed to do was ask Ma. Ma would probably love leaving the city for the country, although Kate knew she'd miss her children.

And Kate would die.

No, no, no. Kate was stronger than that. No matter how much her heart felt as if it were being shredded into bloody strips.

Alex smiled and seemed to relax. "Well, I wouldn't make the suggestion to her if you didn't approve of it. I know better than to cross you, Miss Finney."

Kate didn't think that was funny, so she didn't smile. Nor did she comment.

Alex didn't seem to notice. "I think she'd enjoy it, and I know my mother would be happy to meet her."

"Yeah?" Kate doubted it. She couldn't imagine her own beloved mother having anything at all in common with Mrs. Rich Lady English.

"I'm sure of it. The weather is just about perfect this

time of year, and the apricots and peaches are beginning to bear."

"Are they?" So what? Did he want Ma to pick his fruit for him? "Um, I don't think Ma's in any condition to do any work on a farm, Mr. English."

He blinked at her. "Beg pardon?"

Nuts. She'd gone and done it again. "Nothing."

It wasn't nothing, though, as she recognized when Alex began looking sort of thundery. "Miss Finney, if you think I'm inviting your mother to visit my farm because—"

"No!" She held out a hand. "I'm sorry. I didn't think that. Not really. It's only . . ." Blast. It was only what? Opting for honesty because she didn't know how else to put it, Kate blurted out, "It's only that I can't imagine anybody wanting us Finneys visiting unless they need something done that we could do." There. Let him chew on that one. This was so embarrassing.

"I see." He still looked angry. What a surprise.

She jumped when he leaned over and poked the table in front of her with his forefinger. "For your information, Miss Finney, neither my mother nor I are snobs, as you obviously believe us to be. And my sister, who is fourteen years old, would love to have company. She's bored to flinders on the farm."

"Really?" Kate smiled when she thought about Alex English having an adolescent sister. She couldn't feature him as anybody's brother. "Kids that age can be a pain."

His eyes went kind of squinty. "Were you? When you were that age, I mean. Were you a pain?"

Heck, no, she hadn't been a pain. She'd been too busy going to school, working, and trying to keep Ma out of her father's way. "Probably." She didn't meet his gaze. Fortunately, the waiter had refilled her coffee cup—and if that wasn't a fancy custom, Kate didn't know what was—so she could take a sip of coffee to occupy herself.

Alex stared at her for a moment before he said, "Hmmm."

Hadn't anybody ever told this man that it was impolite to stare? Kate was about to inform him of this pertinent fact of life when he transferred his scrutiny to his own coffee cup. Kate sagged inside with relief. "At any rate," Alex said, "I wanted to ask you before I proposed the trip to your mother. I'll have to consult with the doctors first, of course, in order to ascertain if she's strong enough to travel."

"She's not very strong," Kate admitted. She wanted to say that she didn't want her mother traveling anywhere without her, too, but was afraid Alex would think she was angling for an invitation to his stupid farm for herself. Now that the shock of his proposal was wearing off, she had to admit, if only to herself, that the notion of spending some quiet time in the country appealed to her frazzled soul. She'd never say so to Alex.

"Do you think she'd be willing to travel that far?"

Kate shrugged. "I don't know. She doesn't like to be away from us kids very much."

"Oh, well, the invitation is extended to you and Bill, too. And your other brother, of course. I'm sorry. I guess I didn't mention that before."

"No. You didn't." Kate told her heart to stop leaping around and doing stupid things. It was only an invitation to visit a farm, for pity's sake.

"So, what do you think? I think a change of scenery, especially to the countryside, where the air is fresh and everything's green and pretty, might be beneficial to a sick woman. I was hoping you'd think so, too."

Kate studied Alex and his proposition for several moments, wondering what could possibly be wrong with it. On the surface, Alex didn't appear to be the kind of gent who would use underhanded tactics to get a woman to succumb to his charms. He was too stuffy and proper

for that and anyhow, he didn't seem inclined to view
Kate as appealing as a woman. Then again, Kate absolutely couldn't fathom why he should be going to such
trouble for her family. Heck, her own father didn't give
a rap about his wife and kids; why should Alex English
care? They were almost complete strangers.

Before she'd managed to wrestle all her convoluted
thoughts into some sort of ordered conclusion, her
mouth spoke the words she hadn't agreed to yet. "Sure.
I think Ma would enjoy it."

Darn. What was the matter with her, anyhow?

But Alex didn't know anything about her inner turmoil. Rather, a smile lit his face, making Kate gasp
slightly. He was a *very* good-looking man when he wasn't
hollering at her or in a tizzy about something.

"Wonderful! I'm so glad you agree with me. I'll talk to
your mother's doctors this afternoon."

"Swell." Kate wasn't sure what she'd gotten herself
into, but she feared the worst. Then again, what could
happen on a farm with Alex's mother and her own
mother there to chaperon?

"Are you ready to tackle telling fortunes now, Miss
Finney?" He pulled out the pretty gold watch he carried
and glanced at it. Kate would love to get a watch like that
for Billy. He'd love it. "We haven't used up too much of
your work time."

"Sure." She folded her napkin and set it beside her
empty plate. It was funny, but now that she'd finished,
she sort of hated leaving the restaurant. The meal hadn't
been entirely peaceful, but it had been delicious, and
she'd felt sort of . . . at ease or something. She didn't
know why, but she wasn't keen about walking away from
Alex and his money and facing her world again. Alex's
world was so much less stressful than Kate's.

It was all money, she told herself. Money could buy
peace and quiet, even if it couldn't buy happiness. All

things considered, Kate decided she'd settle for peace, quiet, and plenty. Happiness would probably take care of itself after that.

"Say, Miss Finney," said Alex said as he politely held her chair. "Why don't I meet you outside the Egyptian Palace after you dance this evening. I'll tell you what the doctors say about a visit to the country for your mother, and drive you to the hospital. We can talk about it then. I'll ask your mother how she feels about a trip to the countryside after I chat with her doctors."

Kate's trouble-sensing antennae quivered. She told herself not to be stupid. "Sure. That would be fine." She should probably thank him, but she'd wait until later when she was better able to judge whether or not he deserved her thanks. In Kate's world, it was sometimes difficult to tell.

She felt ever so much better when she went back to Madame Esmeralda's Fortune-Telling booth. Madame looked up from the palm she was reading when Alex opened the door for Kate. Kate didn't like the grin that spread over Madame's face when she entered the booth, but she couldn't do anything about it.

"I'll see you this evening, Miss Finney."

Kate took the hand Alex held out and shook it. "Right," she said. "This evening."

She shot Madame a scowl as she hung up her jacket and scooted to the back of the booth to don her Gypsy paint and garb, feeling as if she'd somehow been manipulated into doing Alex English's will and not quite understanding how it had happened.

Seven

Alex sent a telegram to his mother that afternoon after he left Mrs. Finney's hospital room and before he hopped into his conveniently waiting carriage and headed back to the Exposition.

Mrs. Finney had been stunned by his invitation, but she'd also been pleased. He remembered how she'd held onto his hand and whispered, "Oh, Mr. English, Katie needs to get out of the city. This is so kind of you."

It was, rather, and Alex was proud of himself for thinking of it. Not that he'd done it for Kate's sake. He'd offered the Finneys his family farm because he thought Mrs. Finney needed some fresh air. His heart twisted when he thought about how this would probably be the last look she ever got of the countryside she loved so well.

But aside from the inescapable problem of human mortality, he was feeling fine. Absolutely fine. "Daisy, Daisy, give me your answer, do. I'm half crazy, all for the love of—"

He quit singing abruptly as he approached the Egyptian Palace and saw the crowd gathered there. His smile faded. Dash it, there were always dozens of men hanging about outside the back door of the Pavilion. Alex knew why they were there, too, and their motives infuriated him. They all thought Kate Finney was a strumpet who'd be delighted to warm their beds for an appropriate sum of money or gifts of jewelry and so forth. If the notion didn't gall him so much, he might have laughed.

They didn't know Kate Finney or they wouldn't entertain the idea of Kate succumbing to such lures. Not for any longer than it took her to set them straight, at any rate.

Alex squinted into the gathering gloom of night, trying to make out the individuals who composed the masculine cluster at the door. Something was going on there, but he couldn't tell what. Unsettled, he quickened his pace. As he neared the Pavilion, he heard voices.

"Aw, come on, girlie. Just one little drink. I'll treat you real fine."

"Get out of my way, you drunken lout!" Kate's voice— and it sounded to Alex as if she were in one of her better and more serious rages.

"Who you calling a drunken lout, girlie?" The slightly slurred voice was the same one Alex had heard before.

"You, you lousy bum!"

"Bum? You're pretty mouthy, you know that, girlie?"

"Yeah. I know it." Kate sounded grim.

A yelp of pain. A surge of movement among the men surrounding the Pavilion's back exit. A shout.

Kate's voice again. "Try it again, and I'll do the same thing, you stinking pig!"

That was enough for Alex. He broke into a run.

The group of men seemed to be heaving erratically when he burst through the outer layer of humanity, grabbing shoulders and arms and flinging bodies hither and yon. Yowls from his victims barely registered in Alex's brain, which was occupied with terror on Kate's behalf. He was going to kill whoever that drunken fiend was who'd been harassing her, by Gad, or know the reason why. By the time he got to Kate, a large space had opened up around him, and men stood aside, gaping and rubbing spots on their bodies that Alex had manhandled.

He screeched to a halt, his chest heaving and his fists clenched. They ached to connect with a hard object, preferably the jaw of the man who'd been annoying Kate. "Kate!"

Time seemed to freeze for a moment. Alex's brain cataloged the image of Kate, standing over a man lying on the ground, her eyes blazing, her hair tumbling from under her small, sober-hued hat. For perhaps a heartbeat, he thought about knights and witches, lances, maces, and pots of bubbling brew. Then Kate moved.

"Argh!" She jumped back. She looked frightened. Fright was an expression Alex had never expected to see on this particular face.

His heart continued to race, and he continued to loom over her. She lifted a hand and pressed it to her heart, which was, presumably, thundering as hard as his. "Good Lord, Mr. English, you scared me to death."

Alex blinked at her. Somebody groaned at his feet, and he glanced down to see the man who had, he assumed, been bothering Kate. He scowled at him before turning his attention again to Kate. "Are you all right?"

"Sure," said she. "I'm fine."

Her original sentence finally registered on his brain. He goggled at her. *"I* scared you? *I?"* His gaze shifted wildly between her and the man on the ground.

"Yeah. Shoot, I thought you were a madman or something when you came tearing through that bunch of idiots, punching and shouting." She dropped her hand from her breast.

"A madman?" Insulted, Alex barked out, "Dash it, Miss Finney, I was trying to help you."

"Yeah? Well, thanks, I guess."

"You guess? You *guess?"*

The men who had been gathered around Kate began fading away. Alex observed their retreat with relief. He had no doubt of his abilities—he'd been wrestling cattle for most of his life; surely he'd be able to roust a gaggle of loutish young men—but he didn't really want to create a scene at his own fair of which he was so proud.

"Well, I mean . . ." Kate hesitated, then looked down at the man at her feet. He was beginning to writhe a bit. "Um, thank you, Mr. English, but I really don't need anybody to come to my rescue. I've had to take care of myself all my life."

Alex opened his mouth. He shut it. When he opened it again, he still wasn't sure what to say. He guessed she was right, dash it. But according to the rules governing *his* world, such things as women having to defend themselves against cads and scoundrels didn't exist. The fact that they existed in Kate's world bothered him.

It was true that he'd never much thought about life in the slums before he met Kate. When slum life had intruded itself on his consciousness, it had generally been via the newspapers through articles about crimes and human degradation. Sometimes his lawyer spoke to him about various charities, to which Alex donated sums of money. Now that he'd met Kate and her kin, however, he knew more about who the people living on the "bad" side of town were. They were a lot like him, in fact, and the revelation had come as a rather unpleasant shock. And when his mother had told him about her own poverty-stricken childhood, well . . . Alex just didn't know.

That being the case, he gave up thinking now. He squinted at the man on the ground. He was a well-dressed chap. Alex guessed his age as being in the mid-twenties. He was either well set up in the world, or had a good job. He was, in other words, exactly like other men in Alex's station in life, but without Alex's moral fiber. Obviously, this creature, under the influence of bravery enhanced by alcohol, had been trying to seduce Kate. Alex suppressed a strong urge to kick him in the ribs.

He asked Kate, "How did you get him to fall down?"

Kate, also watching the man on the ground and frowning at the sight, said, "Billy taught me how to flip a man over my shoulder. This one hit another man on the way down, or he'd probably be out cold." She sounded disappointed.

"I see." He wondered if she'd ever done that particular flip to her father. The thought both saddened and sickened him. He hated knowing that people like Kate, who was just like anybody else in the world only poorer, had to endure such difficulties.

Suddenly Alex was tired of the man on the ground. The idiot was wheezing and groaning and generally behaving badly, and Alex wanted him gone. Therefore, he bent over, grabbed him by the front of his coat, and hauled him to his feet. He had to hold on while the man swayed in front of him.

The man said, "Ung."

Alex, shaking him hard, said, "Get out of here, you. Now."

The man said, "Arg."

"And if I ever see you at the World's Columbian Exposition again, I'll have you arrested for assault and battery."

The man said, "Ba'ry?"

Gripping the man in his right hand, Alex reached back with the same hand, as if he were about to throw a baseball, then flung the man, hard, away from him. He watched with satisfaction as the man spun off, his arms windmilling, his feet stumbling, his face a picture of shock and terror. Alex brushed his hands together. "Good riddance to bad rubbish." He turned to Kate again. "Are you all right, Miss Finney?"

She'd taken to hugging herself, and Alex noticed that she seemed a little trembly, a reaction he wouldn't have anticipated in Kate Finney, who put on a good show of being impervious to doubt and fear. "I'm all right," she muttered.

After glancing around and deciding the world was safe for ladies for another little while, Alex held out his arm. "Here, you look shaky. Let me take you to a concession stand for a cup of tea or something. I understand hot, sweet tea is good for shock."

She shook her head. "No, thanks. I don't need any tea. I want to get to the hospital." She took his arm, though, and Alex felt a thrill of triumph. Then she looked up at him, and his heart tripped and wobbled when he saw the worry in her eyes. "Did you see Ma today?"

He reached for the hand she'd placed on his arm and patted it. He didn't dare squeeze it very hard for fear she'd take the gesture, which was meant to be one of reassurance and friendship, the wrong way. Kate seemed to take everything the wrong way. These protective impulses that attacked him every time he was in her presence needed some outlet, though, so he allowed himself a small pat. "Yes. She's doing—well." That was a lie. The woman was dying. Alex sensed that Kate wasn't ready to admit the truth yet, so he let the lie stand.

She glanced up at him, and Alex knew she'd caught him in the fib. She didn't let on. "Good. Did you ask her about going to the country?"

"Yes. She wants to talk to you about it."

"Yeah?"

She looked pleased, and Alex got the strong impression she hadn't anticipated her mother's reaction to his invitation. It struck him as incongruous, but he had an impulse to reassure her of Mrs. Finney's devotion to her only daughter. "Your mother depends on you, Miss Finney. She'd never do anything without consulting you first."

"Really? Do you really think so?"

Now how, Alex wondered, did this woman, who appeared at first glance to be about as soft as old leather and horseshoe nails—maybe chain mail—come by her 'inner insecurities? Were they another product of her environment and upbringing? Alex, who had never had occasion to think about such things before he met Kate, thought about them now. "Of course," he said. "You're the mainstay of your family. Surely, you know that."

He felt her shrug. "I guess."

Shaking his head, he led her out through the main gate to the Exposition. His carriage awaited his pleasure a few feet away, and he considered how lucky he was. That's another thing he hadn't bothered to think about much: luck. He'd always assumed his successful life and business career were the products of his own hard work and intelligence. Since he'd met Kate, he'd started questioning that assumption. In fact, Kate Finney had managed to tip his world sideways quite effectively, and she'd done it by her mere existence in his sphere. Strange, that.

They didn't speak again until he'd guided her into the carriage and climbed in after her. He sat across from her and noted with interest that she didn't seem ill at ease in his company any longer. If she'd get over being so all-fired defensive, they might actually be able to hold a civil conversation one of these days.

He heard her take a deep breath.

"You're not going to hold that against me, are you?"

His nerves twitched. "I beg your pardon?"

She hooked a thumb over her shoulder. "That scene back there. That wasn't my fault."

"Of course it wasn't. Why would you even think that I'd hold it against you?"

She huffed softly. "You were going to kick me out of the fair because of my father. He's not my fault, either. And neither were those guys back there. They're always standing around the exit. Most of the time they don't know I'm the dancer because I change and take all that makeup off. I wasn't so lucky tonight."

He felt his lips tighten and told himself not to be a

fusspot. Recollecting Gil MacIntosh's brother Henry, Alex made a conscious effort to be as unlike Henry as he could be. "Bad luck."

"It sure was." Her expression turned ferocious. "Even if somebody did recognize me, he shouldn't assume I'd entertain such vile suggestions."

"Yes, well, I expect they think only a certain type of woman would dance that way." Was that the wrong thing to have said? He sighed. Probably. It also sounded like something Henry might say, and he was annoyed with himself.

"Yeah? What type of woman is that, Mr. English? One who has to make a living? Is that the type you mean?"

"Hold your horses, Miss Finney. I didn't intend any slights. It's only that most people don't think about dancing as a—well, as a proper or desirable way for a woman to make a living. Don't throw anything at me. You know it's the truth."

"Maybe, but it pays a heck of a lot more than working in the slaughterhouses or the department stores." She was back to being belligerent. Alex wondered if he'd ever knock that chip off her shoulder. "I know it for a fact, because I did both of those things before the Exposition opened."

Good Gad, had she really? A slaughterhouse? An internal shudder rattled him. Kate Finney's life sounded like pure hell to Alex. He spared a moment to marvel that his opinions about her had undergone such a profound change in the short time he'd known her. "I see."

She glared at him. The light in the carriage was dim at best, but Alex felt that glare through his entire being and braced himself. He was beginning to anticipate Kate's reactions to what she perceived as slights or insults.

"You don't, either, see," she said sharply. "How could you? You're a rich man, not a poor woman."

"Right." He pondered the futility of trying to explain

himself and decided he might as well. Why not? The hospital was still a few blocks away. Who knew? He might even get through to her one of these days, although he doubted it. "I'm a man who is comfortably situated in the world." He spoke judiciously, hoping not to rile her any more than usual.

She muttered, "Huh."

"I know you think I was born rich, but I wasn't. My family's circumstances have always been comfortable. I understand that yours were not. That, as you're fond of pointing out, isn't your fault. It isn't my fault, either, however, and I find myself becoming rather tired of being picked on because I wasn't born poor. You're a real snob, Miss Finney, did you know that?"

"Me? A snob?" Her voice rose. "What are you talking about?"

"You. You look down your pretty little nose at everyone who wasn't born in your same circumstances. That's not fair of you. I'm doing my best, given my circumstances. You're doing your best, given yours. I'd say we were pretty equal."

"Equal. Sure. We're about as equal as the queen of England and a mud lark."

"Which one of us is the mud lark?" He smiled.

Kate didn't. "You are."

"I figured as much." Alex thought about giving up and decided not to. "You're a lot of work, Miss Finney. Did you know that?"

"I am not! It's not my fault you decided to help my mother!"

He smiled. "Your mother isn't any work at all. You're the one who causes all the trouble."

"Nuts." She turned her head, probably to look out the window. Alex had pulled the curtains, however, so there was nothing to look at but cloth.

"No nuts. It's the truth. Every time anybody tries to do

anything at all for you or a member of your family, you suspect them of underhanded motives. Every time anybody says anything, you assume they mean something else." He made an effort to keep his expression mild as she gave up staring at the curtain and glared at him. "You know it's the truth, Kate."

"Huh."

Silence settled over them, much to Alex's relief. Deciding not to break into it because he knew speech from him would only precipitate another argument, he contemplated his traveling companion. She presented a complex problem, did Kate Finney.

Truth to tell, he was beginning to wonder why he even tried with her, but something inside him kept propelling him. He liked Bill Finney. He liked Hazel Finney. Kate Finney was a major challenge, but one that Alex found intriguing. It had become important to him, sometime between the day he'd met her and now, that he break down her defenses. Not in a bad way. Not in a way that would hurt her. He wanted to get through to her, to prove to her that not everybody in the world was against her and her family. He thought it would be to Kate's benefit to learn to trust someone someday, and why shouldn't that someone be Alex English?

And how he was going to accomplish that monumental task was presently beyond his ken. She was a woman who had grown up living in fear of the one man in her life who was supposed to have been her protection and haven. Her defenses were thick and solid. It would take a lot of patience and endless endurance, and he wasn't sure he was up to it. Or even why he cared. She was wearing him out.

He didn't have to worry about it for more than another few minutes, because his carriage arrived at the hospital, and his coachman pulled as close to the front stairs as he could. Recalling the first time he'd driven Kate to the hospital, Alex was pleased to note that she didn't seem inclined to leap out of the carriage and run away from him this time. Rather, she waited for him to open the door, let down the stairs, and take her arm to assist her. Just like a real, honest-to-God lady.

It wasn't much, but it was something, and he felt irrationally encouraged.

Kate hurried down the hospital corridors in front of Alex, unwilling to walk at his side or allow him to hold her arm. Embarrassment and rage seemed to be her constant companions around him, and they were wearing her to a frazzle.

She'd always pretty much accepted the way she had to live before she met *him*. Nowadays, every time anything bad happened to her—like that guy outside the Egyptian Palace—Kate saw it as a reflection on her way of life, her moral worth, her character, and her overall unfitness to be among the living. It wasn't fair. Nothing was fair.

And now he was taking her mother away from her.

Aw, nuts. She was being totally irrational. Ma would never abandon her Katie. Never.

She pushed open the door before Alex could open it for her like the gentleman he was, and tiptoed into the room. She noted with relief that her mother was sitting up in bed, talking to a nursing sister. She looked awful, but maybe not quite as awful as she had that morning. Kate took heart.

"Hey, Ma," she called out in the cheeriest voice she could create, given her state of nerves and exhaustion. "You're sitting up." Sitting up was an encouraging sign; Kate knew it in her bones.

Her mother's face brightened. "Katie. I'm so glad you came."

"I always come, Ma. You know that." She took her mother's hand, bent over to kiss her cheek, and stood again. She smiled at the nun, who had stepped back and was beaming down upon them, as if she were witnessing a touching family reunion. Little did she know.

Kate told herself not to be sarcastic, or she'd turn into a bitter old woman before she was out of her twenties.

"And Mr. English came, too." Mrs. Finney's cheeks took on a tiny bit of color. "You're too good to me, Mr. English. But I'm so grateful."

"Nonsense. It's good to see you looking more the thing." Alex came over to the bed, took Hazel Finney's hand in one of his and patted it with the other.

Kate experienced an uncomfortable twisting in her gut and tried to ignore it. She turned to the nun. "How's she doing?" Kate had become accustomed to taking on the responsibilities her mother and father would have assumed if her mother had been healthy and her father a decent human being. She didn't really mind—well, except about her father—and she'd be darned if she'd relinquish her duties to Alex English, a man who had been a perfect stranger until he got a bug in his ear about her.

"Much better."

The nun had a soft voice and a slight accent. She was kind of pretty, and Kate wondered why a pretty woman would give up the chance to have a husband and family in order to marry Jesus and join the church. Then again, maybe the woman had been born on the wrong side of the tracks and had been cursed with a father like Kate's. Kate's father might affect anybody's willingness to undertake the bonds of matrimony.

There she went again. Kate scolded herself for being cynical.

"Did the new doctor come to see you today, Mrs. Finney?" Alex asked.

"New doctor?" Kate glanced from the nun to Alex, her worry gauge quivering. "What new doctor?"

"I have a friend whose brother is a physician, Miss

Finney. I asked him to recommend a doctor who specializes in tuberculosis. I wanted him to examine Mrs. Finney before we take a long trek to the country."

Blast and hell! The damned man was, by God, taking over her life. Kate had been in charge of things relating to her family for as long as she could remember. She'd only met Alex a couple of weeks ago, and already she felt as if everything was slipping from her grasp. She didn't like it. "I see."

"He was a very nice doctor, Katie. He only wanted to make sure I was getting the proper rest and medications."

The tone of worry in her mother's voice smote Kate on the conscience. Nuts. She forced a smile. "That's good, Ma. I'm sure he was nice." It cost her, but she had to ask. "Did he say you were getting the right medication?"

"He prescribed a cough syrup he thinks will be better for soothing the spasms."

"Good. That's good." It was good; Kate couldn't deny it. Turning once more to Alex, she said through her teeth, "Thank you."

"You're welcome."

He looked as if he recognized her attitude as one of jealousy and resentment, softened by unwilling gratitude, and found it amusing. Kate didn't think anything about her mother's situation was amusing. She really didn't like strangers outside her family taking over, either. Oh, yeah, sure, he had money and Kate didn't, but that was no reason to do things without consulting her, and she aimed to tell him so as soon as they left her mother's room.

Alex pulled up a chair and indicated with a gesture that Kate should sit on it, so she did. She tried to unclench her teeth at the same time. She didn't want to show Ma how upset she was. The nun murmured something and left the room. Kate was glad to see her go.

"Did you discuss our proposed trip to the country with Dr. Daugherty, Mrs. Finney?"

There he went again. Taking over. Because she didn't want to start a fight in front of Ma but wanted to show Alex who was the boss here, Kate stuck in an oar. "Yeah, Ma. Mr. English told me he'd talked to you about a trip to his farm. What do you think?"

"I think it sounds heavenly," Mrs. Finney said. Her eyes were shining, which was something they hadn't done very often in Kate's lifetime.

"Did the doc think so?" Kate squeezed her mother's hand, determined to resume her proper role as leading lady in her family's own personal play on the stage of life.

"He said that if I don't overdo, the country air might be good for me."

"Good!"

Alex's hearty voice startled Kate. She glanced over to find him rubbing his hands together. He reminded her of The Great Fontini, a man who called himself a magician and who used to play the street corners in her neighborhood. People tossed coins at him when he did his tricks. After he collected enough coins, he went to the corner saloon and loaded up. "Yeah," she said. "That's real good, Ma."

Mrs. Finney's strength gave out soon after Kate and Alex arrived at the hospital, so their visit didn't last long. Alex felt exceptionally good about Mrs. Finney, though. He was doing all the right things for her, and the knowledge made him glad. Even if the younger Finney woman didn't appreciate him.

He knew—and he knew Mrs. Finney knew—that the eventual result of her illness was death, but he was doing all he could to make her final days as pleasant as possible. Thanks to him, they were going to be a lot nicer than she must have expected. He couldn't understand why Kate was in such a fuss this evening, though. She ought to be pleased that her mother was looking forward to something for once in her unhappy life.

They'd exited the hospital and were approaching the stairs down to the street. Alex's coach awaited his pleasure, as usual, and he anticipated driving Kate to her apartment. He was curious about how and where she lived. She couldn't afford much of a place, he supposed, and he wondered if her brothers helped her out. From his viewpoint, Alex thought the men of the Finney family ought to make her live with one of them, although his own experience with their sister had taught him how little Kate cottoned to the roles most people accepted as appropriate for males and females.

Before she set foot on the cement steps leading to the street, Kate turned around and stopped walking. Alex, wondering what had prompted this action on her part, looked around to see if anything was amiss. He knew something was wrong, or Kate wouldn't be looking like a pot about to boil over.

Kate enlightened him. "Listen here, Mr. English, I don't like it when you do things for Ma without talking to me about them first."

He goggled slightly. "I—I beg your pardon?" What in the name of mercy had he done this time to annoy the infuriating Kate Finney? Dash it, everything he did for Kate's mother was . . . well . . . for Kate's mother, dash it!

"You had no right to call one of your friends about my mother! Pick on your own mother if you want to send doctors to somebody!"

"What? Miss Finney . . . For heaven's sake, you're making no sense!"

"Oh, yeah? Well, how'd you like it if some stranger waltzed into your life and took it over? You wouldn't like it any better than I do!"

"Take over your life? Good Lord, woman, are you crazy?"

"No!" Kate turned precipitately and ran down the stairs.

Alex followed her, more slowly. "Miss Finney, come back here. We need to discuss this." She was a mad-woman. Alex was sure of it this time. He could account for her behavior in no other way.

"I don't want to discuss anything with you! The time for discussion was before you sent a strange doctor to see Ma."

This was idiotic. Alex sped up when she detoured around his coach. Obviously, the wench intended to walk home, whether the streets were safe for ladies after dark or not. It was as if she didn't care to accept even a ride from him. And all because he'd had a specialist visit her mother. Lunacy. That was the only explanation.

His legs were considerably longer than Kate's. She'd managed to skim around the horses, her little feet pumping like pistons, when he caught up with her. Since she didn't appear inclined to wait for him, Alex reached out and took her arm. She tried to wrench herself away, but couldn't break his hold.

"Wait a minute, Miss Finney. You can't walk home in the dark."

She swirled around so fast, Alex almost lost his grip on her arm. "I can, too, walk home in the dark, damn you! I've been doing it all my life! Let me go!"

This was really quite distressing. "Dash it, why are you in such a rage? I didn't and don't intend anything but kindness to you and your mother."

Her whole body seemed to be trembling. Alex's be-fuddlement grew. "Doggone it! Go find some other poor people to help, will you? Leave me and my family alone. We don't need you!"

"Like fun you don't." Alex's own temper was shred-ding fast. "Before you met me, your mother was languishing in the Charity Ward. I can't understand why you're being so irrational about accepting my help."

"Oh! You . . . You . . . *Damn* you!" Kate wriggled and

pulled, and still she couldn't loosen Alex's grip. He feared he was bruising her wrist, but he didn't dare let her go for fear she'd dash out into the street and get run down by a newspaper wagon or a milk truck or something.

"Stop squirming, dash it." He absolutely hated scenes. He'd never been a part of one until Kate Finney showed up in his life. But Kate seemed hell-bent on creating a spectacle of herself—and him—every time they were in each other's company. "Come here, to the coach. We can talk in there."

"I don't want to talk to you!"

If he weren't so occupied, Alex might have rolled his eyes. "Nonsense. You just said we need to discuss things. Well, I'm not going to stand here while you discuss things at the top of your lungs. We'll get into the coach, I'll have my man drive you to your lodging, and we can talk on the way."

"No!"

Good God, people were beginning to notice them. Frustrated beyond anything and tired of being Kate's target, Alex finally gave in to temptation, plucked her right up off the street, and carried her to his coach. He noticed Frank, the coachman, grinning, but decided to take him to task later. Kate was enough of a problem for any man to tackle at one time.

She fought like a fiend, but was so much smaller and lighter than he that Alex had no trouble getting her into the coach. Once inside, knowing she couldn't get out except by the door she came in, he let her go and blocked the door. With a furious bellow, Kate wrenched herself away from him and flung herself on the carriage seat. She glared at him savagely for approximately ten seconds, during which precious few moments Alex tried to catch his breath.

Feeling sour and not caring to disguise the fact, he snapped, "There. Are you sane again yet?"

"Damn you!"

Kate leaped up from the bench cushion like an en-raged fury, stood stock-still for a heartbeat, her mouth gaping and her eyes wide, then crumpled to the floor at his feet.

"Good Gad."

As he picked her up and laid her on the coach seat, Alex thought darkly that at least life around Kate Finney wasn't dull.

Eight

Alex had learned Kate's address from Hazel Finney. After he was pretty sure Kate was out cold—he didn't suppose one could ever be completely certain about anything around Kate—he leaned out the window and told his driver where to go. Frank, who still sounded as if he were finding all this vastly funny, said smartly, "Yes, sir!" and drove off.

As far as Alex was concerned, nothing about this latest incident was at all funny. Irate and frustrated, he crossed his arms over his chest and frowned at Kate as the coach jolted along.

She was a pretty thing once one got past her prickles. He knew she had bright, bright blue eyes. He also knew she had a sense of humor, although she was so defensive about everything, sometimes the humor got buried under the strain of all the other things going on around her. That she had a capacity for great love and loyalty was a given. That she'd suffered greatly in her life was also a patent truth.

Evidently, she was the only girl in a family of boys. A violent, dipsomaniacal father, a sick mother, two brothers, and Kate. Quite a family. From talking with Hazel Finney, Alex had learned that Kate had pretty much run things for most of her life. That was a load of responsibility for such a small thing. He couldn't figure out why she was so dashed reluctant to allow anyone to help her.

She stirred, and he leaned over, ready to catch hold of her if she tried to bolt. He wouldn't put it past her to leap out of a moving carriage if she was still mad at him. A small white hand lifted to her brow. Alex frowned at that hand and that brow. She ought to be wearing gloves. Ladies didn't go out of doors without gloves. He wondered if she didn't wear them because she was stubborn and difficult, or because she couldn't afford them.

Her wrist was awfully tiny. He frowned at it, too, thinking it was smaller than it should be, although he didn't have vast experience with ladies' wrists. He wondered if she skipped meals. Probably. Young women always seemed to be obsessed about their weight. But Kate Finney didn't appear to have any extra fat on her at all.

Visions of a couple of the young women he'd grown up with flitted through his mind's eye. He hadn't paid a whole lot of attention to them, since he hadn't been in the market for a wife, but he didn't recall them being all sharp edges and spikes, as Kate was. His own sister, Mary Jo, was nicely rounded—too nicely, he sometimes thought. All of the other females he knew were softer than Kate Finney, in speech, attitude, and shape.

As long as Kate was immobile, Alex decided to examine her more closely. She always seemed to be in motion when they were together. She never allowed herself to relax in his company. Dash it, why weren't her brothers more involved in their mother's care? Mrs. Finney had given birth to all her children; surely, it shouldn't be Kate alone who cared for her.

He'd managed to work up quite a fit of pique against Kate's brothers, when she stirred and moaned softly. Her eyelashes fluttered. Because he couldn't seem to help himself, Alex reached for her hand and held it gently in his. "Are you all right, Miss Finney?"

She moved, as if she were going to try to sit up. Alex tightened his hold on her hand. "Don't shift around.

You fainted, and you shouldn't sit up too quickly, or your head will swim again."

"No." She gave her head a weakish shake.

"No, what?"

"No, I don't do things like that."

"Like what? Fainting? I can assure you that I didn't knock you out, if that's what you're going to say next." Dash it, she'd scarcely awakened and he was already feeling oppressed and picked on.

She stopped struggling and again pressed a hand to her forehead. "I didn't think that." She shut her eyes.

"Does your head ache?"

"A little. I feel sort of light-headed."

A suspicion that had occurred to him before occurred to him again. "When was the last time you ate anything, Miss Finney?"

"Ate? When did I? . . . Heck, I don't know."

"We had breakfast this morning. Did you eat again today?"

"Oh. Yeah, I remember that. It was good."

"Answer my question, dash it, and stop equivocating."

"I'm not! I don't even know what that word means." She shut her eyes again. Before Alex could blow up, she muttered, "I don't guess I ate again. I think I forgot."

Alex buried his face in the hand not holding Kate's. "Good Gad, Miss Finney, you're a true piece of work, aren't you?"

"I don't know what you mean," Kate said sullenly. "Stop holding my hand."

Alex obliged, although he didn't want to. What was it about this infuriating girl that stirred all of his gentlemanly instincts, anyhow? She certainly didn't appreciate them. She didn't appreciate *him*. Be that as it may, he found himself again leaning out the coach window and directing a command to his driver. "Take us to my hotel, Frank."

"What?" Kate's shock propelled her into a sitting position.

As Alex had anticipated, her abrupt change of altitude made her head swim. She uttered a small cry, pressed her hand to her head, and leaned back against the cushion. "Nuts." Her voice had sunk to a whisper.

Irked—Alex knew exactly what she feared from him, and he resented it—he said, "Don't fret, Miss Finney. I don't plan to ravish you. The only place where it would be proper for us to eat together this late in the evening is the restaurant in my hotel, so that's where I'm taking you."

"But . . ." She didn't finish her sentence. Perhaps she'd begun to think sensibly, although Alex doubted it.

"No buts. You need to be fed, and I'm going to feed you."

She turned away from him. Alex presumed from this that his expression was rather forbidding. He didn't alter it. This was the first time Kate Finney had been too weak to fight him, and he aimed to cling to any advantages, however slight.

"You don't have to do that," she murmured after a minute.

"I don't have to, but I'm doing it." He leaned over, took her chin in his hand, and turned her face so that he could look her in the eyes. "Dash it, Miss Finney, are you trying to kill yourself? What do you suppose will happen to your family if you don't take care of yourself?"

"That's what Madame said."

"As well she might. And what did you answer her?"

"I didn't."

"Well, it's about time you thought about it, young woman. Your mother needs you."

"She doesn't. She's got you now."

"For God's . . . I don't understand you, Miss Kate Finney. If you think for one minute that I would be a satisfactory substitute for you in the eyes of your mother, you're even more daft than I took you for. And, before you ask, I already thought you were about the craziest specimen I've ever come across."

She frowned at him. "Nuts."

"It's not nuts. It's the truth. You're absolutely infuriating. One minute you're telling me you don't need any help, the next minute I find your mother languishing in the Charity Ward of Saint Mildred's, the next minute I meet your brother, who's trying to invest what little money he has to help your family, and the next minute, you're fainting at my feet for lack of food. Now you tell me. Is that crazy or not?"

"Not," she muttered, but she didn't sound as if she meant it.

Alex let go of her chin. She didn't look well to him. His health, always robust, had accustomed him to thinking little about health in general. His life, unlike Kate's, however, wasn't fraught with challenges other than those he encountered in his farming business. His challenges were plentiful, but not especially dire.

Kate's entire life looked dire from where he sat. Kate Finney shook up his notions about life in general, as a matter of fact. Her existence in his world had rocked his serenity and buffeted his complacency. Dash it, she was worse than a thorn in his side. She was more like a broken leg. Or a violent toothache.

But he was getting away from the present problem. "That's not the point. The point is that your mother needs you more than she needs me or anyone else in the world. It has become painfully obvious to me that you're about the only person in your family with a brain and a modicum of common sense, although—"

"I am not!"

Alex squinted at her. She looked as if his words had stung. Curious. "You're the one who bears all the responsibilities," he pointed out.

She sucked in a breath. He expected her to use it to revile him. Therefore, when she spoke after hesitating for a few seconds, her words surprised him.

"That's not fair to Walter and Bill, Mr. English. They aren't very good with sick people, but they both help a lot with food and rent and stuff. And they keep a watch out for our father, too. That's the most important thing anybody can do at the moment."

"Is it? Do they?" Alex was glad to hear it, although he opted not to withdraw his condemnation of her brothers until he learned more about them. So far, the only thing he'd noticed that either brother had done for Kate was make a few investments.

"Yes, they do. Darn it, they've supported the family for years. We all have." She glanced away from him. "You know good and well that our father's no good. It isn't fair, but it's the truth, and my brothers and I know it. We all pitch in, and we have done forever."

The more Alex heard about Kate's father, the more he disliked the man. "Isn't there something the law can do about your father, Miss Finney?" He didn't soften his voice, sensing that Kate would get mad if he indicated by so much as a hint that he felt sorry for her.

She heaved a huge sigh. "Naw. They don't care. They might care if Ma was rich, but even then they probably wouldn't. They don't like to interfere in domestic situations."

"Domestic situations?" Alex could barely wrench his teeth apart far enough to poke the two words out of his mouth.

"Yeah. That's what Sergeant Maguire calls it. It's a domestic situation, according to him. The home is sacred, according to the Chicago Police Department. Never mind that a father is a drunkard who regularly beats up his wife and kids. They don't interfere because the home is not the province of the police department, so they say."

"That's absurd."

"Tell it to the police."

Alex didn't inform Kate, but he intended to do exactly that. Dash it, the home might be sacred, but as far as he was concerned Mr. Finney had violated his right to sanctuary. The man was a brute and probably should have been drowned at birth, as people did with unwanted kittens. Too late for such a merciful solution now.

"But see here, couldn't your mother get away? Don't you have relatives who might have taken you in?"

Her eyes opened wide in mock incredulity. "A sick woman and three kids? I don't know if all of your relatives are as rich as you are, Mr. English, but mine don't have room or food enough to accommodate four more people. Not to mention the fact that my father would probably come over roaring drunk every night until they threw us out of the house in order to get some peace."

"I see." Alex sat gazing at Kate and brooding over life's injustices. If one only looked at it, life was merely life. It had no meaning, really. It was neither good nor bad. It simply was. Life was what one was given to work with for a number of years, and then it was over. It didn't seem complicated on the surface. It was when people started doing evil things with the lives they were given that everything got confused.

"Stop staring at me."

Kate's voice, coming to him, surly, out of the dark, made Alex realize he'd been watching her as he brooded. "Sorry. Didn't mean to stare."

She patted her hair. Her hat had tilted considerably during the past half hour or so, either during her struggle, her faint, Alex's carrying her, or as she lay on the bench. She pushed at it and fumbled with the brim. "Darn it."

"What's the matter?"

"Can't find my hat pins."

"Sit still. Perhaps I can help." He moved to the opposite bench and sat beside Kate, who stiffened. Irked, he snapped, "I'm not going to do anything but try to find your dashed hat pins, Miss Finney. What do you take me for, anyhow?" Ah, there was one of the little devils. It was hanging, caught in a lock of Kate's pretty hair. He worked it out, trying not to pull. "Here's a pin. How many more are there?"

"There's only one more."

"Hmmm. I don't see—Ah, yes! There it is. Here. Hold still for a minute." This one was still stuck in the hat, but it wasn't doing much good since that part of the hat dangled from the ribbon tied under her chin. Alex got the pin loose. "Here. I guess that's it."

She took the pin, and he moved to the opposite bench. She looked ill at ease, and he wondered what her problem was now.

"I'm sorry. Thank you."

The two statements, uttered in a muted voice and with humility behind them, hit Alex hard. He leaned over slightly and stared hard at Kate. Her head was bowed, and her hat sat in her lap. Her hands, one of them holding the two hat pins, were still and rested on the hat's brim. She didn't glance up at him.

"There's no need to apologize," he said, surprising himself. "And you're welcome."

Her head bobbed once. Alex decided the bob had been intended as a nod. She still didn't lift her head or look at him. Nor did she rearrange her hat. Or her hair. It looked as if it were tumbling from its pins. She really did have beautiful hair, thick and shiny. It was a lovely reddish-brown, and Alex would have liked to see it unbound, in the sunshine.

He wondered what the sanitary conditions were at Kate's place of residence. He'd bet she didn't have indoor plumbing or running water. He'd never had to live

like that himself, and the thought of Kate doing so bothered him.

Her shoulders twitched once. Alex leaned forward
slightly. "Miss Finney?"

She shook her head but didn't speak. Good Gad, she
wasn't going to faint again, was she? "Are you feeling ill?"

Again, her head shook once.

It wasn't until he heard a muffled sob that Alex realized she was crying. Kate Finney! Crying! He could
scarcely credit it. Reaching for her arm, he said urgently,
"Miss Finney! Please, Miss Finney, don't do that!" He
hated it when women cried at him. And Kate Finney, of
all people. Crying.

He couldn't stand it. With a lunge, Alex moved to
Kate's side of the carriage. With another lunge, he threw
his arms around her. "Please, Kate, don't cry. Everything
will be all right. Truly, it will. I'll see to it."

For only a moment, she tried to pull away from him, but
he was too strong for her. At last she collapsed in his arms,
sobbing as if her heart would break. Alex felt absolutely
awful. He did, however, realize somewhat to his shock, that
he'd meant exactly what he'd said to her. He was going
to make everything all right for her or die trying.

Dramatic, he told himself. *Entirely too dramatic.* The
problem was, he decided a second later, that, dramatic
or not, he couldn't make himself not mean it.

Kate had never broken down in front of a stranger before. Heck, she'd never broken down in front of
anybody before, if it came to that. Kate wasn't the break-
ing-down type. The fact that Alex's arms had felt so good
wrapped around her, and that she'd wanted to stay there
for the rest of her life, she knew was a bad sign.

"Are you ready now?"

And he was being so nice about it, too. That made it

worse. "Almost." Her throat was scratchy from tears, and her hands shook. Alex said it was from lack of food. Kate feared he was right, too. Darn it. She hated it when people were right about something she'd done wrong.

"There's no rush."

"Stop being so nice to me, will you? I'm not used to it." She stabbed a pin in her hat and grazed her scalp. "Ow."

"I will not stop being nice to you, so you'd better get used to it."

"Huh." Shoot, that had hurt. She hoped to goodness the scratch wouldn't bleed and get her hat dirty. She imagined she looked like the wrath of God, even without a dirty hat. After she'd arranged her hair and her hat, she forced herself to face Alex.

He smiled at her. "Ready?"

"Listen, Mr. English—"

"Please call me Alex."

Huh? After one quick spurt of trepidation, Kate realized she didn't have the strength to work up a good froth of suspicion. Rather, she sighed—she'd been sighing a lot this evening—and said, "Okay. Call me Kate."

He nodded, still smiling.

"Okay. Alex. Listen, you really don't need to do this. I've got some bread and cheese at home I can eat."

"You're not eating a supper of bread and cheese, Kate. Stop fighting me, and come along if you're ready."

She mumbled, "I'll never be ready for this."

"Why not?"

She flung out her arms. "Because I look like hell! That's why."

He squinted at her critically. "No, you don't. You look fine."

"I'll just bet."

She couldn't see very well in the dark carriage, but she imagined he was rolling his eyes. "Listen, Kate, if it will make you feel better, you can stop off in the ladies' room before we dine. You can wash your face or do whatever you think needs doing."

Ladies' room? Dine? Lordy, she really, really wasn't ready for this. Feeling small, insignificant, and overwhelmed, she said, "Okay." It obviously wouldn't do her any good to balk. She'd already tried that. Nothing seemed to alter Alex English's course once he got his mind made up. Pigheaded son of a gun.

She didn't really mean that. To prove it, she said, "Thanks."

"Stop thanking me."

He held out an arm, she took it, he helped her down the carriage steps, and kept her arm in his as they walked toward the Congress Hotel. Kate stared at the elegant facade of the brand-spanking-new building and decided she wasn't surprised to discover Alex was staying in it. She'd seen this hotel from a distance. In passing, as it were. She'd never been inside. People like her didn't go into hotels like this, unless they were maids hired to clean up after the rich people who stayed here. She'd worked as a hotel maid before, but dancing and telling fortunes paid better. She guessed she was still in a debilitated state when her heart started pounding in trepidation.

Telling herself that she was as good as anyone even if she was poor, that she was in the company of Alex English, who was possibly the most respectable human being on the face of the earth, and that nobody, not even the snobbiest and most high-handed maître d'hôtel would kick her out as undesirable, she braced herself for an unpleasant experience. However unpleasant it was certain to be, it would also contain food. Obviously, Kate needed food or she'd never have fainted—and how humiliating that had been—so she would endure.

"The restaurant in the hotel is quite fine," he told her, as if that would be of interest to her.

It was, actually, but not in the way he meant, Kate was sure. She didn't want to dine in a fine hotel restaurant. She wasn't made for that sort of thing. "Good."

He leaned over slightly and whispered, "Please don't be ill at ease, Kate. This is just a place to get food for people who aren't in a position to cook their own. Trust me, eating dinner here is not anything to be uneasy about."

"Easy for you to say."

For some reason, when Alex chuckled, she not only didn't take umbrage, she actually even smiled a little. Maybe Alex was right. Maybe she really *did* have a chip on her shoulder. A tiny one. Virtually invisible.

Alex squeezed her hand. "That's the way. Keep smiling and you'll do fine."

"Thanks."

"Stop thanking me."

This time it was Kate who rolled her eyes. Nevertheless, he'd managed to ease her apprehension enough for her to make an entry into a hotel that was at least a hundred times more classy than she was used to with more aplomb than she'd anticipated. She wasn't even embarrassed when Alex pointed out the ladies' room.

"Here," he said, pressing a coin in her palm. "If there's an attendant, give that to her."

An attendant? Holy cow, fancy ladies didn't really need help peeing, did they? Kate didn't ask. She did accept the coin, considered thanking him, decided not to, and went into the ladies' room. As she'd feared, she looked like the wrath of God. But a little soap and water, and another stab at her hair and hat, and she guessed she'd do all right.

In spite of the glamorous surroundings, which took more than a little getting used to, the meal was better than any other Kate had ever eaten; it was even tastier than breakfast had been. Alex watched over her like a mother hen, forcing her to eat her salad and most of her beef Stroganoff, which she'd never heard of before, but which tasted delicious. Alex told her that some grand duke in Russia had invented it, and Kate was impressed. She, Kate Finney, was eating something with a better pedigree than her own. It was kind of funny, really, but when she told Alex, he didn't seem amused.

"Stop talking about yourself like that," he said sternly.

She lifted her head and gawked at him. "Like what?"

"Like that. You're always disparaging yourself, and I want you to stop it. Starting now."

She chewed on a piece of the butteriest, most marvelous dinner roll in the world and stared at him. After she'd swallowed, she said, "Hey, Alex, you're the one who first said I was no good, remember?"

His glare was quite good. Made him look formidable or something. With more practice, he'd be able to intimidate people with more than his wealth. "I did not say you were no good. I said we didn't want disturbances like the one your father caused at the World's Columbian Exposition. That wasn't your fault, as you were quick to inform me."

"I did, didn't I?"

"Yes. You did. Several times. And, whether it was your fault or not, we still don't want disturbances like that at the Exposition. The Exposition is meant to be a showcase of American ingenuity, spirit, and know-how. It's supposed to exhibit the very best in America, and I'm afraid that incident directly contradicted the fair's purpose."

"I guess it did." She grinned at him. "I was really scared of you, you know."

His eyebrows arched like rainbows above his really quite handsome green eyes. "I don't believe it for a minute. You stood your ground like General Lee at Appomattox."

Kate forked up a piece of beef and a noodle. "I thought Appomattox was where Lee surrendered to Grant."

Alex's eyes narrowed. "Educated wench, aren't you?"

Kate grinned some more. "Surprised?"

"A little," he admitted.

Kate tried to be indignant, but couldn't work up a good head of steam. She wasn't surprised that Alex hadn't expected her to have any schooling. She guessed she did act kind of like a hellion sometimes. Oh, very well, most of the time.

"Did you go to school in town here?"

She guessed the look she gave him was pretty sour, but she couldn't help it. "Where the heck else would I go? Some boarding school in France? The nuns run a school for poor kids in my neighborhood."

"Ah. The nuns. You're Catholic?"

He said the word as if he didn't like it much. "Yeah. You got something against Catholics?"

"Of course not."

She didn't believe him. She also didn't blame him, although she hated herself for the prejudice.

As with everything else amiss in her life, she blamed her opinions about the religion of her forebears on her father. The Holy Roman Church wouldn't allow a woman to divorce anyone even as evil as Herbert Finney. Not only that, but every time he went crazy and hurt her mother, he claimed the Bible told him such actions were justified because a wife was the property of her husband, and the priest had said there was nothing her mother could or should do to stop him. He'd also said that her father should stop beating up on her mother, but her father never bothered to listen to that part.

Kate knew she shouldn't hold Catholicism responsible for her father's reprehensible actions, but she couldn't help it. "Shoot, Alex, I'm Irish. We're pretty much all Catholic. More or less."

"I see. And do you attend church regularly?"

She shrugged. "I go with Ma when she's up to it. I don't go on my own." Lifting her chin and giving him a scowl of defiance, she added, "I don't believe in that stuff. I think the church is wrong about a whole lot of things."

"My goodness."

"Are you laughing at me?"

"Don't climb onto that high horse you're so fond of, Kate. I'm not laughing at you." He hesitated for a moment. "Ah, do you mind my asking you how old you are?"

"Why?" She tried to fight it, but Kate felt suspicion inching its way up her spine.

"Because you act like you're a hundred and ten more often than not."

If her mouth hadn't been full of sour-cream sauce and noodles, it might have fallen open in shock. Before she could swallow and respond to his outrageous allegation, he went on.

"I suspect your life has aged you quickly, and you don't look very old, but you must know that most young women your age aren't supporting their parents. It usually works the other way around."

"Maybe where you come from." Darn it, she was on the defensive again. For a few minutes there, they'd actually been communicating like—like friends, or something.

Alex heaved a big sigh. "I suppose you're right. I'd still like to know your age. I understand it's an impertinent question and that gentlemen aren't supposed to ask ladies such things, but I'm curious. You have to bear so much responsibility."

"I'm twenty-five," Kate said, lying.

"Really? You don't look that old."

"Bother. You're a real pain, Alex English. Did you know that?"

He only grinned.

"Oh, all right, I'm twenty-two. Turned twenty-two last November." She scowled at him defiantly. "Happy now?"

"Relatively. In case you wondered, I'm going to be thirty on my next birthday."

"Shoot, really? You don't look that old."

His grin vanished, and his frown looked pretty serious. "Oh, heck, Alex, you know what I mean."

"No," he said. "I don't."

"Nuts." She flung out a hand. It was the first spontaneous gesture she'd made since entering the Congress. "Most men in my neighborhood are dead before they're thirty. Or roaring drunks."

"Good Gad."

She shrugged. "It's the truth. I don't like it, either."

His expression softened. "Are you worried about your brothers, Kate? Do either of them seem inclined to take strong drink?"

Strong drink? Kate had never met anyone who used words so nicely. In her neighborhood, booze was booze. "No. I think our father cured us of any inclination toward the booze." She grinned. "And I threatened them with an awful death if either one of them so much as looked at a whiskey bottle."

"Good."

Her grin vanished and she eyed him sharply. "My brothers are both good men, Alex. I guess you think they don't do enough for Ma, but they do what they can. Walter works two jobs, and he wants to get married. He's been putting it off for a couple of years now because Ma's been so sick."

"He must have a very understanding fiancée," Alex said dryly.

"Don't sound so sarcastic, darn it. He does. She's a very nice person. I grew up with her."

"Ah. And does she work as a fortune-teller, too?"

"Darn you." If they weren't in a fancy restaurant, Kate might have thrown a noodle at him. "No. She works at Wanamaker's as a ladies' wear clerk. I make a lot more money than she does, but she doesn't have my—" She broke off abruptly.

"She doesn't have your what?"

She'd been going to say "guts," but guessed that might give Alex too much ammunition. "She doesn't have my responsibilities. Her father is a nice man, and he supports his family."

"Ah, I see. That makes sense." His expression seemed strange to Kate, although she didn't know exactly why. "You're an unusual young woman, Kate Finney."

"By unusual, do you mean weird, Alex English?"

He grinned, making Kate's heart do strange, leapy things in her chest. He had a heck of a grin. He didn't look at all stuffy when he grinned. "No. I don't mean weird. I mean unusual. I've never met anyone like you before."

She frowned at her carrots. "I'll just bet."

"That wasn't an insult."

"No?"

"No."

She didn't quite believe him, but she wanted to. She really, truly wanted to.

Kate had a quivery feeling in her middle as Alex's coach approached her neighborhood. Although she knew she was being not merely silly, but totally impractical, not to say insane, she had a mad urge to jump from the carriage and run home so he wouldn't see the dump she lived in.

Reminding herself that she was as good as anyone, even though she didn't feel like it more often than she did, and also that her circumstances weren't her fault and that she was doing her very best to better them, she still felt bad about Alex witnessing this godawful part of town. Garbage lay everywhere. Sanitation was a laugh. Ladies of the night paraded their wares. Drunken men shouted and laughed. Dirty, half-naked children played on stoops. The whole area was characterized by filth, poverty, and desperation, and Kate wanted out so badly, she could taste the longing every time she came home. She was glad for the dark of night because the neighborhood was even uglier with the sun shining on it.

That was one of the main reasons she loved working at the World's Columbian Exposition. Everything there was clean and tidy. It was the only place in Kate's whole life where everything worked the way it was supposed to work. Even her.

She wasn't there now, however, and the carriage was rapidly approaching her little corner of the world. Kate sometimes thought of her tiny room as a refuge in a storm-tossed sea. It might be small, and it might be falling apart in spots, but she kept it clean, and nobody bothered her there. And that, as she well knew, would last for as long as her father remained in ignorance of her address. The mere thought of her father made her lift her hand and finger the fading bruises on her throat. With luck, he was locked up. Kate wished she believed in luck.

Girding her loins, so to speak, she said, "We're not too far away now. It's just down this street and to the left."

Alex grunted something, and Kate shot him a glance. As she'd expected, he was glaring out the window, looking as if he disapproved of everything he saw. What the heck. She didn't approve of it, either. She didn't say anything.

After another few seconds, she muttered, "It's that big gray building over there. The one with the sign painted on the window. The butcher's shop." It might smell bad, but Kate would be forever grateful to the old German couple who allowed her to rent the room over their shop. The Schneiders were nice folks.

Without a word to Kate, Alex leaned out the window and gave a command to his driver. The coach pulled up to the curb in front of Schneider's Meats. With a sigh, Kate prepared to climb down from the high life and reenter her own low place in the universe.

"I'll see you to your door." Alex's voice was gruff.

"You don't have to do that. I know the way."

"Stop being stubborn, dash it! I'm going to see you to your door." He pushed the door open, flipped down the stairs, and reached for Kate's arm.

She allowed him to help her down. Why not? It was kind of fun being treated like a lady for once. "Thank you."

As if the words were pushing past his restraint, Alex snapped, "Stop thanking me! Dash it, I can't even imagine you living in a place like this."

The words hit her like a slap across the face. Stiffening, Kate snapped back, "It's better than where I came from."

"Good Gad."

Before she could wrench herself away from him and dash up the stairs, humiliation burning inside her, a loud roar made Kate stop in her tracks. "Oh, God, no!"

Alex tightened his grip on her arm. "What is it?"

As if life wasn't hard enough already. Kate's heart sank into her resoled shoes. In a voice shaking with rage and shame, she said, "It's my father."

Nine

Alex whirled around, putting Kate behind him, and saw a huge barrel of a man heading straight at him, his head lowered, as if he intended to ram Alex in the stomach like a bull. "Good Gad."

"Oh, Lord, Alex, please don't let him hurt you!"

"Hurt me?" The remark wounded Alex in a sensitive place: his pride.

"He's a monster," Kate cried. She'd started tugging on his coat sleeve, trying to get him to run away.

Alex would be damned before he'd run away from this lout. "Don't be absurd," he barked. "Stay here." Yanking Kate's hand away from his arm, he straightened and stepped away from her, hoping her maddened father would aim for him instead of her. His ploy worked.

With a roar of fury, Mr. Finney lurched toward Alex. Alex, who had plenty of experience in felling animals bigger and heavier than himself, stepped nimbly aside as the charging bull of a man reached him, whipped his arm out and up, thereby catching the other man around the throat, and felling him. Mr. Finney hit the pavement with a thud that rattled the Schneiders' front window.

Time seemed to stand still for a moment as Alex stared down at Mr. Finney, who lay there, his sides heaving, looking confused and in pain. Alex glimpsed Kate from the corner of his eye, her back against the butcher shop window, her hands pressing her cheeks, her eyes huge. He turned to her. "Are you all right, Kate?"

"Me? Am I all right?" She gaped at him.

She had such beautiful eyes. If Alex wasn't otherwise occupied, he'd have been happy to stare into them for several hours. Under the circumstances, her evident inability to understand his question annoyed him. "Yes! Are you all right? For God's sake, this man is twice your size!"

"I know." He heard Kate gulp. "I'm okay."

Alex hadn't experienced violent urges very often in his life. He understood now, as he had never done before, that this was a product of his privileged life and background. He felt extremely violent at the moment. It was all he could do not to pick up Kate's father by the scruff of his neck and beat him to death.

Kate took a tentative step toward him. Alex snapped, "Stay back. I don't know what this animal is going to do next."

"He's going to try to kill somebody," Kate said in a shaky voice. "Probably you. Then me."

"Damnation." The word, coming out of his own mouth, shocked Alex. He shook himself. No matter how bad circumstances were, profanity was no answer. "We've got to do something with him, then."

"What?"

Alex shot Kate a frown. "There's no need to sound so hopeless, Kate. We only need to think for a bit."

He hadn't noticed the crowd gathering until the murmurs and exclamations finally penetrated his concentration. Glancing around, he saw a mob of faces, all looking on with varying degrees of fascination, outrage, and relief. He heard somebody say, "About time somebody leveled that ox," and took heart. Evidently, the crowd wasn't going to lynch him for felling one of their own.

Since they seemed to be on his side in this issue, Alex

decided to press his luck. "Does anybody have a suggestion what to do with him now?"

"Shoot him?"

This suggestion, offered by a toothless man who grinned down at Herbert Finney, prompted laughter from the crowd.

"I wouldn't mind," Alex told him, "but I don't think the police would like it."

Mr. Finney, gaining strength, muttered a profanity and started climbing to his feet. He'd made it to his hands and knees when a young man in the crowd stepped forward and whacked him with the lunch pail he carried. Mr. Finney collapsed again.

"Thanks, Benny."

Alex turned to find Kate smiling feebly at the young man with the lunch pail. The boy couldn't be any older than Alex's sister.

"Sure thing, Kate," said the boy Alex assumed was Benny. Benny looked from Mr. Finney to Alex. "Why don't I go and try to round up a policeman."

Alex contemplated the problem. "Do you think it'll do any good? I was under the impression the police don't take much of an interest in Mr. Finney and his family."

"They don't," said Benny in a matter-of-fact voice, "but they wouldn't like it that Finney tried to hurt a swell."

From the murmurs of approval that went up from the mob, Alex realized they all agreed with Benny. "That's terrible," he growled.

Benny shrugged. "Maybe, but it's true."

"Good Gad." There was no time to worry about the inequities of Chicago law enforcement, since Mr. Finney was beginning to make challenging grunts from the sidewalk. Alex gave himself a short mental shake and barked, "Anybody have a belt or some rope?"

The men standing around exchanged glances. A woman, quicker to understand Alex's intent than her male companions, jerked forward, untying the scarf wound around her neck as she did so. "Here, you can use my scarf."

"No, Rose," Kate said, causing Alex to whip his head her way. She took a shaky step toward him. "Use this, Alex." She took a black ribbon out of her handbag. Alex recognized it as the one that had encircled her neck during her dance performance; the one she used to hide the bruises this same man had inflicted days earlier.

"Don't be silly, Kate," said the woman named Rose. "That wouldn't keep a baby's hands tied. Use this." She thrust her scarf at Alex.

The men in the crowd finally caught on to the purpose of Alex's request. Several of them nudged Rose aside and handed Alex items appropriate for securely tying up a large, drunken man. When Mr. Finney's alcohol-fogged wits allowed him to understand that Alex had deftly tied his hands together—he'd had lots of practice on bulls of another variety—he set up a roar of vile curses and epithets.

Without pausing in his deft movements—he had started binding the drunken man's feet together—Alex said out of the corner of his mouth, "Somebody give me a gag." Several men's and ladies' handkerchiefs were thrust forward instantly. Alex grabbed at the one he saw first and jammed it into Mr. Finney's mouth. When he was through binding and gagging Mr. Finney, he stood up, taking Kate's father with him by means of Rose's scarf, which he'd tied around the man's neck. Alex thought it was fitting, and if Mr. Finney struggled and managed to strangle himself thereby, that would be fitting, too, not to mention convenient.

"All right, you son of a bitch." He heard Kate gasp at his use of such foul language, but didn't care. "We're going to wait right here, and as soon as the police come, I'm sending you with them. Tomorrow, after you sober up and before you can get sprung from the clink, I'm filing charges."

Mr. Finney's eyes bulged, although Alex judged the emotion behind the bulge to be ire rather than worry. Because he was so furious himself, he shook Mr. Finney, hard. Fortunately for all, Rose's scarf held up under the pressure of such violence. Mr. Finney's face turned an alarming shade of puce. Alex didn't care about that, either. Still holding Kate's father in what he wouldn't have minded had it turned out to be a death grip, he turned to Kate. "Are you all right, Kate? Do you need anything?" Shaking her father for emphasis, he added, "This ape won't be bothering you again tonight."

She shook her head. "Yes. I mean, no, I don't need anything. Thank you."

Like hell she didn't need anything. She looked as if she were about to faint and her eyes were huge, too, with what Alex judged to be a combination of shock, anger, and mortification. Potent combination, that, and he deeply regretted the fact that Kate was forced to endure it. Of course, it was all her father's fault. He actually grinned when he realized that's what Kate had told him in the first place.

"I swear to you, Kate, that I'll take care of this. I won't let this man terrorize you or your mother again." Even if he had to kill the bastard with his own bare hands. He didn't add that part, but he silently vowed it, to himself and to Kate.

This time she nodded, although Alex clearly read the doubt on her vividly expressive countenance. Little did she know that Alex never promised things he failed to deliver. She'd learn, though; he'd see to it.

Benny had evidently hurried to fetch a policeman, because a grumbling man in uniform showed up at that precise moment. Alex presented Mr. Finney to the uniform with a vicious thrust forward. Mr. Finney staggered, but Alex held him upright by the scarf around his neck. As soon as the policeman saw who was behind the drunkard, he stopped grumbling and straightened.

"Jaysus," the policeman muttered. "What's this? Finney's been at it again, has he?"

Before Kate or anyone else could respond to this less-than-caring commentary by the law, Alex said in a voice of ice, "Yes. Finney's been at it again, and this time I'm going to make sure he never has a chance to hurt his daughter or his wife again."

The policeman frowned. "And you are?" He didn't take Mr. Finney from Alex's care, a fact that fueled Alex's irritation to a degree he hadn't believed possible. Did Kate and the people in this neighborhood have to endure this sort of thing from official police representatives all the time?

Stupid question. Of course they did.

"My name is Alex English, and I'm one of the directors of the World's Columbian Exposition." The assertion wasn't entirely untruthful. Alex was one of the directors of the fair's Agricultural Forum. "I expect the Chicago Police Department to do its duty in this instance, and I intend to make sure they do it. So if you're not interested in doing your duty, I'll find an officer who is." He gave the policeman a toothy grin and hoped the idiot would choke on it. "And I'm sure the police commissioner will be intrigued to find out how his deputies honor their responsibilities to protect the community they've been hired to serve, as well."

He was pleased to see the uniformed officer swallow hard. "No need for that, Mr. English. I'll take Finney into custody right now."

"And you won't let him out again, will you? I'm going to the station first thing tomorrow to press charges. He attacked me. If he had succeeded, I'm sure he'd have attempted to murder his daughter. Again. We can't have that sort of thing, can we?" Another toothy grin produced another hard swallow.

"No, sir."

"Right. I thought you'd see the situation my way. Remember, don't let him go. I'll file charges tomorrow. You won't fail me in this, will you?"

"Yes, sir. I mean, no, sir. Charges. Tomorrow. Yes, sir."

"Charges. Tomorrow," Alex repeated in order to make sure this flat-foot beat copper didn't forget his instructions.

"Tomorrow."

"Morning."

"Morning."

Alex nodded once. "Good. Take this creature off."

The policeman was so intimidated, he saluted. Alex turned to scan the crowd, which had grown considerably as events transpired. A couple of men glanced at him, lifting their eyebrows in question. He nodded back, and the two men took up flanking positions beside the officer and Mr. Finney. Unless Alex missed his guess, the two aimed to escort Finney to the station in order to make sure the policeman carried out Alex's request. Their show of support, which he supposed they'd offered because they liked and respected Kate and deplored her father's behavior, gratified him.

As soon as the excitement died down, people drifted away, and Alex found himself standing next to Schneider's Meats with Kate beside him. She was shivering, although the evening was warm. Without even thinking about it, he took her arm and leaned down to inspect her face. He was worried about her state of mental health.

She was pale as death, and her pupils were so dilated they made her blue eyes look almost black in the scanty gas lighting in the neighborhood. She licked her lips. "I— I'm sorry, Alex. I didn't know he'd found out where I live."

He stared at her for almost thirty seconds, trying to assimilate the meaning of her words. *She* was sorry? That her father had discovered her place of residence, such as it was? Good Gad.

Alex was experiencing an almost overwhelming compulsion to lift her into his arms and kiss her until all of her cares flew away, so he straightened, hoping the compulsion would die soon. "There's no need for you to apologize, Kate. Your father is at fault, not you."

She nodded again, although she didn't appear to be sure of herself. No longer was she the infuriating Kate Finney who tackled the world and everything in it single-handedly with a hell-bent independence that drove Alex crazy. She bore very little resemblance to that Kate right now. At the moment, she looked like a young woman who, if not defeated, had at least suffered a severe blow to her self-confidence.

Because his protective, not to mention his carnal, urges unsettled him, he sounded more gruff than he intended when he spoke again. "Here. Let me escort you to your apartment."

She shook her head. "You don't need to do that."

"Damn it, Kate Finney, stop fighting me." And, after swearing not once, but twice in a single evening, Alex picked Kate up off the sidewalk and cradled her in his arms. "Where do you live?"

"Upstairs." She was breathless with shock and indignation.

"Stop struggling."

To Alex's great surprise, she did. She released a huge sigh and subsided in his arms. He found out why she'd done so when he walked up the narrow, dark stairway. It wasn't because she liked being in his arms. It was because she feared he'd lose his footing, tumble downstairs, and kill them both if she kept struggling.

The place reminded Alex of a fright house in a circus. The walls seemed to close in on him. The staircase couldn't have been more than a foot and a half wide. No gaslights illumined Kate's place of residence. No friendly, homey smells of cooking food greeted her. The area above the butcher shop reeked of decayed meat, blood, and bone, and Alex would have gagged if he didn't have such rigid control over himself. When he reached the floor above ground level, he blinked into the blackness, squinted around, and thought he discerned two doors. "Which one?" he asked through clenched teeth. He hated knowing this was where Kate lived.

"The one on the right." Her voice sounded funny—soft and strained, as if she, too, were trying not to gag. Or cry. By this time, Alex had no doubt at all that Kate was full to the brim with tears. That she'd only shed a few in his presence, he chalked up to a miracle of fate and Kate's own strength of character.

"Is it locked?"

He felt her shake her head, so he grabbed the knob, pushed the door open, and walked inside, still holding Kate. Although he didn't want to, he set her on the floor. A strange feeling of loss and distress filled him when she immediately scuttled away from him. He heard her moving in the dark. A scratch of flint and a spark preceded a burst of illumination from the kerosene lantern she'd lit. He supposed it made sense that she knew her way around in the dark, since she probably did this same thing—without the preceding melodrama—every day of her life.

The odor of the butcher shop wasn't as strong in Kate's room as it had been on the staircase. Alex looked around with interest, and was not surprised to see that she kept her home neat as a pin and decorated as well as a woman of Kate's means could decorate it. She'd gone to the trouble of placing bowls of sweet-smelling leaves and dried flower petals about, probably in an attempt to disguise the smell of rotting meat. It didn't quite achieve its goal, but Alex felt a spurt of wholly irrational pride on

Kate's behalf that she'd tried so hard to improve her surroundings and succeeded so well, in spite of everything.

"It's not much, but it's home to me."

Alex glanced over and found Kate standing in front of the one window in the room. He suspected she'd made the pretty chintz curtains herself. She'd been through a lot today, he knew, and now she looked both defiant and ashamed. He could understand the defiance part.

"You've done a wonderful job in making a room into a home, Kate. You ought to be proud of your achievements."

She didn't move, although she did frown slightly. "Yeah, right."

Alex tried not to allow his exasperation to seep into his voice. "I mean it." Although he didn't feel much like it, he smiled at her. "You've finally convinced me. None of this is your fault. And your father is a bad man. A truly rotten man, as a matter of fact. You're right. I was wrong."

To his surprise, she bowed her head. "I'm sorry." Her voice had sunk to a whisper. "I didn't want this to happen."

"Good Gad." He couldn't stand it any longer. With two long strides, Alex crossed the room and took Kate in his arms. He held her close. "Kate Finney, you're the most infuriating woman I've ever met in my entire life."

"I am not."

"Don't argue with me. You don't know how many infuriating women I've met."

"I guess not."

Alex's heart swelled when she gave a soft laugh. Kate didn't laugh enough. "You're also the bravest."

"I am?"

She lifted her face to look at him, and Alex saw tears in her eyes and a tremulous smile on her face. "Yes," he said. "You are." And he kissed her.

* * *

Kate was as limp as a rag. The door had just closed behind Alex—he hadn't allowed her to leave her room in order to see him downstairs, even though she knew how dark the staircase was and how unaccustomed to her neighborhood Alex was.

He'd kissed her. Kate had never allowed a man to kiss her before. She was glad she'd waited. Her legs felt shaky when she walked from the door, which Alex had instructed her to lock, and went to the piece of furniture that she used as both a bed and a sofa. She'd made lots of pretty cushions that she propped against the wall during the day in order to allow people who visited—and Kate had her fair share of visitors—to sit and take tea with her.

Her hands shook when she began removing the cushions to the chair where she stashed them overnight. After dropping two of them, Kate decided she wasn't up to making her bed for the night before she'd digested the implications of Alex's actions.

He'd saved her from her father. He'd taken charge of a situation that would certainly have become ugly, perhaps even deadly, if he hadn't been there. He'd probably saved her life.

And then he'd kissed her.

"Oh, Lord, please help me." It had been a long time since Kate had uttered a heartfelt prayer, but she meant that one.

Sitting on the edge of her sofa-bed, her hands clasped tightly in her lap, Kate looked around her room. It was a pretty pathetic place, especially if she compared it to the Congress Hotel, where Alex had taken her to eat. Rather, he'd taken her to *dine* there. Kate supposed she'd actually dined that evening. On beef Stroganoff.

But Alex was right, too, in that she'd done a darned good job in decorating what would otherwise have been even more forlorn a room than it was now. Kate hadn't very often had her efforts to improve herself and her surroundings acknowledged by anybody outside her family. Her heart lifted slightly now, when she realized Alex had meant his comments sincerely.

Not only that, but unlike most times when somebody with money and power said something nice to her, she didn't reject his praise. Rather, she figuratively clasped his praise to her bosom and basked, as she'd basked in his embrace. She hadn't wanted to let him go.

Kate knew it was fortunate for her virtue that Alex was a man of such firm, not to say stubborn, principles. If he wasn't, she was sure she'd have succumbed completely, thereby proving herself to be no better than her circumstances. Kate had determined when she was no bigger than a minute that she'd rise above them. At the moment, she found irony in the fact that it had been Alex who'd kept her determination intact. Not to mention her virginity.

Oh, but that kiss. Kate put two fingers to her lips, savoring the remembrance of Alex's lips there.

"You'd better savor it, Kate Finney, because it will never happen again." She spoke to herself with a good deal of force, because she didn't want to be disappointed when Alex vanished from her life.

She knew she was already too late.

Alex knew it was probably unwise of him to walk back to the Congress Hotel. The neighborhood surrounding Kate Finney's residence teemed with the worst elements in Chicago. Nevertheless, he told Frank to drive the carriage there without him in it.

"Are you sure, sir?" Frank was clearly distressed by Alex's command.

"Yes, I'm sure," Alex snapped. "I'm going to walk."

Dubiously, Frank said, "Yes, sir."

Alex didn't appreciate the expression on Frank's face.

He probably thought that Alex planned to spend the night with Kate. As if he'd ever besmirch Kate Finney or any other woman. He glared at Frank, whose cheekiness was becoming absolutely insufferable, stuffed his hands in his pockets, and set out toward the Congress Hotel before Frank had a chance to do more than release the brake.

How could he have lost control so completely as to have kissed Kate? Alex had never experienced such loss of control before; until tonight, he hadn't thought he had it in him to lose control, as a matter of fact. He knew better now. When he was in Kate's presence, all of his breeding seemed to desert him.

But, how could he have done such a stupid thing? If he'd succumbed to temptation with any of the women his mother had thrust in his way over the years, he'd be married by this time. But Kate Finney? How in the name of all that was holy could he marry a girl from the slums?

He stopped walking abruptly, causing a couple of disreputable-looking passersby to stare at him. He glowered back, and the strangers sped up.

Had he really thought such a priggish thing about Kate?

Yes, by Gad, he had. Scowling at another couple of poorly dressed members of a society that lived on a lower scale than his own and who scurried off in a hurry, Alex experienced a moment of self-revelation that he didn't want to acknowledge because it did him no credit.

Glaring after the retreating men, another unhappy realization struck him. Those men, and the others he'd scared off with his foul mood, were afraid of him. *They* were afraid of *him*, and not the other way around. Alex knew their fear wasn't based on his physical state, which was fit but not especially grand, but because he, as a man of means, could command more worldly power than they.

He, Alex English, could determine their freedom to walk the streets of this city, because the law would pay attention to Alex English. The law, as evidenced by his own experience this evening, paid no attention to the Kate Finneys of the world, unless someone in Alex's station paid attention first.

And he'd just rejected the mere possibility of marrying Kate, a woman whom he admired more than almost any other woman in the world, because she'd been born in impoverished circumstances. He'd been told, and he'd believed, that the citizens of the United States could achieve anything if they worked hard enough for long enough.

It had become painfully clear to Alex in the past several days that this time-honored adage was only true to a degree. If one were a female, one's circumstances defined one's station in life. There were those, like Kate Finney, who fought the world and its inequities like maddened cats, but they were still circumscribed by their sex and stations in life.

And yet his prior thoughts on marriage, based on years' worth of unsubstantiated assumptions, had not only blamed Kate for her birth, but shrank from considering her a suitable partner for marriage with him. Because he was wealthy and she was poor. A convenient wad of paper blew his way, and Alex kicked it hard. He didn't like learning the imperfect truth about himself. That it was the truth, he couldn't deny.

Blast Gil MacIntosh, anyhow. And Kate Finney. She'd waltzed into his life like an opera dancer from a bad musical and managed to turn it upside down and inside out without even trying. Alex had the unpleasant notion that Kate would be happy if she'd never met him.

As for Alex, he'd be happy not to have met her, too, but he had met her, and now he was stuck. Not only had he taken over the medical care of Kate's mother, but he was interested in helping Bill Finney prosper in his investment experiments, and he also intended to take the entire family out to the English family farm as soon as he could possibly arrange to do so.

And then there was the problem of Kate herself. Alex didn't know how he felt about Kate, but he feared the worst. The worst wasn't his sexual interest in her, either. He was a man, after all. Any man would lust for Kate once he saw her. Alex feared his interest in the feisty Miss Finney ran deeper than mere carnal attraction.

"Aw, nuts," he grumbled, unconsciously borrowing a slang expression from Kate. He'd talk to his mother about his state of befuddlement. Ma was a wise woman, and Alex never felt shy about asking her personal questions.

Besides, Ma had been poor once. She'd told him so. Surely, she'd have some good advice.

He didn't even notice his approach to the Congress Hotel until the doorman said, "Uh, Mr. English, are you feeling quite the thing?"

Caught by surprise, Alex stopped and stared at the man. "Beg pardon?"

"I beg your pardon, sir." The doorman looked uncomfortable. "I didn't mean to intrude. I, uh, well—you didn't look quite well."

"Oh." Alex understood at last that the doorman's question had been meant kindly. Until quite recently— say, the past twenty minutes or so—Alex had believed himself to be a rather more kindly specimen of humankind than most. He was ashamed when he couldn't recall the last time he'd actually paid attention to this man, this—Bother. What was his name? Ah, yes. Kaufman. "I'm fine, thanks. Ah, thank you for your concern."

Alex saw relief descend upon the doorman, and he felt like a rat. Did people actually treat the Kaufmans of the world so badly that this particular Kaufman worried about keeping his job when he asked about a man's health? The possibility, which Alex feared was true, bothered him a lot.

What really bothered him, however, was his reaction to the thought of marrying Kate Finney. Was he honestly so arrogant that he would refuse to marry a woman just because she'd been born poor? He'd come to like Kate. A lot. He certainly desired her. While he'd originally believed her to be a woman of low moral tone, he knew better now.

Bother. He needed to get Kate and her mother to the farm; he needed to see how they acted around his mother and his sister. The thought of Mary Jo made his insides give a twinge. Would Mary Jo behave herself with the two Finney ladies? Would she believe herself to be better than they because they were from the bad side of the city?

If she did, Alex would speak to her. By hand, by Gad, if he had to. Mary Jo wasn't too dashed old to be spanked. He wouldn't allow anyone, not even his own sister, to behave less than impeccably to Mrs. Finney and Kate.

Good Gad, there he went again. He was so confused. Thank the good Lord for his mother. Ma would know what to do. Alex could hardly wait to hear what she had to say on the matter, because solving the Kate Finney problem was totally beyond him without help.

It was a glum and exceedingly frustrated Alex English who entered his expensive, luxurious, brand-new hotel room that night.

Ten

Madame looked hard at Kate. "He's taking you where?"

Striving for a nonchalance she was far from feeling, Kate said, "He's taking Ma and me to his farm tomorrow morning. He thinks the country air will be good for her, and the doctors agree."

"Ah. He's concerned for your mother's health. Of course."

Kate, who'd been staring in the mirror and applying greasepaint to her pallid cheeks in her daily effort to make herself look more like a Gypsy, frowned at Madame's reflection. "Yeah. You have a problem with that? I think it's nice of him."

Madame's eyebrows waggled. Kate hoped to heaven the woman couldn't really read people's thoughts, because her own mind seemed determined to dwell on last night's kiss. "Darn it, Madame, there's nothing wrong with this trip!"

"I said nothing." Madame popped a chunk of cheese into her mouth and chewed.

Her grin irritated Kate. "You didn't have to say anything. You look like a darned house cat who's just caught a big, fat mouse."

Madame chuckled and swallowed. "No, no, Kate. I'm only concerned for your heart."

"My heart's just fine, thanks."

"Hmmm." A hot pepper followed the piece of cheese.

Kate knew she'd uttered a huge lie, and she feared that Madame knew it, too. Her heart was a mess, thanks to Alex English. Why had he interfered in her life, anyhow? First he'd threatened her livelihood, then he'd usurped her mother and brother, and now he was threatening her virtue. Oh, it wasn't fair! If she'd been alone, she might have banged her head against the table a few times in an effort to drive out the confusion dwelling therein.

"Darn it," she muttered. "He's being nice to my mother. That's the only thing that matters."

"Ah."

Squinting into the mirror, Kate saw Madame nod. No grin this time. Still, Kate sensed amusement from that quarter. Nuts. Deciding there wasn't anything she could do about Madame, Kate quit trying and resumed applying dark greasepaint to her cheeks. She was really on edge this morning, longing to see Alex, yet afraid of seeing him, too.

He hadn't been at the hospital when she'd visited her mother this morning, probably because he was at the police station, filing charges against her father. The back of Kate's neck burned when she remembered last night's awful scene. She hadn't told her mother about it, because Ma would only have felt bad and worried, and she didn't need more worry. She'd had more than her share of worries in her life already.

Ma had looked better this morning, though, which was the important thing. She'd mentioned the proposed trip to the country three times in ten minutes, and Kate had tried hard to be happy with her. She'd failed. She should be happy. It was a good thing that Ma was going to get out of the city and breathe some fresh country air for a couple of days.

Drat it, why couldn't she keep her priorities straight

anymore? Kate thought grimly that she knew the answer to that one, no matter how little she wanted to admit it. She was beginning to care a great deal for Alex English, and she didn't want to. The fact that she seemed to have no control over her emotions when it came to him bothered her a lot. Kate had made it a policy never to allow her emotions to interfere with her goals. It troubled her that her policy didn't seem to be working any longer.

Lifting her chin to observe her fading bruises and to determine if she still needed that black band around her neck, she thought bitterly that, until Alex English waltzed into her life, she'd been just fine. Oh, sure, she'd been poor, but she'd been working like the very devil to better herself and her family. It was also true that before she met Alex her father had been a constant threat, both to her and to her mother. But Kate was used to those problems. She knew how to deal with them. She'd armed herself long since to do battle with the life she understood.

She didn't understand Alex or his life one iota, yet he seemed determined to drag her into it, whether she wanted him to or not. It was all so confusing.

"It'll be all right, Katie," Madame said after Kate decided she no longer needed makeup or the black band. Her words startled Kate, who glanced at the spiritualist's reflection in the mirror.

Madame was looking particularly mysterious at the moment, even though she was chewing. "Will it?"

"Yes. No worry. Everything be fine."

"Good. I'm glad." She'd be even gladder if she had a modicum of confidence in Madame's predictions.

Alex was still reeling from the battle he and Kate had waged on Friday night when he set out with Frank on Saturday morning to pick her up at her lodging. She'd put up a nonsensical fuss about this part of the weekend's agenda. He'd only prevailed by telling her that if she dragged her suitcase to her mother's hospital room, he wouldn't take her to the country with them. He was certain she hadn't believed him, but she'd given in when he then told her he didn't intend to make a scene on the sidewalk, and if she wanted to continue arguing about it, she'd have to talk to herself because he was leaving.

God almighty, the woman drove him crazy. He couldn't understand why he cared so much about her.

As soon as Frank drove the team around the corner and the carriage approached the butcher shop, Alex glanced out the window and felt his lips tighten. Kate stood on the trash-strewn, unpaved dirt walkway, a shabby carpetbag beside her. Both the bag and the girl were waiting for him.

Dashed woman hadn't even stayed in her room long enough for him to carry her bag down those dismal stairs. The memory of her room caused a shudder to pass through him. He hated the thought of Kate living over that cursed butcher shop.

Alex was frowning out the window when he saw Kate reach down to lift up the bag. In defiance of a lifetime's worth of lessons in manners and deportment imparted by his parents, he shouted at the top of his lungs, "Leave it there!"

She jerked upright as if she'd been pinched and frowned back at him. Furious with her, with himself, and with the forces that had shaped Kate Finney's life, Alex didn't even lower the steps of the carriage when Frank pulled up in front of her. He jumped down, still shouting. "Dash it, let me pick up your dashed bag!"

"It's not that heavy," she said sullenly.

"I don't care how heavy it is. I'll put it in the baggage compartment."

"Fine." She heaved a huge sigh to let him know how silly she thought he was being.

Alex gritted his teeth, lifted the bag, glanced up to see Frank staring down at him with a good deal of surprise, and wondered what was wrong with him—Alex, not Frank. Frank was the one who should be handling the luggage. It was his job. Yet Alex had leaped out of the carriage like a man possessed and grabbed Kate's carpetbag as if it contained pieces of gold. Frank was right: he must be losing his mind.

Consoling himself with the certain knowledge that no man could survive a long acquaintanceship with Kate Finney with his sanity intact, he set the bag in the baggage compartment and tied down the canvas flap. He stopped being surprised to find Kate waiting for him to help her into the carriage as soon as he remembered he hadn't let the steps down. He flipped them down now, and took Kate's arm before she could scramble inside without his assistance. She didn't pull away from him, which he couldn't help but consider some sort of victory on his part, although he didn't expect it to last.

Banging on the carriage ceiling, he said, "Hospital, Frank." Then he sat back and studied Kate, who occupied the bench seat across from him.

Pale face. Pretty brown hair drawn back into a severe bun. Ridiculously small hat with a pink flower attached to it. Well-tailored pink traveling suit that Alex suspected she'd made herself. Old boots, patched and polished and laced with new shoestrings. White gloves.

White gloves?

Yes, by Gad. White gloves. Glory be, the woman was actually wearing gloves for once. Small handbag that she'd made and embroidered herself unless Alex was much mistaken. She looked perfectly respectable and trim. She was, in fact, a living, breathing miracle sitting there across from him.

"Quit staring at me."

Startled, Alex realized he had actually been staring.

He tore his gaze away from her and directed it out the window. "Sorry."

"Hmph."

Frustrated and impatient, he snapped, "Listen, Kate, will you please climb down from your high horse for a minute?"

As he might have expected—actually, as he *had* expected—she bridled. "*My* high horse? What about *your* high horse? Darn it, I wasn't being silly when I suggested meeting you at the hospital! It made perfect sense, and it would have saved a lot of time."

"It made no sense at all, you mean, and the amount of time it would have saved would have been minuscule at best. At worst, you would have strained something, carrying such a load so far, and spoiled the weekend for everyone. How did you expect to get a bag containing clothes for you and your mother to the hospital without help, pray tell?"

"Who said I'd be doing it without help?"

"You did!"

"I did not!"

"Dash it, you—" Realizing he'd started shouting again, Alex cleared his throat and forced himself to moderate his sound level. "At all odds, you didn't let on to me that you had someone who could help you."

"Oh? So, do you think I should tell you everything that goes on in my life?"

Unable to refrain from rolling his eyes, Alex said, "For heaven's sake, no, I don't think you should tell me everything. However, when it comes to excursions in which I'm involved, then yes, I not only think you should have explained your mode of transport to me, but I also believe that you were remiss in not doing so."

"Nuts."

"It's not nuts."

"Hmph. Either one of my brothers would have been

happy to help me help Ma. You know darned well that I have two brothers."

Alex strained to keep his temper from flaring again. "I thought both of your brothers held jobs. Aren't they busy during the morning on Saturdays? I'm sure I saw Bill behind the counter in Schneider's."

He felt a surge of triumph when her lips pursed in frustration. "Yeah, well, I could have found someone to help me."

"You did," Alex said more smugly than he'd intended. "Me."

"Hmph."

"Face it, Kate, I'm concerned about your mother. Being concerned about your mother includes concern for you, whether you want to admit it or not. If anything happened to you, your mother would be devastated."

"I know that. What does that have to do with you picking me up at my apartment?" Her expression took on even more defiance, which Alex would have believed impossible until it happened. "For your information, I'm not proud of where I live, Alex English. I don't *like* having you see where I live. It's ugly, it's poor, it's dangerous, and—well, it just is, is all."

"Oh, for God's sake, Kate. I know what your circumstances are. Do you think I care about that?"

"Darn it, *I* care about it!"

"Oh, for . . ." Alex swallowed another hot rejoinder, and reminded himself that she had a point. Not a good point, in his considered opinion, but he could almost understand her sentiments on the subject. He'd most likely have felt the same if he were in her shoes. God forbid.

She went on. "Do you think I like having some rich swell barge into my life and turn up his nose at me?"

This time Alex considered his outrage more than justified. "I do not turn up my nose at you!"

"Maybe not now, but you did."

"That's not fair, Kate." He felt as if she'd punched him in the heart, as a matter of fact. He was the good guy here, dash it.

"The heck it isn't. Your nose was stuck so high in the air that first day when you wanted to toss me out of the Exposition, I'm surprised you could see where you were going."

"That's ancient history! Surely you're not going to drag that incident into the conversation again, are you?"

Fire flared in her eyes. "Darn it, that *incident,* as you call it, almost cost me my livelihood! And if you'd succeeded in getting me kicked out of the fair, what do you think would have happened to Ma then?"

"But I didn't get you kicked out, if you'll recall. As a matter of fact, since that first meeting, I've been trying to help your mother."

"Yeah, but you didn't want to at first."

He sucked in air and held onto it for long enough to suppress his bellow of outrage. After he calmed down a trifle, he muttered, "You're not a proponent of forgiving and forgetting, in other words."

"I can't forget! You scared me to death! You threatened my mother and me!"

"That wasn't my intention, as even *you* must understand by this time."

"Huh."

"My intention was to protect the integrity of the greatest exposition of American invention and creative expression ever presented to the world. The World's Columbian Exposition is . . . is—well, it's like my baby. I didn't want your father and you to cast inappropriate shadows over what was intended to be a showplace of all things wonderful in our country."

She glowered at him. She had a great face for glowering: small, vivid, and glowing at the moment with bright flags of fury. "My father isn't—"

"Your fault. I know. I admit, and have admitted before, that your father isn't your fault. You're doing everything in your power to overcome your father's influence in your life, and to remove your mother from the brute's clutches."

"Yeah, well, it took you a while to admit it."

"Oh, for . . ." Gritting his teeth and feeling persecuted—he didn't enjoy remembering his first antagonistic meeting with Kate, since he believed it portrayed him in a less-than-stellar light—Alex said, "I'm sorry that I didn't understand your situation before we met, Kate. But how could I? And how many times must I apologize for that one mistake? Besides, you must admit that as soon as I learned about your problems, I've been trying to help."

"Hmph." She turned her head and commenced glaring out the window.

Alex studied her profile, wondering why they were fighting. More, he wondered what they were fighting about. Was it because Kate still resented his misjudging her character and moral fiber before they met? That wasn't his fault, as even she'd probably admit if she ever admitted anything.

Was it because she was afraid he was taking over her life and her mother? This possibility had some merit. She'd even more or less said it outright once or twice, although since he'd come to understand her extreme sensitivity regarding certain aspects of her life, he'd tried very hard to ease her insecurities on the subject. It gratified Alex that he could help Mrs. Finney and, by extension, Kate and her brothers. They were a worthy family, except for the father, and they deserved a break.

Or was it that kiss? Alex stared moodily out the window and thought about it. He didn't know about Kate, but he hadn't forgotten that kiss. Dash it. He didn't think he'd ever be able to forget it, as a matter of fact. Every time he remembered it, his unruly manhood stood at attention and saluted. He wanted her badly. Very badly.

Although Alex had spent some time in recent months vaguely reflecting on the subject of marriage, he hadn't considered the sexual aspects of such a union. Except in terms of providing heirs to keep the family business going, he hadn't bothered to consider the appeal of certain women on a carnal level. He'd always believed that marriage stood apart from carnality, rather as an ideal of perfection. Alex hadn't considered that the perfect marriage should include sexual compatibility, mainly because such topics never intruded into conversations and he'd never had to think about them. Until that kiss.

Because he didn't care to brood too long on the kiss, with Kate only a foot or so away from him, Alex decided to review the list of ladies who would make appropriate wifely candidates for him. His lip curled when he thought about Mabel Howell, and he made it stop.

Poor Mabel. She was an all-right sort of lady, but she had a dreadful giggle, buck teeth, and, Alex would swear it, she'd never produced an original thought in her life. Not that Alex believed that women necessarily *should* be original thinkers. Still and all, he unquestionably required a woman who wouldn't bore him to death within ten minutes of the conclusion of the wedding ceremony. Besides, the brighter the mother, the brighter the children, and Alex didn't care to sire dolts.

Then there was Julia Bigelow. Julia was quite pretty. No buck teeth in her mouth. And she was smart, according to all the teachers in the small school both she and Alex had attended during their growing-up years. Alex held no prejudices against ladies who wore spectacles, and he didn't think Julia's own eyewear detracted from her overall attractiveness. She did have a rather declaratory pattern of speech, however, and one always got the feeling Julia was bestowing a particularly gracious condescension upon a fellow by speaking to him.

No. Alex didn't think he'd enjoy marriage to Julia. In truth, and totally without partiality, Julia was a prig and a pedant; she considered herself superior to pretty much everyone else in the world, and she'd make a very uncomfortable wife.

The notion of Julia rearing his children caused him a pang, as well. He didn't think children needed to be condescended to and treated like inferior boobies. The notion of Julia treating a child of his loins the way she treated her friends made his blood run cold. Any child of Julia's would grow up thinking he—or she; Alex wouldn't mind having girl children—was undeserving and unwanted.

Not that children didn't require discipline. However, Alex preferred his mother's mode of discipline, which was delivered with gentleness, love, and a guiding hand, to what he expected Julia would mete out to her offshoots.

So. That eliminated Mabel and Julia. Who else was there? Alex brooded over prospects as he continued to gaze absently out at the city.

Imogene Hamilton. Ah, yes, Imogene. She was a sprightly sort; totally unlike Julia, who was as stiff as a stick, and less giggly than Mabel, who was a brainless nitwit. Alex supposed Imogene was a possibility.

But, really, as much as Alex liked and appreciated Imogene, he'd always thought of her more as another sister than as a sexually attractive female or a viable future wife for him. Imogene and Alex's second-youngest sister, Elizabeth, had been the best of friends. Still were, he guessed. Alex had been a big brother to both of them, and he didn't think he could suddenly begin thinking of Imogene as a wife.

And . . . But this was a ridiculous exercise. Alex knew why he'd been wasting time thinking on it, though. He was trying to downplay his attraction to Kate Finney. Although he hated admitting it, he feared the Kate problem was going to require more than a few idle moments spent contemplating other women. Not only did Alex not give a fig about the other women he knew, but the notion of bedding anyone but Kate left him feeling empty. The notion of bedding Kate and degrading both her and himself left him feeling sick.

"There's the hospital."

Kate's simple comment succeeded in dragging his brain back from the dismal contemplation of impossible options. "Ah, yes."

"I hope they have one of those wheeled chairs, so Ma doesn't have to walk down all those stairs. She can take a little exercise, but I don't want her to wear out before we get to the country."

"I've arranged for a chair."

The skeptical glance she shot him didn't escape Alex's notice. He sighed. "I'm not trying to take over your position in your mother's life, Kate."

"I know that." She didn't sound like it.

"I only want your mother to be as comfortable as possible. It will be a long ride for her."

"I know that."

Alex heaved another sigh. Frank drew the carriage up to the front steps of Saint Mildred's, hopped down from his seat—Alex guessed poor Frank didn't want him usurping any more of his duties—and flipped the stairs down. Without speaking again, Alex held out a hand. After a hesitation so brief he might not have noticed if he weren't so exquisitely aware of everything she did, Kate took his hand and descended the steps. Alex followed her, sighed yet again, and walked with her into the hospital.

Mrs. Finney, in a wheelchair, with Sister Mary Evodius standing next to her and beaming like the sun itself, awaited them in the hospital's lobby. Alex noticed two

Introducing Ballad,
A LINE OF HISTORICAL ROMANCES

*A*s a lover of historical romance, you'll adore Ballad Romances. Written by today's most popular Romance authors, every book in the Ballad line is not only an individual story, but part of a two to six book series as well. You can look forward to 4 new titles each month – each taking place at a different time and place in history.

But don't take our word for how wonderful these stories are! Accept our introductory shipment of 4 Ballad Romance novels – a $23.96 value – and see for yourself! You only pay for shipping and handling.

*O*nce you've experienced your first 4 Ballad Romances, we're sure you'll want to continue receiving these wonderful historical romance novels each month – without ever having to leave your home – using our convenient and inexpensive home subscription service. Here's what you get for joining:

- *4 BRAND NEW Ballad Romances delivered to your door each month*

- *30% off the cover price with your home subscription.*

- *A FREE monthly newsletter filled with author interviews, book previews, special offers, and more!*

- *No risk or obligation...you're free to cancel whenever you wish... no questions asked.*

Passion–
Adventure–
Excitement–
Romance–
Ballad!

*T*o start your membership, simply complete and return the card provided. You'll receive your Introductory Shipment of 4 FREE Ballad Romances. Then, each month, as long as your account is in good standing, you will receive the 4 newest Ballad Romances. Each shipment will be yours to examine for 10 days. If you decide to keep the books, you'll pay the preferred home subscriber's price – a savings of 30% off the cover price! (plus shipping & handling) If you want us to stop sending books, just say the word...it's that simple.

A $23.96 value — **FREE** No obligation to buy anything — ever.
4 FREE BOOKS are waiting for you! Just mail in the certificate below!

Get 4 Ballad Historical Romance Novels FREE! ❖

BOOK CERTIFICATE

Yes! Please send me 4 FREE Ballad Romances! I only pay for shipping and handling. After my introductory shipment, I will receive 4 new Ballad Romances each month to preview FREE for 10 days (as long as my account is in good standing). If I decide to keep the books, I will pay the money-saving preferred publisher's price plus shipping and handling. That's 30% off the cover price. I may return the shipment within 10 days and owe nothing, and I may cancel my subscription at any time. The 4 FREE books will be mine to keep in any case.

Name _____

Address _____ Apt. _____

City _____ State _____ Zip _____

Telephone (____) _____

Signature _____

(If under 18, parent or guardian must sign)

All orders subject to approval by Zebra Home Subscription Service.
Terms and prices subject to change. Offer valid only in the U.S.

DN102A

If the certificate is missing below, write to:

**Ballad Romances,
c/o Zebra Home
Subscription Service Inc.**

P.O. Box 5214,
Clifton, New Jersey
07015-5214

**OR call TOLL FREE
1-800-770-1963**

Passion...

Adventure...

Excitement...

Romance...

Get 4
Ballad
Historical
Romance
Novels
FREE!

lll..l.l.lll....lll.l.l.l.l.l...l.l.l..ll.l..lll..l

BALLAD ROMANCES
Zebra Home Subscription Service, Inc.
P.O. Box 5214
Clifton NJ 07015-5214

PLACE
STAMP
HERE

spots of color in Mrs. Finney's cheeks, and prayed that they signified eagerness to begin this country trek and not fever. He watched Kate rush up to her, smiling as if she hadn't a care in the world, and kiss her mother's cheeks. Mrs. Finney glowed at her daughter.

"You look swell, Ma."

"Thank you, Katie, darling. Sister Mary Evodius has been taking good care of me."

"It's a good thing." But the grin Kate gave the nun held nothing but gratitude and friendship.

"Good morning, Mrs. Finney. You're looking bright and pretty this morning."

Mrs. Finney acknowledged Alex's comments with a brilliant smile. "This is so kind of you, Mr. English. I'm so looking forward to getting out of the city for a while."

"I'm glad." Alex smiled at the nursing sister. "Here, Sister, let me take over this operation."

"There was no need for the chair," Mrs. Finney murmured. "I'm not completely helpless."

"I'm sure of it, but there's no need to overexert yourself." He was sure of no such thing. For all the color blooming in her cheeks this morning, Alex could swear she grew smaller every time he saw her. It was as if she were fading away before his eyes, and his heart ached for Mrs. Finney and Kate.

"I can push her." Kate's voice was sharp.

Alex considered telling her not to be foolish, but thought better of it. "If you want to." He stepped aside. Kate gave him an odd look, almost as if she were embarrassed, although Alex wasn't sure about that. Embarrassment seemed unlikely from this source.

Mrs. Finney glanced from her daughter to Alex, sighed, and said, "I'm looking forward to meeting your mother, Mr. English."

"Please," he said, "call me Alex. And my mother is looking forward to meeting you, too. I'm sure you two will find many things in common." That wasn't even a lie, although it sounded funny, even to his own ears.

"Yeah?" said Kate. She sounded absolutely skeptical.

Her mother murmured, "Katie."

Alex didn't react. He was getting used to being abused by Kate.

Kate mentally swore at herself to stop being such a witch to Alex. It wasn't his fault he was a nice man to whom she was wildly attracted. She knew good and well there was nothing in a future with him, because he was rich and educated and socially prominent, and she wasn't. She was dirt. She was nobody from nowhere.

Actually, she was nobody from the slums, which was probably even worse than being from nowhere. If she'd been born to a poor ranching family in Texas or somewhere, she might exude a tolerable bit of cachet to the folks in Alex's circle. But, as ever, her luck ran true. It was uniformly bad.

Perhaps not totally. Her father was in jail again, and with Alex pressing charges, maybe he'd stay there long enough for her to relocate. Again. Maybe her luck was turning. Probably not. Pa would probably find her wherever she went. It irked her that if anybody did the world a favor and shot him dead, it would be the perpetrator of that act of mercy who got sent up the river. If justice prevailed in the world, her father would have died before he'd been allowed to cause so much trouble and terror and pain.

She bit her tongue and didn't utter a word of protest when Alex gently lifted her mother into the carriage. She even smiled at him. A little bit. He gave her an ironic salute, and she knew he understood her smile had been forced. *What's the matter with me?*

An answer eluded her and continued to do so as Alex

settled a lightweight blanket over her mother's knees, then turned and assisted Kate into the carriage. He was a prince of a guy, really. She shouldn't resent his attentions to her mother, since they were making Ma happy. Ma's happiness mattered more than Kate's state of confusion. A lot more.

The carriage ran pretty smoothly on the paved streets of Chicago. Kate had noticed before this that Alex's carriage rode more smoothly than any cab she'd ever been in. Money could sure work wonders. She shot a peek at her mother's face, and wished money could work a wonder of a permanent nature for Hazel Finney.

"This is so nice," Mrs. Finney murmured as the carriage rolled along the highway.

Kate watched with fascination as the houses got farther and farther apart, and green stuff began showing up at the sides of the road and in people's yards. She'd seen fancy houses before, so she knew that many people who were wealthy enough actually grew grass in their yards for no better reason than so the kids in the families could play there.

A grass lawn sounded sort of like a poor girl's version of heaven to Kate Finney, who'd grown up playing on the streets. Heck, she'd learned to dodge the milk wagon and the delivery carts by the time she was three. Walter and Bill and the Griswold kids used to make a game of it.

"This is really pretty," she said, hoping the comment would serve as an offering of some sort to Alex, who didn't deserve her bad temper.

"You think so?"

He sounded merely curious, so Kate didn't snap at him. "Yeah. We don't get much green growing stuff in my neighborhood." She spoke lightly, because she didn't want her mother to start feeling guilty.

"True, true," Mrs. Finney said upon a sigh that set her to coughing. The spasm didn't last long, although it made Kate's heart skip and her fear rise up like a monster in her breast.

"You okay, Ma?" Her voice was breathy with worry.

"I'm fine, Katie." Mrs. Finney took a small flask out of her handbag and sipped from it. "The doctor gave me this. It helps to calm the spasms."

"I wish we'd had more rain recently," Alex said, sounding as if he, too, were concerned. "There's so much dust being kicked up by the horses and the carriage wheels. I think I ought to let down the isinglass windows until we get farther out into the country."

He moved to do so, and Mrs. Finney laid a hand on his arm. "Please don't do that, Mr. English. I mean Alex." She gave him such a sweet smile, Kate would have wept if she did things like that. "I'd rather see the countryside than worry about my health right now. I—well, I don't know how many more opportunities I'm going to have to see this."

Kate uttered a strangled noise that she hoped didn't sound like a sob as Alex sank back down onto the seat across from her and her mother. "Of course," he said. "I understand."

So did Kate, and she hated it. Very seldom did she allow herself to admit that her mother was dying. When Kate thought about Ma dying, she felt as if her heart were being gouged out of her chest by a monster's claws. If Ma died, she'd die.

Or she wouldn't die, which would be worse, because then she'd be left to face the world all by herself. Sure, she'd have Bill and Walter, but they always looked to her for everything. She'd have no one left to whom she could talk, of whom she could ask advice, to whom she could cry if she needed to. And sometimes, although she hated to admit this, too, Kate Finney cried.

Oh, God, please don't take Ma away from me.

As usual, God paid no attention to Kate Finney.

Eleven

Mrs. Finney managed to stay awake almost the whole way to the English farm, but nodded off during the last portion of the trip. Alex had thought to provide pillows for her—the darned man thought of everything—so Kate propped a couple of them next to her, and her mother lay her gray head there. Kate wanted to cry but, naturally, didn't.

"We're almost there," Alex whispered after several minutes of silence on the part of the coach's occupants.

Kate realized he'd been watching her mother and herself closely during the preceding couple of hours as his fancy carriage rolled them out of Chicago and into paradise. It looked like paradise to Kate, at any rate. She nodded. "I think Ma's getting kind of tired."

"Evidently." Alex smiled, nodding toward the sleeping woman, and Kate's insides fluttered.

Because she knew she'd been unjustly snappish earlier in the day, and because she truly appreciated what Alex was doing for her mother, she said, "It's really pretty around here, Alex. I'm surprised you ever want to leave it to visit Chicago. I'd want to stay here, where it's so pretty and clean."

"I like visiting the city sometimes, but this is my home."

Kate wished she could say that. She'd kill to be able to live in the country. And wouldn't Billy and Walter love it? They would. She could envision her brothers working behind plows and doing other farmerly things of a similar nature. They, unlike their father, were hard workers.

Also, Kate didn't know about Walter, but Billy loved animals and horticulture. She couldn't even remember all the strays he'd taken in over the years. And even though he lived in a room not unlike Kate's, in a boardinghouse for young men and located in an even worse neighborhood, he liked to grow vegetables in a box he'd built and set up in his window. He brought Kate carrots and radishes quite often, and had even managed to grow beans on a trellis he'd rigged.

Recalling something Alex had said to her a few days ago, she said, "How long has your family lived here?"

"We're into the fourth generation."

He didn't sound proud exactly, but Kate heard what she identified as satisfaction in his tone of voice. She didn't resent it. If she could claim sixty or seventy years of family farming in so gorgeous a setting, she'd be satisfied, too. "That's a long time. My family was in Ireland three generations ago." She shrugged, grinned, and added, "One generation ago, too, come to think of it."

Darn it, why did he have to go and chuckle like that? Every time he chuckled, everything inside her curled up and started purring. "I remember your mother telling me she was from Ireland."

"Yup. So's my old man." Kate wrinkled her nose, a reaction that had become automatic for her over the years whenever her father intruded himself into the conversation.

Alex was silent for a moment or two. "I'm sorry, Kate. I'd give anything to free you from your father's influence."

She'd been looking down at her mother and thinking how pale and exhausted she appeared, but Alex's words made her head snap up. "Thanks, but you're doing plenty already."

His lips thinned as he pressed them together, and

Kate wanted to slap herself upside the head. She hadn't meant to sound so defensive. It was only that every time he did or offered to do something nice for her or her family, she reacted badly. She wasn't used to people being nice to her, darn it. Because she knew she'd managed to offend him again, she said, "Thanks for filing charges. I think that'll help some."

"Not enough," he said grimly.

She sighed. "Nothing's ever enough when it comes to him. I guess we won't have any peace until he kicks off. With my luck, that'll be years from now."

He looked at her for long enough that she got to feeling uncomfortable, then said only, "We'll see."

Whatever that meant. He sounded like Madame. She didn't trust him.

Oh, who are you trying to kid, Kate Finney? she asked herself nastily. *You know darned well you trust him. He's one of the only people earth you do trust.*

The thought didn't comfort her appreciably. She didn't want to begin counting on Alex to be there for her, because she feared for her state of mental health once he vanished from her life. She had no doubt whatsoever that he would.

"It's right there."

His brief comment jolted her out of the bitter contemplation of things that could never be. Kate turned her head, trying not to jostle her mother, and looked out the window toward where Alex pointed. The carriage took a slow, sweeping turn and passed through a gate that Kate could only consider picturesque. It reminded her of a gate belonging to a huge estate, pictures of which she'd seen in a book at the church school she'd attended. Sister Benedict, who'd taken a liking to Kate, had let her look at it whenever she wanted to. The book contained photographs and paintings of famous English castles and mansions. Kate had spent hours pretending she lived in one of them.

"Oh, boy," she said for lack of anything more original popping into her head. "This place is great."

She wasn't fibbing. Trees bearing all different kinds of fruits lined the drive leading to a huge white house. To Kate, the place looked like a castle in disguise. She knew castles were supposed to be made out of stones and had battlements and crenels and so forth, but this place was big enough to be a castle, even if it was crafted from wood and painted a bright, sparkling white. Dark green shutters looked perfect against the white.

The porch was something wonderful. Kate had daydreamed about porches like this one. She could imagine sitting out there on a summer evening, sipping lemonade and listening to owls hoot and watching cows graze, or whatever it was cows did. The only part of the cow with which Kate was familiar was the decaying odor of it once it went to the slaughterhouse.

"Thanks," said Alex, and the genuine pride ringing in his voice caught her by surprise.

When she tore her gaze away from the house and directed it at his face, she saw the pride there, too. It wasn't vanity; it was honest-to-goodness, genuine, true pride—in his family, in his heritage, and in himself for maintaining the former two. Kate didn't blame him. She'd be proud if she'd managed to hang onto something like this, too. Heritage was good, if it was this type. Her own brand of heritage stank.

She saw a woman and a girl step out onto the gigantic porch and wave at the carriage. "That your mother and sister?" An imp of nervousness began dancing in Kate's chest and chipping away at her self-confidence. She wasn't sure she was up to meeting the high-class English ladies.

"Yes. They're both looking forward to meeting you and your mother."

I'll just bet. Kate wondered how many arms Alex had had to twist in order to get them to agree to have a couple of women from the slums visit their precious farm.

Lordy, there she went getting snappish again, and it was all due to nervousness. She advised herself to calm down and tried to take her own advice. It wouldn't do to approach those two ladies with a bad attitude and a chip on her shoulder. Kate knew how to behave. Her mother had tried her best to rear her with an appreciation of proper manners and deportment. The fact that her father had always interfered with these attempts, and the fact that they lived in a neighborhood where such qualities as manners and deportment weren't honored or valued, didn't matter now. At this particular moment, Kate needed all of her mother's teachings, and she aimed to use them.

She jiggled her mother's shoulder gently. "Ma? Ma, we're here."

Mrs. Finney stirred and struggled to sit up. "Oh, my," she murmured, rubbing her eyes. "So soon?"

"Yup. It's really pretty, too."

"Did you have a good rest, Mrs. Finney?" Alex's smile was as soft and tender for her mother as Kate's had been. Kate appreciated him a lot just then.

"Yes. Thank you. What a wonderful carriage you have."

"I'm glad you were comfortable."

"Oh, my, yes, I was comfortable. I'm sorry I slept, though, since I really wanted to see everything."

"I'll be sure that you do," Alex assured her. "Now I'd better let them know they've been spotted. He leaned out the window and hollered, "Ma! Mary Jo!" in a voice so loud it made Kate jump and Mrs. Finney laugh.

It was moderately encouraging to know that even so sophisticated a swell as Alex English could holler when he was excited about something. Heck, it was encouraging to know he could *get* excited about something, for that matter. Kate spoke softly to her mother. "You ready for this, Ma?"

"I'm looking forward to it, Katie." Mrs. Finney patted her daughter's hand. "Mr. English's family must be exceptionally fine, for him to have turned out so well."

Hmmm. That put a new light on things. Kate said, "Right. Sure. Makes sense." So, what did that make her? She was the product of a sainted mother and a devil of a father. Nuts. She didn't want to think about her miserable beginnings now.

Alex drew himself inside the carriage, laughing, and sat back with a *whomp*. "They're excited about your visit. I'm afraid Mary Jo thinks farm life is dull and boring. I promised she could return with us to Chicago. I'm going to show her the Exposition."

Mrs. Finney laughed. "You sound as if you're a very good brother to her, Alex."

"I try to be."

"My brothers are good to me, too," Kate said, feeling defensive on her brothers' account.

"They are, indeed." Mrs. Finney patted her hand again.

"I've only met the one, Bill, and he's a brick," agreed Alex. "He's smart, too. I wouldn't be surprised if he'll be making his fortune before he's too much older."

Kate searched his face for signs that he was attempting to humor his companions, but didn't see any. "You really think so?"

Alex shrugged. "He's smart and ambitious. He wouldn't be the first man in America to turn his circumstances around and create a fortune for himself and his family. This is really the land of opportunity, if a person uses the opportunities available." He grinned. "A little luck doesn't hurt, either."

"I guess not." Shoot, he sounded sincere.

"Brace yourselves," Alex advised before Kate could think anymore. "Mary Jo is a pistol."

Again, Mrs. Finney laughed. "I can't wait to meet her."

A tiny, pointy dart of jealousy nicked Kate in the heart, and she gave herself a hard mental shake. Was she so insecure that she couldn't allow her mother to like another human female? Brother, was *that* notion a kick in the teeth. Kate decided to do a little self-survey before going to sleep that night. She was discovering all sorts of things about herself that she didn't like.

The carriage entered a sweeping circular drive and slowed to a stop in front of the porch. Both English ladies had descended the stairs to the porch, Mrs. English with the grace and dignity befitting her years, Mary Jo with a whoop and several long bounds. Kate, who hadn't until this minute known proper ladies behaved so enthusiastically, was impressed.

"Alex!" Mary Jo shrieked.

Grinning from ear to ear, Alex paused before opening the carriage door. "Better brace yourselves. My sister takes some getting used to."

Kate, wide-eyed with astonishment, only nodded. Mrs. Finney laughed again.

Alex hollered, "Stand back, you little imp! We have two ladies in here!" He didn't add that one of the ladies was infirm, which Kate appreciated.

"I won't be pushy," his sister promised.

Eyeing her curiously, Kate saw that she was a pretty girl, with curling brown hair and huge pansy-brown eyes. Her dress was pretty, but it wasn't brand-new. It even looked as if someone had lengthened it at one point, and had covered the faded former hemline with a row of rickrack. In other words, someone had done to this girl's clothing exactly as Kate and her mother had been doing for ages now. This seemed strange to Kate, who had assumed all people who weren't dirt poor threw out old clothes and bought or made new ones whenever they felt like it.

Mary Jo had taken to jumping up and down and uttering small, joyful screams, while her mother eyed her and laughed indulgently. Alex's sister, in short, looked as if she could be a handful, and Kate's theories about rich folks suffered another slight wobble. Shoot, maybe rich folks weren't so different from her class of people after all. Of course, having money made a whole lot of difference to the general comfort and health of one's relatives, but that might possibly—Kate wasn't about to jump to conclusions—be the only difference. Or *one* of the only differences.

This weekend should prove to be interesting, if it turned out to be nothing else. Kate only prayed it would be serene and peaceful for her mother. Kate herself was willing to suffer the martyrdom of a saint if necessary in order to spare her mother pain. That being the case, she pasted on what felt like an artificial smile and prepared to meet Mrs. English and Alex's sister.

"Don't attack me, Mary Jo. I'm going to put the steps down." Alex grinned as he said it, but Kate detected steel behind the joking words.

"I won't," Mary Jo promised. "Mother told me that Mrs. Finney isn't well." She clapped her hands over her mouth, as if she were conscious of saying something she shouldn't have.

But Alex only shook his head in mock disgust. Mrs. English sighed and said, "Mary Jo," and Mrs. Finney laughed, so Kate didn't guess she had to reprimand the talkative adolescent. She turned to her mother. "Here, Ma, take my arm."

Alex had descended from the carriage first. Kate acquitted him of doing so for any improper reason. He'd done it not because he wasn't a gentleman, but because he wanted to assist Mrs. Finney as much as possible.

Therefore, with Kate assisting from inside the carriage and Alex taking the sick woman firmly by the arm and guiding her slowly down the stairs, Mrs. Finney finally set foot on the grounds of the English family farm. Kate followed quickly after her mother.

She was shocked speechless when, as soon as she was out of the carriage, Mary Jo threw her arms around her and hugged her hard. "Oh, Miss Finney, I'm so *happy* to meet you! I can't *wait* to talk to you about what you do at the Columbian Exposition. Your jobs sound so exciting!"

"Mary Jo," Mrs. English murmured again. Her voice held an interesting degree of hopelessness, as if she didn't really expect anything she said to curb her daughter's boisterousness.

Kate, who also doubted that such a mild reproof would quell the lively Mary Jo, had been about to say something polite before she was struck speechless by Mary Jo's hug and her artless comment. When she caught her breath and stabilized her hat, which Mary Jo's exuberance had caused to teeter, she said, "Um, really?"

"Please forgive my sister," Alex said, his voice heavy with censure. "She seems to have forgotten all the lessons in manners our mother tried her best to instill in her."

As if she realized she'd committed a social gaffe, Mary Jo leaped away from Kate. This movement was as abrupt as the hug had been. Kate, caught unawares twice in less than thirty seconds, staggered slightly. "Oh, please," said she, "don't scold. I don't mind." It startled her nearly senseless to realize she'd spoken the truth.

"Well," said Alex, unconvinced, "I'd rather not reward my sister for outrageous conduct."

"I'm sorry," a contrite Mary Jo said, clasping her hands behind her back and looking embarrassed. "I didn't mean to be so stupid."

"Don't be silly," said Kate, shooting Alex a quick glare that dared him to say anything else that might wound his little sister. "I don't mind at all. In fact, you made us both feel welcome. I think we ought to meet your mother now, though."

"Of course." Mary Jo stepped back, looking even more chastened than she had before, and Kate wished she'd kept her big mouth shut. She didn't know how to behave in polite circles, and she ought just to observe these Englishes for a while before trying to enter into their conversations.

Alex, apparently satisfied that his sister aimed to behave from now on, stepped aside and presented Kate's mother to his. "Mrs. Hazel Finney, please allow me to introduce you to my mother, Marguerite English." Smiling at his sister, he added, "And, as you've probably guessed, this rambunctious urchin is my youngest sister, Mary Jo."

"How do you do?" said Mrs. Finney.

Kate watched her mother be as gracious as any great lady to Alex's mother and sister, and her heart swelled with love and pride. Marrying Kate's father had been a hideous mistake on Hazel Finney's part, but it had been one Mrs. Finney hadn't anticipated. Kate didn't think that misjudging a person who'd probably misrepresented himself to begin with should be held against a woman forever. She resented the Church, where she'd gone for assistance and guidance once or twice, for telling women it was their duty to remain in miserable, and even dangerous, marriages.

Mrs. English took Mrs. Finney's hand in both of hers and smiled warmly. "It's such a pleasure to meet you, Mrs. Finney. I'm so glad you could visit us. We get lonely way out here on the farm, and it's such fun to have company."

"I hope you'll think so after we've inconvenienced you for two days," Kate's mother responded, laughing.

Holding her breath in anticipation of a coughing fit, Kate couldn't recall the last time she'd seen her mother so perky. It astonished her that Ma could be so natural and comfortable with a woman whose position in life was so far above her own. She decided it might be a good thing if she watched how her mother behaved with these people and took notes. Thank God a spasm didn't follow Mrs. Finney's laugh.

"And Mary Jo," continued Mrs. Finney, her smile becoming more intimate, "it's so nice to be around young people again. My own children are all grown up, and I miss their youthful high jinks."

Mary Jo executed a perfect curtsy and smiled at Kate's mother. "Thank you for being nice about my bad manners, Mrs. Finney. Alex is always scolding me for acting like a hoyden. My mother really *has* tried to teach me, but I keep forgetting."

Alex snorted. His mother laughed. Mrs. Finney squeezed Mary Jo's hand. "I'm sure she's done a wonderful job with you. You only need to get out into the world a little and practice some more."

"That's what I keep telling Alex." Mary Jo further spoiled her mother's lessons by sticking her tongue out at her big brother. "That's why I want to go to Chicago for a visit."

Kate had been taking a gander at the surrounding countryside as these pleasantries went on. When she heard Mary Jo's last comment, she turned and stared at her. "You want to leave this for Chicago?"

"Oh, yes!"

"Um . . . Why?" Kate couldn't conceive of such a thing.

Alex, chuckling again, made a herding gesture to the gaggle of women. "Let's discuss this inside over tea, shall we? It will be interesting for you and Mary Jo to exchange ideas about Chicago, Kate. I have a feeling you're going to have a hard time convincing her that the country's better than the city."

"My goodness," Kate said, stunned.

Mrs. English laughed. Alex took Mrs. Finney by the arm and guided her up the porch steps.

As soon as the quintet entered the house, Kate was struck by several things at once. The first thing she noticed was the overall charm and warmth of the house itself. The front door opened into a large airy room that Alex called the hall. The room's floors were some hard, dark wood, and were sprinkled here and there with rag rugs of the sort Kate's own mother made. The aroma of cinnamon and ginger kissed Kate's nostrils, and blended well with the smell of furniture polish and wax. The room was big and warm and friendly, and made Kate want to live in it.

A woman in a white apron and cap appeared, beaming at the newcomers. Alex said, "Mrs. Gossett, please let me introduce you to Mrs. Finney and Miss Finney. These ladies will be staying with us for the weekend."

Mrs. Gossett dropped a curtsy. "Pleased to meet you both."

"Likewise," Kate murmured, wondering who Mrs. Gossett was in the overall scheme of things.

"Thank you, Mrs. Gossett," said Mrs. Finney.

Mrs. Gossett turned to Mrs. English. "There's tea and gingerbread all ready, Mrs. E. Shall I set it up in the parlor?"

"Please do," said Mrs. English. "And tell Louise to see the Finney ladies to their rooms, if you will."

Rooms? Did this mean they were each going to have a room? Until she'd taken her one-room apartment above the butcher's shop, Kate had never had a room to herself. Heck, she'd never even realized people *had* rooms to themselves.

"Yes'm."

After executing another curtsy, Mrs. Gossett departed. Kate marveled at the speed at which another maidservant appeared. She assumed the newcomer to be Louise.

Kate suspected this routine had been rehearsed or learned over a number of years, since the timing of the servants' arrivals and departures was so exquisite. Assuming Mrs. Gossett to be some sort of housekeeper, she then marveled at the English family being able to afford both a housekeeper and a housemaid. And a carriage driver. Good Lord almighty, the man must be positively rolling in dough.

"Good afternoon, Louise," said Alex, confirming Kate's suspicion as he stripped off his gloves and acted as if the arrival of a housemaid was merely a part of life—which it was, to him—"please take Mrs. Finney and Miss Finney to their rooms."

Louise bobbed a curtsy, smiled at the Finney ladies, and said, "Please follow me." She headed for the stairway, which lay straight ahead of them as they stood in front of the big front door.

Alex said, "Just a minute, Louise." He turned to Mrs. Finney. "Do you need help climbing the stairs? I'll be happy to help you. Carry you, if need be." His smile made Kate's stomach pitch.

"Don't be silly," said Mrs. Finney. "I wouldn't want you to have to do that." She gave a low chortle, as if she'd never heard of anything sillier than Alex's offer to carry her upstairs.

"Nonsense," said Alex. "You can't weigh much more than a feather. I'm sure I have muscles enough for that." He winked at Mrs. Finney to let her know he meant it and that she wouldn't be imposing.

"You're a good man, Alex," Mrs. Finney said, her smile going a little mushy, in Kate's opinion. "But please don't carry me. I hate feeling helpless, even if I am sometimes. Please let me walk as much as I can." She sighed as she gazed at the staircase. "I used to zip up and down stairs like nobody's business."

"I'll help, Ma," Kate said, feeling left out.

"Good. Then I'll go supervise the gingerbread." With another wink, Alex left them with the impression that supervision in this instance meant sampling the cake to make sure it was tasty enough for the rest of them.

Kate tried to resent his assumption of authority over her and her mother, but couldn't do it. He was too darned nice to resent. "Here, Ma, take my arm."

"Thank you, Katie, darling."

Mrs. Finney took Kate's arm and together they walked up the stairs. From out of nowhere, or so it seemed to Kate, a man appeared, lifted Kate's shabby carpetbag—without even sneering at it—and trotted up the staircase before them.

"I'll unpack for the two of you," Louise said brightly. "You can decide which rooms you want. They're both all made up. The missus has been so excited about your visit."

"She has?" Kate would have shaken her head and maybe batted at her ears a couple of times if she'd been alone. She couldn't account for Louise's state of excitement. Maybe Mrs. English really *did* want them here.

"This is so kind of Mr. English and his mother," Mrs. Finney said, gasping only slightly.

"Take it easy, Ma. You can talk once we get upstairs."

"Mr. English was quite crippled toward the end of his life," the chatty Louise informed them. "He talked about installing one of them electrical lift things that they have in grand hotels, but he died before they could have one installed."

"My goodness," said Kate, genuinely surprised. "I didn't know that." Mr. English being crippled didn't fit with her image of a member of the English family.

"Oh, my, yes." Kate had slowed her pace so as not to outstrip the ladies she was guiding. "He was all bent over with the lumbago. His joints hurt something terrible. He used to be such an active man, too. Why, he plowed the fields until he was in his late sixties. Until the lumbago took over."

"That's too bad."

"Indeed," assented Mrs. Finney, who'd stopped walking at the top of the staircase so that she could catch as much of her breath as her lungs would allow. "I'm sorry to hear about his infirmity."

"Yes, well, I guess the good Lord works in mysterious ways. As you should know, ma'am, if you'll forgive me for saying so. Mr. Alex speaks so highly of the both of you. It's a crying shame that you came down with the consumption, Mrs. Finney."

Mrs. Finney smiled. "I think so, too, Louise. Thank you."

"Me, too," added Kate, not quite sure what was going on here. Everybody was so darned friendly. Shouldn't they be looking down their collective noses at her and her mother? And had Alex—Mr. Alex, indeed—actually, honestly and truly, said nice things about them? Her mother deserved them. Kate feared she didn't. She'd actually been sort of mean to Alex since they met. Not that he hadn't deserved her rancor—at first.

"My uncle Harry caught the consumption. He worked in the mines in Pittsburgh. They say that black coal dust kills more men than accidents."

"My goodness."

As much as Kate appreciated Louise's friendliness, she wished the girl hadn't mentioned her uncle's death from black lung. The reference didn't seem exactly diplomatic to Kate. On the other hand, she could forgive verbal missteps as long as the intent behind them wasn't malicious. "Yeah," she said, hoping to turn the conversational topic. "I hear black lung is really bad. Say, are these the rooms?"

"What?" Louise looked startled. "Oh, I see. Yes. Mrs. English had us prepare the two rooms closest to the staircase. She said it'll cut down on the number of steps you have to take and all."

"She's very considerate," Kate's mother said.

"She sure is," Kate agreed. Louise pushed open the door of the first room, and Kate's heart executed another flip. "Oh, my!"

The room was gorgeous. The pretty yellow-trimmed chintz curtains had been drawn aside and the windows had been thrown open to the bright summer afternoon sun. Forgetting for once that her mother was more important than she was, Kate went to the open window and gazed outdoors in something as close to awe as she could get. "Oh, Ma, it's a room with a view!" She felt stupid as soon as the words popped out.

"Isn't it grand?"

When Kate turned at Louise's comment, she saw the housemaid standing in the open doorway, her hands clasped together at her waist and a huge smile on her face. "It sure is. Can you walk over here, Ma? Do you need help?"

"I'm fine, Katie." But it didn't escape Kate's attention that her mother was slipping the flask into her skirt pocket.

Her heart quailed as she watched her mother walk to the window. She was so frail, she scared Kate. The notion of life without her mother filled Kate with a hurt so deep, she was pretty sure it would never heal. In spite of that, or perhaps because of it, she pasted on a jolly smile for both their sakes. "Look. You can see all the trees and flowers blooming, Ma. It's so pretty."

Mrs. Finney put her hand on Kate's shoulder and looked out the window. "Oh, Katie, it reminds me of home."

"Home?" Kate hadn't heard that wistful quality in her mother's voice before. "You mean Ireland?"

Hazel Finney nodded. "Aye, Katie. It's green in Ireland. Just like this. The green just rolls on forever."

Kate gazed out, trying to see the countryside from her mother's point of view. Couldn't be done. She saw great beauty, but the only thing she could relate it to was pictures in fairy-tale books. The nuns had never allowed the children to read fairy-tale books, but Kate had cleaned house for a rich lady with children, and she'd looked in the children's books sometimes. Those books with their pictures had been one of Kate's guilty pleasures, moments of joy stolen from a life of drudgery. As she stared upon the view, the same feeling of doing something she shouldn't be doing washed over her.

"Jeepers." Although she knew she was being irrationally uneasy, Kate eyed the scene with renewed appreciation, not that she hadn't appreciated it before, for her heritage's sake. "Does it really look like Ireland?"

"Very much. In spots." Mrs. Finney laughed softly. Kate held her breath, but her mother didn't start coughing.

"I'm so glad you like the room and the view."

Kate had forgotten about Louise. With a sigh, she turned away from the window, only to find Louise opening her carpetbag. At once, all of her feelings of insecurity attacked her. "What are you doing?"

Startled, Louise jerked upright. "Why, I was going to unpack for you. I assumed your mother would stay in this room since it's the closest to the staircase."

Mrs. Finney, close on Kate's heels, again put a hand on her daughter's shoulder. "Thank you so much, Louise. That's a good idea. I'll be very happy in this room. But Katie packed clothes for both of us in that bag. Perhaps it would be better if you left the unpacking to her. May we see the other room?"

"Of course."

Louise looked a trifle put out, and Kate wished she'd held her tongue. Again. Sometimes she despaired of

ever leaving the slums behind. Even when she had opportunities, like this one, the slums seemed to travel with
her and spoil everything. In an effort to redeem herself
in Louise's eyes, she smiled hard and decided to tell the
truth. Might as well, since it always managed to catch up
with her anyhow. "Thanks, Louise. I'm not used to people doing things for me."

Louise relaxed instantly. "Oh, I know exactly what you
mean, Miss Finney! I'm the same way myself. Come
along. Miss Finney's room is right next door. It's done all
in pink. Miss Mary Jo decorated it."

Thank God they'd got over that one. Kate vowed she'd
watch herself and not step in any more mud of her own
making than she could help. Vigilance was what was
needed here. She'd just be vigilant. She was always vigilant, for that matter, but this weekend, instead of
watching out for her father, she'd be watching out for
herself.

It was an odd and uncomfortable concept, but Kate
feared it was about right.

Twelve

Alex couldn't remember ever fussing over guest accommodations at the farm before. His mother was a supremely capable woman, she loved to have visitors, and she never, ever allowed the least little attention to go wanting where her guests were concerned. He fussed anyway.

"Are you sure the tea will stay hot until they get downstairs? I don't want to serve tepid tea to Mrs. Finney." Frowning, Alex gazed at the table in front of the comfortable, slightly worn parlor sofa. Mrs. Gossett had set out gingerbread, frosted fairy cakes—she said the recipe had come from some Irish ancestor or other, and she thought Mrs. Finney might enjoy them—little tea sandwiches, and a flowery teapot accompanied by flowery cups and saucers. He hoped to heaven the Finney ladies wouldn't be intimidated by all the finery; he was sure they'd consider matching cups, saucers, and plates finery.

"Mrs. Gossett covered the pot with a cozy, Alex." Mrs. English smiled as she arranged teacups on the table. Alex got the feeling her smile wasn't for him, but for something private that she found amusing and didn't intend to share.

Alex gave up on his mother's smile and frowned down on the covered teapot. "Is that what that thing is? What did you call it? A cozy?" Ridiculous name for a piece of quilted fabric.

"Yes, dear." Mrs. English began rolling napkins and fitting them in some brass holders Alex's father had brought to her from a trip to New York. "Everything will be lovely, dear. You'll see."

"I hope so." No longer was Alex able to disparage Kate for her upbringing; not since he'd met her mother and father and had come to understand exactly what her circumstances had been. Now his only aspiration was to make Kate and Mrs. Finney's lives more comfortable, however he could. In the attempt, he especially didn't want to make them feel inferior.

He jumped slightly when Mrs. English patted him on the arm. "Sit down, Alex. Everything will be fine."

When he turned around and saw her watching him, catlike, as if she suspected him of caring more about Kate and her mother than he actually did, he frowned again. "Of course. I just don't want to serve them cold tea. Mrs. Finney's health makes her movements rather slow."

"Of course." Mrs. English's scrutiny didn't fade appreciably.

"I like them," Mary Jo said, snatching a frosted cake before her brother could stop her and popping it into her mouth. "I can't wait to talk to Miss Finney about the Exposition."

Alex turned on his sister, his glower feeling more comfortable than it had felt when he'd directed it at his mother. "I won't have you pestering the Finneys, Mary Jo. Mrs. Finney is deathly ill, and Kate has enough to worry about without you annoying them."

Mary Jo spoke with her mouth full, she was so indignant. "I'd never! I would never pester them!"

"See that you don't."

"I think," said Mrs. English with a hint of a laugh in her voice, "that your brother is worried about making an impression, Mary Jo."

"Nonsense," Alex barked, self-conscious and with his

ire climbing. "I only want to make sure this weekend is pleasant for them both. The two of them haven't had much pleasure in their lives."

"Really?" Mary Jo's eyes went huge, and Alex wished he'd kept silent on the subject of the Finneys' relative absence of pleasure.

"Their circumstances have been unfortunate, Mary Jo," her mother explained. "Alex doesn't want anyone to embarrass them by bringing them up."

"Really?" Mary Jo repeated. She had to swallow twice in order to get the cake down. "What kind of circumstances do they have?"

"Straitened circumstances, dear. They have very little money and no family support, evidently. I was poor when I was a child, too, so I know how uncomfortable it can be."

"Oh." Mary Jo pondered the nature of impoverished childhoods. "I guess we're lucky, aren't we?"

"Yes," said Alex firmly. "We're very lucky." It occurred to him that before Kate Finney and her atrocious father had been thrust into his face by Gil MacIntosh, he'd pooh-poohed the notion of luck having anything to do with his own position in life. What an ass he'd been.

"And here they are!" cried Mrs. English loudly.

Alex presumed she wanted to make sure her children didn't continue the conversation regarding the Finneys and luck, thereby causing the newcomers social discomfort. He walked to the door, smiling up a storm. "Come in, come in, ladies. I hope you found your rooms adequate."

"Adequate?" Kate stared at him as if she suspected him of irony. Alex could get lost in those heavenly blue eyes if he didn't watch himself. "Both rooms are exquisite. Thank you very much."

"Indeed, yes," said Mrs. Finney. She held onto Kate's arm and walked slowly.

Both ladies had on the same gowns they'd worn for traveling, an indication, had Alex needed one, that they were both of limited means and scant wardrobes. They both looked neat and trim, and Kate had tidied her hair. Poor they undoubtedly were, but neither Finney lady allowed her poverty to interfere with cleanliness or resourcefulness.

That being the case, Alex wondered if Kate had sewn her mother's outfit, as well as her own. It wouldn't have surprised him to find out she had, necessity being the mother of invention and all that. Or poverty being a prod to personal industry. Alex knew poverty didn't always breed industry; some folks floundered and sank under the weight of it. The Kate Finneys of the world overleaped their circumstances, or tried to. He knew it was presumptuous of him, but he was proud of Kate.

His heart hurt as he accompanied the pair over to the parlor sofa. Kate looked so damnably exhausted, and her mother looked so damnably sick. If he knew a magic spell that would cure both of them, he'd use it in a minute. Unfortunately, unlike Madame Esmeralda, Alex didn't know any charms or curses. Which reminded him of something he'd been meaning to ask Kate.

After he'd deposited her on a comfortable chair and her mother on the sofa, and his mother had started pouring out cups of tea—which still steamed, verifying his mother's prediction on the subject—he said, "Say, Kate, does Madame really believe in fortune-telling? I've wondered about that for the longest time."

After shooting him a suspicious glance, which he deflected with a lift of his eyebrows and an I'm-not-being-condescending-dash-it shrug of his shoulders, she said, "To tell you the truth, I'm not sure. She said she—" Kate stopped speaking abruptly. "Thank you," she said when Mrs. English handed her a cup of tea.

"She said what?" Alex asked, holding the plate of sandwiches and cakes out to her so that she could take her pick. "I'm only curious," he added, knowing how defensive Kate could get without half trying. "I won't hold anything Madame Esmeralda said to you against you." He laughed to let her know he meant it and that he considered this all in fun.

Kate shrugged and took a small sandwich. "She said she'd put a curse on my father."

"Good heavens!" Mrs. Finney stared at her daughter, her cup halfway to her lips. "Did she really?"

"I'm afraid so. Sorry, Ma." Kate took a bite of her sandwich, looking uncomfortable.

But Mrs. Finney, replacing her cup in her saucer before she'd taken any tea, leaned back against the sofa and laughed so hard, she started coughing. After taking a swig from her flask, she gasped for air and apologized. "Oh, my, I'm so sorry. But, Katie, darling, that's the nicest thing Madame could ever do for any of us." She wiped her eyes with a handkerchief snatched from a pocket. "Oh, my. I must be a terrible person to find such a thing amusing."

"Nuts," said Kate. "You're right. I hope the curse works. And soon."

"I have to agree with your daughter, Mrs. Finney. If you still have feelings for the man, I'm sorry, but I think he deserves a good curse, at least."

"Alex," murmured his mother, "I'm sure I don't know what to think of you." She smiled, though. "I tried to teach my children manners, Mrs. Finney, but you can see how much they learned."

"Oh, no, Mrs. English," Mrs. Finney protested. "Your children are wonderful. You must be so proud of Alex."

"I am."

Alex turned his eyes up and gazed at the ceiling, praying this part of the conversation would end soon.

Mary Jo said, "I didn't say anything about any old curse. I have manners." She grinned. "But I'd love to know how she did it."

The tea break progressed smoothly and with much good humor. Alex was proud of his mother, and even of his little sister. He dreaded the notion of Mary Jo getting Kate off by herself, however, because he didn't trust either one of them. Mary Jo could be offensive without even knowing it, and Kate could become offended even when no offense was meant.

When it became clear that Mrs. Finney's strength was waning, Alex signaled to his mother to do something to end the tea party. As ever, his mother rose to the occasion. "Hazel,"—they were all on a first-name basis by this time—"let me show you around the house a little, and then I think you ought to rest for as long as you need to. It's been a long, tiring trip for you, I'm sure."

"Thank you." Mrs. Finney's pinched features appeared more relaxed than Alex had heretofore seen them. "I do need to rest a good deal. But the trip wasn't difficult at all, thanks to your son and his generous attentions." She smiled at Alex. "You have a such a kind and generous son, Marguerite."

"I think so," said Alex's fond mother.

Alex hoped to heaven the heat he felt creeping up his neck wouldn't be noticeable in his cheeks. He was too dashed old to blush.

"I can see Ma upstairs," Kate said.

Everyone turned to look at her, and she dropped her gaze. "Unless you don't want me to," she muttered.

"Why don't I show you the grounds, Kate," Alex suggested, feeling both protective and appreciative. Her defensiveness had spared him embarrassment in case he *had* been blushing, since nobody was looking at him any longer.

"Oh, yes!" Mary Jo cried. "I'll go with you!"

Bother, thought Mary Jo's affectionate brother. He didn't want her along; he wanted to be alone with Kate. Yet he couldn't think of an appropriate way to rid himself of his pesky sister without making an embarrassing scene. "Fine."

Kate glanced from him to Mary Jo to her mother. "Is that all right with you, Ma? Do you need me?"

"I'll always need you, Katie, but I think I can make it back upstairs with Marguerite's help." The smiling glance she gave her daughter was as full of love as any Alex had ever seen. "You go along with Alex and Mary Jo and enjoy yourself."

Thus it was that Kate, Alex, and Mary Jo, leaving the tea things behind on the table for Mrs. Gossett and Louise to dispense with even though Kate had offered to help and then seemed self-conscious that she had, left the house that afternoon.

Alex discovered himself eager to introduce Kate to his world. He also discovered himself hoping she'd love it as much as he did, which didn't make sense to him. What did it matter to him if she liked his farm or not? Fearing he knew the answer and that he didn't want it to be true, he dropped the subject before it could cause him discomfort.

Mary Jo skipped along merrily, sometimes at Kate's side, sometimes at Alex's, and sometimes ahead of them both. "This is the prettiest time of year," she informed Kate. "Except for the fall, because the leaves are so pretty then. Although winter's kind of nice, too, because the snow is so pretty and white. And I like summer, too, except when it gets too hot."

Laughing, Alex said, "Sounds like you can't make up your mind."

"I guess I can't."

"I think it's good that you can enjoy it all," Kate said, sounding as if she meant it.

Alex glanced down at her and wondered when she'd last been able to relax and enjoy anything.

He was becoming perfectly maudlin about this

woman. He gave himself a hard mental shake and told himself to snap out of it.

"I'm so glad you came to visit! I really want to know all about fortune-telling. How do you do it? Do you read people's palms or something?"

"Mary Jo, don't pester Kate."

But Kate shook her head. "It's all right, Alex. I don't mind." She smiled at Mary Jo. "It's all hogwash, of course."

"Is it?" Mary Jo sounded disappointed. Looked it, too.

"Well," said Kate thoughtfully, "I don't know about Madame. I think she really believes in some of the things she does, but I don't. I only tell fortunes for a living."

"You can't really read palms?" Mary Jo's disappointment intensified.

"Oh, sure, I can read palms, but I don't know how much a person can really read in another person's palm. And Madame taught me to read the Tarot cards, too. I know she believes in what they say, because she casts a fortune for herself every day. I don't know if any of it is true or not, but it's a better living than clerking in Wanamaker's."

"Oh, did you do that?" Mary Jo's face took on an expression of keen interest. "I'd like to get a job someday."

"Yeah?" Kate looked as if she were trying to fight a sardonic expression. "Well, you can take it from me that telling fortunes pays more than Wanamaker's, although I don't know if it would if I weren't doing it at the Exposition. People tend to get their fortunes told for fun while they're enjoying the fair. And I guess I do have to admit that reading palms is kind of fun."

Mary Jo brightened. "Can you read my palm?"

"Mary Jo." Alex would have liked to paddle his exasperating sister. His tone was severe.

"Oh, no," said Kate quickly. "It's all right. Sure, I'd be happy to read your palm."

"Goody!" Shooting Kate a penetrating glance, Mary Jo then said, "Do you just make it all up as you go along?"

"Mary Jo." This time Alex glowered at her. She didn't seem to notice.

"No," said Kate. "There are supposed to be meanings in the configuration of the palm and the fingers and in the lines crossing the palms. Madame had to teach me." Another shrug. "Maybe it's true. I don't know. But Madame taught me what all the lines and the mounds and so forth are."

"Oh, this is such fun!"

"Do you really think so? Shoot, I'd rather live on a farm like this. It's so beautiful here. And peaceful. It's so peaceful." Kate spoke as if she really meant it, and Alex was pleased.

"It gets real boring." A pout marred Mary Jo's pretty mouth.

Deciding to interfere before Mary Jo spoiled Kate's enjoyment of his particular life's love, his farm, Alex spoke up. "It's only boring because you're used to it and you haven't been out much. Kate knows what city life is like. It's not all fun, Mary Jo."

"You can say that again. Where I live, it's no fun at all."

"Really?" Mary Jo's pout faded.

"Really." Kate shot Alex a quick smile. "It's so serene here. And green. There are days when I go a mile out of my way to pass by the park because I need to see something growing. I'd love to see some of your cows and horses and pigs and other animals."

"Cows and pigs? Really?" It didn't look to Alex as if Mary Jo quite believed in Kate's interest in cattle.

"Sure. The only time I ever see a cow is when we use the bones in soup. I think it would be fun to see the soup bones on the hoof, if you know what I mean."

"All right, then, come this way." Alex took Kate's arm. He didn't want her wandering off with Mary Jo, although he wouldn't have minded if Mary Jo had wandered off by herself. Guiding her down a path between some rhododendron bushes, he aimed for the closest pasture. His father had removed the cattle part of his farming enterprise to a location farther from the house than it had originally been, since cows tended to produce smelly residual products.

"Golly," said Mary Jo, apparently aiming to stick to Alex and Kate like glue, "I didn't know anybody actually liked cows."

"I think they're darling. Pigs, too," said Kate stoutly, although Alex got the feeling she was putting on an act for Mary Jo's sake. He admired her for it.

"Darling? Pigs?" Alex pretended to be offended. "Good Lord."

"Sure." Kate gave a little skip. "I think cows and pigs are adorable."

"Well, we've got plenty of both of them, so you can feast your eyes on their adorability until you get sick of them."

"It probably won't take long," added Alex's sister. "Cows and pigs stink like anything. Then you can read my palm."

Kate laughed. Alex said, "Mary Jo," again, sternly. Mary Jo pasted on an innocent expression that Alex didn't believe for a second. He was pretty sure Kate didn't, either, but she only laughed some more.

The fresh country air caressed Kate's skin like a healing balm, and she breathed it in as if it could cure all her psychic wounds. That was probably silly thinking, but she couldn't help it. She loved this place. The notion of actually living on a farm like this, with all this green loveliness growing all around her, was akin to an impossible dream. It was all so beautiful. She was afraid she was going to make herself look ridiculous by showing how much she loved it here.

Therefore, she attempted to appear dignified as they passed by the hedge of huge bushes loaded with gorgeous flowers. Kate had no idea what they were. She paused before a bush covered with bright red flowers. "Would it be all right to pick some of these? For my mother?" Darn it, she was blushing; she could feel it.

"What?" Alex stopped walking and turned, looking bemused. He saw the bush to which Kate referred. "Oh, of course. Pick as many flowers as you want, Kate. These are rhododendrons. They have a lovely flower, don't they?"

"They sure do."

"Why don't you wait until we're walking back toward home," Mary Jo suggested brightly. "That way they won't wilt. And I'll help you pick some roses and peonies, too. My favorites are the peonies."

"My goodness. You know what they all are?"

"Sure." Mary Jo appeared surprised. "My mother taught me all about flowers. Don't you have flowers where you live?"

"Uh, no. I don't have a place to grow flowers where I live. I go to the park when I have time. There are flowers there."

"Kate lives in an apartment, Mary Jo," Alex said, hoping his repressive tone would curb her chattiness. He knew how Kate could get, and didn't want her to blow up at his sister, who was curious out of innocence, not unkindness.

"What's an apartment?"

"It's a room over a shop," Kate told her. "It's not much, but it's mine."

"I wish I could have an apartment," Mary Jo said wistfully.

Kate gawped at her. Alex chuckled. "You might not like it as much as you think you would."

"Bet I would."

Kate could have given her one or two pertinent facts of life that might disabuse her of that notion, but she held her tongue. She considered it a flaw in her nature that she found Mary Jo's innocence irksome. By rights, all children Mary Jo's age should be innocent. It was poverty's fault, and her father's, that Kate's own innocence hadn't lasted past babyhood. Because she suspected her irritation grew out of some kind of jealousy of Mary Jo and her family and her circumstances, she suppressed it ruthlessly. Herbert Finney wasn't Mary Jo's fault any more than he was Kate's.

"I'd rather live here. It's so . . . I don't know. It's alive and growing. Where I live seems to be more . . . Oh, I don't know; dead and dying, I guess. Or something." Kate felt silly after her artless confession, and braced herself for scorn or, worse, pity.

"Golly, I don't think so. I think it's boring here." Mary Jo's own sweeping gaze didn't indicate pleasure in her surroundings.

"I could stand a little boredom from time to time," Kate said dryly. "Anyhow, I think it would be exciting to have my own home, and to be able to sew curtains and cook meals and that sort of thing. I don't really like having to work away from home in order to make enough money to survive. Not that my room's much of a home, but . . ." Her words petered out again. She wished she'd stop blurting out these personal confessions. They made her life sound so shabby. Which it was. Kate heaved a huge, grass-scented sigh.

"I think it would be fun to have a job and earn my own money."

"Hmmm." Kate didn't want to get into that one. Since pretty, spoiled little Mary Jo English didn't know what the heck she was talking about, there didn't seem much point to arguing.

"You only think so because you don't have to."

Kate glanced up at Alex, who had made the comment, and rather sharply, too. "Yeah," she said. "Maybe that's it. I guess if your very life didn't depend on it, working at a paying job might not be so wearisome."

"Maybe," said Mary Jo, clearly unconvinced, but unwilling or unable to argue.

Kate suspected she'd been threatened with all sorts of punishments if she didn't behave herself during the Finneys' visit.

"The trouble with you, little sister, is that you have no responsibilities whatsoever, and Kate has too many."

"Um—" Kate started, but Mary Jo interrupted, which was all right with her because she didn't want to go into her own miserable life situation any more than she had to.

"That's not fair! I do so have responsibilities! I have to feed the chickens and gather the eggs and slop the pigs and do all sorts of other chores!" Mary Jo's cheeks bloomed with indignant color as she flounced along in her made-over dress.

"You don't have the sorts of responsibilities Kate has," Alex intoned haughtily. "No young woman should have to shoulder such burdens."

"Humph." Still rebellious, Mary Jo picked up a stick and threw it as hard as she could.

"Well, now, I don't know about that," Kate said, trying for a placating tone, although she agreed with Alex regarding the disparity of the burdens meted out by a Maker Kate had been told was benevolent. She hadn't believed that one since she was around three or four. A benevolent God wouldn't have burdened the world and its inhabitants with people like Kate's father.

From out of nowhere, a black-and-white dog bounded up to them, Mary Jo's stick in its mouth. Kate jumped back and uttered a small shriek. She wasn't really afraid of the dog—not exactly—but she was certainly startled. She hadn't met many dogs in her life, except a few that were kept by merchants in her neighborhood as guard dogs. Those dogs were worth being afraid of. This specimen, with his vacuous brown eyes, wagging fluff of a tail, and floppy ears, didn't appear to be terrifying. In point of fact, he seemed sort of bouncy and happy and pleased with the world, himself, and the three humans in his vicinity.

"Well, there you are, Conk!" Alex sounded delighted. "I wondered where you'd gotten yourself off to."

Kate's assumption that the dog—Conk? What a peculiar name—belonged to the English family was confirmed by Alex's next action. He reached down, grabbed an end of the stick, and began a growling tug-of-war with the dog for possession of the stick. Kate couldn't distinguish one growl from the other. Her astonishment that Alex English, refined gentleman farmer, could play with a dog warred with her leftover alarm at the dog's abrupt appearance in her life.

Mary Jo laughed with delight.

Kate slammed a hand over her thundering heart and watched man and dog wrestle over the stick. Nuts. She hated being startled like that. Since Alex was occupied, she turned to Mary Jo. "I presume that's your dog?"

"Alex's." Mary Jo shouted when Alex, capturing the prize, reached back and flung the stick about twice as far as Mary Jo had. "His name's Conky. He was one of Romeo and Juliet's puppies, but he was scared of gunfire, so he couldn't be used as a hunting dog."

"Ah . . . Romeo and Juliet?" Kate was beginning to wonder if she'd stepped out of her own personal world and into an alternate one where everything was exactly opposed to anything she'd ever known. Conky the dog, after sprinting heroically after the stick, leaping low brush and bushes growing in his way, made a flying jump and caught the stick right before it landed. It was a spectacular catch, and Kate was impressed.

Mary Jo clapped and hollered, "Good catch, Conk!" She turned to Kate. "Romeo and Juliet are Mr. Howell's hunters. Alex bought Conky from him because Mr. Howell's dogs are supposed to be the best pointers around, but Conky isn't. He's a dunce when it comes to hunting."

"Why did Alex name him Conky?"

Mary Jo's smile widened. "It was because Alex was trying to teach him to catch. You know, when you throw a dog a scrap of food, and he catches it in midair?"

Kate didn't know, but she was willing to accept this tidbit of dog lore on faith. "Ah," she said. "Yes, but . . ."

"It's because Conky didn't understand. He'd wait until the bone or the bit of biscuit conked him on the head before he'd realize it was meant for him."

"I see." She eyed the dog, who was racing back to his master as if the trip was the most important of his life.

"He learned eventually, but, Alex still claims Conky's as dumb as dirt. And he still doesn't have a good hunter, either."

Mary Jo's laughter rippled out on the spring air, reminding Kate of tiny white flowers, from which fanciful imagery she presumed she was losing her mind, if she hadn't already lost it. Kate Finney couldn't afford to get fanciful. "I see. Um, and Alex goes hunting often?"

"Oh, sure." Conky arrived at Alex's feet with a slide and a shower of dirt, and Mary Jo leaped back to avoid getting her skirt spattered with flying pebbles and dust. "He hunts ducks and geese and deer and other game. You know, keeps meat on the table and all that."

"Ah. I didn't know that." She hadn't known that rich men had to shoot their meals, for that matter. She observed Alex and his no-good hunting dog for a few minutes, and came up with another assumption. He probably didn't *have* to shoot his meals. He probably did it because he liked hunting. Or he was miserly and didn't want to pay more for food than he had to.

Scratch that one. Alex English might annoy the life out of Kate on a regular basis, but he definitely wasn't a tightwad. He was more generous than any other person she'd ever met, if it came to that.

Alex held the stick up so that Conky couldn't get it. The dog jumped on him, smearing Alex's trousers with dirty doggy prints, and Alex laughed ruefully. "Down, Conky! Behave yourself. You need to meet someone." He turned to Kate. "Kate Finney, meet Conky English, the low-down, no-good, non-hunter of a hunting dog. But he's a good boy in spite of his defects and shortcomings, and even if he isn't the brightest candle in the box."

To Kate's astonishment, the dog obeyed its master and got down. He even sat on his black-and-white-spotted rump and looked up at Kate, his tongue lolling. She'd never seen a dog do *that*, either. Because the dog was gazing at her with huge, pleading eyes, and because his feathery tail was whipping up a dust storm behind him, Kate said, "Er, hello, Conky. Good doggie."

"Shake, Conk," Alex commanded.

The dog lifted a paw for Kate to shake. She did it, thoroughly charmed. "Did you teach him to do that, Alex?"

"Sure did. It's about the only trick he knows. He's a total failure at what he's supposed to be, which is a hunting dog, but he's friendly and shakes hands like a champ."

"He's an expert at fetching," Kate said, feeling defensive on Conky's behalf.

"He is now." Alex laughed. "We had some awful battles at first. He didn't mind fetching, but bringing things back again was another matter. It took me forever to teach him to return the items he fetched."

"Is that true, Conky?" Kate knelt beside the dog, who indicated his appreciation by licking her face. Laughter bubbled up in her, spontaneous and unexpected. "Ew!"

"Hey, Conk, lay off the lady." Alex spoke sternly, but Kate heard the laugh in his voice.

"He's a good, good doggie," crooned Kate. "And he fetches beautifully now, no matter how long it took him to learn how."

"Huh," said Alex.

When Kate arose, she saw that he was watching her like a hawk, a sharp, assessing look in his eyes. What did that mean? Had she done something wrong? Mary Jo spoke, and she couldn't dwell on her actions and Alex's reactions.

"And he chases Mrs. Howell's cats off, too," said Mary Jo, adding, "I like cats, but Mrs. Howell's cats always try to fight with Minnie."

"Who is Minnie?" Kate felt as though she were swimming in a confusion of names and wanted to sort them out before her brain exploded.

"She's our barn cat. She's real nice."

"Yeah? I don't know any cats. Or dogs, either." Kate wondered how she could have lived to be this old without encountering more cats and dogs. Oh, sure, she saw the same mangy street animals all the time, and the Schneiders let a couple of cats sleep on old towels in the back of their shop. Those felines were tolerated because they kept the rodents out of the butcher shop. Still, Kate didn't think of those working-class cats as anybody's pets. They were only scrambling to survive like everyone else in Kate's neighborhood.

"We've always got lots of barn cats. They kill the mice and rats and gophers and stuff like that." Mary Jo shuddered delicately.

Kate didn't think that a cat doing its duty and killing vermin was anything to shudder about. "That's their job, I guess."

"I guess so. And Minnie just had four kittens."

"Oh."

"Maybe you'd like to have one." Mary Jo looked as if she considered this a brilliant suggestion and a kind-hearted offer on her part.

"Don't burden Kate with any more problems," Alex advised, smiling, but meaning it. "She's got her hands full already."

"Little kittens aren't any trouble," Mary Jo protested.

They would be trouble in Kate's life. Sometimes Kate thought that if she had to handle one more little thing, even something so little as a kitten, she'd crumple up under the weight of her responsibilities. She glanced quickly at Alex, her gaze got stuck on his, and all at once she perceived something that left her breathless.

He understood.

It was impossible—and wonderful. He understood. Alex English, of all unlikely people in the universe, understood Kate and her life and her problems and her need to have no pets.

"Drop it, little sister," he said, tugging on one of Mary Jo's braids. "Kate doesn't want a kitten, and that's that."

"Well, *I* think kittens are more adorable than any nasty old cows or pigs," Mary Jo said with a sniff.

"I'm sure they are, but I don't have room for pets in my apartment." Kate spoke gently, hoping to convey gratitude along with a firm rejection of the girl's offer. She wasn't sure she achieved her aim, but Mary Jo skipped off in front of them, so she guessed it didn't matter.

"Don't mind my pesky sister," Alex said, slowing down even as Mary Jo sped up, followed by the dog, who wanted to play.

"I don't. I think she's nice."

"She's been very sheltered."

"Yeah?" Kate glanced up at him again, hoping she wouldn't get trapped by his beautiful eyes this time. "I wish . . ." But she decided not to finish the sentence because it might sound as if she were whining. It was true, though. She wished somebody'd bothered to shelter her a little once or twice.

She felt Alex's hand on her arm, and her heart sped up and her skin got warm. "I wish you'd been more sheltered, too, Kate." His voice was deep and soft, and it made Kate's insides puddle up and steam. "Life hasn't been fair to you or your mother."

Kate swallowed. "Yeah, well, we're doing okay."

His chuckle did its usual damage to her composure. "Don't get all defensive on me, Kate. You're doing better than okay. You're doing wonderfully, all things considered."

She didn't believe him. Worse, she didn't believe he meant it.

"I mean it, Kate," he said, as if he knew exactly what she'd been thinking. Which he had.

This was a serious problem. Kate feared it was destined to grow larger, too, and she didn't know what to do about it. Sometimes, she thought that meeting Alex English had been the best thing ever to happen to her. At other times, she thought it had been the worst. Most of the time, she feared both statements were the truth, which was absolutely, dreadfully, drastically, miserably awful.

Thirteen

Dinner at the English family farm was served at six o'clock. According to Alex, this was earlier than most society folks dined, but farmers had to get up early in the morning to go out and plow fields and milk cows and do all the other chores that constituted the farming life.

Kate forked up a bite of potatoes and gravy. "So far, I haven't seen you do anything like that."

Mary Jo laughed heartily. So did Mrs. English. Mrs. Finney frowned at her daughter, and Kate got embarrassed. Louise, who was serving the delicious dinner that had been cooked by Mrs. Gossett, sniffed.

"That's only because I've been successful," Alex told her. "And I've been taking a holiday to help organize the Exposition. That's work, too, you know."

Slipping him a surveying glance out of the corners of her eyes, Kate decided he wasn't mad at her for being so undiplomatic. "I didn't mean that the way it sounded. What I meant was that I thought farmers had to do all sorts of hard work, and that they worked from dawn to dark every day, and never had any time off."

"Sort of like you, in other words."

She could tell by the laugh in his voice and the grin on his face that he wasn't mad at her. That being the case, Kate decided not to blow her stack at him for saying something that she considered moderately insulting, although she couldn't have said why, since it was the truth. She grinned back. "Yeah. Sort of."

"Believe me, Kate, Alex and his father and his father's father worked from dawn to dark every day for years and years. Decades. Even on Sundays, before we all went to church. They did that for a little more than a century, actually. Thanks to Alex's abilities and business sense, the farm and his other enterprises have prospered so greatly that he's been able to hire several men. We've got a foreman who oversees the cattle and dairy businesses under Alex's direction, and hired men who do most of the plowing and planting, under Alex's supervision." Mrs. English gave her son a doting look. "Alex has taken off some time in order to work on the Columbian Exposition, but believe me, he works as hard as any of the other men most of the time."

Oh. Well, that was interesting. Kate gazed at Alex, too, although probably not with as doting an expression as his mother. On the other hand, she wasn't sure about that, which was worrisome all by itself. "I see." Sensing danger in Alex's direction, Kate switched her attention to Alex's mother. "This chicken is delicious, Mrs. English."

"It is, indeed," agreed Mrs. Finney.

When Kate glanced at her mother's plate, it didn't look to her as if Mrs. Finney had eaten enough of her meal to form a judgment. Her mother caught her worried frown and stabbed a couple of English peas. "It's a delight to be here in the country, Marguerite." She delivered the peas to their intended destination, and Kate decided she couldn't very well fuss at her mother while they were guests in the English home. Darn it, Ma needed to eat more.

"It's such a pleasure to have you here," Mrs. English countered sweetly.

Kate almost allowed herself to conclude that Alex's mother was a genuinely nice woman, although she didn't dare commit herself after so short an acquaintance, since she didn't think she could stand the disappointment of learning she'd been mistaken. Still, there was no law that said Kate couldn't treat her as if she were nice until she proved herself otherwise. "This is such a pleasant place, Mrs. English. I love your house. It's so homey and large and comfortable."

"It's old," Mary Jo announced, wrinkling her nose. "I want Alex to build a new house."

"Why?" Kate stared at Mary Jo, unable to credit the sentiment that had prompted her statement. "I think it would be a crime to tear this house down. It's—it's—" She swept an arm out as she dug around in her mind for the appropriate word. Unable to find it, she said, "It's absolutely perfect," and thought the two words fell short of the mark.

"Do you really think so?" Alex's expression fairly screamed gladness about Kate's assessment of his home.

"Do you really think so?" Mary Jo, on the other hand, seemed dumbfounded. She glanced around at the walls of the room—they were taking supper in the breakfast room, since it was smaller than the large dining room—and scowled.

Kate, too, glanced around. She took in the shiny plates hanging on the walls, souvenirs from various places members of the family had visited on business or pleasure trips. She thought it was swell that people collected stuff like that. The only thing her room collected was dust. Her family wasn't chock-full of heirlooms, unless you could count poverty and unhappiness. "I do," she said firmly. "I think you have a beautiful home, Mary Jo, and you ought to appreciate it. Shoot, if you had to live where I live, you'd appreciate it, believe me." She smiled at the girl, since she didn't want Mary Jo feeling sorry for her. At the moment, Kate was feeling sorry enough for herself; she didn't need company.

"Ah, Katie," murmured Mrs. Finney.

Kate wished she'd kept her fat mouth shut, a wish she entertained far too often. "It's all right, Ma. I've got a great life." *Liar, liar.* On the other hand, her life could be worse, she guessed.

Mrs. Finney, seated next to her daughter, gave her a sweet, sad smile. "If wishes were horses, Katie."

It was one of her mother's favorite sayings, and Kate smiled back. "I know, Ma. I know."

Alex cleared his throat. "We went out to the west pasture today, Ma. The rhododendrons are going wild."

"Yes. Kate was kind enough to bring me a lovely bouquet," Mrs. English said, smiling fondly at Kate, who didn't know what to do when strange ladies smiled fondly at her, so she ate a bite of chicken as a cover-up. "And she brought Hazel a gorgeous bouquet, too. Mary Jo and Kate added some roses and Queen Anne's lace, too. Isn't the centerpiece beautiful?"

"It's very pretty." Alex smiled at Kate. She didn't know what to do when he smiled at her, either, so she ate some more peas.

After she swallowed, she asked, "Where'd all the plates come from?" Her nerves itched as if a chorus of circus fleas were biting on them. All this fancy stuff was alien to her, although she wished it wasn't. As her mother would say, *if wishes were horses.*

"Oh, my, they come from all over the place."

"That one over there came all the way from France." Mary Jo, undoubtedly defying a lifetime's worth of training in polite manners, pointed at a plate on the wall over her mother's head.

Mrs. English said, "Mary Jo," but she didn't scold.

"France." Kate gazed at the plate pensively. It was pretty, but no more so than many of the other ones. But it had come from France. France, for Pete's sake. Maybe even Paris. "My goodness."

"My father and I visited Europe several years ago,"

Alex said. "It was a business trip, believe it or not. We were looking at some new grain hybrids in France."

"And don't forget the English pigs," Mary Jo told her brother. She giggled.

"Grain and pigs? In France and England? Somehow, when I think of France and England, I don't necessarily think of grain and pigs." Kate and Mary Jo shared a grin.

Laughing, Mrs. English said, "Nor do I. I think of fancy dresses and the queen and the guillotine."

"Maybe we don't, but Alex never thinks about anything but the farm," his sister informed their guests.

"Mary Jo," muttered her mother again.

Kate got the feeling Mrs. English wasn't exactly a stern disciplinarian. That was perhaps the only thing she had in common with Kate's own mother.

"People the world over rely on farms and farming techniques." Alex frowned at his little sister to let her know she oughtn't be impertinent. "And people experiment with new techniques and hybridizing in every place people are fortunate enough to have developed agriculture. Some of the new hybrids, both here and abroad, are much hardier than the older types. And the Shropshire pigs we brought home are the best ever."

Mary Jo, whose face was quite expressive of her inner feelings, wrinkled her nose again. "They're huge and smelly, if you call that best."

"I guess huge is a good quality if you want lots of pork," Kate said doubtfully.

"Exactly." Alex bestowed another smile upon her. She stuffed some potatoes and cream gravy into her mouth in a hurry.

"We got that plate above Ma's head in France. The one over there"—Alex tilted his head to indicate a rose-colored plate to the left of the French plate—"we brought home from Shropshire. In England."

"My goodness. Developing new sorts of pigs and grain

never occurred to me." Kate realized the English plate had a pig on it, and would have laughed if she were at home. An English pig. Imagine that. A *hybridized* English pig. Would wonders never cease?

After supper, the English family and the Finneys retired to the huge, screened-in front porch to sip tea and watch the fireflies. Alex wasn't sure, because he was unhappily certain now that he was besotted with her, but he thought Kate seemed softer and less brittle after her brief sojourn in the country. And they still had another day to go. By Gad, she might even turn human if this kept up.

Kate had darted upstairs to fetch a light shawl for her mother. When she brought it out onto the porch, Alex took it from her. "Let me do that, Kate. You sit there and enjoy the country evening air."

Softer or not, she meant to fight him for possession of the shawl. She reminded him of Conky, but she was nowhere near as good-natured as his failure of a dog. He leaned over and hissed harshly in her ear. "Dash it, go sit by your mother! How much longer do you think you're going to be able to do that?"

Her stricken look didn't shame him much, and he was glad she took his advice without launching a pitched battle. As soon as she'd settled herself on the chair beside her mother, he said, "Here, Mrs. Finney. Please let me drape this around your shoulders. It's not cold, but there's a slight breeze tonight."

"Thank you, Alex. You're such a kind man."

"Nuts," he said in unconscious imitation of Kate. He used to think he was kind. Before he met Kate and her mother, he'd have told anyone who asked that he was a nice man, and a kind and generous one. Then Kate had smashed forever all of his conceptions about himself. But he was learning. So far, he'd learned that true charity doesn't condescend. Nor is it blind. True charity comes from the heart, and it respects its recipient.

Taking the chair closest to Kate, he took a deep breath of fresh air. A hint of manure kissed his nostrils, and he smiled to himself. "Wind's blowing from the east," he observed. "I can smell the cows."

"It smells good to me," said Kate, breathing deeply.

"You should smell it during the heat of the summer," Mary Jo chimed in. "It's awful."

"It's the smell of money." Mrs. English laughed.

So did Mrs. Finney. Alex noticed Kate staring at her mother as if she didn't understand why she considered the smell of money something to laugh about. There were times—many of them, and one of them right this minute—when Alex didn't think he and Kate could ever find a common ground.

But the evening was a fine one, the fireflies came out and blinked up a storm, thereby entertaining Kate and her mother madly, Mary Jo behaved herself for the most part, the two older ladies seemed content, and Alex decided not to worry about common ground. There were other things to do this weekend, the primary one being to give Hazel Finney a pleasant memory to take with her to her grave.

Alex feared that time wasn't far off and decided on the spur of the moment to do some research. He aimed to find a hospital or a group of doctors and scientists doing research into tuberculosis and become a major contributor to the cause. If someone could discover a cure for the white plague, the world would be a much better place.

The night air seemed to stir Mrs. Finney's cough, unfortunately. After only a few minutes on the porch, it became obvious that she was fighting hard for breath. Damnation. If he'd met Kate two or three years ago, he might have been able to do something substantial for her mother. Now, all he could do was watch her die, try to make her last days on earth as comfortable as possible, and feel helpless. He hated that. "Are you all right, Mrs. Finney?"

After hacking into her handkerchief for several seconds and then taking several desperate sips from the flask in her pocket, she turned watery eyes upon Alex. "I'm so sorry, Alex. I guess it's the night air. It's so beautiful here, and I don't want to go indoors, but . . ." She sighed, thereby precipitating another paroxysm of coughs.

Alex's insides tightened. Kate got up from her chair. "Come on, Ma, let me help you upstairs. We can look at the countryside from the window."

"Good idea." Alex got to his feet at once and put a hand on Mrs. Finney's arm. "Please, let me help you." He caught Kate's eyes across her mother's head, and the pain in them made his own heart ache. Hoping a sympathetic—but not a condescending—smile might help her cope, he gave her one. She dropped her gaze instantly. Alex sighed.

"Thank you both." Casting an apologetic glance at Mrs. English and Mary Jo, who had also risen from their chairs, Mrs. Finney said, "Please, you two, don't bother with me. I'll be fine with Kate and Alex helping me."

"You bet," said Kate, her voice a sprightly contrast to the agony in her eyes.

"Absolutely," confirmed Alex.

They walked slowly through the front door and to the staircase. At the foot of the stairs, Alex took matters into his own hands again. "I apologize for the presumption, Mrs. Finney, but I'm going to carry you upstairs." And with a swoop, he picked her up.

Mrs. Finney tried to laugh and ended up coughing.

Kate said, "Alex!" She said no more, but handed her mother her own handkerchief.

Alex wondered how many handkerchiefs Mrs. Finney went through on the average day. He suspected the one she'd carried outside was already damp and bloody. He took the stairs slowly, being careful not to jostle his cargo. She weighed nothing at all, and he recalled how little of her dinner she'd eaten. She's pushed her food around and made a gallant effort, but he knew she hadn't eaten much.

At the top of the stairs, Kate scooted past him and opened her mother's door. "Here, Ma. Lie down, and I'll open the curtains. You can watch the fireflies from the window, and I'll sit next to you."

After setting his cargo on the bed, Alex said, "I'll get a couple of chairs, and we can join you."

"You two are too good to me," Mrs. Finney gasped.

A duet of voices responded to this declaration. "Nuts." Alex and Kate glanced at each other, and Alex suspected they might have smiled if circumstances had been different. As it was, he could see tears in Kate's eyes. He knew she'd never shed them. Not Kate. Not in front of her mother.

"I'll get Ma ready for bed while you go get chairs," Kate said after a moment of stillness, unbroken even by coughs. "Be sure to knock before you come in."

As if he'd ever enter a woman's bedroom without knocking first. Rather than tell Kate so, he said only, "Right," and left the room in search of chairs.

The door closed behind Alex. Kate swallowed the lump in her throat and blinked back tears. Her mother was dying. She knew it. No matter how much she tried to deny it, her mother was dying. Sucking in a deep breath, she turned to the bed and proceeded to do her duty. "Here, Ma. Let me unbutton you. You don't have to sit up or anything. Just roll over."

"Ah, Katie, I hate being so helpless. I wish I could be strong for you."

"Aw, heck, Ma, I'm strong enough for both of us."

"I know it. That's the truly sad part."

Whatever that meant. Her mother struggled to sit up-right, and Kate snapped, "Darn it, Ma. Don't sit up."

A spate of coughs greeted this admonition, and Mrs. Finney sank back onto the bed, defeated. "I'm sorry, Katie."

"Nuts."

By the time Alex's knock came at the door, Kate had managed to get her mother's daytime clothes off her and had slipped a flannel nightgown over her head. The nightie was one Kate had made with her own two hands, out of cheap white flannel, and it had little red rosebuds sewn around the neckline and hem. Chinese Charley had sold her about a million of the fabric rosebuds at a real bargain. Kate still had a ton of them. "Don't move, Ma. It's probably Alex."

Her mother nodded without opening her eyes. Kate had to swallow more tears when she went to the door and opened it. "She's really weak," she whispered as a greeting.

Alex didn't move to enter the room. Kate saw two comfortable-looking chairs behind him. "Do you think we ought to forget the chairs?"

Glancing over her shoulder, Kate took in the sight of her mother's slight frame lying still under the covers. Her body was so wasted, it hardly made a lump, and she was so weak, she hadn't made a wrinkle in the counter-pane. She needed rest. More, she needed her family. Kate shook her head. "No. Bring them in. I think she needs companionship right now."

With a nod, Alex turned and lifted both chairs. They looked heavy, and Kate made a move to help him with one, but his scowl stopped her. Pinching her lips, she decided to let him be a hero if he wanted.

What a nasty thought. Shoot, when had she become so unfair to everybody? Since forever, she guessed. And to Alex, of all people. The only man she'd ever met, aside from her own brothers and a couple of friends, who was worth more than a bucket of spit. And that was character-wise. Money-wise, he was worth God knew what. Thousands, certainly. Could she actually have met a millionaire? Kate supposed stranger things had happened in the world, but never to her.

"Why don't you set them up over here?" she suggested, rushing past him to the window.

He set the chairs to one side of the window and gazed critically at the room. "I'm going to move the bed."

"You're what?" Glancing from him to the bed, Kate doubted it. That thing was heavy.

But Alex had already moved to Mrs. Finney's side. "Would you like to see out the window, ma'am?" He winked down at her.

"I'd love it," Mrs. Finney whispered.

"But you can't . . ."

Alex interrupted Kate's protest. "I'll just slide the bed over so you can see outdoors."

"Thank you, Alex." It looked to Kate as if her mother would have liked to say more, but she shut her mouth fast, undoubtedly to stop coughs from leaking out.

"But . . ." Again, Kate didn't get her protest out.

"I'll just have to move it a little bit," Alex said, and proceeded to do it.

Kate was impressed. Not only was he nice, but he was strong as an ox, too. Maybe that's what farming did for a man. Kate approved, if so.

After he'd positioned the bed so that Mrs. Finney could look out the window if she only turned her head, Alex set the chairs beside the bed. He gestured to one of them. "Kate?"

She hesitated for a moment, then gave up. She didn't even know why she'd been going to fight. Habit, most likely. A bad one, in this case. Generally, Kate needed to keep her wits sharp and the ability and readiness to fight for what she needed was an admirable attribute. In this place, this farm that had belonged to Alex English's family for more than a hundred years, she didn't need it. Shoot, if this kept up, she'd lose her edge.

Vowing not to let that happen, Kate sat. It might get complicated, but if she were only pugnacious in Chicago and remembered that she didn't have to be when she went places with Alex, things might go easier for her. After thinking about it for a moment, she snorted softly and decided she was being stupid. Again. There was little possibility that she'd be going very darned many places with Alex.

"What is it, Kate?"

Alex's soft question jerked her attention back to the bedroom. "Nothing. I was just thinking how—how pretty everything is."

"Beautiful," Mrs. Finney murmured.

Kate peeked at her mother and found her gazing out the window. When Kate did likewise she saw only night, and would have said something to that effect only she stopped herself. Because she realized she was probably being unnecessarily hostile out of habit—again—she looked harder into the darkness.

After a moment, she came to the conclusion that, even though night had fallen and the gorgeous greens and flower colors of the countryside could no longer be discerned, the scene held great beauty and serenity, two commodities unavailable to Hazel Finney on a regular basis. Small wonder she liked this view. It was pretty, all right. The sun had set, and the moon hung in the sky like a silver dollar. It tipped the trees with silver and dimmed the stars twinkling against the blackness of the sky. You could never see the stars in Chicago, although they were as clear as anything out here.

Kate heaved a deep sigh of . . . Good Lord, could it be contentment? Searching within herself for answers, Kate

decided that, by gum, it was contentment. How unusual.
Not to mention unsettling.

"It's pretty here, isn't it?" Alex asked. She heard contentment in his voice, too, but his didn't surprise her. He
deserved it, because he lived here.

"Beautiful," whispered Mrs. Finney once more.

"Amen," agreed Kate.

They sat in silence for a long time. Kate didn't know
how long, and she didn't care. Every now and then she'd
glance at her mother's face, pale and drawn in the moon-
light, and found her gazing out the window as if she
couldn't soak up enough of this precious peace. It made
sense to Kate, who made a quick swipe under her eyes to
catch stray tears. She'd never been weepy before; she
couldn't afford to be. It annoyed her that tears seemed so
close to the surface now, of all inconvenient times.

She needed to be tough. She needed to be strong for
her mother. And herself. And her brothers. Kate was the
rock and the mainstay of her family; she couldn't fall
apart now. Not now, when her mother was dying.

Oh, God.

The next time she glanced at her mother, Mrs.
Finney's eyes were closed. Kate stared hard, unable to
discern a rise and fall of her chest. Rising slowly, she
reached out to her mother, in a panic for fear she'd
died. Alex caught her hand before she could touch her
mother's cheek.

"Just a minute, Kate. We don't want to disturb her rest."

She hadn't realized he'd already arisen from his own
chair. "But . . ."

"Let's just do a little test." He pressed two fingers
lightly against the side of Mrs. Finney's neck. Kate knew
from experience that he was searching for her mother's
pulse, and that the skin was dry and brittle and felt like
old leaves. When he smiled, Kate released a gust of
breath. "She's asleep." He kept his voice quiet.

Kate allowed her head to droop for a second as relief swept through her. She knew that one day, and probably soon, she wouldn't hear such good news, but she was grateful for it now. "Thanks, Alex."

He stood beside the bed, gazing down at Kate. "Come with me, Kate. I have a question for you."

"Yeah?" She stepped away from the bed, only then realizing how exhausted she was. In Chicago, she never seemed to get tired because she needed her strength to carry her from hospital to job to job to hospital to home every day. Now that the tension had drained from her during this fresh-air-and-country-filled day, her knees wobbled when they tried to support her.

Alex's hand darted out, he put his arm around her, and she didn't withdraw from his embrace. With another sigh, she murmured, "Thanks. Guess I'm all in."

"I guess so."

He sounded stern. Under Chicago circumstances, his tone of voice would have provoked Kate into a full-fledged rebellion. Since she'd come to the country, she'd figured out that his stern voice was the one he used when he was trying to get a point across to a recalcitrant female. Kate imagined he'd honed that tone of voice on Mary Jo, and she laughed softly.

"What's so funny?" He still sounded stern.

"Nothing." She allowed him to lead her into the hallway outside her mother's door. "Thanks for being so nice to Ma, Alex. I really appreciate it, and so does she. I'm afraid . . ." But she couldn't voice her fears. It was now possible for her to acknowledge her mother's impending death to herself, but she couldn't talk about it. Not yet. Not now. Not here.

"I have a question for you, Kate." He didn't sound so stern now.

"Oh?" She yawned and slapped a hand over her mouth. "Beg pardon."

"Don't be silly. You have every right to be totally exhausted. But I'd still like to ask you something tonight. Before you go to bed. That way you can think about it and give me an answer tomorrow."

All of Kate's protective barriers went up and quivered, on the alert. "Yeah? What kind of question?"

"Not that kind."

Oh, good, now she'd offended him. With a sigh, she said, "I beg your pardon. As you must know by now, I'm not used to people doing nice things for my family. And I'm not used to entertaining questions of a polite nature from men."

"For God's sake, Kate! What do you take me for? I'm not that kind of man. As *you* ought to know by now!"

She held up a hand to stop his outraged spiel. "I'm sorry. I know you're not that type. What do you want to ask me?"

"Let's go downstairs."

She hung back. "I don't like to leave Ma alone. Can't you ask me here?"

He frowned. "No. This might take a while. You're probably going to protest, and I'm going to have to explain my reasons, and then you'll argue about it, and it will doubtless take a while for you to understand and agree to my point of view."

Was she *that* bad? Probably. "Well, come into my room, then."

Now it was he who looked shocked. Kate sighed. "I'm not going to seduce you, Alex. I just want to be here if Ma has a coughing fit or something."

"Of course." He still sounded shocked, but Kate didn't care. She opened the door and led the way into her room. Someone had turned the counterpane back and plumped up the two feathery pillows. Kate supposed it had been Louise, since it was the maid's job to do stuff like that.

Although it still boggled her mind to know that people could afford to hire other people to do such things, she thought it was nice to walk into a bedroom and have everything already prepared for her. She considered the possibility of getting a job like Louise's, here, in the country. She probably wouldn't make as much money as she did dancing and telling fortunes, but the air was better, and the working conditions were superb. And she wouldn't have to fend off the advances of disgusting men who thought she was easy.

After Ma died, Kate would have only herself to support, so she wouldn't need to earn as much money. She almost sobbed aloud, and covered this uncustomary lapse into emotionalism with a show of opening the curtain covering her window.

When she turned around, Alex had drawn two chairs over so that they could peer outside. "Have a seat," he said, gesturing.

With a deep sigh, she took his suggestion. No fight about that. Truth to tell, Kate didn't feel up to fighting about anything at all. She kept her gaze on Alex as he sat down, too. She realized he was bracing himself for battle. She felt bad about that, since he didn't deserve all the hardness she'd flung at him since they'd met. Not all of it; only a little bit. She didn't want to lose her edge, which was important to her everyday life, so she didn't say anything by way of apology.

"Now," he said, his voice firm, "we need to talk about your mother."

"We do?"

"Yes. I think she'd be better off here in the country than in the hospital in Chicago."

Kate stiffened. "She wouldn't have to stay at the hospital. She could stay—"

Alex forestalled her. "At your place?"

"Well . . . Yes." Bristling, Kate said, "It's not that bad, Alex. It's clean and warm."

"It's a room above a butcher's shop!"

"It may be a room above a butcher's shop, but it's home! Not everybody can have a grand palace like this!" The gesture she made with her hand was about as choppy as the commotion in her heart. "She needs to be with her family!"

"She wouldn't be with her family! She'd be alone all day, every day. If she stays here, she'll have people with her constantly."

"But it wouldn't be her family." The words came out taut since she had to squeeze them past the ache in her throat.

Alex's gaze was intense. "You can stay with her, Kate."

Shocked, Kate stared at Alex, her open mouth spewing no words.

"I know you need to earn a living. I can pay whatever you earn at your two jobs at the fair."

"But—but that's not possible."

"It is, too, possible. Listen, I want to help you. Neither of us knows how much longer your mother can last, Kate. You must know that."

"No! I don't know that." She was lying through her teeth.

Plainly exasperated, Alex barked, "For God's sake, Kate, you claim to want the best for your mother, but you reject offers of help at every turning of the road."

"Darn it, Alex, I don't need your charity!"

"The hell you don't!"

Kate was so shocked by this slip into profanity that she could only stare at him for several seconds. She noticed that he appeared rather shocked himself.

He cleared his throat. "I beg your pardon. I didn't mean to swear."

She waved her hand. She heard worse than that tiny little "hell" every day of her life.

"And I know you don't need my charity. I like your mother, Kate, and I know she's had a hard and sometimes brutal life. I'd like to make her last days on earth a little easier on her, and on you, too. The doctor lives only about a mile down the road, and I can see that he checks on her every day."

"She'll miss her family," Kate muttered, wondering even as she spoke if Walter, Bill, and Kate herself were worth dying in Chicago for. Kate didn't think so. She'd rather breathe her last out here in the open, with fresh air and flowers blooming. On the other hand, she knew Ma would want her children around her at the end. And Alex had offered to pay her her regular salary and let her stay here with her mother.

"Oh, God!" Unable to control her emotions, she buried her face in her cupped hands.

"Kate!" In an instant, Alex had her in his arms. "Don't cry, darling. I know how hard all this is for you. And I don't want to take your mother away from you. But she's so ill. And she seems to enjoy the country so much."

"I know she does." Kate tried and failed to control her tears. Her heart was breaking, and she couldn't help it. "Oh, Alex, she's dying." There. She'd spoken the truth out loud. It made her cry harder.

"There, Kate, I know, I know."

"No, you don't. You don't know anything." Her words were so thick, she could scarcely understand herself. "She's had such a hard life, and she's such a saint. It's not fair."

"I know it's not," Alex soothed, not bothering to contradict her statement about his not knowing anything.

Kate knew it was because by this time he knew better than argue with her when she was being irrational. She even admitted—to herself—that she was being irrational. How she'd changed since she'd first met Alex English!

His big hand stroking her from her head to her waist felt good. Kate had developed a lot of respect for Alex's hands. They were capable hands, and Alex used them for good. He was about as unlike her father as a human male could get, and she loved him.

"I don't want to go back to Chicago and leave her here," she said when she could push the words past the ache in her throat.

"You wouldn't have to," he told her patiently. "You can stay here with her."

"I can't let you support me. That would make me a . . ." She couldn't say the word.

"For the love of—" She felt him take a deep breath. "You will *not* be my mistress, Kate. For heaven's sake, this is my mother's home. And your mother will be here, too. Do you suppose I'd take advantage of you under these circumstances? Or any other circumstances," he added, sounding cranky.

Kate feared his unwillingness to take advantage of her spoke more of her own unpleasant personality than his nobility of character. "I can't let you do that. It's too much. But if she stays here, I might never see her alive again. And what about my brothers? They deserve to see their mother again."

She felt his chest heave with another sigh. "I'll make sure your brothers get to see your mother, Kate. I'll drive them out here every day if you want me to."

Lifting her face, she actually managed a crooked smile. "How can they come out here every day? We all have to work."

"I know that, damn it. I'll fix everything. Trust me for once, will you?"

She stared at him through tear-filled eyes. His face came in and out of focus as she blinked. It was a strong face—a good face. She loved his face. Without her conscious consent, her hands lifted to frame his face. "You're so good to us, Alex."

"God knows, I try to be."

It sounded to Kate as if he were attempting to maintain his firmness in the face of her tears. She didn't want him to be firm. She needed more than firmness from him tonight. She needed his love. And if she couldn't get that, maybe she could get a little temporary affection.

That being the case, Kate lifted her face to his and kissed him.

Fourteen

Alex knew he shouldn't be kissing Kate. This was a dangerous thing to do, it being that they were in her bedroom, everyone else in the family had gone to bed, and her own bed was only a couple of feet away. "Kate . . ." But he couldn't tell her to stop. He wanted her too much. He loved her too much, heaven save him.

"I know, Alex," she whispered. "I know this is wrong. I guess I'm bad clear through, because I don't want to stop."

"Don't say that. For God's sake, Kate."

"Then why am I doing this?" Her voice broke on a sob.

Alex couldn't stand it. He wanted to make everything better for her. He wanted to stop her mother from dying and give her brothers money and make sure Kate herself never wanted for anything again. And the only thing he could do was to offer her some sort of solace in her time of distress. He lifted her in his arms and carried her to the bed. "You're doing it because you need comfort. And I want to give it to you."

She'd buried her face against his shoulder. Alex didn't want to let her go, but he was an honorable man, in spite of all obstacles. "You need rest, Kate."

"Don't go," she pleaded.

Alex thought he detected torment in her voice. "I won't go. Lie down and try to get some rest, Kate. You're totally exhausted. You work too hard, you know."

"I have to."

"I know it." And he hated it. He laid her tenderly on the bed. "Here, Kate, let me take off your shoes."

To his surprise, she didn't argue. Rather, she lay back against the fluffed-up pillows with a deep, shuddering sigh. "I'm scared, Alex. I don't know what I'll do when Ma dies."

"I know, sweetheart, but we'll think of something."

"We will?"

"We will." It was a promise he aimed to keep. He dragged over one of the chairs and sat on it, thought about taking her hand, but didn't trust himself.

She heaved another ragged sigh. "Thank you."

"I hope you'll consider my proposition carefully, Kate. I'm not trying to take advantage of you."

"I know that. But if I took you up on it, I'd be taking advantage of you."

"Nonsense." Because he had to touch her or die, he placed his hand on her forehead and brushed back a few stray strands of hair. "Would you like to take your hair down, Kate? Would you be more comfortable?" He'd been wanting to see her hair down for a long time now.

Her head moved back and forth slowly, and Alex sighed with disappointment. "Just close your eyes, then. I'll get a quilt for you if you need more covers."

"No, thanks. I'll get up in a bit and put on my nightgown. Right now, I'm just so tired. So tired."

"I know, sweetheart. Go to sleep. You need rest."

"Sweetheart?" She didn't open her eyes, but she smiled. Alex's heart lurched and stumbled.

"Yes." *I love you, Kate.* He couldn't say that—wasn't even sure he meant it—but he did deposit a kiss on her forehead. "Go to sleep now."

Her eyelids fluttered, as if she wanted to protest or acknowledge the kiss, but they didn't open. She only nodded slightly. "I'm so tired."

"Sleep now."

It didn't take long for her to fall asleep. Alex watched her, longing to hold her, to pet her, to make love to her, but unable to do anything about it. He couldn't. He was a gentleman.

He could if he married her.

The notion had sneaked up behind his back and attacked him so suddenly he jerked in his chair. Marry Kate Finney? Alex English? Impossible.

He watched her sleeping and wondered about impossibility or the lack thereof. Perhaps his judgmental instincts were still operating on notions no longer valid. He'd learned a lot, about himself and Kate, in the last few weeks. It was still true that she wasn't from his social class, but did it matter? He gave himself a mental whack. Of course it mattered. It mattered almost more than anything else, and it mattered to Kate even more than it did to him; he'd learned that much long since.

His mother had come from a poor family. Granted, it had been a poor farming family, thereby enabling her to understand his father's way of life a whole lot better than Kate and Alex understood each other, but that might not be an insurmountable obstacle to a happy union. For that matter, what constituted a happy union? Was happiness in marriage largely a matter of chance, as Jane Austen had written in *Pride and Prejudice?* Might be, although he'd always been taught that if two people were compatible, they'd be happy in marriage.

Very well, then, what constituted compatibility? He supposed people coming from similar backgrounds might have some grounds for compatibility. He supposed that, if a child were exposed to a happy union between his parents, he'd be better equipped to create and maintain a happy union in his own life, provided he received help in the endeavor from his spouse. He and Kate had no similar experiences in that regard. As he stared hard at her, he contemplated the notion of Kate's family as opposed to his own.

There would surely be problems there. How could there not be? His father had been a loving and supportive gentleman. Her father had been and still was a son of a bitch. Therefore, Kate was accustomed to men being a hindrance to her happiness rather than an aid thereto. Could a person unlearn life's lessons and accept another set of values? Sounded like a hard road to him, and he wasn't sure he was up to it since it would be up to him to teach her that he could be trusted. She was as prickly as a cactus in some ways—ways that occasionally drove him almost to violence, which would make him no better than her father.

Alex spared a moment to be resentful that Kate might possibly, if she tried hard enough, turn him into a son of a bitch, too, then told himself not to be ridiculous. Still, her experience with her father would indubitably create problems of trust in so close a union as marriage.

That being the case, marriage probably wasn't such a good idea. But Alex didn't want to lose touch with her; he felt as if his heart were being ripped in two when he considered such a parting of the ways, actually. So perhaps he could make Kate his mistress? That way they could enjoy each other, but remain free at the same time.

His entire being clamped down and rebelled when he considered *that* possibility. No. No mistress. Not Kate. Not anyone, for that matter. Alex English wasn't the mistress-gathering type, and Kate would certainly shoot him dead if he so much as hinted at such an alliance.

Anyhow, Alex despised men who neglected their families for the sake of their own pleasures. If he made Kate his mistress, assuming she'd even consider such a thing, which she wouldn't, he would be dishonoring his own family, his personal code of ethics, and her, too. He couldn't abide that.

As he watched Kate sleep, he saw the lines of care and worry on her face smooth out. He ached to help her, to ease her burdens, to make her life easier. And she didn't want him to, because she didn't trust his motives, not because of him, but because of her short life's teachings. That hurt. What more could he do to prove to her that he wasn't like the other men in her life? What else could he do to prove to her that he only wanted to help her?

Maybe that was it. She didn't want what she called charity. Could he help her without making her feel as if she were accepting too much from him?

His head began to ache, and he decided that Kate and her prickly personality aside, all this thinking was too much for him. Propping his elbows on his knees, he sank his chin into his hands and stared out at the night sky from across Kate's sleeping form. He had a feeling his life would be much easier if he'd never met her, but it would also have been a life flawed and barren.

If he'd never met Kate, he'd have ended up like Gil MacIntosh's brother Henry, sure as check, and probably pretty soon if what Gil had said was true. Alex feared it was.

Not that Henry MacIntosh was a bad man. On the contrary, Henry was known for doing his duty. Doing one's duty was an admirable quality. The trouble was that Henry did his duty out of a feeling of obligation; he didn't do it out of love.

That sounded like a sappy sentiment, so Alex mulled it over for several seconds before coming to a conclusion.

Dash it, it wasn't sappy. It was the truth. Alex didn't want to turn into a stuffy stump of a man who didn't understand anything except his own narrow life. He didn't want to be a man who threw money at charities while despising the people he was helping thereby. He didn't want to consider himself superior to his fellow beings, when the truth was that he was only more lucky and, perhaps, a trifle more provident, than most.

Good Gad, but Kate Finney had taught him a lot of things about himself. Many of them were dashed uncomfortable, too.

A strange sound from the room next door had just penetrated Alex's concentration when Kate sat up with a jolt. "Ma!" She scrambled toward the edge of the bed.

Understanding struck Alex. Kate's mother was in distress, and Kate, whose senses had been honed during months—perhaps years—of listening and worrying, had discerned it in her sleep before Alex, fully awake, had done so. He reached out and caught her before she could fall out of the bed.

"What?" She turned to look at him, groggy-eyed, then shook her head as if she didn't know where she was.

"You're all right, Kate. Here, let me help you out of bed. The bed's tall, and you're not, so you might have a drop." With exquisite care, Alex lifted her down from the bed. She swayed slightly, but steadied herself at once. Again, Alex got the feeling she'd had lots of practice in bounding out of bed and being alert. She'd had to be.

"It's Ma," she said in a voice gravelly with sleep.

"Yes," said Alex. "Here, take my arm."

"I don't need help."

Alex sighed. "I know. Take my arm anyway. It's dark, and I know my way around the house better than you do."

Evidently that made sense to her, because she didn't argue but hurried to the door, not quite allowing him to lead her, but not trying to shake him off. The lamp in the hall had been turned down. Alex didn't bother to turn it up, figuring he could do that after he got Kate to her mother's side. Mrs. Finney was still coughing and gasping. It hurt to hear her. Alex knew how exhausting these coughing fits were for her. She had so little strength to begin with, and then to choke like that seemed to sap what energy she had left. He discovered himself sucking in breath in an attempt to help the sick woman, and made himself stop.

"I should have made her sleep sitting up. I know better than to let her lie down flat like that."

"It's not your fault, Kate. You always do the best you can," Alex assured her. "You can't think of everything every time."

"I should have thought of that this time." She pushed the door open and rushed inside, bumping her hip against a table set against the wall next to the door. She didn't even seem to notice, so Alex winced for her. He almost grinned, thinking what useless occupations wanting to breathe for her mother and assume Kate's pain were.

"Ma!"

Mrs. Finney couldn't talk for coughing, so Alex turned up the light. It didn't illuminate the room much, but he could see that Kate had flung herself on the bed and put her arms around her mother. She lifted Mrs. Finney into a sitting position and held a handkerchief to her mouth. Mrs. Finney's eyes didn't open, although tears of stress leaked out through the tightly squeezed lids. Watching and wishing he could do something—anything—to help, Alex understood that the ordeal of Hazel Finney's life was almost over.

What an awful pity her life had been, too. Until this minute, he'd never fully understood how cruel and unfair the Fates could be. He allowed himself to wonder if there was any order to the universe, or if everything worked by chance. He didn't like thinking of life as a haphazard affair, over which one had no control. Shaking off the thought, he asked, "Is there anything I can do, Kate?"

Kate didn't turn around. "No. Thanks, Alex."

"Some hot tea with honey? Something to soothe her chest?"

"Tea? Yeah. Sure. That would be nice. Thanks."

She was humoring him in the hope he'd go away and quit pestering her. Alex heard the impatience in her voice. With a short shake of his head, he did her a favor, left the room, and went downstairs to the kitchen. He was by no means an expert on where things were stored in that room, but he found the brandy bottle his mother kept in a high cupboard for medicinal purposes. Alex was absolutely certain that Kate wouldn't approve of dosing her mother with alcohol, but he figured Mrs. Finney wouldn't live long enough to become addicted to the demon that had ruined her husband, and he'd heard more than once that brandy soothed a cough.

In fact . . . Drawing from snippets of conversations he'd heard between his mother and Mrs. Gossett, Alex poured some brandy into a glass, stirred in some honey, boiled some water in the kettle, added hot water to the mixture, stirred, and shrugged. Couldn't hurt. Might help. If anything at all could help Hazel Finney, Alex would like to provide it for her. This was little enough, God knew.

He trotted back upstairs and into Mrs. Finney's room. She'd stopped coughing in favor of gasping for breath. His soul hurt for both of the Finney ladies when he saw them. Kate still held onto her mother as if she didn't want to release her for fear she'd slip away from her forever. Mrs. Finney looked as if she were dead already, although she fought hard for breath. He walked softly over to the bed. Kate wasn't crying. As far as he knew, Kate never cried unless she was caught unawares or so overwhelmed as to forget herself.

"I brought some medicine," he said, wondering if he were lying. Deciding it wasn't quite a lie, he amended it. "I mixed up a tonic."

Shaking her head, Kate said, "She can't take anything yet."

Without arguing, Alex pulled up a chair. "I'll set it on the table. Perhaps she'll be able to drink it in a while."

Kate nodded her acquiescence. Alex allowed himself a very short feeling of triumph. At least she hadn't hollered at him to take the glass away and lose himself somewhere. Knowing he was courting a sharp retort, he asked his next question anyhow. "How's she doing?"

Kate didn't snap at him. "Not very well." She turned bleak eyes to him. "Not well at all."

He shook his head, knowing any words from him would be superfluous.

Thirty minutes later, when Mrs. Finney was nearly unconscious with fatigue, Kate managed to pour a little of Alex's tonic down her throat. "Does that help any, Ma?"

Alex was amazed at how firm and jolly Kate's voice sounded. The circumstances were so dismal, he'd have expected them to vibrate in her tone of voice. Not with Kate Finney. Kate was superior to circumstances, sort of like she was superior to logic. He'd have laughed at his little joke if it weren't for the aforementioned circumstances.

A murmur of assent came from Mrs. Finney. Alex hoped she wasn't just agreeing because she thought she should. Before she offered her mother his tonic, Kate had forced her to sip from her flask. It was almost empty, and Alex's heart suffered a sharp spasm when the knowledge that the medicine, which was supposed to have lasted all weekend, had been consumed in a mere day. She was sinking fast, there was nothing anybody could do about it, and the knowledge ate into him like acid. He couldn't even imagine what Kate must be going through.

At last, Mrs. Finney fell into an exhausted sleep. Watching her and listening to her labored breathing, he knew what he had to do. He reached for Kate, but she shook her head.

"I'd better stay here for the rest of the night, Alex. She's in pretty bad shape tonight. I guess the day was too much for her."

A pang of guilt smote him. "I'd hoped the country air and relaxed country living would help her."

"It's not your fault. She wanted to come out here. She loves it out here. The trip helped her heart and mind, Alex. At this point, that's the most important thing."

"Thanks, Kate. That's a generous thing to say."

As he might have predicted, Kate said, "Nuts."

Acting upon his prior resolution, Alex said, "Stay here with her, Kate."

"That's just what I said I was going to do." She rubbed eyes that must have been gritty with lack of sleep.

"That's not what I meant. What I meant was that you should stay with her and not go back to Chicago. You can't go back to the city and leave her here, and you can't take her back to Chicago with you. The trip might—It might be bad for her health." He'd been going to say that the trip might kill her, but good sense kicked him in the head and he modified the statement before it left his lips.

Kate bowed her head. "I can't let you take over my responsibilities, Alex."

Dash it, there she went again. With rather more force than was necessary, Alex hauled another chair up next to Kate's. Fortunately, a thick braided rug, pieced together by his grandmother more than forty years before, prevented the chair legs from clunking against the wood floor. He placed a hand on her arm, squeezing slightly so she wouldn't try to escape before he'd said his piece. "You're going to marry me, Kate Finney, and I'm going to take care of your mother and you from now on."

That caught her attention. Her head jerked up so fast, Alex was surprised he didn't hear her neck snap. "What?" Fortunately for her mother and Alex, a frog had taken up residence in Kate's throat, so the word didn't come out as a shout.

"You heard me."

She blinked at him, as if she were in a thick mist. "I—I don't think so."

"You don't think what? You don't think you heard me, or you don't think you're going to marry me?"

After a significant pause, Kate muttered, "Both."

He was having none of that. "You heard me, and you are going to marry me. You have no choice. I won't allow you another choice."

"Alex . . ."

"No arguments, Kate. You need me. I want to help you. You're going to marry me. I'll help your mother and your brothers and you, and my mother will be ecstatic. She thinks you're a peach."

"She doesn't know me."

He grinned. "True, but I won't tell her."

Her eyes narrowed and her face began to take on its customary rebellious cast. Alex braced himself. This was one argument he didn't plan to lose.

"I can't marry you, Alex."

"Why not?"

Again, she stared at him for several seconds before answering. Then she spoke judiciously. It was the first time he'd ever heard her be judicious. "Marriage is a lifetime commitment. It's not something to be taken lightly."

"Marriage to me would mean a lifetime of comfort for you."

She shook her head. "You don't know what you're talking about if you think marriage is comfortable for a woman, even if you're rich." Her tone was as dry as her mother's flesh.

He felt his lips tighten and endeavored to relax them. He didn't appreciate her sarcasm under these circumstances. "Dash it, Kate, you know very well that I can offer you a better life than the one you have. And I've already told you I'll help your mother and your brothers, too."

"Marriage is about more than helping people, Alex."

She'd adopted a lecturing tone, as if she were trying to impart a lesson to a slow student.

"Of course, but it encompasses helping each other, too."

Although he couldn't account for it, she seemed to be getting angry. Now why, he wondered, should a proposal of marriage from a personable and well-to-do young man create a mood of anger in a young woman who needed help? He knew the answer to that one. It was because this was no ordinary young woman. This was Kate Finney, a female who carried a chip on her shoulder the size of Gibraltar and who was about as irrational and outrageous as a young woman could get. It was good luck for him, he supposed, that they were in her mother's sickroom, or she'd probably have started hollering at him by this time.

"Marriages are supposed to happen between people who have affection for one another, Alex. And you can't very well say you have any affection for me."

"That's not true, Kate. I have a good deal of affection for you."

She eyed him skeptically, which irked him.

"I do," he declared. He didn't dare say he loved her. While it was true—or he thought it was—he was absolutely positive she wouldn't believe him. He didn't quite believe it himself.

"Well," said she, "I still won't marry you. I guess it would be best if Ma stayed here, but I won't stay with her. I need to get back to Chicago and my jobs. I've never depended on anyone else in my life, and I don't intend to start now. I—" She sucked in air thick with her mother's illness and her own despair. "I can't."

"Nonsense. I'm offering you a much better life than you can achieve on your own, and you know it."

She eyed him as if she didn't know what to make of him, and Alex thought suddenly that she might have a point. He wasn't altogether sure what to make of himself, actually. Although her hesitation aggravated him, it did serve to point out to him, as if he needed another pointer, that marriage to Kate Finney could easily turn out to be a mighty uncomfortable proposition.

He hadn't intended to take no for an answer, but her refusal, while irritating, had also served to shake his confidence. All of the obstacles to a happy union between them rose up in his mind's eye. He stood suddenly. "I want you to think about it, Kate. Seriously." She still looked skeptical, so he growled, "I mean it, Kate."

"Right." She saw him bridle and hastened to add, "I mean, I will, Alex. I will. Honest."

He stood looming over her for another minute or so, but she didn't give any hint that she aimed to change her mind anytime soon. Again Alex wondered if this might not be a lucky escape for him. He shook his head hard, not liking the implications of that thought. After hovering for long enough to make himself nervous, although his tall presence didn't seem to trouble Kate, he turned on his heel and marched out of the room.

Kate stared after him, not sure if she was awake or asleep. She feared she was asleep, since she couldn't honestly believe Alex English would have proposed to her in real life. If that could be considered a proposal.

"Nuts," she muttered. It *had* been a proposal, but it wasn't the type Kate had ever contemplated receiving in the rare moments when she allowed herself to daydream. The proposals that had danced in her head, before she'd learned better, had included declarations of undying love and passion and threats of suicide if the offers were refused. Not once had she entertained the possibility of a proposal prompted by pity. She hated being pitied.

But she loved Alex English.

Feeling overwhelmed, depressed, and bereft, Kate buried her face in her hands and wished it were she who was dying, and not her mother. She was sick of life. Besides, her mother was worth a dozen of herself. Why couldn't God take her instead of Ma? If there was such a thing as God. Kate grimaced when she thought about what the nuns would say to her if she voiced that thought aloud.

Before she could drive herself into a full-fledged session of self-pity and loathing, Kate fell asleep in her chair. It was a comfortable chair, but it wasn't intended to replace a bed. She awoke with a jerk when her body slipped sideways and she almost ended up on the floor. After a huge yawn, Kate inspected her mother closely.

Mrs. Finney still slept. Her breath came hard. Kate heard the gurgle in her lungs, and wished she were a weaker person and could break down and cry whenever she felt like it. She felt like it now.

But there would be lots of time for tears after Ma was gone. Kate decided she might as well go to her own room and sleep for a while. She'd had enough experience with Ma's illness to judge that her mother probably—there were no guarantees with consumption—wouldn't wake up before morning. Kate had propped pillows behind her back, giving the fluids clogging her lungs less of a chance to accumulate and suffocate her.

She tiptoed across the room, opened the door, unsqueakable since the hinges were so well oiled by Louise, and bumped smack into Alex. His arms went around her instantly, preventing her from bouncing off his chest and falling down. She peered up at him. "Where'd you come from?"

"I've been waiting for you."

"How come?"

"I just wanted to be here if your mother needed help."

He was so darned nice. In spite of herself, knowing she shouldn't, Kate sighed and rested her head against his chest. She felt so good in his arms. Protected. Cared for.

She loved him so much. If he loved her, too, she'd agree to marry him in a second, in spite of the trouble she'd surely cause him. Trouble seemed to follow her around like a stray dog. Kate knew Alex didn't deserve to have to deal with her problems. He was too good for the likes of her.

"I was almost asleep on my feet," he confessed. She heard the smile in his voice. "But I was pretty sure you'd come out eventually."

"You were right."

"So, have you thought about my proposal?"

She didn't want to think about his proposal. She wanted to pretend that everything could be right for once. Accepting his proposal wouldn't be right. It would be cruel to a man who'd been nicer to her than anyone else in the world, including all the nuns and priests she'd ever known.

He prodded her. "Kate?"

She sighed again and tried to draw away from him, but he didn't let her go. "Yeah," she said. "I've thought about it."

"And?"

"And I can't marry you, Alex. Thanks a lot, but—I just can't, is all."

"Nonsense. Certainly, you can. You won't, is what you mean."

"Nuts." She was going to cry in another second or two. And if she did that, she knew she'd fall apart completely. She might even accept his proposal, thereby ruining his life. Kate couldn't stand that.

Therefore, because she loved him so much, wanted so much to be his wife, and knew that marrying him would be the worst thing she could do to repay his kindness, she reached up with her arms, snaked them around his neck, stood on tiptoe, and kissed him with all the love she had in her.

Fifteen

Alex responded to her boldness as Kate had hoped he would: he misunderstood her intentions completely. "God, Kate, I'm so happy," he murmured into her tumbling hair. "I knew you'd see reason eventually."

She made a soft, encouraging noise as he deepened the kiss. She was going to reward him for his many kindnesses to her and her family in the only way she could. She wouldn't wreck his life by marrying him, but she could give him her body. The good Lord knew, it seemed to be in demand, her body. Other men wanted it. She had reason to believe Alex did, too.

Kate was no starry-eyed innocent who couldn't tell when a man was excited. She'd remained a virgin because she possessed a strong mind, a logical brain, and the intelligence to know that throwing away her virginity was the sure path to ruin where she came from. If there was anything she didn't need more than she didn't need poverty, it was a flock of little bastard children to rear. Until she met Alex, she'd never met a man who wanted anything from her but sex. The men in her life, with very few exceptions including her brothers, didn't stick around to support the leavings of their lust. Kate's brothers had honor, but few of their contemporaries did.

A low rumble in Alex's chest preceded his next words. Kate loved his voice. It was deep and melodious, unlike most of the other male voices in her life. The male voices in her life were hard, desperate, and resonated with anxiety, too little money, and too much pain. Or they were loud, malicious, drunken shouts.

"I've wanted you from the moment I first saw you," Alex admitted.

It didn't come as a complete surprise to Kate, but she was pleased to know it. "I want you, too, Alex."

He held her so hard, her ribs ached, and she laughed softly. "You're squishing me, Alex."

"Sorry." He laughed, too, and eased up on her ribs.

Kate let her arms slide down his and took his hand. "Come with me, Alex." She tugged lightly, and he obeyed.

He drew back when she opened her door. "Kate . . ."

"I want this, Alex." She turned and looked him in the eye. His eyes had gone dark with passion and soft with—well, Kate guessed it was affection. That was nice. It pleased her to know that Alex English, a man whom at first she'd believed to be a hard-hearted stuffed shirt, had turned out to be so open to life that he actually liked her in spite of herself. She knew good and well that she hadn't given him much reason to care about her. Not at first.

After hesitating at the door for a moment, it looked to Kate as if Alex decided something. "It will be all right," he murmured, following after her. "We'll be married soon."

That's what he thought. Kate knew better. She didn't let on, but led him to her bed. "You'll have to pick me up," she said after eyeing the bed for a moment. "I can't climb that high."

"There's a footstool," he said, grinning, and he stooped and dragged it out from under the bed.

"Shoot, you climb stairs to bed? Now that's what I call class."

He chuckled.

As ever, his chuckle sent warm shivers through her. She climbed the two steps and bounced on the bed. Patting the space next to her, she said, "Want to join me?"

"More than anything."

That was nice. This was the biggest, scariest step Kate had ever taken in her life. It even surpassed moving out of her parents' home and getting a room of her own. It might lead to her absolute ruin, although she didn't think so. If she should get pregnant as a result of this night, she knew Alex would support his child. He'd probably want it to grow up on his farm. And Kate would want that, too, although it would kill her to let a child of her womb go.

Lordy, what was she going into that possibility for? Alex knelt in front of her, surprising her into allowing her thoughts to scatter. That was a good thing.

He took both of her hands in his. "Are you sure about this, Kate?"

"Yes." She spoke more firmly than she felt. Alex deserved this. So did she, actually.

He didn't respond, but gazed into her eyes for several seconds. She'd expected him to ask her if she was sure again, but he didn't. Rather, he stood up and yanked at his tie. "I'll get rid of these." He gestured at his coat and vest.

"All right. I guess I will, too." That didn't make sense, but Kate knew he understood. She started unbuttoning her shirtwaist. She'd made it herself, from fabric she'd bought from Chinese Charley. She'd also recently made her chemise and drawers, and was ever so glad she'd brought them with her this weekend. She might have brought her dingy, overwashed underwear that she'd made last year, but she'd decided even her underthings should be special this weekend.

Alex threw his tie, vest, and jacket anywhere. He didn't even look as he tossed them aside. "Let me help you, Kate."

"Gladly." She shoved her shirtwaist down, unbuttoned her skirt, and laid both neatly over the footboard of the bed. Alex might feel free to jumble his clothes in heaps and piles, but Kate didn't. He'd knelt before her again, and reached for her leg. She let him and saw him swallow when she placed her foot in his hands. "Want to unroll my stockings?"

"Yes."

The word came out in a croak, and Kate took heart. Clearly, Alex wasn't as composed as he wanted her to think. Perhaps he wasn't as experienced a man of the world as she'd believed him to be. Maybe he was nervous about this step, too. Unlikely, given what Kate knew about men in Alex's station in life.

Then again, Alex didn't act like any of the men who'd wanted her for a mistress. Maybe he really *wasn't* like them. He'd said he wanted to marry her; maybe he did. His hand on her leg caused her thoughts to scatter again. She gasped and his hand stilled. She didn't want it to.

"Are you all right, Kate? Are you afraid? Do you want me to stop?"

She sucked in air and forced herself to smile at him. "Yes, yes, and no, in order."

It took him a second to decipher her answer. When he did, he smiled, too. "I'll be very gentle, Kate. I'm not the most experienced gent in the world, but I know what to do."

So much for *that* question. "I'm glad to know it." She allowed her smile to broaden into a grin.

"I'm glad you're glad."

With torturous slowness, Alex untied her garter. She'd made that, too, out of a yard of satin fabric Chinese Charley had on sale because it was stained. Kate had worked around the stains and embroidered roses over the ones she couldn't avoid. They were pretty garters. She didn't wear them as she danced, but reserved them for church and other formal occasions. She wasn't sure this counted, but she viewed it with reverence, so she was glad she'd tied her stockings with them this weekend.

"These are pretty, Kate," Alex said, holding up the first garter.

"Thank you." She expected him to ask her if she'd made them herself and was relieved when he didn't. She always felt like something out of the gutter when he asked her if she'd sewn her own clothes. She knew that was unfair of her and unkind to Alex. Most women, except those who were wildly wealthy, made their own clothes. Heck, even Alex's own sister wore hand-me-downs.

It didn't help. She was still ashamed of her circumstances and was grateful that he didn't ask her if she'd made her garters. Her mind went blank when Alex kissed the inside of her thigh. Good Lord! Were men supposed to do that?

"You're a beautiful woman, Kate," he said huskily. "Very beautiful. Inside and out."

"Thank you." Her voice was shaking. Terrific. It would. But . . . Did he honestly think she was beautiful? Everything inside her glowed as if someone had turned on a light.

He'd begun rolling down her stocking. Shivers of delight suffused Kate's body. She'd thought about what it might be like to make love before, but she'd never imagined it would feel so good, mainly because she'd never envisioned herself with Alex. She whimpered in spite of herself, and Alex's hand went still instantly. Panic-stricken, Kate blurted out, "Don't stop!"

He grinned, and she started breathing again.

"Please don't stop, Alex. It—it feels good."

"It feels good to me, too, Kate. Your skin is as soft as a baby's."

"You have a lot of experience with babies, do you?"

He glanced up at her as if he wondered what she meant. Kate wished she hadn't said it, even though she'd meant it as a joke. "Well, only my younger brother and sisters," he said at last. He didn't stop his tantalizing work with his hands.

"It was a joke, Alex," she said when she could catch her breath.

"Ah. I thought you believed me to be a roué or something."

"No. I don't. I never did. Not even when I hated you."

Again he glanced up at her. "You don't hate me any longer?"

Lord, no. Kate shook her head. As he started rolling down her other stocking, she whispered. "No. I don't hate you any longer, Alex."

"Good."

I love you. She didn't say that. Couldn't. Felt too stupid about it.

She didn't feel stupid about the sensations he was creating in her body. He'd gently tugged her second stocking off and was depositing soft, sweet kisses on her calf. She braced herself on the bed, fearing she might float straight up and bounce off the ceiling if she didn't.

When he scrambled up off his knees and sat beside her, she turned into his embrace as if they'd been doing this since the beginning of time. His kisses were hot and sweet and made her head swim. His hands drove her to the brink of madness. Her nipples pebbled instantly under his touch. When he took one tip between his teeth she thought she might swoon. Imagine that. Kate Finney, child of the streets, swooning in a gentleman's arms.

Because she had some basic knowledge of how the act of love was carried out, even if she'd never been involved in it herself, Kate returned Alex's caresses with all the passion that had been building in her for twenty-two years. Until this moment, she'd half expected to go to her grave without having expressed any of it. But this was Alex. She loved him. She gave him everything.

He had muscles like Hercules. She didn't know why she

should be surprised. He'd told her often enough that farming was hard, physical work, and she'd watched with her own eyes as he'd leveled her scoundrel of a father. She guessed it was because he always dressed so stylishly. Kate had always thought of rich, stylish men as flabby and self-indulgent. And there was always the truth that he was a farmer, and when she'd thought about farmers, which she'd seldom done before she met him, she'd thought of them as skinny old men with white beards and stooped shoulders. Showed how much she knew.

His mouth traveled from her breast to her stomach, and Kate gasped. "Oh, Alex!"

"Does this feel good, darling?"

After she gasped again, she breathed, "Stupid question."

His chuckle did its usual damage to her self-control. Not that she had much left.

"Here. Let me take care of this impediment."

Only then did she realize he'd been unlacing her corset. He flung it aside and began unbuttoning her chemise. She was glad to part with both.

Kate was gratified to be able to view the muscles she'd only felt seconds earlier. His chest hair was like curly silk when she ran her fingers over his hard torso. "You're like a god, Alex," she whispered, feeling foolish.

"I work at it," he said, laughing, but obviously pleased. Kate's feeling of foolishness evaporated. "You're pretty much of a goddess yourself."

She smiled and said, "Thanks," in a joking tone, but she was glad he thought she was pretty. And suitable, even, more or less—although she didn't believe he truly wanted to marry her. He was only being nice about that. She'd worked hard to rid herself of the outward vestiges of her low-class heritage. For years, she'd dressed properly, spoken properly, and tried to behave properly, although that one often eluded her.

Slowly, he lowered her to the bed so that she was on her back, and he held her and kissed her hard. Her arms wrapped around his back and she caressed the rock-hard sinews hewn by hard labor that were Alex's own heritage. It seemed strange to her that she'd never considered people in other walks of life from hers as having to work hard. Maybe hard work wasn't the sole provenance of the lower classes. Maybe some folks worked hard to achieve their exalted stations in life. By this time, she was willing to grant Alex English his place in society as having been achieved, rather than having been bestowed as a birthright.

He was working faster than her brain could assimilate all the new experiences and sensations he was evoking in her. Because she felt left behind, she decided to assume a more aggressive role in what should, by rights, be a joint enterprise. She reached for his trouser buttons.

"Oh, Lord!"

His cry sounded like one of anguish, and Kate drew her hands away as if they'd been burned. "Alex! Oh, Alex, did I hurt you?"

He'd sunk his head onto the pillow next to Kate's head and looked as if he were in agony. But he shook his head no. Confused, Kate whispered, "Alex? What's wrong?"

Still shaking his head, he moaned, "Nothing. I didn't expect that."

Uh-oh. "Um, did I do something wrong?"

"Lord, no. Feel free. Everything you're doing is right."

He sounded as though he were in pain. Kate didn't understand, but she was willing to take him at his word. Reaching once more for his trouser buttons, she hesitated momentarily when he groaned again. She decided this must be part of the routine, although she still didn't understand, and proceeded to unfasten the buttons. His erect member pressed hard against them, and Kate had to struggle. After the second button popped free of its buttonhole, she realized that, rather than pain, Alex was experiencing some sort of pleasant torture as she moved from button to button.

"Um," she said, "I've never done this before. Let me know if I do something wrong."

"I will." He was short of breath, and the two words escaped on a gasp of pleasure.

Kate began to feel rather powerful when she understood the effect she was having on Alex. And then he removed her drawers and cupped his hand over her most secret place, and all power fled in a rush of sensation. "Alex!"

"This is good, Kate. This is perfect. This is what men and women do. And to think we'll be married soon and can do it anytime we please."

She couldn't speak. She scarcely heard him. His fingers had started rubbing, very gently, over the center and core of her femininity. She was wet down there, and Alex was using her own moisture to lubricate his movements. She crammed a hand into her mouth for fear she'd scream and wake up the whole house. A very few seconds later she was glad for her caution when Alex's magic fingers drove her to a pinnacle of pleasure she'd never dreamed of before this night.

For what seemed like forever, Kate's body reacted to Alex's ministrations. Wave after wave of sensation rocked her. She seemed to float out of herself for a moment. It was Alex's voice that brought her back to earth again.

"Ah, Kate, that was beautiful. You're beautiful. My darling, darling Kate. You're perfect. We're perfect together."

They were what? She was what? The sentiments he was expressing seemed so opposed to everything she'd believed since she'd met him that Kate couldn't take them in. Then he was kneeling over her and guiding his rigid sex to the seat of her pleasure, and her thoughts scattered yet again.

With a powerful lunge, Alex conquered her virginity. It wasn't a painful capitulation. Kate was more shocked than hurt, and then she held on for dear life as Alex moved in her, harder and faster, until his release came with a shout he muffled in the pillow. Kate still held tight, feeling his hard muscles slip under her fingers because of his perspiration. She loved him so much. Burying her face in the hollow of his shoulder, she allowed herself to wish for his love in return. Kate wasn't one to spend time in idle fancies, but she allowed herself that one, knowing it wouldn't last long.

Tomorrow she'd go back to Chicago and start working her two jobs again and try to start to forget. Fat chance of that ever happening. Still, she'd survive. She always had, and she always would.

"God, Kate."

Alex's voice was ragged and almost inaudible, muffled as it was in the pillows. She squeezed him as tightly as she could—his skin was slippery with sweat and her arms slid, but she didn't care. In fact, she laughed. "I'm so happy, Alex." It was a confession she hadn't meant to make, but she didn't think it would hurt—at least not yet. Kate had learned a long time ago that one had to pay for one's moments of happiness. Sometimes the price was high, sometimes it wasn't. She feared the price for this was going to be higher than any other she'd had to pay so far.

"Me, too." With what seemed to Kate like a huge effort, Alex heaved himself to her side. Without giving her a chance to think about anything, he wrapped her up in his arms and drew her tightly to his body.

"Alex . . ."

"Hush, Kate. Just be quiet now, and go to sleep. This is the beginning of a beautiful life together. We'll talk about it all tomorrow. I'm too exhausted to think right now, much less talk."

That suited Kate fine. She didn't want to talk anyhow.

So, instead of talking, she turned her head as far as her neck would allow her to, and kissed what she could reach of Alex's face, which turned out to be the tip of his nose. "'Night, Alex."

He laughed softly and kissed her back. He could reach her hair, so that's what his lips touched. "Good night, Kate. Sleep tight."

"Don't let the bedbugs bite," she said, drawing from a childhood joke, although it hadn't been a joke for the Finney children.

Alex chuckled, then yawned. It wasn't long before Kate heard his deep, regular breathing. With a sigh, she decided to shelve all her questions and problems and take Alex's advice for once, without arguing. It wasn't long before she, too, slept.

Alex woke up early the morning following his night with Kate, feeling better than he'd felt in a long time. Maybe ever. He wanted to leap out of bed and dance around the room but didn't want to wake Kate, who needed her sleep.

What a wonder she was. And how lucky he was to have caught her. She'd make an excellent wife. A *perfect* wife. She had none of the flaws possessed by the other ladies he'd considered. Kate Finney wasn't a giggler. And she wasn't a pedant. Nor was she stupid.

She was not merely smart and pretty, but she was self-sufficient—perhaps a little too self-sufficient at times. That might be considered a flaw, but it wasn't a huge one. Anyhow, it was overwhelmed by the fact that she had an unsurpassed capacity for love and loyalty. And besides all that, he . . . well, he loved her.

As he darted around the room picking up his clothes, Alex knew he must have a sappy grin on his face. He was going to do something even sappier. He was going to rush downstairs to the barn and take the cover from the two-person bicycle he'd bought for his parents in a fit of filial idiocy several years before.

His father had been amused but disapproving. Mr. English didn't condone spending money foolishly.

Alex's mother had thought it was a precious, albeit silly, gift. Alex thought he recalled them riding it twice. Maybe only once. Neither of his parents possessed the ability to appreciate something that might be considered out of the way. Kate did. She'd love the absurd bicycle. He knew it.

Kate wouldn't think it was a nonsensical thing. She'd adore it. Alex knew her pretty well by this time, and he knew darned well that there wasn't a single stuffy thing about her.

Because he felt a tremendous sense of responsibility toward Kate's mother, after he'd washed up and donned fresh clothes, he tiptoed into Mrs. Finney's room to assess her condition. As he leaned over her while she slept, he had the unpleasant knowledge that her condition, as it had been yesterday and weeks earlier, could only be assessed as mortal. His heart crunched. Mrs. Finney was on her last legs. Her breathing had eased a bit as she slept, but she still labored to draw in enough breath to sustain her feeble hold on life.

Alex's determination to get that bicycle out of the barn intensified. Mrs. Finney would love watching her daughter and the man she was going to marry riding on that thing. It would make her happy. Therefore, it was good that Alex had splurged on the bicycle, no matter what his father had thought.

After he'd determined that Mrs. Finney still lived, even if she was sicker than any other person he'd ever seen, including his father, who had died suddenly of a stroke, Alex tiptoed out of her room, raced down the stairs, and out to the barn. He flew to the bicycle propped against the far wall and yanked off the blanket that had covered it for a year or more. Dust and hay particles flew every which way, but—Alex hooted with delight—the bicycle was as clean as a whistle and the tires were still full of air. He wheeled it out of the barn and up to the porch, where he propped it against the house.

Whistling happily, he reentered the house. Kate stood at the top of the staircase, clad in her bathrobe, clutching it to her chin. Her hair tumbled around her shoulders, and she looked worried. Fearing his departure had caused this state of apprehension in her, Alex ran up the stairs, taking them three at a time.

"Kate!" He grabbed her in his arms, whirled her around, and ended with a smacking kiss on her lips.

Her apprehensive expression melted into giggles. "Put me down, you ridiculous man!"

"I might be ridiculous, but I'm happy."

"I'm glad, Alex." She hugged him hard, and he felt about a hundred feet tall. It was odd how loving someone could affect a fellow so strongly. Of course, he had no idea if she loved him, but she would. He'd see to it. Alex had faith in himself and his persuasive abilities. He'd be so wonderful to her, she wouldn't be able to help herself after a while.

He put her down with a thump that rattled her teeth. "Kate!" He lifted her in his arms again. "Did I hurt you?"

She was laughing so hard, he could hardly understand her answer. "No. You didn't hurt me."

"Good." He let her down more gently. "Get dressed, Kate. I have something to show you."

"Oh? What?"

"You'll see." He smirked at her.

She didn't smirk back. "I dunno, Alex. I'm not fond of surprises."

Her comment startled him. "You're not? Why not?"

"Most of the surprises in my life haven't been great."

"Ah." His heart did a back flip. "We'll change all that, Kate. You just wait and see."

Her grin eased his aching heart some. "Well . . . All right. I'll get dressed. But before I see your surprise, I want to make sure Ma's all right."

He sobered at once. "Of course. I'll go with you."

"After I get dressed." She laughed again, and turned pink.

Completely charmed, Alex sighed. He knew he had a huge, foolish grin on his face, and he couldn't have cared less if he'd tried. "I'll go sit with her while you get dressed."

"Thank you, Alex. You're truly a good man." She reached up, cupped his cheek in her hand, and Alex wanted to purr like one of Mary Jo's stupid barn cats. He watched her turn and go to her room, and had to shake himself out of a Kate-induced trance.

Mrs. Finney had awakened by this time, although she hadn't tried to sit up. She looked even sicker today than she had the day before. Alex wouldn't have thought such a thing possible until he saw her. Her head barely turned on her pillow and her eyes, sunken and watery, belied the smile she forced for his benefit. It hurt his heart to know how much she had to struggle for the least little amenity—like smiling at somebody in the morning.

To counteract her misery and his own knowledge of her perilous condition, Alex put a bounce in his step and a broad smile on his face. He felt akin to Kate and decided that was appropriate. "How's Mrs. Finney this morning?"

Rather than speak—Alex presumed she didn't dare speak for fear she'd precipitate a coughing fit—she nodded her head about an eighth of an inch.

"I've got a surprise for your daughter," he informed her, keeping his tone jolly. "After breakfast, you and Mother can sit on the front porch and see it, too." He winked. "Mary Jo will be jealous."

She still didn't talk to him, and he guessed he'd have to get serious at last. "Do you need some medicine, Mrs. Finney? Can I help you sit up?"

She nodded twice, from which Alex guessed both suggestions would be helpful to her. "I'll pour you out some cough syrup," he muttered, heading to the night table. She must be wretchedly weak if she couldn't even reach that far. "Let me put my arm at your back."

"Thank you." The words were a mere breath of air.

His smile broadened, although he felt like shrieking imprecations to the heavens about the unfairness of life. "Here we go." As gently as gently could be, Alex lifted her. She didn't weigh more than ninety pounds. Probably less. His heart cramped again when the movement provoked a spasm of coughing.

Damn, damn, damn, damn, damn. He hated this.

"Here. Use this, Mrs. Finney." He whipped the clean handkerchief from his jacket pocket and pressed it into her hand.

Then he politely turned away and poured a dose of medicine into the glass he'd brought up the night before. He couldn't stand to watch the poor woman cough like that, and he knew the bloody phlegm she produced embarrassed her. As if any of this were her fault.

"Ma!"

Alex started when Kate barreled into the room. He whirled around, miraculously not spilling a drop of the precious syrup. "Good Gad, Kate, you scared the life out of me."

"Sorry." She didn't even look at him as she raced to her mother. "Take it easy, Ma. Let me help you."

Feeling superfluous and ignored and knowing he was being an ass, Alex swallowed his emotions. "I poured out a dose of her medicine."

"Thanks." Without even looking, Kate held out her hand. Alex put the glass into it and told himself this was her mother and it was her right to dose her. He watched as Kate held her mother tight and tilted the glass to her blue lips.

Blue lips? Good Gad, they were. Mrs. Finney's lips had taken on an unhealthy bluish cast. What did that mean? Alex thought he knew, and decided Dr. Conners was going to pay the sick woman a visit this afternoon if Alex had to kidnap him and bear him to the English farm bound and gagged. Not that Dr. Conners was a recalcitrant sort of man, but Alex didn't plan to accept any excuses. If any woman happened to go into labor during the time Mrs. Finney needed the good doctor, she could just do so on her own.

"Can you swallow it, Ma?"

Mrs. Finney didn't even try to nod this time. Alex heard her swallow, then gasp for breath. He shut his eyes against the terrible sight and sound.

"That's the way. Take another little sip."

How did Kate do that? How could she sound so encouraging and cheerful as her mother lay there, dying in her arms? Alex's respect for Kate Finney almost matched his love for her. She was so strong. And so *good*. He could no longer even conceive of how badly he'd misjudged her at first. What a total idiot he'd been.

Kate shooed him out of the room after that. "I've got to help Ma get dressed, Alex."

"Would you like me to bring a tray up to you, Mrs. Finney?"

Still unable to talk, she shook her head.

Kate frowned at her mother. "Are you sure, Ma? Can you walk downstairs?"

This time she nodded. "In a minute."

Alex held his own breath as she struggled for hers, as if she wanted to say something more.

Kate forestalled her by turning to Alex. "I'll bring her down in a few minutes."

"Good. I'll tell Louise and Mrs. Gossett to expect a ravening horde."

She laughed. "You do that."

Mrs. Finney's eyes actually managed to twinkle, and Alex descended the staircase feeling like some sort of hero.

Sixteen

Kate gaped at the bicycle Alex was holding upright at the foot of the porch steps. "It's a bicycle built for two! Just like in the song!"

Mrs. English laughed. Mrs. Finney tried to. Alex said, "Brilliant, Kate. You got it on the first try."

"Smart aleck," she muttered, feeling silly.

"That's smart Alex, if you please. Hop on."

"Hop on?" She goggled at him this time. "I can't ride a bicycle!"

"It's not difficult, especially with me doing all the work."

Feeling small and foolish, Kate clasped her hands behind her back. "I don't know, Alex . . ."

"My husband and I rode it, Kate." Mrs. English looked up from her embroidery.

"They sure did," agreed Mary Jo. "And if Ma could learn how to ride a bike, anybody can."

Kate cringed inwardly at this bit of non-diplomacy, but Mrs. English only laughed and said, "True, true."

"Go on, Kate," urged Mrs. Finney. "I've always wanted to see one of those tandem bicycles in action."

It had taken her mother a long time to recover from her troubled night. Kate wondered if that meant Hazel Finney's time on this earth was nearing its end. Probably.

That being the case, and as little as Kate liked feeling ridiculous, she supposed it wouldn't kill her to give the bicycle built for two a whirl. If it would make Ma happy, her own embarrassment would be worth it. "Well . . . All right." She heaved a huge, dramatic sigh. "If I fall off and break a leg, Alex English, you're going to have to fill in for Little Egypt for me."

Mary Jo shrieked with hilarity. Alex gave his sister a mock ferocious scowl. "I'll send my sister to do it."

Like heck. Alex would shoot somebody before he'd allow his baby sister to appear in Kate's Egyptian costume, and everybody knew it. He took care of his family, unlike some men Kate knew. "I'll bet," she grumbled. But she flung her leg over the body of the bicycle. "I hope my skirt doesn't get caught in the spokes."

"It won't." Alex's voice fairly reeked with confidence.

Kate wasn't so sure about that, and she didn't much want to sacrifice this skirt, which was the same one she'd worn yesterday and which she'd made by hand, to the cause.

"Hold onto the handlebars," Alex commanded.

"Right. Handlebars." Kate knew what those were because she'd seen lots of people ride bicycles and had gleaned the pertinent information. She'd never done so herself, since nobody in the family owned a bicycle. She'd never thought she'd missed much, transportation in Chicago being so easy to come by.

Without another word, Alex pushed off and started peddling. Shocked, Kate uttered a brief shout of alarm and held on tighter. When she realized her feet were going up and down and around and around, she nearly lost her footing.

"Pedal!" Alex hollered.

The wind hit her face at the same time his yell hit her ears. "How?" she screamed back, terrified.

"Just do it!"

He was laughing at her. Kate would have hit him except that she needed both hands to keep herself upright. How humiliating it would be to tumble off the bicycle and end up with her skirt over her head.

"Yay, Kate!"

That had come from Mary Jo, who, Kate assumed, was still on the porch. She didn't dare turn her head to look for fear she'd unbalance the whole act.

"That's the way!" Alex cried.

It was? But she wasn't doing anything. Daring hugely, Kate glanced down at her feet. By gum, they were going around on the pedals. As an experiment, she exerted a little pressure. The bicycle sped up and she shrieked again.

"Good!" shouted Alex. "That's the way!"

And it was. Without understanding exactly how, Kate soon discovered herself peddling away behind Alex, laughing and screaming with joy. She'd never done anything so exhilarating—except for last night, but that was personal and not to be shared. When she felt secure enough to glance over to the porch, she saw that both Mrs. English and her own mother were laughing, Mrs. English heartily, her mother more or less just smiling. But Kate knew a laugh when she saw it, and she shouted out again with pure glee.

They rode for almost an hour, and Kate couldn't remember ever having so much fun. And her mother had been able to share it with her. She knew she'd never be able to express enough gratitude to Alex and the rest of his family for giving Mrs. Finney this opportunity. And Kate. Kate wouldn't have missed it for the world.

"We're good at this, Kate," Alex hollered back over his shoulder.

Kate, her hair having fallen out of its pins and now streaming in the wind the two of them were creating, and her skirts frothing up around her knees, had to agree. "We got the rhythm going, for a fact."

"Can I take a turn?" Mary Jo had to shout to be heard

over the laughter of the two mothers and the whoops from the two cyclists.

"Nuts," said Alex.

Kate was more gracious. "Absolutely! I'm exhausted." She poked Alex on the shoulder blade when he didn't seem inclined to stop peddling. "I mean it, Alex. I'm not used to this kind of exercise."

"Nuts," Alex said again. "You dance for a living. You're in great shape. I know it for a fact."

Kate poked him again when he waggled his eyebrows at her from over his shoulder. "Stop that!"

Alex heaved a huge sigh of mock distress. "Oh, very well. If I must."

Kate scrambled down from the bicycle and staggered to the porch. "Whew!" She winked at Mary Jo. "Good luck, kid. Your brother's a slave driver."

Mary Jo giggled as she made a move toward the bicycle, then stopped and turned back to Kate. "I'm so glad you visited us this weekend, Kate. I'd never have gotten to ride this thing if you hadn't come."

With another laugh, Kate flopped down next to her mother on the chair Mary Jo had vacated. "Glad to help." She glanced at Mrs. Finney. Her heart lurched when the harsh spring sunlight revealed the extent of her mother's ill health. Not only was she pale and drawn, but she looked to Kate as if she were only hanging on to this life by sheer effort of will. Kate got the impression her mother was breathing for Kate's benefit alone; that she'd lost all interest in living for herself. Reaching over to pat her mother's thin, dry hand, she said, "You all right, Ma?"

Mrs. Finney turned her hand over and squeezed Kate's. "I'm fine, Katie. Just fine. This has been the best weekend of my life."

"I'm glad, Ma."

When her mother's attention veered to the brother and sister on the bicycle, one of whom was squealing like a piglet and the other of whom was roaring like a lion and bellowing at his sister to shut up and pedal, and both of whom were being pursued by a stupid black-and-white dog that couldn't hunt, Kate passed her other hand over her eyes to make sure none of her tears would leak out and make Ma feel bad.

"Are you sure you don't mind?"

Alex rolled his eyes. "Will you stop asking me that, Kate? For God's sake, my mother and your mother have become practically like sisters during the past two days. Her staying here will be good for them both. Ma needs an interest in life besides her children, and since Mary Jo's going to Chicago with us, this is the perfect answer."

Kate knew it. But she didn't want to leave Ma here. She was afraid she'd never see her alive again. And what about Billy and Walter? Oh, God, she didn't even want to think about what her brothers would say to her when they found out Kate had left Ma on Alex's farm. Would they think she had abandoned Ma to the mercy of strangers?

On the other hand, Kate's father had finally managed to find out where she and Ma lived. When he got out of jail—which might already have happened, given the law's indifference to husbands beating up on their wives—her mother would no longer be safe at Kate's apartment. And Ma would be much happier here on the farm, where she could watch the birds fly and the squirrels chatter and the cows moo, than she'd be in that ghastly, white hospital room. "I know," she muttered.

"Then stop fighting me about it."

Kate heaved an aggrieved sigh. "You must know I'm only worried about Ma, Alex. I'm not trying to be difficult."

"You don't have to try," he grumbled, flinging his sister's wicker bag into the baggage compartment of the carriage. "Being difficult comes naturally to Kate Finney."

"That's not fair."

She saw Alex's teeth clench as he grimaced and picked up another piece of luggage. "Nothing's fair. If you haven't figured that out by this time, you've been living life with your eyes closed."

Peeved, she snapped, "How come you're so grumpy today, anyhow? *I'm* the one who's going to be late to work."

She'd expected Alex to have driven her back to Chicago yesterday evening, but he'd postponed the trip until today. After he rearranged the baggage to his satisfaction, he turned on her. "Dash it, Kate, you don't have to go back to work at all! I can't understand you."

"I know you can't." She sucked in air and told herself not to throw a tantrum just because her heart was broken and she felt as if she were dying and she didn't think she'd survive the day at all, much less a day of telling fortunes and dancing to squealy Egyptian music.

She hadn't yet informed Alex that he was mistaken in assuming the two of them were destined to be wed. She aimed to delay the announcement until they were alone together. Mary Jo would be in the carriage heading to Chicago with them. Kate really didn't want a witness to what she knew would be a huge fight between herself and Alex, especially since she had a hunch Mary Jo wouldn't understand Kate's position on the matter. "But I need to explain everything to Madame. And they're depending on me at the Egyptian Palace, too. It wouldn't be fair to them if I just didn't show up again. I thought you were such a stickler for principles."

"Huh." He heaved the last piece of luggage into the baggage compartment and dusted off his hands. When he turned this time, he placed his hands on her shoulders and grinned down at her. Kate nearly melted into a puddle at his feet. She loved him so much. "Kate, my darling, you're right and I'm wrong. There. Does that make you feel better?"

"Yes." She swallowed so as not to sob aloud.

"Good." He hugged her hard. Kate hoped nobody was watching. "You're absolutely correct in that you ought to inform your employers that your circumstances are about to change. I'm sorry I urged you to neglect a responsibility."

"That's okay," she mumbled, struggling to free herself.

With a loud exhalation of breath, Alex let her go. "Let's see if Mary Jo is ready to set out for town. If she's still dithering, I may just leave her behind."

"You'd never be so cruel to your sister." Kate smacked him on the arm on the off chance that if she acted playful, she'd feel playful. It didn't work, but Alex misinterpreted her mood, so the gesture worked out all right anyway.

"I don't know about that. Mary Jo can be a pain in the neck sometimes."

He grabbed her hand. Kate didn't resist because she wanted to experience as many of these tokens of his affection as she could before she delivered the news. She knew he felt obliged to marry her now that they'd been intimate, but she also knew that if he'd only think about it he'd agree that she'd make the worst possible wife for him. He needed some high-society lady who understood his station in life, not a worm like her, who'd have to learn how to be a lady. "You promised her you'd take her to the fair," Kate reminded him, trying her best to sound pious.

"I know it." He heaved a melodramatic sigh. "And I never go back on my word."

"It's a good thing, or I might have to sic one of those big Egyptians on you."

They were both laughing when they trotted up the porch stairs and entered the house. The entryway was abustle with activity. Kate saw her mother in the wheeled chair Alex had either rented or bought for her, laughing along with Mrs. English, Mrs. Gossett, and Louise as Mary Jo dashed here and there, dropping things, picking them up, trying to straighten her hat, losing her hat pins, and generally behaving like an addlepated adolescent.

Alex released Kate's hand, put his fists on his hips, and frowned at his sister. "For heaven's sake, Mary Jo. Aren't you ready yet?"

Mary Jo yanked on a glove, stabbed a pin into her hat so hard that Kate winced in sympathy, and skidded to a stop before her brother. "Yes!" She slapped a hand over her heart and panted.

Kate laughed, although she didn't feel like it. She'd surveyed her mother's face during the last act of Mary Jo's show, and she didn't like what she saw. She was afraid—terribly afraid—that if she left now, she'd never see Ma again in this lifetime. And, since Kate wasn't sure a hereafter even existed, much less that she herself was destined to go there since she considered herself a less-than-stellar human being, she hated to leave Ma here, even with the knowledge that Ma would be better off in this lovely place with all these helpful people surrounding her than she would be in the city. Alex even managed to get the neighborhood doctor to visit the farmhouse twice a day to make sure she had everything she needed. Within reason. What she needed was good health, and nobody could restore that. And God, if He existed, didn't seem inclined to waste his time on such as Hazel Finney.

Making her way to her mother's chair, Kate knelt beside her. "You sure you're going to be okay, Ma? You can come with us if you want to go back to Chicago." *To die.* Naturally, she left out that part.

Hazel Finney kissed her daughter's cheek with lips that felt like dried rose petals. "Please don't fuss about me, Katie. You've done more for me than any mother should expect from a daughter. You've even brought me to this beautiful place and introduced me to the kindest people I've ever met. I'll be fine, lovey. Please don't worry."

Kate had meant to give her mother one of her usual good-humored, saucy quips. What she did do was break down. Laying her head on her mother's lap, she sobbed, "Oh, Ma, I'm so scared."

"Ah, Katie, Katie. I know you are, darling, but please believe me when I tell you that I'm not. I'm ready for whatever happens. And you've made it possible for me to spend a few of my last days in heaven—even before I get there." She began laughing, and the laugh turned into a painful fit of coughs.

Kate felt terrible about losing her control. She fumbled for her handkerchief and brutally wiped her eyes. "I'm sorry, Ma. Here, take this." She handed her mother her tear-stained hankie. Mrs. Finney nodded her thanks and pressed the embroidered—by Kate's own fingers—piece of cotton to her lips.

Sensing Alex close by, Kate lifted her head and found him gazing at the two of them, concern plain to read on his face. She tried to smile. "Sorry, Alex."

"Don't apologize, for God's sake." He knelt beside her and put one of his big warm hands on Mrs. Finney's shoulder. Kate knew from experience that her mother's shoulders were skeletal, all the excess flesh having been vanquished years ago by hard work and ill health. "Will you be all right, Mrs. Finney? I'd be happy to leave Kate here, but she insists on going back to the fair."

When she finally caught her breath, Mrs. Finney gasped, "My Katie knows what she has to do, Alex. That's one of the things that makes her special."

"I suppose so."

Kate heard plenty of doubt in his voice. She knew he wasn't doubting her code of honor; he doubted her common sense. She did, too, but she also knew that it was important, both to herself and to her mother, that she fulfill her commitments.

"I'll be back soon, Ma. Promise."

"I promise, too, Mrs. Finney. I'll bring her back to you as soon as possible."

"Thank you, Alex."

Kate wondered if she was reading more into her mother's expression than was really there. She could have sworn some sort of silent communication was taking place between the two people she loved most on earth. She shook her head as she stood up, telling herself that she was only being fanciful. Still, Mrs. Finney clung to Alex's hand for a long time before they finally departed the English farm and headed back to Chicago.

Mary Jo chattered the whole way about what she wanted to see at the fair and what she aimed to do there. Her babbling made Kate's head spin, and her mood went from depressed to itchy to incredibly crabby before they'd been rattling along the road to town for an hour.

Finally Alex, either sensing Kate's mood or, more likely, becoming tired of his gabby sister on his own, told Mary Jo to pipe down. "I know you're excited, kid, but why don't you give the two of us a break. We've got other things to think about than seeing the sights at the Exposition."

Mary Jo lifted her chin. "That's because you've seen it before."

"No," Alex snapped. "It's because we're both worried about Mrs. Finney."

If Kate weren't so grumpy, she might have felt sorry for Mary Jo. As it was, she could only be glad the girl stopped chattering before Kate blew up and said something nasty to her. *I've got to work on my temper,* she told herself. Maybe most of the people she knew deserved to be yelled at, but the Englishes didn't. Not even self-engrossed, adolescent Mary Jo.

The rest of the trip passed more or less in silence. Kate tried to respond appropriately to the speaking glances Alex sent her way, but she only felt tired and cold and alone, and it was difficult for her not to wish she'd never met him. It was a selfish wish, because Kate's introduction to Alex was the best thing that could ever have happened to Ma, given her health. As for Kate, she loved Alex to distraction, but since they were destined to part forever soon, she'd as soon have spared her heart and soul the pain of that parting.

She was getting morbid. Life would go on, no matter what happened to Kate's own personal feelings. It didn't seem fair to her, but as Alex had noted not long before, life wasn't fair. A body would think that a girl would know better than to leave her heart vulnerable as Kate had done. Fool. Idiot. She was so darned stupid.

Before Kate was done vilifying herself, the carriage drew up in front of the Congress Hotel. Kate wished Alex had taken her home first. On the other hand, she didn't want Mary Jo to see where she lived. It was probably better this way, even if it prolonged Kate's state of misery.

"We'll get you settled," Alex said cheerfully. "After I take Kate home, I'll be back, and we'll decide what to do first."

"I want to see the Columbian Exposition first. I want to ride on the Ferris wheel! Then I want to see Buffalo Bill's Wild West show!"

Even Kate couldn't help but produce a smile for this bit of enthusiasm. The Ferris wheel had become the most popular attraction at the fair. Buffalo Bill's Wild West wasn't even an official part of the Exposition, but was housed on the grounds outside the fair. It was as popular an attraction as the fair itself. It was said that some folks came to Chicago, saw the Wild West, and went home thinking they'd seen the entire Exposition. Kate didn't know about that, and she'd never seen Buffalo Bill's offering to the world's inquisitive mind, but she didn't fault Mary Jo's choices in entertainment.

"We'll all three go to Buffalo Bill's Wild West tonight," Alex declared, winking at Kate. "Kate doesn't have to go back to work until tomorrow."

"But—"

"I'll see to it," Alex interjected loudly, trampling Kate's protest as if he were swatting a bothersome fly.

"But, what about—"

Again Alex forestalled her. "I'll talk to the Egyptians and Madame Esmeralda as soon as I see you home. Stop fretting."

Kate gave up. She might as well. Alex had an answer for every one of her complaints and equivocations. Therefore, nothing more provocative than social pleasantries passed her lips as she and Alex went with Mary Jo to the room Alex had taken for her. It was next to his. Kate had to suppress a gasp when the bellboy, who had been summoned to carry Mary Jo's luggage, gestured them into a cage, pressed a button, and the cage began moving upward. She didn't want to look like a booby, but she'd never been in an elevator before, and the experience was almost as exciting as riding the Ferris wheel.

The suppressed elevator gasp was nothing compared to the gasp Kate had to suppress when the bellboy turned the key in the door to Mary Jo's room and pushed it open. Why, the room was bigger than Kate's entire apartment! She gazed with wonder at the luxurious appointments. It was all so plush and modern.

"Oh, my," she murmured. Then she felt foolish.

"Oh, Alex!" Mary Jo exclaimed, easing Kate's qualms, somewhat, about being a booby. "This is so pretty!"

"The Congress is a brand-new hotel, sister mine. All the appointments are modern."

"It's bee-yoo-tiful, Alex!" Mary Jo ran to the bed and flung herself on it, bouncing twice. "I love it!"

Kate, who had believed the luxury of the English home could hardly be surpassed, stared in wonder at Alex's sister. Fancy that! A young, spoiled, rich girl could be impressed by something. Would wonders never cease?

It didn't take long to get Mary Jo settled, and although she begged to be allowed to go with Alex to see Kate to her apartment, her entreaties were rejected. Kate guessed she was glad of that, but wasn't sure, given the nature of the news she aimed to impart unto Alex during the carriage ride.

But she didn't impart it. She couldn't. And it was all because he was so happy.

He grabbed Kate's hand and held it tight as soon as she was settled in the carriage. "I'm going to take you and Mary Jo up on the Ferris wheel tonight, Kate. And after that, we're all going to see Buffalo Bill's Wild West."

Kate opened her mouth to refute Alex's assumption of her evening's time, but didn't do it. Couldn't do it. This was the man who was responsible for making her mother's last days on earth happy. She couldn't spoil the evening for him. There would be time tomorrow to inform him she wouldn't marry him.

He anticipated her. "Don't say a word, Kate. I'm taking you and Mary Jo to dinner in the hotel, and then we're going on the Ferris wheel, and then we're all going to see Buffalo Bill's Wild West. I'm only taking you to that ghastly room so that you can have a few hours of rest."

She expelled a gust of air and gave up completely. "Thank you, Alex," she said meekly.

He eyed her skeptically. "That's all?"

She blinked at him. "That's all of what?"

"That's all you're going to say to me?"

She thought about it. "Um . . . Yes."

"Good Gad." He gaped at her.

Kate felt her temper beginning to spark, sort of like when she touched something and got an electrical

shock. It took all of her willpower to hold a sarcastic retort inside and not blurt it out in Alex's face. This was
the man she loved, she told herself. This was the man
who was being kinder to her and her family than anyone
had ever been.

As if he understood, Alex squeezed her hand. "I'm
sorry, Kate. I oughtn't tease you. I know you're facing
some difficult times."

She stared at him. Never, in all of her twenty-two years,
had anyone been so nice to her. Turning her hand over in
his, she returned his pressure. "Thanks," she said simply,
loving him and wanting him, and wishing she were someone else and could marry him with an easy conscience.

They reached her room a few minutes later. To Kate,
the ride from the Congress to her street was like a descent
into hell. From the bright, clean streets surrounding the
luxurious hotel, the neighborhoods got dirtier and less
sanitary and shabbier and uglier, until the carriage took
the familiar turn around the corner, and the smell of the
slaughterhouses and butcher shops smote their noses. The
odor was so foul, it made Kate's eyes water. She couldn't
fathom why she'd never noticed it before.

Silly Kate. She'd never noticed it before because she'd
had nothing with which to compare it. Not for more
than a few hours at a time, anyway. After three days in
the country, her senses had been clarified. Now she
could completely understand the horror of where she
lived. With all her heart, she wished Alex didn't know of
her ignominy.

Too late. With a sigh, Kate decided it was past time she
resumed the cocky, don't-tread-on-me demeanor she'd
perfected in her several years in the slums. "Aha. The
sweet smell of home."

Alex squeezed her hand again. "Not for long, darling.
Not for long."

She gave him a long, steady look and almost broke her

vow not to burden him this evening. But she couldn't spoil his first evening in the city with Mary Jo. That would be too unkind, even if Kate knew it would ultimately prove to be the best course of action. She wouldn't allow herself to ruin the life of the only man who'd ever shown any kindness to her and her family. Rather, she smiled sweetly after only a very few moments of hesitation—nowhere near long enough to make him suspicious. "I'm looking forward to it."

"Good." Although Frank the coachman knew by this time where Kate lived, Alex thumped on the carriage ceiling as they approached the Schneiders' shop. When he turned back to Kate, he wore a frown. Kate braced herself.

"We've got to get you out of this place before your father gets out of jail."

Kate shrugged, feeling a wash of defeat. "He's probably already out."

"We'll see about that."

His face was grim. Kate recognized that look and was surprised it still had the ability to shock her. She should have learned by this time that his elegant demeanor hid a will of iron and a heart of gold. Not to mention fists of steel, God bless him. If there were any justice in the universe, her father would have landed on his useless head and killed himself when Alex punched him. She patted his knee. "Don't worry about me, Alex. I know you don't like to hear it, but I've learned to take care of myself, you know."

"I know." His scowl didn't abate appreciably. "And I think it's a dashed awful world that demands such sacrifices from young girls who ought to be loved and protected."

Until Kate met Alex, she'd have considered such a sentiment not merely maudlin and silly but absolutely unheard of. Nobody in her whole life had expected to have to protect Kate Finney. Not even her brothers, mainly because they were all born within a four-year span, and had grown up protecting each other. Kate could recall helping Billy drag Walter out of their father's reach during drunken rages. And they'd all tried to protect their mother. "Yeah," she said. "That would have been nice."

"We'll take care of it," he promised her.

Kate believed him. That is, she believed he meant it. Again she smiled.

Alex hefted her carpetbag as if it weighed nothing and toted it up the stairs to her room. When she pushed the door open, the shabbiness of her living quarters smote her full in the face. Astonishing how one could get accustomed to the least felicitous surroundings, especially if one didn't know any better. Although Kate had never thought twice about her apartment except to be grateful she had it, this time the thought of moving back into it after a weekend in the country made her stomach roll.

She stood beside the bag Alex had set down. "Thanks, Alex. You've been so good to us."

"Nonsense. I don't think my mother has had a better time since my father died. You and your family are a blessing to us, Kate."

Right. And pigs could fly. Rather than say so, Kate smiled again. "Thanks. Talk about blessings, you're the tops when it comes to blessings, Alex. As well you know."

"Aw, Kate."

He had a silly grin on his face when he closed the distance between them and took her in his arms. Kate and her unruly body responded to his embrace instantly. She'd have given her eyeteeth, had anyone offered for them, to be able to consummate another act of love before Alex left her life. *Maybe tonight,* she thought, even though she knew another intimate joining would only be taunting fate. She wasn't going to marry Alex; she'd be a benighted fool to go to bed with him again anyway.

He deepened the kiss. She pressed against him shamelessly, wanting to feel his warmth for however much longer she had.

"Gad, Kate, I want you so badly."

She already knew it, because she could feel his arousal pressing against her stomach. "I want you, too, Alex. But you need to get back to your sister." It almost killed her to add that.

Alex groaned as he pulled away from her. "Soon," he promised her. "Soon we'll be able to love each other anytime we want to."

She stared at him, the word "love" having caught her by surprise. But no. She told herself not to be frivolous. He didn't mean he *loved* her. Not the way she loved him. Rather, he was using the word as a—what was that word? Euphemism? Kate wasn't sure, but she thought that was the one—for desire. "Yes," she said at last, figuring she was probably damned anyhow, so what did one more lie matter at this point?

He hugged her hard once more. "I don't want to leave you here, Kate."

"I know you don't." She didn't add that she didn't want to stay, because she didn't want to sound like a whiner. Besides, she had to get in touch with her brothers as soon as possible.

"I'm going to the Exposition before I go back to Mary Jo. I'll talk to Madame Esmeralda and the Egyptians."

"Tell them I'll be back to work tomorrow."

He didn't like it. Kate could see it clearly as his expression turned mulish. She said sternly, "Alex."

Throwing his hands in the air, he cried, "All right! I'll tell them you'll be back to work tomorrow—or maybe the day after. But you aren't going to be working any longer than I can help, Kate."

"Don't tell them that, please. If you dare—"

"I won't." He rolled his eyes. "For the love of heaven, Kate, I've learned not to usurp what you consider your privileges by this time."

"Privileges? *Privileges?*" She embraced her rage as a fortunate alternate to grief. "Nuts to privileges! I have the right to live my own life without your interference, darn it!"

"Oh, Lord, not again."

She could tell his temper was tattered, too, and was contrite, although not enough so to moderate her tone when she spoke again. "Yes, darn it. Again. I'm not a compliant little rich girl, Alex. I'm Kate Finney, and I'm used to taking care of myself."

His expression softened, and Kate's heart lurched painfully. "I'm sorry, Kate. I know you're an independent female. I guess we'll have to work on getting used to each other's . . . ah . . . quirks."

In spite of herself, Kate grinned. "That's a good word for it. Diplomatic. You're good at that, Alex."

"You bet. I'm good at lots of things."

He bent down and kissed her again, although she didn't allow the kiss to linger. She wanted to. But she knew better. Life had taught Kate Finney that if a girl in her situation once allowed herself to fall victim to a man's blandishments or her own heart's longings, she was done for.

"I'll pick you up in three hours, Kate. Be ready!"

"I will."

He kissed her one last time before he departed. Kate flopped down on her bed that served as a sofa during the day and wished she could just die now and get it over with. If God could only take her instead of Ma . . .

But no. Kate knew that her own passing would wound her mother. She guessed she was the stronger of the two of them. Therefore, it ought to be Kate who endured the pain of living. Her mother had taken enough abuse in her life. She'd probably be better off dead.

And, on that dismal thought, Kate removed her clothes and began washing herself, using cold water left over from before she left for the country, and wishing she were somebody else.

Seventeen

Alex felt as if he were walking on air as he strolled through the Columbian Exposition, his feet fairly bouncing with the weightlessness of his soaring heart, heading for Madame Esmeralda's booth. He flung the door wide and marched right in, heedless of any possible future-seekers who might be concentrating within.

The booth was empty. Alex looked around, peeved. Experimentally, he said, "Madame Esmeralda?"

The beaded curtain at the back of the booth rattled, and Madame appeared, stuffing what looked like bread and cheese into her mouth. Although he didn't know the woman well, he beamed at her. She looked as though she might have beamed back, had she not been chewing.

"I'm sorry for detaining Miss Finney from her work Saturday, Madame." He felt a little silly calling her that, but he had no other name with which to work. "We both felt it would be better for her mother to remain at the farm for a while."

The medium swallowed audibly and brushed her fingers against her striped skirt, as if to rid them of crumbs. "Aha. Is Mrs. Finney still in this world?"

What an odd way to ask the question. Nevertheless, having become remarkably tolerant in the short time he'd known Kate, Alex offered another smile to Madame. "Indeed, she is. Not stout of health, of course, but still on the earth."

"Ah." Madame walked over to the table holding her crystal ball and her deck of fortune-telling cards. Kate had told him they were called Tarot cards, but he didn't know that of his own accord. "She won't be here for long, though. You going to take care of Kate?"

The question took him aback. "Take care of her? Why . . . Well, yes. As a matter of fact, I've asked Kate to marry me, and she's accepted." As soon as the statement left his lips, he furrowed his brow, trying to recall exactly when Kate had accepted his proposal.

Oh, it didn't matter. She had to marry him now. Not that she wouldn't have done so even if they hadn't jumped the gun and lain together before they officially became man and wife. But Alex decided he'd best not think about them having lain together because the memories sparked too many desires that, having once been fulfilled, now clamored to be fulfilled again. And again and again.

Madame looked at him hard for a few seconds, then made a small gesture with her head that came across to Alex as a shrug might have done. "Ah," she said again.

A woman of few words, evidently. Alex, uncertain what to do now, recalled that he hadn't conveyed Kate's message, so he leaped to do so. "Kate will be back to work tomorrow, Madame. She wanted to come back today, but, as I said, we remained in the country for another day."

"Ah."

The woman seemed completely untroubled by silences in conversations. At least she appeared less nervous about the silences in this particular conversation than Alex was. She just sat there looking at him. He shuffled his feet, wondering how a foreign woman in so dubious a profession as fortune-telling could have the capacity to make him, a well-to-do young man of the world and a sterling citizen, nervous.

Fiddlesticks. Alex had removed his hat when he entered the booth. Now he plopped it on again with a dashing flair and grinned at Madame. "Well, now that I've delivered a message to you, I need to tell the Egyptians that Kate won't be dancing tonight. My sister has come to Chicago to see the fair, and Kate and I plan to show her around this evening."

Madame nodded. "Ah." Her eyes narrowed. She pointed at Alex. He suppressed an itch to press a palm over the area of his chest at which her fingernail pointed. "You bring your sister here. I tell her what's what."

Alex felt his eyebrows lift. "You will?"

Another nod. "Yes."

"Ah . . . Why, certainly. I'm sure Mary Jo would think that was fun."

One of Madame's black eyebrows rose above one of her black eyes. It looked to Alex as if she considered his choice of words inapt.

But that was nonsensical. She was only a fake Gypsy fortune-teller. What did he care what she thought? With that happy notion, Alex touched his hand to his hat in a gesture of farewell, bowed slightly, grinned, and said, "I'll see you tomorrow, Madame, when I escort Kate back to work."

Her eyebrow didn't lower, and she still looked as if she considered Alex something of a figure of fun, but at least she smiled at him as he took his leave. Alex felt uncomfortable for only a couple of seconds after he left her booth. As he aimed himself at the Egyptian Palace, his spirits resumed their buoyancy, and he was soon whistling.

"Daisy, Daisy, Give me your answer, do. I'm half crazy, all for the love of you. We won't have a fancy marriage . ." Alex, unlike the gentleman in the song, could afford to spring for all the luxuries Kate might want for their own marriage ceremony. He thought she'd look sweet in an ivory gown. With a long train.". . . but you'll look sweet upon the seat of a bicycle built for two."

She had looked sweet. She'd looked adorable, with

her hair flying in the wind and her skirts blowing up around her knees and her sober walking shoes pumping the pedals of that ridiculous bicycle. Alex wondered if Kate would consider taking a bicycle tour of England. Bicycling was all the rage these days, and he knew that the Cook's people advertised bicycling tours in all sorts of European countries.

Perhaps Kate would like to see Italy. Now there was an idea with merit. After all, she'd started out in life as a Roman Catholic, even though Alex had his doubts about her acceptance of most Catholic doctrine, which was just as well, given he'd been reared in the Presbyterian church and didn't cotton to popery.

In fact—why should he scrimp on a wedding trip? After all, a man only wed once in his lifetime, if he was lucky—why couldn't they travel the world around? Now *that* would be a trip to remember.

"Katie, Katie, give me your answer, do. We will travel from England to Istanboo." Alex's newly revealed streak of nonsense made him laugh.

"My God, Alex, I never thought to see you laughing at nothing!"

So involved had Alex been in his own happy thoughts that he didn't notice Gilbert MacIntosh approaching with his pretty wife on his arm. Alex's train of thought snapped in two, and he smiled broadly at the newlyweds. "Gil! And Mrs. MacIntosh! What a pleasure to see the two of you!" He pumped Gil's hand with a vigor that seemed to take his friend by surprise.

"My Lord, Alex, what's got into you? You look as if you've just won a million dollars in a sweepstakes." But Gil grinned from ear to ear, which was a distinct improvement over the grim expression Alex had left him with the last time they'd spoken.

"Better than a sweepstakes, Gil, old boy. Much better

than that. I've got to thank you, by the way, for making me see Kate Finney before throwing her out of the fair."

"Kate Finney? Who's . . . Oh, the fortune-teller?" Gil appeared puzzled, which wasn't hard to understand. "You're quite welcome, but . . . Well, why?"

"Mr. English," Mrs. MacIntosh said with a sly smile. "Are you trying to tell my husband something?"

It was on the tip of Alex's tongue to reveal his marital plans, but suddenly Madame Esmeralda's ironical expression seemed to rear up in front of him, and he didn't. Instead, he said, "Yes, indeed, Mrs. MacIntosh. I'm trying to tell him that he averted a nearly fatal tendency in my character. And I appreciate it."

"I must say, you do seem a trifle less rigid, old man." Gil grinned at Alex. "A *lot* less rigid, actually."

"I am! I am!" Alex bowed to the couple again. "But I have an errand to run, and have to get it done. Such a pleasure seeing you both." Again, he was on the verge of telling the two that he'd see them at his wedding, but he held his tongue. Dash it, Madame Esmeralda was enough to spook a man.

His step was jaunty when he reached the Egyptian Palace, however, and he managed to convey his message about Kate's absence with a minimum of fumbling, considering he didn't speak Arabic and the members of the Egyptian community he bumped into didn't speak much English.

When he'd completed his errand, he went back to the Congress, checked on his sister, found her in a fidget to get going, told her to hold her horses, went to his own room, washed, changed clothes, and returned to his sister's room.

"I want to go with you!" Mary Jo cried indignantly when Alex explained to her that he was setting out to fetch Kate and would return to get Mary Jo so that they could dine at the hotel.

"You might want to go, but you're not going," he said in his stern-big-brother voice. "You still have to change into something appropriate for dining at the hotel and then cavorting at the fair. It's going to be a long evening, sister mine, and I won't have you spoiling it by whining about too-tight shoes or a corset that's stabbing you in the ribs."

"Alex!" But Mary Jo giggled.

He left her with a jaunty salute and whistled in the carriage all the way to Kate's place. As it always did, his mood slid downhill as he approached the vile alleyways of Kate's neighborhood. But he didn't stay there long since Kate, unlike his beloved sister, didn't believe in making people wait for her. She was standing at the curb when the coach drew up. Alex frowned to see her thus, wishing she'd stay indoors and let him walk up that dark and dingy staircase and protect her on the way down.

With a laugh, he told himself to stop dreaming. If she were the type of woman to do that, she wouldn't be Kate. And he loved Kate. If a man loved a woman, it seemed a silly conceit for him to want to change her into something else.

She looked tired. She also looked distracted and unhappy. But Alex told himself that even if he'd begun thinking up silly lyrics to songs, he shouldn't allow himself to go overboard in creating moods for people. She was probably worried about her mother. Alex had made arrangements for quick notification should anything happen to Mrs. Finney.

Because he wanted to show Kate only the best of everything, since until now she'd been exposed only to the worst of everything, he greeted her heartily. "Kate, my darling! You're looking fine this evening." It wasn't much of a lie.

With a smile that seemed a trifle wan, she acknowledged his robust greeting. "You're looking pretty swell yourself, Alex. You sure do have a fine wardrobe."

He eyed her warily. "Are you being sarcastic, my sweet?" Still, he smiled.

She looked genuinely shocked. "Good Lord, no! I mean it, Alex. You always dress like the cat's meow. I wish my brothers could wear such fine clothes. You know what they say. Clothes make the man." His smile tilted, and she fairly tripped over herself to add, "Not that it's true in your case. You're a saint on earth. But you look nice, too. That's a bonus."

Her grin appeared as genuine as her shock had, so Alex relented. "I suppose I should thank you."

"It's a compliment. Trust me."

He took her hand and placed it on his arm so that he could cover it with his other hand. "After we're married, I'm going to take your brother Bill under my wing, my love. He's got a good head on his shoulders and was on the right track with his investments. I'm sure he's going to make a mint if he took my hint about investing in the various Exposition ventures. Then he'll be able to buy his own fancy duds."

"But that's just it. You don't wear fancy duds. You always look absolutely elegant and never flashy."

Since she was serious, Alex didn't laugh. Instead, he spoke in a chastened tone as he guided her into the waiting carriage. "Ah. I see. Well, then, perhaps I can advise him about the intricacies of securing a good tailor."

Watching him enter the carriage with a suspicious eye, Kate demanded, "Are you laughing at me, Alex English? Because if you are—"

He held his hands up in a please-don't-shoot-me gesture. "No. Never. I'm not laughing at you and never will. Cross my heart." To prove it, he did exactly that. "But tell me, Kate, is your older brother as bright as Bill?"

"Oh, yes." She sighed and sank back against the well-padded cushions. "He's probably the smartest one of the three of us. He's working hard to better himself, too."

"Ah." He'd like to know, but didn't dare ask, if either of her brothers showed any tendency toward succumbing to their father's weakness. He'd find out eventually. He only hoped he'd have the patience to cope if either one of them turned into a miserable drunkard. He had a feeling his darling Kate wouldn't disown her kin without a good deal of misery first. He wanted his Kate to be spared further misery in this life, and aimed to see to it if he could. Her family was something over which he had little, if any, control, unfortunately.

Because it was true and it troubled Alex, he said, "You look tired, Kate."

She sighed again. "I am. I found Billy and told him that Ma's staying in the country for a little while. He . . ." The word drifted out, as if it had expired of its on accord.

"Was he angry?" Alex hoped the lad had better sense than to be angry, but family relationships were touchy things, and Bill might consider that Alex had usurped some of his own privileges regarding Mrs. Finney.

Again Kate appeared surprised. "Angry? Good heavens, no. Why would he be angry?"

Alex shrugged, having no verbal answer handy. At least, he didn't have one that wouldn't rile Kate.

"No. He was grateful. But he's afraid he'll never see Ma alive again." She gazed out the window as if to gather her thoughts.

Since he still didn't know what to say, sensing that to agree with Bill might be too brutal, he remained silent. He did reach over and pat Kate's knee to let her know that he loved her and was on her side.

She turned and peered at him again. "He's going to tell Walter. They live in the same boardinghouse." Fingering the small beaded bag in her lap, Kate was quiet a moment and then said, "Can they both go see her over the weekend, Alex? Billy's sure they can both get the time off."

Alex was so startled by the question and the tentative,

fearful way in which it was asked, he spoke too loudly. "Of course! Good Gad, Kate, I'm not trying to keep your mother from you or your brothers. I'm trying to make her last days as comfortable as they can be." He tried hard not to be offended.

"I know it, Alex. But don't forget that Billy's only met you once. And Walter's never met you at all. It's not so difficult to understand their feelings, is it?"

"I guess not." He didn't like it, though. "Will you be going to the farm with them?"

"I . . ." She swallowed.

Alex couldn't figure out why she appeared so uncomfortable. After all, they were engaged to be married and she was going to quit both of her jobs as soon as she could, so there should be no problem in getting time free to visit the farm.

After a moment, she said, "Yeah. Sure. I'll go with them."

She turned her head and stared out the window, and Alex could have sworn she was about to cry. Women. He'd never understand women if he lived to be three hundred years old.

They had fun that afternoon and evening, though. After Mary Jo joined them and they retired to the dining salon, Kate seemed to perk up. She and Mary Jo enjoyed each other, although Alex couldn't understand why. Kate was so wise about the world and its problems, and Mary Jo was so naive and so unaware of her total ignorance, he'd have expected Kate to react with contempt to his sister's idiotic pronouncements, all rendered with the air of one habituated to the world's tragedies. Little did Mary Jo know.

Kate, however, was unfailingly kind to the pestiferous child.

"Um," she said after one such statement about the fumbling nature of the serving staff, "I think you need to give the waiters a break, Mary Jo. They're working awfully hard to earn their keep. Besides," she added with a wink, "if you're not nice to them, there's no telling what they might do to your food behind your back."

Mary Jo's eyes grew huge and her mouth fell open, and Kate burst out laughing. So did Alex. He loved the way Kate handled people, even silly, ignorant people like Mary Jo. She didn't use her beat-'em-up pose with Mary Jo, knowing that the girl was still only a child and could be forgiven—usually—for her blindness regarding the world's cruelty. Rather, she used a teasing tone that couldn't possibly offend its recipient.

"Merciful heavens!" Mary Jo cried. "Whatever do you mean?"

Kate grinned like a fiend. "Shoot, Mary Jo, when you have no social power, you take your revenge any way you can. I have a friend who waits tables at a chophouse near the docks. When the sailors are rude to her—and they're rude a lot, being sailors, you know—she'll spit in their beer. It doesn't do the sailors any harm, but it makes her feel better."

"Ew."

Alex laughed until his eyes watered.

Mary Jo's feet scarcely touched the ground when he paid her way into the Exposition. He and Kate exchanged a glance. Kate was amused. Alex was resigned.

Kate smacked him lightly on the arm. "This may be old news to you, Alex, but it's the first time Mary Jo's seen it."

"I know it. I'm prepared." He sighed dramatically. Since Kate already had her little hand on his arm, he shoved his hands into his pockets, hunched his shoulders, and tried his best to look like a man sorely abused. Since his heart was almost as light as Mary Jo's, he wasn't sure how effective his pose was, but Kate laughed, so that was all right.

After Mary Jo had *oohed* and *ahhed* her way through

the White City and seen the Grand Basin and they'd listened to John Philip Sousa direct his band in one of his more stirring marches, Alex led them to the building that housed historical treasures of Chicago. They all stared with varying degrees of wonder and sympathy at the photographs taken during and after the great fire that had razed the city in 1871.

"My goodness," breathed Alex's sister. "What a terrible thing."

"Sure was," agreed Kate. She hadn't removed her hand from Alex's arm, bless her, and Alex realized he'd started to feel about ten feet tall.

When she turned to stare at Kate, Mary Jo's eyes had gone huge again. Alex realized that his sister might be a pretty woman one day—if she managed to grow up before somebody killed her in a fit of pique fostered as a reaction to her irritable qualities. "You mean, you *lived* through it?"

Kate grinned at Mary Jo. "No. It happened in 'seventy one, but my mother told me all about it. It was pretty bad, I guess."

Mary Jo blinked, realizing her question had been thoughtless. "Well . . . I mean, I didn't know your family lived here then."

"Sure. My mother's lived in Chicago since shortly after her family moved here from Ireland."

"Oh."

Alex pinched his sister's cheek. "You're a goose, Mary Jo. You know that, don't you?"

She flushed, her attention having shifted back to the photographic display. Even Alex had to admit the photographs depicted a terrible event in the life of Chicago and its citizens. The fire had killed hundreds and leveled square blocks of buildings. It had been a ghastly tragedy and was certainly nothing to laugh about. Nevertheless,

Kate laughed. He wondered if she laughed because otherwise she'd be crying.

"Don't pay any attention to your brother," she advised. "And consider yourself lucky that you live on that beautiful, peaceful farm. This city's a terrible place to live, even when it's not on fire."

"Really?"

Alex wondered if Mary Jo's eyebrows would stick in an upraised position. Ever since they'd set out this evening, she seemed to be in a perpetual state of awe.

"Really." Kate's brow furrowed as she thought for a second, then she said, "Well, I guess if you have lots of money, it's not so bad. There are some grand houses by the lake that must be nice to live in. Or even work in," she added judiciously. "Heck, if a house servant could make as much money as a dancer, I'd rather be doing that."

"Really?" Mary Jo said again.

"Really." Kate turned a wry glance upon Alex's sister. "Being poor isn't much fun, Mary Jo. Even if you've got a regular job, nobody pays women as much as they pay men."

"They would if the women were doing the same job, wouldn't they?" Mary Jo thought she had a point.

Kate immediately set her straight. "Don't kid yourself. I know lots of women who do the same jobs men do— and better, too—and they get paid less than half of what a man makes." She shot Alex a peek from the corner of her eye, daring him to contradict her. Kate knew her ground here. She had experience.

"That's not fair."

With a grin, Kate said, "Your brother would say you sound just like me."

Alex held his arms up, as if he were surrendering to superior forces. "Not I," said he. "Never."

Kate gave him a sharp frown, and he said sheepishly, "Well, hardly ever."

"Huh." Turning back to Mary Jo, Kate said, "You ought to consider yourself lucky that you have a good family, Mary Jo. Having to fend for yourself can be a mighty tricky business."

"I guess so."

For approximately ten seconds, Alex's sister seemed subdued. Such was her delight at finally being brought to the World's Columbian Exposition, however, that her reserved demeanor didn't last long. By the time they'd left the building and were aiming for the Egyptian Palace—Mary Jo had bullied Kate and Alex into allowing her to see Little Egypt dance—her mood was bright again.

"I can't wait to see Little Egypt," she babbled. "It must be so exciting to dance like she does."

Eyeing Mary Jo skeptically, Kate muttered, "Uh-huh. Wait'll you hear what these guys call music."

She congratulated herself for having warned her audience. As soon as the Egyptian bagpipes began squealing, Mary Jo would have clapped her hands over her ears, except that her brother, anticipating her, grabbed her hands and stopped her. Kate heard him whisper harshly, "Stop that this instant, Mary Jo. It's rude." With a smirk, he added, "Besides, you're the one who wanted to see this."

Kate heard Mary Jo whisper back, "I didn't know it would sound like this."

"I warned you," Kate reminded her.

Outnumbered and unappreciated, Mary Jo sat back and crossed her arms over her chest. Her posture remained defiant until Little Egypt danced out on stage. Then she forgot her dudgeon in favor of watching, fascinated, as Fahreda Mahzar, known to the fascinated public as Little Egypt, did her famous "Egyptian Muscle Dance." When the number was almost over, Mary Jo leaned over to Kate and said in her ear, "Do you *really* know how to do that, Kate?"

"Sure do."

"My goodness. Will you teach me?"

Kate was so startled she turned to Alex, expecting to find him about to explode. She couldn't imagine the prim and proper Alex English allowing his sister to dance like that. She was surprised when he only winked at her. Supposing correctly that his wink settled the question of propriety, she turned back to Mary Jo. "Er, sure. I guess so."

But Mary Jo, hands clasped and held under her chin in an attitude of rapture, was watching Little Egypt again. Kate did likewise. It really was kind of a spectacular dance, if she looked at it objectively. It certainly didn't look like anything a body could see at a regular dance hall. Kate didn't suppose even rustic folks living on those big ranches out West danced like this. She wondered if the so-called hoochie-koochie dance would be all the rage soon. Probably. People loved new stuff. Especially people like Mary Jo, who had lots of money and nothing in particular to do with it or themselves.

She told herself to stop being snide. As soon as Little Egypt writhed her way offstage and the music shrieked to a stop, she said, "Would you like to meet Miss Mahzar?"

Mary Jo blinked. "Miss Who?"

"Miss Mahzar. She's the dancer you just saw."

"I thought her name was . . . Oh. I see. People just call her Little Egypt. Is that right?"

"That's right."

"Let's hurry it up, if you're going to meet her," Alex said, hauling out his beautiful gold pocket watch. "We still have a lot of things to see and do. I want to take you on the Ferris wheel tonight. It's great to see all the lights at night from way up there."

"I want to see Kate's fortune-telling booth, too." Mary

Jo's round eyes were glittering with delight as Kate shoved her way backstage.

"Good Gad," her brother growled under his breath.

Kate gave him a speaking look. "Of course. Madame Esmeralda will be delighted to meet you, Mary Jo."

"Can she tell my fortune?"

"Don't know why not."

Alex opened his mouth, Kate was sure to protest, and she smacked him sharply on the arm. He jerked and glowered down at her, then gave up. "Oh, very well. Madame asked me to bring you, anyhow. I guess I'm surrounded by willful females tonight and might as well not fight it."

"Exactly," said Kate.

Mary Jo only laughed. Kate got the feeling she wasn't used to getting the better of her brother and didn't want to press her luck.

When Kate introduced the brother and sister to the Egyptian musicians, Mary Jo seemed to shrink. Alex was gracious and polite. When she introduced them to Fahreda Mahzar, Mary Jo was tongue-tied. Alex, as ever, was gracious and polite. Kate marveled at his ability to meet people from all walks of life and treat them all alike. When she'd first met him, she'd believed him to be stuffy. Now she understood that Alex operated by some sort of gentleman's code, and that it fit any occasion.

In other words, he had manners. It had never occurred to her how pleasant the world might be if everyone only had good manners.

If—and it was a big if, given the state of her mind and heart—she ever had children, Kate was going to be darned sure she taught them good manners. Good manners could see you through pretty nearly anything. And if, as was almost inevitable in life, you ran into a brutal beast like her father, you could put the manners up, haul out your gun, and simply shoot him.

Her thoughts were so out of the ordinary that Kate burst into laughter. Amused by her spontaneous outburst, Alex said, "What's so funny?"

She shook her head. "Nothing. I was just thinking about my father."

"Is he funny?" Mary Jo asked naively.

Kate shook her head. "Not very."

Alex watched her keenly. "I've never seen you laugh about him before, Kate."

"I guess not." Which made her thoughts veer onto an entirely different path. How wonderful it would be, thought she, to have a dependable and lovable man in one's life. Someone like Alex, who could act as a buffer between one and the world. Until she met Alex, Kate wouldn't have dreamed anything even remotely concerning her father would make her laugh.

But his presence in her life gave her some relief from the hardness of the world. Just knowing he was there, and that she wasn't entirely alone any longer, gave her a little space in which to think absurd thoughts. And laugh.

Was she losing her edge? With a sigh, Kate decided it didn't matter. As soon as Alex left her life, she'd get it back again. It was get the edge back or die, and she'd be damned before she'd allow life to get the better of her.

It sure would be nice to have someone in it with her, though. Too bad it couldn't be Alex.

Kate's brothers found Alex, Mary Jo, and Kate as they left the Ferris wheel area, all three laughing and exhilarated from their ride. "It was such fun!" Mary Jo cried happily.

Alex said, "Glad you liked it," in a satisfied sort of voice.

Kate was about to agree with her two companions when she spotted Walter and Bill. She stopped in her tracks and felt as if her insides had been hit by a blast of arctic air.

Mary Jo had no inkling a problem lurked until Alex stopped walking, too, and by doing so jerked her backward against his side. "What?" she demanded, plainly annoyed.

Alex said nothing, although he nodded at Billy, who nodded back and said, "Good evening, Mr. English."

Kate rushed to her brothers. "What's the matter? Is it Ma?" She knew it was her mother. What else could it be?

But Walter shook his head. "It's Pa. They let him out, and Bill and I don't want you to go home."

"He's out of jail?" Kate's heart took a nosedive that left her feeling sick.

"Yes. The damned, er, blasted police wouldn't keep him."

"Damn," said Alex. He didn't bother to correct himself or apologize.

Mary Jo's eyes grew huge. "Your father? But, what . . . ?"

Since everyone was ignoring her, she stopped speaking. Kate was grateful, not having anticipated cooperation from Mary Jo in the keeping-quiet department. "Darn it, where can I go? Either of you have room?"

"You can't stay with us because we live at that boardinghouse on Fifty-first Street, and it's only for men," Walter said. "But Bill and I have money for a hotel room for you, and we're both taking off work tomorrow. We'll find you another place and move you in."

"You can't do that," Kate said, touched by her brothers' concern and loyalty. "I'll bet I can stay in Madame's booth for a couple of days until I can find a place."

"I'll take care of it," Alex said, breaking into the conversation and stopping it dead.

Walter, who hadn't even looked at Kate's companions until now, wheeled toward Alex, frowning. "Who are you?" His voice held an edge of challenge.

"Calm down, Walter," Bill advised. "This is Mr. English. He's the one who gave me that advice on the Exposition stocks. Be nice to him." He grinned his impish grin, and Kate decided it was past time for her brain to get busy and start working.

With that in mind, and remembering how handy manners could be when properly used, she hastened to say, "I'm sorry, Alex and Mary Jo. These are my brothers. Mary Jo English and Alex English, please allow me to introduce you to my brothers. This is Walter Finney, and—well, you already know Billy, Alex. Mary Jo, this is Billy."

Mary Jo executed a pretty little curtsy, even though she was obviously confused. Manners again. What a blessing they were, to be sure.

Walter and Alex shook hands, and everyone mumbled appropriate greetings. When that was done, Walter turned back to the matter at hand. "I don't want you paying for my sister, Mr. English, if you'll pardon my saying so. It's not your affair."

An awkward pause followed Walter's unfortunate choice of nouns. Alex stepped into it. "Of course, not. I do, however, feel a touch of obligation. After all, your sister and I are—"

Fearing he was going to announce their impending— and fictitious—nuptials, Kate said, "We've become very good friends, and Ma is staying at his farm. I'm sure Alex will have a good suggestion."

Alex looked at her oddly, but said, "The best. I think Kate and Mary Jo can stay in the Congress together. They can share Mary Jo's room. It's big enough for an army, and Kate doesn't take up much room." He winked at Kate.

He was awfully darned full of winks this evening, Kate thought, wishing she'd been allowed to be happy for an entire evening, but knowing she was being ungrateful.

"Oh, yes!" cried Mary Jo, obviously delighted by the prospect of sharing her room with Kate.

"But . . ." Kate glanced from Mary Jo to Alex, and then to her brothers. Truth to tell, she couldn't think of too many reasons not to accept the kind offer.

"Please," begged Mary Jo. "I've never been alone before, and even though I know it's a new hotel and Alex is there, too, it would be such fun to have you stay with me."

Billy grinned. "Sounds good to me."

Walter wasn't so instantly won. "Well . . ."

"I promise you, I won't allow any harm to befall your sister, Mr. Finney."

It seemed strange to Kate that Walter should be addressed as Mr. Finney. The only person she'd ever heard addressed thus was her father, and he didn't deserve the *Mister* part. Manners. They were priceless.

Thus it transpired that Kate Finney spent the night in the absolute pinnacle of elegance for the first time in her life.

Eighteen

Alex liked Walter Finney almost as much as he liked Bill, although Walter was stuffier than his brother. He considered this circumstance—the liking, not the stuffiness—extremely encouraging. There had lurked in the back of his mind a niggling doubt about Kate's siblings. After all, they were the products of a vicious drunkard. It was interesting to Alex that the influence of a good woman like Hazel Finney could be more powerful on the characters of two growing boys than the influence of a bad father.

Or maybe it wasn't. If he followed the thought to its natural conclusion, Alex might have to admit that women were as powerful as men, and he didn't believe it. Or maybe he did. *Nuts,* he said to himself as they reached the door to Mary Jo's room.

"I really wish we could have stopped to get some of my things," Kate muttered when Alex turned the key in the lock and pushed the door open.

"I'll go to your room and pick up some things for you, Kate. I don't want you anywhere near that place until I know what's going on with your father."

She heaved a huge sigh of what Alex pegged as exasperation and annoyance. He braced himself for a verbal lashing in reaction to his usurpation of her apartment and the things therein. He wasn't about to back down, though. It had taken him dashed near thirty years to find her, and he wasn't about to allow her snake-mean drunk of a father to kill her before he married her.

"Let me at least go with you."

"Not on a bet. I don't want you anywhere near your room."

"Darn it, Alex, I don't want you pawing through my things!"

Mary Jo gasped. Alex presumed she'd never heard anyone speak to her big brother like that. Little did she know. Once she got better acquainted with Kate and realized how vulnerable to insult he was, Alex feared for his position of command over his little sister.

"Too bad. I'm not letting you go to your apartment." He spoke with authority, and hoped like mad Kate wouldn't argue with him for the rest of the night.

What she did was turn to Mary Jo and say politely, "Will you please excuse us for a moment, Mary Jo? I need to talk to your brother."

"But . . . You can talk in front of me. I don't mind." Mary Jo smiled sweetly, hoping, Alex knew, to be privy to the argument.

"Um . . ." Kate was flustered, apparently unaccustomed to putting off vexing younger siblings with finesse.

Alex, who knew Mary Jo didn't deserve finesse—after all, she was his little sister—said, "No. We'll speak in my room." And with that, he shut the door in Mary Jo's face. He laughed at her expression, which was one of indignation.

"We don't need to go to your room," Kate said, resisting as he tugged on her arm.

"I'm not about to wage a fight about this in the middle of the Congress hallway. My room's just next door." Because he didn't want her escaping, he kept hold of her arm as he fished for the key in his pocket.

"Oh, for heaven's sake," Kate grumbled.

Alex still didn't trust her not to bolt. As soon as he'd

opened the door, he yanked her inside, kicked the door shut with his heel, and grabbed her into his arms. "Dash it, Kate, I'm not going to expose you to danger." Then he kissed her, as he'd been longing to do all day.

The real reason Kate hadn't wanted to go to Alex's room was her fear of this very thing. She wasn't sure she could control her unwieldy emotions, not to mention her body's cravings, if he kissed her this way in a private room. Darn it all, she knew she couldn't.

Kissing him back with all the love in her heart, Kate gave up resistance. She'd probably never get another chance to do this. She knew the dangers; none knew them better than she. If a baby resulted from this idiocy, so be it. Kate had supported her mother and herself for darned near five years; surely she could support a baby and herself if she had to.

"Dash it, Kate, I want to protect you." Alex was panting when he stopped kissing her.

Fortunately for Kate, he didn't release her from his embrace or she'd have fallen on the floor, having lost control of her leg muscles. Not to mention her brain muscle. She told herself that sarcasm wasn't appropriate at the moment. She couldn't catch her breath, so she didn't say anything.

Alex went on. "We'll be married soon, and then I'll have the right to do so. I'm claiming the right now, as your affianced husband. I'm telling you that you can't return to your apartment again."

Dear God. She couldn't allow him to continue in this vein, or she'd be lost. It would be criminal of her to marry him. Kate couldn't bear the notion of ruining the life of the only man she'd ever loved. Taking her courage and all her strength in her own two hands, she stepped away from him, using a good deal of force to break his hold. She felt cold when his arms fell away. She scooted across the floor and behind a chair as if all the devils in hell were pursuing her.

He looked at her in confusion. "What is it, Kate? I won't dishonor you again. I'm gentleman enough to control myself."

Oh, Lord, he sounded snippy. Kate realized she was trembling and wrapped her arms over her chest, trying to hug the shakes away. It didn't work. Because she didn't want to get distracted from her purpose, she blurted out, "I can't marry you, Alex."

He gaped at her, as if he couldn't credit his ears to have heard her correctly. His eyebrows soared nearly into his hairline, his head jutted forward, and his mouth fell open.

Seizing the moment of silence engendered by his astonishment, Kate rushed on, still hugging herself, trying with all her might to hold herself together. Her voice shook, but she couldn't help that. "I can't marry you. If I married you, I'd be an evil person, and I'm not, darn it, whatever you think!"

He snapped to attention. Now he looked outraged. "I don't—"

But Kate cut him off. "No. Let me speak. Darn it, I'm a girl from the slums, Alex! You can't marry a girl from the slums! What would your friends think? What would your mother think? I'm so far below you in the scheme of things, it's not even funny. I wouldn't have a clue how to act around your fancy friends."

"Kate . . ."

"No!" She wished she could hold her hands out, as she'd seen policemen do when controlling traffic on Chicago's busy streets, but her hands were currently occupied in holding herself together. "Darn it, will you *think* for a minute? If you married me, you'd end up hat-ing me, and I—" Her voice broke on a sob. She forced herself to finish the sentence. "I couldn't stand that."

Alex took two quick steps forward, but she shouted at him. "No! Don't come any closer! Darn it, I love you, Alex. I didn't want to, God knows. I tried not to. I tried to hate you, but it didn't work. When we first met, you thought I was an immoral strumpet. Well, guess what? I'm almost what you thought I was. But I have enough character left to know I'd be ruining you if I allowed you to marry me, and I won't do it. I won't." She swallowed another sob and took a huge breath. "I won't."

He glared at her for almost a minute. Kate was grateful for the space of silence, because she was having a good deal of trouble keeping the boulder of pain out of her throat and her tears contained. She'd learned early that tears served no good purpose to someone like her; she could kick herself for having forgotten this important lesson during the time she'd known Alex.

When she saw that he was drawing in air in order to speak, she braced herself. Her crossed arms were about all that seemed to be keeping her inner turmoil from bursting out and humiliating her, so she kept them tight around her and leaned against the back of the chair to give them added support in their monumental effort. His words took her completely aback, not having been those she'd expected.

"You love me?"

Since he was still frowning and looking as if he'd as soon shoot her as talk to her, Kate only nodded. She'd spoken her piece. If she said anymore, she'd only confuse the matter. She needed to be firm on this issue since it was the most important of her life, except for that of her mother's health, and God had taken that one away from her. Sometimes, even though she knew it was blasphemous to do so, Kate hated God.

Alex had tossed his hat on the chair next to the door

as soon as he'd dragged Kate into his room. He snatched it up again now and slammed it on his head. "Wait here. Don't move. Don't even think about escaping." And with that, he wheeled around, jerked the door open, and marched out as if he were going off to slay a dragon.

Damn the woman. She was the most exasperating, irritating, aggravating, annoying female Alex had ever met in his entire life. He hurtled down the stairs of the Congress Hotel, ignoring the fancy new brass-cage elevator gleaming at him from across the way. He even ignored Frank, his coachman, who was walking across the lobby floor after having stabled the horses and parked the carriage.

Out of the corner of his eye, Alex saw Frank stop and make a move as if to waylay him and ask him if he needed his services, but Alex forged onward. He pushed the huge double doors open as if they'd done him a personal affront, and barreled down the steps of the fancy hotel, charging past the liveried footmen, and bellowing for a cab himself. Damnation, a body would think a gentleman was totally unable to fend for himself in the world, with all these servants hovering around, getting in the way.

Well, Alex English could fend for himself. He'd done so all his life, and he intended to continue doing so. And if he wanted to marry Kate Finney, admittedly a girl from the slums, he'd dashed well do so, whatever she said. Damn her. How dare she think he was unable to make such a momentous decision by himself? How dare she say she'd ruin his life? Nobody was going to ruin his life unless he said they could, and he wasn't going to.

When he gave the cabbie Kate's address, he barked it, daring the man to make a comment on the unsavoriness of Kate's neighborhood or Alex's ability to take care of himself there. Damned fool. They were all damned fools.

"Wait here," he snapped when the cabbie drew up in front of Schneider's Meats.

"Say, mister, this ain't a good neighborhood to be waiting in," the cabbie said. He, too, was evidently in a mood to ignore others, since Alex's bad mood didn't seem to faze him.

"Wait anyhow," Alex commanded. When he turned to look where the cabbie had his attention fixed, he realized a crowd was gathered outside Schneider's. Dash it, what now? Reaching into his pocket and thrusting several dollars at the cabbie, he barked, "Wait."

The cabbie scratched his chin. "Well, hell, mister, I reckon I can wait for five bucks. But I'm pulling down the street a ways. I don't want no trouble."

"Fine." Dismissing the cabbie, Alex forged through the crowd. Spying a woman who looked faintly familiar, he said, "What's going on?" He had a sinking notion that he already knew.

The woman confirmed his suspicion. "Herbert Finney." She spat into the gutter, giving Alex a fair notion what her opinion of Herbert Finney was. "He's looking for his wife and daughter."

"Aw, hell."

Shoving his way through the crowd of onlookers gathered around the door opening onto the stairway to Kate's apartment, Alex took the steps three at a time. He found the man charging around Kate's room, giving Alex a good idea where the expression "bull in a china shop" came from. A few men were attempting to dissuade Finney from smashing Kate's furniture and flinging her belongings around, but Mr. Finney was a powerful man. In his present fury, he reminded Alex of what an enraged grizzly bear might do, although he admittedly had no experience of bears, grizzly or otherwise. He wondered if Finney was drunk and decided it didn't matter.

"Get the hell out of here," Alex roared, causing the good-intentioned men to jump and Herbert Finney to shake his head, this time reminding Alex of an enraged bull. He'd seen enraged bulls a time or two.

"Who the hell are you?" Finney bellowed.

"Never mind who I am. Get out of Miss Finney's apartment, now."

"I'm her father!" Finney shouted, beating his chest, as if he thought siring a child gave him unspecified but unlimited rights to do whatever he chose to do to said child and his or her possessions.

"I don't give a damn who you are." Because he was almost as big as Herbert Finney, and because he was every bit as angry, and because he'd had lots of practice in leveling maddened cattle of various sorts, Alex didn't hesitate, as had Kate's other defenders, to approach her father.

Striding straight up to Finney, he grabbed him by the shirtfront, startling the man into staggering sideways. "Get out of here," Alex commanded once more, lowering his voice into a threatening rumble.

"Lemme go."

Finney attempted to jerk away from Alex, but Alex wouldn't let him. Instead, he hauled him around and shoved him at the door. The other men, who had been watching with varying degrees of approval and amusement, although what they could find amusing in this situation, Alex couldn't fathom, scattered aside so as not to be bumped into by Herbert Finney. Finney rolled toward the door, unable to get his feet to operate properly.

Rage seemed to bring him to attention before he sailed through the door, however, because he grabbed the jamb and stopped his forward momentum. His body, taut with fury, swayed in the doorway until he drew a bead on Alex with his light blue, bleary-looking eyes.

Alex couldn't recall ever having such hatred directed

at him. That was fine with him. He'd never truly hated anyone in his life. Until now. Now, as he gazed upon the man who had ruined Hazel Finney's life and done his best to ruin the lives of his children, Alex hated Herbert Finney absolutely. Because this was so, and because Finney had once again violated Kate's life, he actually found himself gesturing the man to come forward and fight him. He wanted to feel his fists crunching against that ugly jaw.

"Damn you," Finney muttered in a low, threatening voice. "Damn you."

"Come on," Alex challenged. "Face me like a man. I'm bigger than your daughter. I suppose you only beat up on women, don't you?" Alex then did something he'd never done in his entire adult life. He spat on the floor of Kate's apartment. "You don't like to fight people who can fight back, do you? You're a coward and a bastard, aren't you?"

Finney's eyes opened so wide in shock and wrath that Alex could see the individual red veins standing out against the yellowed whites. "What are you saying to me?" Finney's eyes thinned to mean-tempered slits. "Who the hell are you, you son of a bitch?"

And with that, he heaved himself away from the door frame and lumbered at Alex. The man was huge. Alex suspected that when Finney did work, he worked at hard manual labor because his hugeness didn't look as if it were composed of excess fat. That being the case, he braced himself on wide-apart feet, knees loose, thigh muscles tight, and prepared to do battle. He was more than ready.

Finney's arms didn't windmill violently. He approached Alex like a trained boxer, his bulging arms supporting fists the size of a side of mutton. But he was older than Alex and, Alex expected, not completely sober.

Alex dodged Finney's first blow with agility and landed a quick jab to the man's stomach, which was almost as hard as Alex's own. That surprised him, but didn't make him lose his concentration.

Finney roared like a lion and turned around. In his ire, his face had turned a deep red. He reminded Alex of street boxers he'd seen once or twice, and it flashed through his head that Mr. Finney might even have been one of those men, who earned drinking money by daring other men to bouts of fisticuffs. The notion didn't frighten Alex.

"Come on," he taunted. "Come and try to take on a man for a change, instead of a woman. I know you're used to beating up on women, but give it a try. Come on, *Mister* Finney."

Another roar propelled Finney away from Kate's window at Alex. Alex had been hoping for this opportunity. The older man was clumsy in his fury, and Alex had plenty of time to draw his right arm back and deliver a punch that crunched like ice breaking up on Lake Michigan. Finney's arms windmilled this time, as he staggered backward.

It was only when Alex realized the other man was unable to stop himself that he lurched after him, reaching out to grab some piece of Finney's clothing or an arm or a leg. He felt the other men, who'd clumped up to watch the excitement, rushing forward, but didn't see them.

What he saw seemed almost as if it had been choreographed. Finney staggered across Kate's floor, his heels bumping against things he'd previously tossed about in his anger. But there wasn't anything to stop him. When he hit the window, his weight didn't stop him, either.

Alex couldn't shut his eyes. He saw and heard everything. He saw the expression of terror cross Finney's face when he realized he'd hit the window. He heard the loud smash and crunch of glass as the pane shattered. He saw blood spurt out onto the floor and walls as shards of splintered glass speared Finney's flesh. He saw Finney's mouth open in horror, and he heard the shriek of terror. And then he saw Herbert Finney disappear out the window.

A tinkle and smash of glass hitting the street below preceded the muffled crunch of Finney's body landing on top of it. The cry they'd all heard as he fell ended abruptly. Alex stood in a void of darkness and silence and stared at the empty space where once a window had been. It seemed like eons that he stood there, but it couldn't have been.

All at once, someone bumped him from behind. He felt hands on his shoulders and his arms. People were clapping him on the back. He blinked and understood through some automatic process over which he had no control that he had responsibilities to fulfill regarding this—this—

God, there was a lot of blood. Where had it all come from? Surely, Herbert Finney couldn't have bled that much. Unless the broken glass had severed an artery. Alex shook himself.

Good God, he'd killed Kate's father. Alex shook his head hard and began to make sense of the words tumbling out of people's mouths and assaulting his eardrums.

"That's the best right—"

"Damn, I think—"

"Good job!"

"Congratulations! That's the best—"

"Thank God somebody finally—"

He shook his whole body then, knowing he had to suppress his emotions and take charge. "Uh . . . Somebody'd better run and get a policeman." His head felt fuzzy. He knew there must be something else that needed to be done. Reaching deep within himself, he added, "And a doctor. Somebody'd better fetch a doctor."

"A doctor ain't going to help him this time," said a grinning man.

"I sure as hell hope not," said another.

Alex glanced at his companions, puzzled. Why were they all so damned happy? Again, he shook his head, wishing the fog inside it would clear. "Um, he doesn't need a doctor?" That meant he was dead.

But the man who'd rebuffed the doctor idea only grinned harder. "I don't know. Let's go see."

And Alex felt himself being tugged along, out through Kate's door, and down the miserable, skinny, dirty, smelly staircase from Kate's apartment to the street below. An even larger crowd had accumulated since he'd gone up those stairs. How long ago had it been? Not long. Not more than ten minutes. Good Gad, but it didn't take long to kill a man, did it?

He commanded himself not to think like that. Finney was probably still breathing. Certainly, a fall out of a— He looked up. Kate's apartment was on the second floor. How far a fall would that have been? Sixty feet? A hundred? And there had been all that blood. Oh, Lord.

The crowd seemed to melt before him. Alex heard buzzing in his ears, as the people whispered to each other. He imagined some of them pointing him out as the perpetrator of the villainy.

Or was it villainy? For all Alex knew, there wasn't a soul alive who'd mourn the passing of Herbert Finney, if he was dead.

And if that wasn't a sad commentary on a man's life, he didn't know what was. By this time he'd made it to the body. He glanced down and instantly averted his gaze. Herbert Finney was dead. Nobody could lie like that, with his head twisted at that crazy angle, and not be dead.

A shudder passed through him, and it was all Alex could do not to rub his hands over his face. Considering that such a gesture would denote weakness, he kept his arms at his sides, stepped away from the body, and waited.

He didn't know how long he stood there, not quite sure what to do and hoping other people were doing it

without him. At last, somebody came up with a uniformed policeman in tow. The officer took in the
situation as if such things happened every day of his
week, asked a few questions, received a few answers, then
walked up to Alex, his expression sober.

"I guess you'd best come with me, sir," the policeman
said.

Alex could only be glad his elegantly tailored suit and
gentlemanly air led the policeman to refrain from clasping manacles around his wrists.

Still and all, this was it. He, Alex English, was going to
be arrested and tried for murder. Good Gad. He could
hardly believe such a thing could happen to him. And
it had all come about because he'd taken pity on Kate
Finney.

Kate didn't know what to do. Alex had been gone for
what seemed like hours, and she was not merely frustrated and sad, but was getting angrier by the second.

Mary Jo, naturally, hadn't waited demurely in her
room as her brother had told her to do. It wasn't more
than fifteen minutes after Alex had run out on her that
Kate heard his sister's discreet tap on the door. Feeling
abandoned and mistreated, she stamped to the door
and flung it open. "Yes?" The word came out more tartly
than she'd intended it to, but she didn't regret it. As far
as Kate was concerned, it was past time Mary Jo learned
a few hard lessons about life.

Alex's sister blinked at Kate and stammered, "Um,
where's Alex?"

Throwing the door wide, Kate walked back into the
room, leaving Mary Jo to follow or not, as she wished.
"Beats me. He tore out of here a few minutes ago. I guess
he's headed to my apartment to get my things."

"Oh." Stepping uncertainly into her brother's room,

Mary Jo asked, "Um, are you coming back to my room, Kate?"

Kate flopped into the chair she'd recently vacated. She didn't feel like being badgered by Alex English's kid sister. Still, she didn't suppose Mary Jo deserved out-and-out rudeness just because she was an annoyingly young and gullible young lady. If the world were a just place, Kate Finney herself probably would have been gullible. "Alex told me to wait here for him. I guess I will."

"Oh." Still looking uncertain, Mary Jo eyed her brother's room.

Kate was pleased that she and Alex had not been indiscreet and that his room remained as the hotel maids had left it earlier in the day. It would have been embarrassing had Mary Jo seen any dropped items of clothing scattered about. She waved a hand. "Want to sit down?" She didn't want her to. She wanted her to go away and leave her to fume and fuss on her own. Darn Alex, anyhow.

"Um, I guess I'll go back to our room and change into my night things," Mary Jo said after thinking about it.

"All right." *Thank God, thank God.* "I'll wait here a little while. Until Alex brings my stuff to the hotel." Unless, of course, he was so mad at her for declining to marry him that he stayed away all night. Kate didn't know what she'd do then. Sleep in her clothes, she reckoned, and go to work wrinkled. With a sigh, she saw Mary Jo to the door, then went back to the chair and sat some more.

Unaccustomed to having nothing with which to occupy her hands and her mind, Kate soon rose from the chair and scoured the room for something to read. She found a novel that Alex had stashed in the night table drawer: *A Connecticut Yankee In King Arthur's Court,* by Mark Twain, and decided it would have to do.

She'd read as far as the fifth chapter when a knock came on Alex's door. Startled, Kate slammed the book shut and lost her place. "Nuts," she muttered as she rose from the chair and went to the door. Because she couldn't conceive of Alex knocking on his own hotel door, and because she'd learned caution in a hard school, she leaned toward the crack between the door and the wall and said, "Who is it?"

"It's me, Kate," Mary Jo answered. "Your brothers are here."

"My brothers? Billy? Walter?"

"Open up, Kate," came Walter's voice. He sounded worried. "Something's happened."

Oh, God. Fearing the worst—that her mother had died—Kate flung the door open. Sure enough, her brothers stood there, flanking Mary Jo, whose face still appeared flushed from sleep.

"They asked at the desk for my room," Mary Jo explained. "I said you were waiting for Alex in his room."

"Yes," Walter said in patent disapproval. "But we can discuss that later. Right now, we need to talk about something even worse."

Even worse than what? Kate didn't ask, knowing what her brother meant. He didn't approve of Kate's residence in a single gentleman's room, no matter how innocent the reason, and even if the young gentleman wasn't there. Kate stepped aside, allowing all three people entry. "What's wrong?"

"You'd better sit down, Kate," Billy said. Always more sympathetic than his older brother, Billy smiled at Kate in understanding.

She appreciated him a lot. Nevertheless, she declined his invitation. "I don't have to sit down. Is it Ma?"

Both of her brothers shook their heads. "It's Pa," said Billy.

In spite of herself and her unwillingness to be thought to be doing anyone else's bidding, Kate sank into her chair. "What about Pa?" The only thing she could think of that would have put the serious expressions on her brothers' faces was that Pa had done something horrid. Like hurting Alex. Her heart began aching like a sore tooth.

Walter had been standing beside the bed as if checking to make sure no one had been doing anything unsavory on it. With his back still to Kate, he said stiffly, "He's dead."

Kate's brain executed a twirl of confusion. "Um . . . I beg your pardon?" If their father was dead, why were the boys looking so worried? Kate would have expected them to be dancing in the streets.

Billy heaved a gigantic sigh. "It's Alex," he said, fuddling Kate the more.

"Alex? I thought you said it was Pa?"

Walter turned around. "It's both of them. The police are questioning Alex about Pa's death. Evidently, they were fighting, and Pa fell out the window of your apartment."

Mary Jo gasped.

So did Kate.

"So," Billy said, taking over from his older brother, "I think it would be a good idea for you to come down to the police station with us. We just left there. Sol Schneider's the one who fetched us. Micky O'Brien called on him as soon as it happened."

Kate was having a hard time making heads or tails of this story. "But what was Pa doing in my apartment?"

"Tearing it up, apparently," Walter said drily. "You know Pa."

"Yeah," said Kate, pushing herself up from her chair. "I know Pa, more's the pity."

"Well, I guess none of us will have to worry about him any longer," Billy said brightly, as if he were trying to cheer up his siblings.

Mary Jo gasped again and clutched her dressing gown at her throat. Sliding her a look, Kate understood why she'd gasped. Innocent little Mary Jo couldn't conceive of anyone being pleased about a parent's passing. Which just went to show one more time how their lives differed in every single particular.

Because she felt she owed at least a partial explanation to this child, this sister of the man she loved, Kate went over to her and put a hand on her arm. "I'm sorry, Mary Jo. I guess I'll have to go with my brothers. We'll be back as soon as possible."

"But what about Alex?" Mary Jo sounded panicky.

"I guess he's at the police station." Kate slid a glance at her brothers, both of whom nodded. "Yes. He's at the police station. I'll—we'll—" They'd what? Kate had no idea. Feeling helpless, she looked to her brothers for assistance.

"I'm sure it'll be all right, Miss English," said Walter politely. "I'm sure it was all our father's fault, and that any misunderstandings can be cleared up presently."

"Absolutely," Kate agreed with more force than she felt. She couldn't even conceive of Alex doing something wrong, but anything having to do with her father must be suspect.

"Our father's a no-good buzzard," Billy said, grinning as he did so. "And Alex is a good guy. I'm sure there's not going to be a problem."

Kate wished she shared her lighthearted younger brother's optimism. "Right. I'll walk you back to your room, Mary Jo. Just wait there, and I'll be back as soon as possible."

"Well, I really think I ought to go with you," Mary Jo said, sounding as if she was going to be stubborn about it. "After all, we're talking about my brother, too, don't forget."

Kate eyed her without favor. Her nerves were crackling like fat over an open fire, and she didn't want to have to fuss with a spoiled, adolescent rich girl right now. "Listen, Mary Jo. My father just died, and I want to find out what happened. I don't want to wait for you to get dressed. We'll be back as soon as possible, bringing Alex with us." She prayed she hadn't just lied.

But Mary Jo was having none of it. She said, "I'm going with you. It will only take a few minutes for me to dress. Don't go without me. Alex will be furious if you leave me here alone."

Kate knew that was only one more argument and that it probably held no weight, but the notion of Alex getting mad at her didn't appeal. "Oh, for heaven's sake! All right, I'll help you. But if you dawdle, I'm leaving without you."

Kate hustled Mary Jo to her room and threw clothes at her. She blessed her brothers for not scolding her about being impatient with the girl. Both Walter and Billy were inclined to get chivalrous at inconvenient times, and Kate didn't feel like being scolded any more than she felt like waiting.

Before they left Mary Jo's room, Kate plucked up her own hat and shawl and threw them on, willy-nilly. Then the Finney siblings and Mary Jo English hurried out of the hotel, into the cab Walter and Billy had waiting, and rattled on to the police station.

Kate, who had no decent gloves to wear, chewed on her nails all the way there. Mary Jo looked as if nothing this exciting had ever happened to her, and it was all Kate could do not to shout at her.

Nineteen

The police station was a depressing and dingy place. And it smelled bad. Alex's nose wrinkled at the aroma, which reminded him of despair: old sweat, carbolic, and vomit. *Drunks,* he deduced, and was glad he'd never taken to drink. A pang of regret that his beloved Kate had grown up in such difficult circumstances smote him.

Kate. He'd like to lay her over his lap and paddle her luscious rump for being so idiotic and obstinate. Imagine, refusing to marry him because she thought she'd ruin his life. As if she had the power to do that.

Hell's bells, he'd managed to ruin his life all on his own, by killing Kate's dipsomaniacal, revenge-obsessed father. Although what Mr. Finney thought he needed to be avenged for still eluded Alex.

With a sigh, he decided he'd better pay attention to the questions being asked of him.

"So, you're saying Mr. Finney was already in the room when you got there?" A bushy-mustachioed police sergeant was asking the questions, and a younger policeman, who seemed to be in awe both of his sergeant and of Alex, was taking notes.

The relative courtesy of his inquisitors led Alex to believe that he was being treated better than most of the people who ended up being taken to the police station on suspicion of murder. "Yes."

"And you say there were other people there, too? Witnesses, that is to say?"

"A crowd had gathered there, yes, and some of the men were trying to get him out of the room." Alex knew good and well that other policemen had questioned the bystanders, but he didn't point this out to the sergeant, sensing the man would react negatively to such statements from him.

"And the room is his daughter's place of residence. Is that correct? Her apartment, that is to say?" Mustache squinted at Alex, as if he were trying to catch him in a fib.

"Right. I'd gone there to get some things for her to wear, because she's staying with my sister at the Congress Hotel."

The policeman seated next to the sergeant allowed his eyebrows to lift. Alex turned a quelling stare upon him, and the young man's eyebrows behaved again at once. Good thing, too. "Miss Finney and I," said Alex in a voice as lethal as he could make it, "are engaged to be married."

"Is that so?"

The sergeant probably could have looked more surprised, but Alex doubted it happened often. He was pretty certain the other policeman was as astounded as he'd ever been.

"Yes," he said. "That is so." His tone dared either man to say anything about his proposed marital plans.

"I see." The sergeant cleared his throat. "Do you believe you said anything to provoke the man, Mr. English?"

Alex snorted. "He was already provoked. He was behaving like I've seen infuriated bulls behave. He was throwing Miss Finney's belongings everywhere. I'm surprised he didn't paw the ground."

The sergeant frowned, but the younger policeman grinned. He didn't look up, apparently not wanting to risk his superior's disfavor, and he kept writing.

Alex went on. "Her brothers had warned us that their

father had been released from jail, and we were worried for her safety and that of their mother."

"Her mother?" Mustache squinted at Alex.

"Yes. Mrs. Finney is at present staying at my farm with my own mother." There. That ought to give both men pause.

"I see." The sergeant's squint thinned further, and Alex decided to become more aggressive.

"We took her there because her health is bad and her husband is a menace." This time he directed his killing stare at the sergeant. "The police evidently don't believe in guaranteeing the safety of Chicago's citizens unless the citizens have lots of money, and the Finney ladies don't."

The sergeant cleared his throat, stroked his mustache, and tried to appear dignified. "Now, Mr. English, that's not so. It may seem so to some, but it's not."

"Right," said Alex in clear disbelief.

The sergeant chose not to argue, and went back to the matter under investigation. "So, would you say Finney was drunk?"

Alex shrugged. "I don't know. I understand that's his standard of behavior. He drinks and then beats up his wife and children."

"Yes," muttered the sergeant, as if he didn't want to admit it. "We're familiar with Finney at the station. *Too* familiar with him for my comfort."

Alex grunted.

"Guess we won't be troubled by him again, though, Sarge," said his younger, more guileless companion cheerfully. The sergeant glowered at him, and the young man sobered and turned his attention back to his notebook.

"But you took a swing at him?" The sergeant looked as though he'd finally asked the most important question in this entire interrogation, the one he'd been building up to and one from which he expected to achieve results.

"He swung at me first," Alex said promptly. "There

were lots of witnesses. I assume other police officials have already questioned them."

"Yes, well . . ." The sergeant cleared his throat again. "Right now we're talking to you, Mr. English."

"Right." Alex would have rolled his eyes, but he didn't want to aggravate his slow-witted inquisitor.

"So, in essence, what you're telling me is that this whole thing was an accident," the sergeant said. He directed a scowl at his associate, who licked the point of his pencil and wrote something else in his notebook.

"I guess," said Alex. "He challenged me when I told him to get out of Miss Finney's room. He was tearing it up. I don't know if he was looking for something in particular, or if he only wanted to destroy her things, but I suspect the latter. From what I've heard of him, he was a resentful, belligerent bully, and he didn't like the fact that Miss Finney had taken the care of her family unto herself." There. Let the police argue about *that*, if they dared. "He charged at me, I dodged, then he swung, I hit him, he staggered back, and went out the window." And there was all that blood. Alex suppressed a shudder when he remembered that arcing rainbow of blood.

"Yes. So others have said." The sergeant and the other policeman exchanged a glance.

A knock came at the door of the interrogation room in which Alex had been taken. The younger policeman rose and went to the door. Alex heard another officer standing outside the room say, "It's the Finneys and Mr. English's sister. Come to see the sarge and the prisoner."

"I'm not a prisoner," said Alex, feeling cranky. Damnation, what were Kate and Mary Jo doing here?

"Of course not," said the sergeant. He'd risen and gone to the door and now frowned at the policeman there, who cowered back.

"Sorry, sir."

As he faded away, Kate burst into the room, right

smack past the sergeant, who was taken aback. She was followed by Mary Jo, Walter, and Bill, who also ignored the sergeant, whose dignity suffered as a result, and who scowled after them.

"Alex!"

Ignoring the policemen, his sister, and both Finney boys, Alex surged up from his chair and caught Kate in his arms. "God, Kate, I'm so sorry about all this."

When she hugged him hard and didn't seem inclined to let him go, Alex mentally revised his statement. If killing her father had this effect on his darling Kate, he wasn't sorry at all.

He'd never say so.

"It's not your fault, Alex. I know it wasn't your fault."

"True. Let's hope the police see it your way."

"They will." And with that, Kate disentangled herself from Alex's embrace and turned on the sergeant like a whirlwind. Alex hadn't seen her in her full-fledged Kate-from-the-streets, just-let-me-get-at-him mode since shortly after they'd met. He watched with interest and a fair degree of amusement.

"Sergeant Maguire, you know darned well that Alex didn't do anything wrong. You've arrested my father how many times for being drunk and disorderly? And how often have you had to chase him out of our house after he hit my mother? And how *dare* you keep Alex imprisoned in this filthy police station? Darn it, you let my father out time and time again when he'd almost killed people. You ought to give Alex a medal for finally ridding the world of some bad rubbish!"

Since Mary Jo had gasped in horror and astonishment shortly after Kate began her tirade, Alex decided to go to his sister's side. He frowned at her to let her know he wouldn't countenance any interference from her. Besides, this was classic Kate, and he loved her for it.

"Oh, for Pete's . . ." Walter muttered as he and Billy hurried to flank their sister.

It looked to Alex as if Walter and Bill weren't so enamored of their sister's assertive tendencies. Walter tried to take her by the arm, but she shook him off. "Kate," he said, a placating ring to his voice.

Placation wouldn't work; Alex would bet money on it. He watched as Bill tried it anyhow. "Kate . . ."

"Leave me alone!" She shot her brothers such a vicious glower that they both backed up a couple of paces. Turning back to the beleaguered sergeant, she poked him in the chest with her finger. "You know good and well that my father was a worthless piece of—" casting a quick glance at Mary Jo, Kate went on, using words Alex imagined she'd edited on the spot—"junk. He was a no-good drunk, and from what my neighbors have told me when we were coming in here, he was tearing my place apart. Alex was defending me, which is a darned sight more than any of *you* people have ever done."

"Now, Miss Kate, that's not—"

"It is, too, true, and you know it!"

Her cheeks had taken on a pure-fury crimson flush. To Alex, she was the most beautiful, desirable woman in the world. Since he was pretty sure the sergeant didn't agree with him, he felt it would be prudent to interfere before Kate got arrested for annoying an officer of the law. "It's all right, Kate. The sergeant was only asking a few questions."

She whirled around again and faced him, her chest heaving and her body trembling. "Are you sure, Alex? Because I won't allow you to suffer for my father's sake. Or mine. Darn it, you've been so good to us. They can't possibly believe you killed him for no reason, can they?"

"Actually, I didn't kill him at all. It was an accident."

"Oh." She appeared disappointed for no more than an instant. "Well, then, it's even more ridiculous that they're holding you in this filthy hole! They aren't going to try to pin a murder charge on you when it was an accident, are they?"

"Of course not," Sergeant Maguire muttered. When Kate gave him a withering scowl, he spoke no more.

Alex said, "I don't know how they could. There were too many witnesses to what really happened."

"Even if there weren't witnesses," Kate said firmly, sending another glower at the sergeant, "they couldn't actually believe it. Herbert Finney was an animal."

Mary Jo pressed a hand over her mouth. Her eyes were bulging in shock and disbelief. Alex patted her on the shoulder, but spoke to Kate. "But if anybody'd had that much sense, you wouldn't be here, Kate." He grinned, hoping he wouldn't further rile her, but unable to help himself.

"As if that mattered," Kate grumbled. With lowering brows, she spoke again to the sergeant. "So, are you planning to keep Mr. English here all night, or are you going to pin a medal on him and let him go?"

Sergeant Maguire sighed heavily. "He can leave, I guess." Turning to Alex, he said, "Will you be staying at the Congress Hotel, Mr. English?"

"Yes."

"If we have any more questions, we'll be in touch with you there."

"Good enough."

"You'll have to sign a written statement." The sergeant looked as if he didn't approve of having the subject of his inquiries leave before he told him he could go, but didn't quite dare protest.

Alex wondered if it was his good reputation or Kate's hellish disposition that had swayed the sergeant. He thought he knew. "That's fine." He experienced a twist of cynicism. If he were a poor man, the sergeant would doubtless have used force to detain him. Policemen didn't dare beat up on rich men.

Alex remained polite in spite of everything. Breeding showed, he told himself. "Thank you, Sergeant."

Still overtly unhappy about losing control, Sergeant Maguire said stiffly, "This is most irregular, sir. Under the circumstances, however . . ." He guided a look of disapprobation to Alex's sister and Kate's brothers.

"I can't tell you any more than I've already told you, Sergeant. Mr. Finney went backward through the window after I punched him. He tried to hit me first. End of story."

"Hmmm," said Sergeant Maguire, and said no more.

He probably didn't dare, which added one more bit of unfairness to the pile of them Alex had gathered since he'd first met Kate. If Alex were poor, he'd have been charged with manslaughter, at least, by this time, even if the charges had to be dropped later.

But Alex could think about the unfairness of life all he wanted later. Right now, there were more important things to attend to, the primary one being to explain himself to Kate and her brothers. He knew the Finney children detested their father. It seemed vital to Alex, perhaps for that very reason, that they know exactly what had happened in that dismal little room over the dismal little butcher shop.

While he couldn't even imagine having a father like Kate's, and would have loathed him if he'd been so unfortunate, he also knew that the death of a parent must be a blow no matter what. That being the case, he took Kate by one arm and his sister by the other, and nodded at the Finney boys. "Let's get out of here. We need to talk." Sending a significant glance his sister's way, he added, "Without any nosy Parkers listening in."

"I'm not a nosy Parker!" Mary Jo cried, stung.

"Right. But I'm dropping you off at your room anyway.

I guess we can hold a conference in my room or in the hotel restaurant."

Walter pulled out a pocket watch that was nowhere near as fine as Alex's and squinted at it as they exited the police station. "I don't suppose there's a restaurant open in the entire city of Chicago at the moment. It's almost three in the morning."

"Right. My hotel room it is, then."

"What about my apartment?"

Alex realized Kate still trembled, as if the emotions trapped inside her were seething and roiling and trying to get out. He squeezed her arm. "Do you want to see it? It's—" He remembered the blood splattered on the floor and on the wall beside the window. He'd been thinking a lot about that blood. A shard of broken window glass must have severed an artery for there to have been so much of it. He didn't want Kate to see it. "I think there will be time to see it tomorrow."

Walter caught his eye and shook his head. Alex felt curiously akin to Kate's older brother in that instant, and he appreciated Walter for wanting to spare his sister the sight of her father's blood. Walter said, "Mrs. Schneider and Mrs. Brewster are cleaning it up, Kate. Mr. Schneider's going to hammer a board over the window until the glazier comes to replace the glass. You don't want to see your room now."

"Right," said Bill, and shuddered involuntarily. "It's—it's a mess."

Kate stopped walking suddenly, pulling Alex up short. "Why?" Her gaze flew between her brothers and Alex. "Why don't you want me to see it? I thought he just threw things around and then went out the window and fell to the ground. Is there anything else? *Tell* me, darn it!"

Walter looked at her blankly. Bill shuffled his feet. Mary Jo didn't know what was going on, and stared at the knowledgeable parties with fascination. Alex knew it was up to him. He expelled a gust of breath. "There was some blood, Kate."

"Blood? Like a bloody nose or something?" She gave a shaky laugh. "Wouldn't be the first time."

"It was more than that."

Kate stared at Alex, demand plain to read in her blue, blue eyes, and Alex gave up. What the hell. She'd lived through hell already. What was a little blood? "I think maybe a piece of glass severed an artery when he hit the window. Might have been in his throat or his arm or anywhere. I know I didn't look hard at the body. But blood sprayed everywhere inside your room." There. He'd told her.

Her body went still. Not a tremble shook her. "I see." She nodded. "I see."

Walter kicked at the wall outside the police station. "It was a mess, Kate. You don't need to see it. It's being taken care of."

She nodded again. "Was he drunk?"

That was enough for Alex. Roughly, he tugged her into a walk again. "We're going to talk all about it as soon as I get my sister stowed. Until then, let's just be glad it's over. We're going to have to tell your mother, too, and we'll talk about that at the same time."

"Right." Kate walked like an automaton to the carriage Walter and Bill had waiting. It was crowded, but they all fit. They were as still as statues as the carriage rattled them back to the Congress Hotel.

"I don't know why I can't sit in," Mary Jo grumbled. "I won't say anything or get in the way."

"Stop being a pain in the neck," her fond brother advised. "You're going to go to your hotel room and stay there."

Kate blessed him for it. She really liked Mary Jo, sort

of, but she didn't feel like putting up with her right now. "I'm sure we won't be long, Mary Jo. I'll have to borrow a nightgown, I guess." She tried to shake off the exhaustion threatening to smother her. In truth, she didn't care about nightgowns or day gowns or anything else. She only wanted to sleep.

"Are you ready, Kate?"

Alex's voice was all solicitude and it made Kate want to cry, which was stupid and irrational. She revised her emotions and decided she actually wanted to scream at herself and stamp her feet. And then sleep. "Yeah. I'm ready." She sighed down to her toes.

"Walter and Bill are waiting for us. I had them pick up some sandwiches from the kitchen."

Kate perked up slightly. "You mean somebody's still awake in the kitchen at this hour?"

"It's a brand-new, top-of-the-line hotel, Kate. They're there to offer their services for money, and I have money."

His sister appeared shocked by this audacious statement, which she probably took as a boastful one. Kate knew better by this time and only gave him a wry grin. "Must be nice."

Alex was firm but gentle when he deposited his sister in her room. Mary Jo stuck out her tongue at him, but he only closed the door in her face.

"It is. Now come along with me. I think they got some tea and coffee, too."

"Tea," Kate mused. "I could use a cup of tea."

"Good." He took her arm and tugged. "Then come with me."

She did. As Alex had told her, Walter and Bill awaited them in Alex's room. She tried to smile at her brothers, but it was a feeble effort. Billy popped up from the chair he'd been holding down.

"Come over here, Kate. I've got a cup of tea ready for you, just the way you like it."

Kate doubted it. She took nothing in her tea, and Billy always used milk and sugar. She eyed the teacup and saucer he held out to her. Sure enough, the cup was filled to the brim with tea laced with milk and, she had no doubt, liberally dosed with sugar. She was about to protest when Alex thwarted her.

"I told him to give you sugar and cream, Kate. Hot sweet tea's good for shock."

She felt her shoulders slump as her gaze went from the teacup to Alex. "You think I'm in shock?"

"If you're not, you're inhuman." Alex didn't sound as if he cared a whole lot. He took a cup of coffee from Walter, who was manning the coffeepot. "Thanks."

Walter only nodded and gulped from his own cup. "Sit down and quit fighting, Kate. We all need to talk about what's happened and what we need to do now."

Before she even knew what was happening, Kate felt tears well up in her eyes. Because she'd slit her wrists before she'd cry in front of these three men, she swallowed them and sat with a flounce intended to demonstrate her state of bravado and indignation. Somehow or other during this performance, she managed not to spill her tea.

"Exactly," agreed Alex. "And what I propose is this. I had expected that Kate and I would marry in a few months in order to allow for all the folderol usually attendant upon such ceremonies, but after this night's work, I think we'd best speed up the process."

"What?" Kate cried, all inclination to weep having vanished.

"Good idea," said Walter, sounding judicious and ignoring his sister.

"Right. It would be best to do it soon," said his brother, likewise ignoring his sister. "Then Katie won't have to worry about where she'll be living and so forth, and *we* won't have to worry about *her.*" Bill turned his head and grinned at his sister in a manner intended to let her know how much fun he thought it was to override her in every particular.

Kate was so offended, she couldn't even find words to fling at him.

"Glad we agree," said Alex complacently. "I recommend we hold the ceremony at the farm in a couple of weeks. That way your mother won't have that tiring trip back to Chicago. Besides"—he winked at Kate's brothers—"my mother and yours will have a grand time with the decorations and so forth."

Walter nodded. "Women love that sort of thing."

"Yeah," said Billy. "They seem to, all right."

This was too much for Kate's independent soul. She'd been the mainstay of her family for too many years to put up with having her fate decided by three interfering men in this outrageous way. She stood up with even more of a flounce than she'd sat. "Now you all wait just a minute here! I'll have you know that I have absolutely no intention of marrying—"

An imperative knock came at Alex's hotel room door, cutting Kate off in mid tirade. All four of the room's inhabitants turned abruptly and stared at the door.

Alex moved first. With a jerk, he launched himself out of his chair and headed to the door. "If that's my interfering sister, I'll—" He flung the door wide and blinked at the uniformed messenger standing there, holding out a tray upon which lay a yellow envelope.

"Telegram for Mr. Alex English," the bellboy said. Then, taking in Alex's furious face, he gulped and braced himself.

But Alex, as Kate might have told the boy had she been asked, wasn't one to relieve his anger on innocent strangers. At once his expression softened, although he still appeared rather worried. Reaching into his pocket, he withdrew some coins and exchanged them for the telegram on the boy's tray. Relieved, the boy smiled and hot-footed it away from Alex's door.

Kate, Walter, and Bill, as if propelled by the same force of nature, all rose from their seats. Kate's heart, which had taken a real beating lately, began hammering out a funeral dirge. Telegrams *always* meant bad news.

Turning at the door and shutting it absently behind him, Alex tore open the envelope and took out the message. He read it, looked up at his guests, then reread it.

Kate bit her lower lip. It was about Ma. It had to be about Ma.

Alex cleared his throat. "Um, it's about your mother."

Kate pressed a fist to her mouth.

"Ma?" Billy sounded like a little boy.

Walter said nothing.

"It's from my mother. It says, 'Mrs. Finney has taken a turn for the worse. Dr. Conners recommends her family come at once.'" Alex looked up from the telegram, straight at Kate, as if he knew what she wanted to know. "My mother sent one of the farm boys to Centreville on our fastest horse, where the telegram was dispatched. The message is no more than an hour old, Kate."

"I'll have to make arrangements at work." Walter turned to his younger brother. "You go with Katie, Bill. I'll clear your absence with Mr. Schneider."

Kate heard Billy answer Walter, and she turned to say she'd go with Bill to the English farm. A strange, muted roaring in her ears interfered with the thought, and she didn't get her statement out. The last thing she heard was Alex's sharp, "Kate!" Then she heard no more.

Kate awoke in Alex's arms. He held her cradled gently, and he sat in one of the chairs in his room. Billy hovered over her. When she rubbed her eyes and glanced around the room, she didn't see Walter.

"She's awake!" Bill sounded unutterably relieved, which seemed rather an overreaction to Kate, mainly because she had no idea why he was reacting at all.

"Kate." Alex's gentle murmur seemed to draw Kate closer to him.

"What . . ." What, what? Oh, yes, she remembered. "What happened?"

"You fainted," Alex crooned. "My dear, darling Kate. You actually fainted."

"I never faint," Kate declared stoutly. She struggled to release herself from Alex's arms, although she didn't really want to.

"Nuts," crooned her beloved. "You've fainted twice in the short time I've known you."

"I have?" Bother. There went that illusion of strength and determination. Then she remembered the telegram and her heart gave a huge, lurching spasm. She sat up in spite of Alex's attempts at restraint. "What about Ma?"

"Walter's gone to send a telegram back to Mr. English's farm, Kate," Billy said. He was such a nice boy. Kate really loved her little brother. And her big brother. "Ma's taken a bad turn. Mr. English is driving us all out there tomorrow. He's sending a telegram to the preacher from his church, too. You two can be married in front of Ma, Katie, as soon as it can be arranged. That will make her happy."

"Married?" What was all this talk about marriage? She couldn't marry Alex. She'd ruin his life, for heaven's sake.

"Married," Alex said firmly, as if he intended to consider no more arguments from her.

"But we can't get married, Alex." She felt feeble, as if all the strength in her body had fled sometime between this morning and right now. "I can't allow you to make that sacrifice."

"Sacrifice?" Bill looked honestly bemused.

Alex gave him a wry glance. "She thinks she'll be ruining my life if she marries me, because I have more money than she does."

"That's not the reason, and you know it, darn it!"

Bill eyed his sister with disfavor. "Shoot, Katie, that's the stupidest reason I've ever heard. If any two people were made for each other, it's you and Alex."

Kate's mouth fell open.

Alex grinned at Kate's brother. "Exactly. My thinking to the last degree. I knew you were a smart man from the moment we met, Bill Finney."

"Likewise," said Kate's brother, who looked to Kate like Mr. Carroll's Cheshire Cat in full meow.

"Besides," Alex said in that reasonable tone Kate hated, "it will make your mother happy to see you and me attached permanently. She can go to her grave with the full knowledge that her children will be cared for."

It was absolutely the only argument Kate would have accepted. And Alex knew it, the rat. She heaved a gigantic sigh. "Oh, nuts."

"Exactly," said Alex.

Bill got up and sauntered to the door. "Now that that's taken care of, I'll go downstairs and collect Wally. We've got some packing to do."

"I'll pick you both up tomorrow morning. Or this morning." Alex yawned. "You know what I mean."

"I know," said Bill. Before he shut the door behind himself, he winked at them both.

As soon as they were alone, Alex began nuzzling her neck. "We'll make the happiest couple in the United States, Kate. You'll see."

"I'll make you miserable," she grumbled, although it was difficult not to purr with his warm breath melting her bones.

He chuckled. Kate thought that, in a well-run world, Alex's deep, velvety chuckle would be outlawed. As she had reason to know, though, the world wasn't well run, and there was no escape for her via that road.

That being the case, she decided it would be foolish to fight. Turning into his embrace, she flung her arms around him and completed her abject surrender. "I love you, Alex."

"I love you, too, Kate."

The words were so sweet to her ears that she almost fainted for the third time in her life.

They made sweet love that night, in Alex's hotel room, leaving his innocent sister to fend for herself. Alex told Kate that Mary Jo wouldn't dare say a word, and Kate believed him. Why shouldn't she? He'd been right about everything so far.

"I love you, Kate," he whispered as he entered her.

She lifted her hips to welcome him home and clung to his shoulders as if to a lifeline—which is pretty much what she considered him. "I love you, too, Alex."

He drove her past the point of desperate hunger, up a ladder of craving, until it seemed to her as if her entire being exploded in a shower of brilliance. The experience was so exquisite that tears leaked from Kate's eyes when Alex, too, achieved release and collapsed at her side. She held onto him almost desperately as an odd sense of understanding seeped through her.

"You know," she mused after they'd both caught their breath, "I'm beginning to understand how a woman could cleave to a man even after he'd ceased to behave as a human being."

Alex grunted and turned over so that his body cocooned hers. "You're thinking about your mother and father?"

"Yes. I always wondered how she could have loved him, because to me he was always a monster."

"Mmmm. But you're thinking he must have been a different man when they met?"

She nodded. "If Ma had ever loved him the way I love you, well . . ." Her words faded out. Even with this new understanding on her part firing her imagination, she couldn't conceive of Alex turning into a drunken monster like Herbert Finney.

Alex squeezed her to him, and she felt his sex begin to stir to life again. Good. To Kate, the life-affirming act of sexual union was a blessing, and she hoped to do it as often as Alex was able.

"I swear to you, Kate," he said solemnly, "that I'll never, ever behave in a manner that will make you ashamed. Or in a way that will make you hate me. I couldn't stand that."

She turned in his arms and pressed her breasts against his chest. "I couldn't, either."

Twenty

Alex took quite a bit of ribbing from Gilbert MacIntosh when he asked him to serve as his best man in an emergency wedding ceremony to be held at Alex's farm is five days' time. He didn't mind. He was besotted and didn't care who knew it.

Kate, who didn't invite many people to the wedding, was able to persuade Belle Monroe, the woman who'd rescued her from her father's attempted strangulation, to visit the farm and serve as her maid of honor. Since Belle worked for a couple called the Richmonds, they came, too. Fortunately for everyone, the Richmonds came complete with a little boy and a little girl, one of whom served as a ring bearer, and the other as a flower girl.

Win Asher, the official photographer for the World's Columbian Exposition and a friend of Kate's, agreed to take pictures of the ceremony. Kate got the feeling Mr. Asher came more for Belle's sake than hers, but she didn't care.

Mrs. Finney's health was so poor that she had to recline during the ceremony, but Kate saw to it that she wore a beautiful new gown, and Alex saw to it that she was propped up on a chaise and had a clear view of everything.

Kate's brothers looked uncomfortable in their new suits, bought at Wanamaker's ready-made men's wear department, but Kate thought they were stunning. She came from a handsome family, in spite of her father's deplorable set of weaknesses.

She wished she could stop resenting her father. She knew her resentment was childish and did her no credit, especially now that he was dead and couldn't cause any more trouble for anyone. But she couldn't help it. He'd been awful, and even though she almost understood that he might not have always been awful, she couldn't help but be glad he was dead and unable to interfere with her family any longer.

Mrs. English was about the dearest woman Kate had ever met, barring her own mother, and Mary Jo was so excited about having the wedding in her own house that she nearly drove everyone to distraction. Kate was becoming accustomed to Mary Jo's adolescent transports. She no longer felt like slapping the child every time she behaved like a silly young girl, mainly because she *was* a silly young girl.

Mary Jo, unlike Kate herself, hadn't been forced to accept responsibilities greater than her years warranted long before she was ready to do so. Kate honored the strong family bonds that had allowed such a state of affairs to exist. She aimed to create one along with Alex, as a matter of fact.

Madame Esmeralda came to the wedding. She arrayed herself in all of her Romanian Gypsy finery, and finally got around to telling Mary Jo her fortune at the reception. Three of the Egyptian musicians and Miss Fahreda Mahzar attended, too. Along with Madame, the Middle Eastern contingent was the hit of the show, according to Alex, who claimed he'd not anticipated his wedding to be such an extravaganza.

Kate smacked him on the arm and told him not to be sarcastic.

Peering down at her with such a loving look it almost made Kate dizzy, he said, "Believe me, my darling Kate, before I met you, I hadn't anticipated anything but boredom and decay from marriage."

Her eyes popped open wide. "Boredom? Decay? What the heck did you think marriage was, anyhow?"

Alex thought about it, then shrugged. "A bore. The beginning of a decline into old age and decrepitude."

Kate stared. "Good Lord."

He grinned. "See how much you've taught me? Not only am I being spared becoming a stuffy old man, but I'm even welcoming Gypsies and Egyptians into my home."

"Not to mention three Irish kids from the Chicago slums."

"Ah, Kate." He grabbed her up and swung her around. "I'm hoping we can do something about that. I've talked to my attorney about creating a lung center at Saint Mildred's in your mother's name."

Kate buried her face in his shoulder and offered up a prayer of thanks for sending Alex English into Madame's booth that day in May.

Hazel Finney died two weeks to the day after her daughter was united in holy matrimony with Alex English. She faded away one night as Kate sat beside her bed, embroidering pillow slips by candlelight.

Her last days on earth had been happy, and Kate blessed her new husband for that, even though she knew she'd always miss her mother. Fortunately, Mrs. English, who was brokenhearted at her new friend's demise, was there for her and made a good substitute.

Alex had spent the two weeks following his wedding making plans. A month after Kate and he said "I do," he swept his bride off on a world tour. Kate was especially fond of the Pyramids, about which she'd been told by her musician friends, although her pregnancy made descending into one problematic. Alex told her not to fret.

"We'll have decades and decades together, Kate. I'll take you to Egypt again when the kids go off to college."

Kate thought that was a spectacular plan.

From Best-selling Author
Fern Michaels

__Wish List	0-8217-7363-1	$7.50US/$9.50CAN
__Yesterday	0-8217-6785-2	$7.50US/$9.50CAN
__The Guest List	0-8217-6657-0	$7.50US/$9.50CAN
__Finders Keepers	0-8217-7364-X	$7.50US/$9.50CAN
__Annie's Rainbow	0-8217-7366-6	$7.50US/$9.50CAN
__Dear Emily	0-8217-7365-8	$7.50US/$9.50CAN
__Sara's Song	0-8217-5856-X	$6.99US/$8.50CAN
__Celebration	0-8217-6452-7	$6.99US/$8.99CAN
__Vegas Heat	0-8217-7207-4	$7.50US/$9.50CAN
__Vegas Rich	0-8217-7206-6	$7.50US/$9.50CAN
__Vegas Sunrise	0-8217-7208-2	$7.50US/$9.50CAN
__What You Wish For	0-8217-6828-X	$7.99US/$9.99CAN
__Charming Lily	0-8217-7019-5	$7.99US/$9.99CAN

Call tool free **1-888-345-BOOK** to order by phone or use this coupon to order by mail.

Name_____

Address _____

City_____ State _____ Zip _____

Please send me the books I have checked above.

I am enclosing $_____

Plus postage and handling* $_____

Sales tax (in New York and Tennessee) $_____

Total amount enclosed $_____

*Add $2.50 for the first book and $.50 for each additional book.

Send check or money order (no cash or CODs) to: **Kensington Publishing Corp., 850 Third Avenue, New York, NY 10022**

Prices and numbers subject to change without notice.

All orders subject to availability.

Come visit our website at **www.kensingtonbooks.com.**

Thrilling Romance from Lisa Jackson